CHAINS OF FEAR

Alex opened his eyes again, and he was in a huge open barn. He focused his eyes where a man sat, studying him. Alex tried to speak, but his voice rasped. He coughed to clear his throat.

"Where am I?" he managed to say.

The small, thin man chuckled, then stood. A long chain clinked when he moved. It was secured to a manacle circling his left wrist. . . .

Alex rolled up on his elbow, testing his strength. Other than nausea and stiffness from lying on the cold, hard-packed dirt floor, he was all right, everything worked. Of his clothing, only his pants remained. Metal clanked and his arm hurt him. He was shocked when he looked down. His own left wrist was manacled, and a similar chain was attached to it. He studied the unforgiving steel. The end snaked behind a block of concrete.

"What the hell is this?" he asked, holding up the chain. He jerked it, but it was solid.

The other man looked over and smiled, then said, "Welcome to the club."

DEADLOCK

Also by William Cross

CUTUP

DEAD LOCK

WILLIAM CROSS

JOVE BOOKS, NEW YORK

For Ginny
A much better woman than I deserve.

Thanks to:
Barbara Roberts
Belmon Hall
Don MacRae Sr. and the Western Writers Group in Eatonville (wherever that is)
Doctor Norman (Jim) Dreher and his charming wife, Angela
Judge Kip Stilz

DEADLOCK

A Jove Book / published by arrangement with
the author

PRINTING HISTORY
Jove edition / August 1994

ISBN: 0-515-11433-2

A JOVE BOOK®
Jove Books are published by The Berkley Publishing Group,
200 Madison Avenue, New York, New York 10016.
JOVE and the "J" design are trademarks
belonging to Jove Publications, Inc.

PRINTED IN THE UNITED STATES OF AMERICA

10 9 8 7 6 5 4 3 2 1

1

"Well, picture this then, boy. You alone in the Oak Bucket Beer Hall, and three scraggly, hard-assed, slack-jawed Skaggits, just in off the mountain, calling you names and pushin' you for all they're worth. What do you do then?"

Patrolman Josh Warren took his eyes from the road and glanced a challenge at Alex Gregory in the passenger seat. Josh's open-necked uniform shirt stretched at the buttons and showed sweat around his neck and arms as he gripped the steering wheel with both hands. He was in his early thirties, and his waist was beginning to show the effects of too many biscuits with gravy.

"Wouldn't draw my gun even then," Alex said as he stared into the distance at the setting sun. It colored the sky with ribbons of red and violet as the cruiser bounced and jostled its way down the narrow gravel road. In the warm glow, the reddish dirt along the road took on a pinkish cast.

"So, what if one of them not only calls you names, but pulls a knife?"

Alex was amused because he knew Josh wanted different answers. "Well, if I couldn't reason with him, I guess I'd just have to go back to the patrol car and call for backup according to regulations." Alex continued to gaze at the sky.

"Regulations? Why the hell wouldn't you whip out

that shiny-new hog-leg you're carryin' and draw down—
threaten to blow 'im out from under his filthy hat. Sure
as hell save a passel of screwin' around.''

"Because I don't believe in ever pulling a weapon on
another human being unless you intend to use it. It could
lead to an undue escalation of violence," Alex said. He
brushed an imaginary speck off the shoulder of his new
uniform and leaned forward to hide the grin that almost
escaped.

"Undue violence!" Josh spat tobacco out the window
as though ejecting the aftertaste of the statement. "Hell,
boy, you don't know the meaning of them words. If you
give them Skaggits half an inch they'll be pissin' on the
piece of dirt you're layin' under. The only thing those
inbreeds respect is a kick in the ass and the barrel of a
gun.''

"Look, you're entitled to your opinion. I simply feel
differently. Everyone has his rights. I think most con-
frontations can be avoided if we take the time and use
reason.''

Josh shook his head and downshifted as the car slewed
through loose gravel on the shoulder of the road.

They drove along the two-car dirt lane in silence; Josh
frustrated, Alex still smiling to himself.

This has gone too far, Alex thought. *I've got to stop
teasing him.*

"I know you think I'm a tight-ass. I've got to confess.
I don't really believe all that garbage I've been feeding
you the last couple of days." Alex chuckled and glanced
across at him. His boyish face lit up in a wide smile.
"I've just been kidding you, Josh. Guess I carried it too
far. Sorry.''

"You're shittin' me. You been pullin' my leg all the
time?" Josh asked.

"Just having a little fun. I believe in respecting folks'
rights, of course. But when it comes to taking guff, I
draw the line just like you.''

"Damn, well now, that's a relief. Thought I had me a
real by-the-book J. Edgar for a partner." Josh looked over

at him, smiled, and punched his shoulder. "Boy, you had me going for a while. Didn't know what the hell I was gonna do with you. You sure got some weird sense of humor."

"How about if we take a few minutes after we drop off the car and have a beer . . . on me," Alex said. Josh nodded and they both looked out the window in silence. Alex was twenty-five, tall and lean with dishwater-blond hair. His wife, Jenny, had teased him about looking like Huckleberry Finn with his freckles and dimples. Josh was short, with a round face and thinning hair.

In front of them, the shadows of the green Appalachian hills were getting longer. It would be light for two hours yet, but the sun would hide behind the rounded peaks in minutes. Off to the east, below the descending layers of green, were the flatlands that harbored Picksburg, a small town huddled under aging oak trees.

Alex glanced up at the darkening mountains in the distance where a misty white haze hung between the aqua peaks, seeming to connect them like a vaporous rope. Up in the haze, on those pristine slopes, it was easy to imagine prehistoric shapes with snapping maws and whipping tails, standing tall to challenge anything that dared to move across the spongy forest floor. A land where time had been frozen for eons, where anything was possible, where anything could live.

"What would you say the humidity is today, ninety percent?" Alex asked, trying to be friendly. After the arid heat he was used to in California, this was incredible.

"After you're settled in . . . for twenty to thirty years," Josh answered, "you won't notice it at all." They both chuckled. Alex continued to stare at the rainbow of hot colors in the sky. He decided he was going to have to sit on his sense of humor. Fortunately for him, Josh had thought his kidding was funny. Some of these other country boys might have taken serious offense.

Alex allowed his mind to drift back to three weeks ago when they'd driven into town. *Pop. 1,458,* the sign on the outskirts said when he and Jenny had passed with their

U-Haul loaded to the gunwales. As they drove into the heart of Picksburg, they doubted the figure as they cruised through the quiet streets lined with scattered, tree-sheltered homes.

"God, look at how old those houses are!" Jenny yelled. The central section of town was populated with utilitarian, drafty, wood-sided houses with paint-sealed, wooden-sashed windows and coal-eating furnaces—like the house they now lived in—dinosaurs in their own right, anachronisms from the beginning of the century. The houses had the expected porches and swings, and there were grape arbors and picket fences in various states of disrepair.

Main Street was a smattering of tired brick retail stores with fading signs. They were mixed in with two markets, one at each end of town, two gas stations, and Merrill's Dry Goods Store. Most of the buildings had shingled roofs sheltering worn wooden sidewalks running the length of the two-block business section. The downtown streets were black-topped, the surface sprinkled with gravel carried in by cars from the gravel-covered county roads. *Crazy. Giving up California for this,* he thought.

Josh snorted as a prelude to changing the subject. "We been so busy, haven't had time to ask. You and the missus settled in yet?"

"Sort of, but we've had trouble getting anything to work at the house we're living in," he said. "Tough on a city kid."

"The old Hackett place?" Josh asked. "Boy, that spider trap hasn't heard a voice for five to six years I know 'bout."

"How did you know where we were living?" Alex looked away from the sky and at Josh for the first time.

"Hell, son, this ain't L.A., you know. Can't sneeze around here without a God-bless-you from everyone within five miles. Likely as not they'll have your humpin' and shittin' schedule on the grapevine within the week."

Alex laughed and leaned back. *This town is going to take some getting used to,* he realized.

Alex was six months out of the police academy in L.A. He'd graduated with honors and planned to follow his father in a long career serving the citizens of L.A.—until Jenny. She'd finally convinced him to change that plan, with her back-to-the-roots fervor and change-the-world social science degree.

They'd decided to pull up roots and move here because they couldn't afford to buy a home in California, and they had no intention of waiting five to ten years until they could. In Picksburg, they could buy a house for what a down payment would have been in California. Besides, Alex loved to write and the history and ambience of the South fascinated him. When he started writing novels, he wanted to frame them in Southern urban settings, and God knows, he had as much of that as he could handle within driving distance. The clincher for Jenny had been that her family was only about an hour away.

"It's beautiful, Alex," she'd exuded. "Just seventy-five miles from Charleston and my family, but it has the social structure of a nineteenth-century mountain town. You'll love it—we'll love it. I know I was raised in Wheeling, but I love the country. We can plant a garden and preserve what we can't eat, raise some animals. It'll be wonderful! Please . . . we'll be so happy there." She'd bounced up and down with excitement. "You can work for the police department, I can teach at the primary school. We'll have two point three children and live happily ever after." He shook his head as he reflected on the conversation, still uncomfortable with his decision to move from Los Angeles, unsure it was going to work. His father had given him a hard time about it, but if it made Jenny happy . . .

The dusty black-and-white patrol car jostled off the dirt road into a long driveway and pulled up in front of a country store, where it jerked to a stop. When the cloud of dust cleared, Alex read the crudely lettered sign nailed to the siding that said *Allen's*. It was the only indication the unpainted, clapboard structure was anything more than a deserted house with a dirt yard. It had a long, planked porch across the front and right sides, shaded by a sagging roof. At the back of the building, chickens and goats wandered aimlessly, heads pressed to the ground, picking at and between the blades of grass. Cars in different stages of undress littered the field fronting the trees, their age indicated by the accumulation of rust and the length of the weeds growing through the windows.

The lawmen thumped up onto the porch, opened the squeaking screen door, and walked inside. Alex smiled as he looked around. Farm implements lined one of the store's walls. Alex recognized only a plow. Most looked well used, and he guessed that they predated the twentieth century. He reflected on the rocky soil in these foothills, and wondered at the amount of effort it must have taken for those people to nurture a crop in these hardscrabble fields.

Have to keep Jenny out of here, he thought. *She'd have one of those cleaned and polished up and hanging on a wall at home in a flash.*

He smiled at the thought of her at home, working, fixing supper, like a long-married housewife. This was the middle of his first week on the job and going home to her was the highlight of his day.

Barrels were randomly spaced along the base of the walls, and a long, handmade counter ran the length of the back. Behind that, sagging, unpainted shelving contained everything from blue-and-red boxes of ammunition to iron skillets and pipe tobacco. The odor of grains, leather, and mildew intermingled pleasantly. One bare bulb hung on a long wire and lit the rear of the store.

A greeting came from the left. "Josh. Evening." A bulky man opened the side screen door and walked in. His gaze flitted to Alex, then dismissed him. He walked over to the counter, his movements slow and ponderous, his voice the same. The man rubbed his hands on a dirty shirt that barely covered his stomach. His round face bristled with stubble, and his thinning hair was askew. "Caught a four-pound big-mouth this morning," he said to Josh without the inflection of pride. "Coupla walleye yesterday."

"What'd you use, Earl?" Josh asked.

"Grubs," the man said as he scratched his stomach again. "What'll it be?"

"Drivin' the boonies. Introducing Alex here to the folks here'bouts."

The man nodded without looking at Alex.

Friendly, thought Alex. The man's reaction was typical of the people he'd met driving the foothills leading up to the mountains. Aloof, distant. Alex wondered if unpacking the last of the boxes at the house was such a good idea.

"This here's Earl Allen," Josh said to Alex as though the man's behavior were normal. Alex considered stepping forward and shaking his hand, but Earl continued to stare at Josh without acknowledging Alex's presence.

"Stayin' at the Hackett place," Earl said in a flat voice, then let his blank eyes drift over and fix on Alex. This dirty man knowing where he lived was somehow disturbing to Alex.

"Yeah, we plan to fix it up, then plant some—"

"Anything else you want?" Earl interrupted, then looked back at Josh.

"That'd be it for now," Josh answered. Earl grunted, then lumbered over to the screen door, opened it, and walked through without looking back. He let it bang behind him.

"Good to meet you," Alex said to the closed door.

"Don't pay him no mind. He's a good man, only a little short on words, that's all."

"Little short on manners is more like it," Alex said.

"Give it some time, boy. You're an outsider right now. Folks ain't goin' to invest much energy in you 'less they see you're goin' to be around." The men clumped out onto the dusty porch.

Alex jumped when he turned to his right. Two men

stood glaring at them, their repeater rifles tilted with a hint of threat. They wore nondescript dark clothing, wrinkled and covered with dust. One man ruminated a plug of tobacco, revealing glimpses of brown-stained, fragmented teeth.

"Jed—Seth," Josh mumbled as he nodded to the men. They just scowled in return. Their piglike eyes were recessed into their heads, and their oversized, scabrous ears extended out through their shoulder-length, baby-fine hair. Alex hesitated for a moment, fascinated. *Strange eyes,* he thought. *Pinkish lids with no eyelashes or brows, eyes flat with no life, like a shark's.*

Receding chins added to the evidence of inbreeding. Genetics had been one of his minor subjects at SC, but these men had an almost vacant look, bordering on retardation.

Alex sidestepped toward the car after Josh tugged on his shirtsleeve, then looked to Josh for assurance. Josh shook off his questioning glance and motioned to the cruiser. Turning his back on those guns made Alex nervous, so he watched them as he edged away. Something feral in the men's eyes told him that killing him would as easy as swatting a mosquito.

"Mountain folks hereabouts get a might touchy 'bout staring," Josh suggested as he swung his door open. "Don't mean it to be critical, just offerin' advice."

"Sorry. I'll remember that."

The two policemen climbed into the car and drove at a measured pace toward the dirt road. The mountain men remained frozen like statues and followed the car with their small pink eyes, guns canted at the ready.

"Skaggits," Josh said. "Family goes way back. Most of 'em live up on the other side of Cason's Ridge."

"Can they talk?"

"Just a word here and there."

"They dangerous?"

"Not 'less you rile them. Folks around here have learned to let 'em be, give 'em space. They'll soon disappear back into the hills an' we won't see them for a piece."

"Should they have those guns? They don't look capable of handling weapons like that."

Josh laughed, revealing his own even but brown-stained teeth. Alex tried not to cringe. Getting used to people who chewed tobacco was going to take a while.

"Those boys can center the eye of a coon from fifty yards. 'Sides, there ain't no law against them carryin' a rifle—'specially not up here. Only real trouble we've had, beside a little fight here and there, is back when two of the boys killed a college kid outside of Picksburg. Blew twenty-some holes in him with their Remingtons."

"Jesus! They must have really been pissed. What'd they kill him for?"

"Killed him for makin' fun of 'em by usin' big words they didn't understand."

"You're kidding—killed him for that?"

"You're right."

"Right that they killed him for that?"

"No. Right that I'm kidding." Josh guffawed and slapped the steering wheel.

"Touché," Alex muttered.

"See, what a coincidence! That's the very same word he used just 'fore they shot him the first time!" This time Josh laughed so hard tears ran down his cheeks. "Kiddin' aside," Josh continued. "There was a college kid killed, and we did suspect those Skaggit boys, but there weren't no witnesses so we couldn't take 'em in."

Alex shook his head and chuckled as they rolled back onto the gravel road, eight miles from the blacktop, ten miles from the town. The spray of pebbles peppered the underside of the car as they drove along in silence for another mile, Alex still thinking about the hill people and the unpacked boxes at his house. He liked some of the people he'd met, but he'd be out of here in a minute except for Jenny, and leaving would be like giving up. The only way he'd been able to handle this place was to not think about what he'd left behind in L.A.—family, friends, and the constant sunshine that was a part of everyday life. And dry heat. Unlike this sweatbox, there was almost no moisture in the air at all.

Alex leaned forward and squinted into the shadows ahead. Alongside the road, a vintage car sat in the shade of a copse of trees. An old woman stood at the rear of the car with her arms crossed, watching the road as though waiting for someone. A young girl slumped on a rock next to a tangle of bushes.

A wave of apprehension rippled through Alex, then he shrugged it off. "You going to stop?"

"Yep."

"Want me to call it in?" Alex asked as he touched the mike.

"No need. Shouldn't take no more'n a minute." They pulled in behind an ancient Packard, the gravel crunching under their tires.

Josh said in a serious voice: "More Skaggits, look smartly. Can't tell about these people, even the women." Alex reached down and unsnapped the safety strap on his holster.

The woman's head turned. She glared at them from the hollows of her eyes as they drove nearer—

Damn! This woman sure looks like trouble, thought Alex.

2

Jenny let the screen door slam behind her as she walked into the kitchen from the backyard. She walked to her stove, picked up her flower-decorated teapot, and filled it with water. Setting it on a burner, she turned on the propane and lit it with a stick match. The odor of sulphur mixed with gas was strange after cooking with electric all her life. She smiled at the feel of the white ceramic handles and wondered how many stories they could tell. It had taken her almost a full day to clean the stove to the point she felt comfortable cooking on it after they'd found it deteriorating in the backyard under a pile of discarded furniture.

Sweating from the humid afternoon, she wore jeans, a loose blouse, and a bandana tied around her hair to keep it from blowing in her eyes when she turned the rich earth for her garden. She was short and trim at 115 pounds. Her face was oval with large, expressive eyes.

The soil had been soft, loamy, and black between the rocks, and was alive with life-giving insects and earthworms.

A puff of breeze ruffled the lace curtain on the window above the chipped sink. The old house was light and airy, and the kitchen was still redolent of the fragrant bread she'd baked that morning.

All the walls were freshly painted off-white in Sears Best, and even the chipped woodwork was coated with white enamel. They kept the windows open as much as the changeable September weather would allow the paint fumes to dissipate.

She rubbed her arms and smiled. Digging in the ground was hard work and it made her muscles sore, but it was a pleasant sore—satisfying almost. As she waited for the water to heat, she studied her hands for blisters. She'd worn gloves, but the telltale signs of redness were there. She said, "Darn," under her breath, then walked over and held her right hand in the cold stream of water. After a few weeks, calluses would form, and gloves would be unnecessary.

Those gardening programs back in California didn't say anything about blisters, she thought.

A horn sounded from the front yard, and a car door slammed. Jenny smiled with anticipation of Alex's return. She brushed her long black hair back and trotted to the front door. Smiling widely, she opened it, and stepped out onto the porch.

A young woman in stylish slacks and silk blouse bounded up the steps two at a time and said, "I do declare, you've become a bona fide shit-kicker!" Carole Redding beamed as she approached the door. "My God! And it only took you three weeks—has to be a record."

"Thank goodness. A civilized voice in this bastion of barbarism," Jenny said as she opened the screen door for her. "Come on in. I have some tea on. The storm trooper will be home from a hard day of cracking skulls in a few minutes." They stopped and hugged at the door, smiled, then walked into the spacious country kitchen where the teakettle was whistling. Jenny took a canister of loose tea from her cupboard, filled a tea ball, and dropped it into the pot. Carole watched from the dinette table.

"Well, how's Alex like our local yokels?" Carole asked.

"I think the jury's still out for him. This town's a strange mix. Young urban expatriates like us, the stolid apple-pie majority who make up the backbone, and the fringies who slink down out of those hills like ghosts on a moonless night. I give them a ten for weird."

The two young women had bumped shopping carts two weeks earlier in the Triple-A Mart on Hudson Street, and after a couple of awkward comments, they were soon chatting like old friends. They were stunned that they had both gone to college in Los Angeles: Carole to UCLA, Jenny to USC. Friendly enemies, they'd observed, then made a date for lunch the following day.

"Two lumps, honey," Carole said. "That's how I stay so sweet." Jenny smiled, set two cups on the table, and poured the tea. Carole was a short brunette with a round, animated face and a ready smile.

Since they'd first met, they'd seen each other almost every day. Carole and her husband, Don, owned a small farm on the outskirts of town where they bred midget horses and pygmy goats. Like Jenny, Carole's family lived in Charleston. Carole and her husband had bought acreage in Picksburg because the land was cheap and the scenery was out of a travel brochure—pretty much for the same reasons *they* had.

"Sure stinks in here," Carole said, referring to the fresh paint. "Bread smells great, but it doesn't cover the odor. How can you stand it at night when you have to close the windows?"

"We've been thinking of pitching a tent in the rear yard," Jenny said, "but hopefully, it should be manageable in a couple more days." She smiled and sipped her tea.

Outside, the sky had darkened and the crickets began their rhythmic serenade, masking the sound of the cicadas. The rasping was syncopated by throaty bullfrogs. When night came to this land behind the mountains, it came quickly. One minute twilight, the next, an impenetrable black umbrella laced with pinpoints of light. Jenny closed the window above the sink and locked it because the breeze wisping in had an uncharacteristic chill.

"Alex is usually home by now, isn't he?" Carole asked.

"Usually. But I don't worry. What could happen in this town? They roll up the sidewalks at dark." She cradled the warm cup in her abraded hands. It felt comforting. "We're having a small party Saturday night at my place. A celebration."

"Wonderful! I love parties—I love it, I love it. Celebrating what?" Jenny's expressive face lit up and she leaned forward.

"A conception."

"A baby! Oh, congratulations. How marvelous!" Jenny stood and paced in her excitement.

"Calm down—the mother's a horse."

"Don't be so hard on yourself, you're only a few pounds overweight," Jenny said with a smirk as she lowered back into her chair.

"Idiot. It's Lisa, our little thirty-inch-high Appaloosa mare."

Jenny giggled, then asked, "When's she due?"

"We weren't even sure she was capable of conceiving when we bred her. She's just a little over a year old, you know."

"So, how long is their gestation period?"

"Vet says the big event will be approximately ten and a half months from now, give or take. Needless to say we're pretty excited ourselves. We've done nothing but lay out bucks for these little eating machines. Setting up breeding stalls, buying hay, building fences, paying vet bills, and so forth. It'll be slick to start getting a return."

"What do they go for on the market?"

"If you have to ask, you can't afford it," Carole said archly. "Five big ones a copy."

"Five hundred?"

"Thousand."

"Ouch. Many people afford that?"

"Sure. Believe it or not, we already have a waiting list."

"Holy smoke. I'm out scratching in the dirt for blisters

and turnips while your animals are fornicating you into
Guccis and a Mercedes.''

"Relax. There's a lot more horse manure to haul and
vet bills to pay before we show a profit. It's a long way
to break even. Don will have to commute to his day job
in Charleston into the foreseeable future to keep food on
the table." She chuckled. "I'll let you know when to start
envying us."

Jenny stood, walked to the front door, and looked out
onto the dirt road meandering off through the trees. The
shadows in the yard were so dark she had trouble picking
out Carole's dark blue TransAm under the tree. She
hugged herself against a sudden chill.

"I'm getting a little nervous," she said. "Alex hasn't
been late before."

"I wouldn't worry. It's probably just a shoot-out at the
Oak Bucket Beer Hall, or something."

"Thanks, I needed that," Jenny said, and smiled as she
took one last look out the door. If he was coming, she'd
be able to see his lights well up the road, but it was inky
black. "Speaking of shoot-outs, have you seen those
weird people in town the last few days?"

"You mean the mountain people? Yeah. Understand
they creep down out of the hills about once every six
months or so. First time I saw them, I thought they were
going to a damned Halloween party or something. I hear
there's a whole clan of them living in virtual isolation
on the other side of Cason's Ridge. Only come down
when they need supplies. They're like something out of
Deliverance. Give me the willies."

"Somebody ought to do an anthropological study of
those people. They almost look like a separate race. Have
you noticed their genetic anomalies?"

"Hell, no. I'm too busy checking out the guns they
carry. That shouldn't be legal." Frowning, she sat back
down.

"Unfortunately, you don't need an IQ over fifty to buy
and carry a rifle, all you need is money."

Carole took in the dregs of her tea. The cup clinked

when she set it in her saucer. "Want me to wait with you?" she asked more softly. Jenny's concern about Alex obviously bothered her.

"Don't be silly. He'll come dragging in in a few minutes with lipstick on his shirt and beer on his breath—not to worry."

"Sure. I'd have to see that. Mister By-the-book-never-had-a-hair-out-of-place-in-his-life." Carole laughed. "Not that he won't get some offers in this burg. He's quite a hunk."

"God, don't tell him that. He thinks he isn't good enough for me. Can you believe it?" Jenny chuckled. "Besides, he's not uptight. That's only a facade. Underneath, he's a marshmallow." They both stood, then ambled toward the door with their hands around each other's waist. "Thanks for the invitation. What time?" Jenny asked as she squeaked open the front door and screen.

"Sevenish. There's going to be a couple of people from the state democratic committee there. Hope you don't mind."

"What's that about?"

"Don's thinking about running for the House of Representatives. They think he has a good chance."

"This isn't a fund-raiser, is it?" Jenny arched her eyebrows with an accusing look.

"Hell, no. I wouldn't do that to my friends. You only ask strangers for money." Carole laughed.

"Of course. We'll be there with bells on," Jenny said as they walked out onto the porch. The night swallowed up the attempt at putting a light timbre in her voice. In the brisk evening air, bugs tapped the porch light next to Jenny's head as she watched Carole make her way to her car. Jenny waved into the dark after Carole was inside her car and had turned on her headlights. Then she closed the door and snapped off the porch light.

Jenny suddenly felt alone and restive. Outside, Carole's horn honked a good-bye as she disappeared down the road.

Jenny went to the phone, picked it up, then hesitated. *I'll wait another half hour before I call,* she thought. She replaced the receiver and ticked it rhythmically with her fingernail.

I don't want them to think I'm a worrier.

Lights flashed, and a roaring like thousands of waves crashing on rocks filled Alex's mind. He was sick and could feel his body convulsing, but he had no sense of where he was, or even what position he was in. He was cold and his body felt light. Hands touched and fondled him and he had the sensation of drifting off into the night air.

Voices. Several different voices, some loud and strident, some mumbling confusing words. Voices ululating inside an echo chamber—colliding and vibrating—destroying the meaning.

Words—demanding.

Hands—pulling, shoving, grabbing.

Something smashed hard into his body, and he was aware he should be in pain from the impact, but there was none. He was in a different place now, no longer moving, but his body still had the sickening sensation of motion.

Drifting again and colder now; pressure against his side. *Must be lying on something hard,* flashed through his mind. A whirlpool formed and he spun around and around, faster and faster, out of control, then spiraled toward the light of consciousness. As he was about to reach the surface, his stomach violently forced hot, scalding fluid up his throat. Choking. Coughing. Searing hot bile filled his nose, and his eyes burned with pinpoints of fire. Hacking, wracking, savage explosions from his lungs ejected it from his passageways. Then he could gulp in air, gloriously cool air on his burning throat.

Voices again—echoing. Then hands tore at his clothes and he heard loud, penetrating sounds of metal clinking and clanking on something hard behind him. His body shook with overwhelming sickness, and he wanted to—actually hoped he would—die. Then, mercifully, he drifted off into a blackness that was smooth and comforting. He reached out and it enveloped him, softening the sickness at first, then absorbing the pain and nausea.

He floated into a dark, quiet place where there was no sound or feeling at all. . . .

Police Chief Cody Brighton stared straight ahead at the dirt road and maintained a steady speed in his pickup truck. In the distance he could see the flashing lights of a parked cruiser. When he got closer, he could make out another darkened police car parked in the headlights of the second one. An officer sat with his door open, gumballs atop his cruiser rotating and illuminating the surrounding fields and trees with pulsing color.

The chief stopped, climbed out, and walked up to the other officer. The man stood and nodded, lit a cigarette, inhaled deeply, and rubbed his forehead in frustration. His radio scratched in the background as a woman's voice talked in fits and starts to another car, directing them to this location. The night sounds of crickets, bullfrogs, and cicadas came from both sides of the dark country road.

"Ain't nothing, anywhere, Cody. Checked it inside and out. Even shined my light down into that there field and ain't no evidence of tracks. Brush's so high you couldn't walk down there without leavin' a trail a Boy Scout could follow."

The chief hiked up his gunbelt and walked to the abandoned police car, opened the door, and looked inside. He sat in the driver's seat and turned on the radio. It blinked on and crackled with static. He twisted the key and the powerful engine rumbled to life. Shaking his head, he switched it off and night sounds returned.

"Damn wonderment, ain't it?" he mumbled to himself. It had been two hours since they'd heard from Officer Warren and his new partner. Dispatch had tried to raise them on the radio, and after what they'd considered a suitable wait, they had started a grid search centered around Allen's store, the last place Josh and Alex had checked in.

The chief opened the back door and ran his hands across the seat and floor with the same negative results, then went to the rear of the car and opened the trunk. Nothing but a spare tire and tools and dry cleaning with Josh's name on the ticket.

"What do you reckon happened to them?" the officer asked.

The chief glared down at the shorter man, and grumbled: "Probably one of them spaceships, come down, beamed 'em off to another planet. One of them that has only naked women on 'em, where they eat fruit and screw all day."

"What? What do you mean?" The man laughed nervously.

"What I mean is, I don't know jack shit, any more than you, boy. You think I got some crystal ball stuck up my ass that I can just whip out when I need it?"

The officer nodded and shuffled his feet, obviously undecided about whether to continue to grin or not. "What do you want me to do, Cody?"

"You mean after you stop asking stupid questions?"

The officer nodded again.

"Wait here for Jeffers to show up from off duty, then you two do a search along this road in both directions. Take your time and look for anything, and keep in touch with me. We don't find anything, at daybreak we'll bring out the dogs, see what we can turn up. Be out there now, but I already called Clarence and he can't bring the dogs over till morning. Meanwhile, I'm going out to this new guy's house and see his wife. She's been calling the station every fifteen minutes."

"So, what do you think happened to them?" the officer asked. The chief looked at him, shook his head in exasperation, and walked to his truck. He gunned his engine, did a U-turn, and his tires spit gravel at the man as he headed back toward the town.

Checking along the side of the road as he moved, the chief could see faint glimmers from houses here and there back in the fields, but nothing that would indicate where the officers had disappeared to.

Maybe the idea of a spaceship wasn't so damned far-fetched, he thought. He had only eight men total on his small force, and this would make a major dent in his ability to function in the town. But that's *if* they were gone. He had some ideas, but he'd think on them later.

It was ten minutes before eight o'clock, and the lights of Jenny's house were bright as he idled his truck under the canopy of a huge tree in her front yard. The curtain next to the door ruffled, then the porch light flicked on. Jenny stepped out. Even in the shadows, he could see the anxiety in her face. He knew she was expecting Alex.

"Sorry," he said as he clomped up the steps. "Didn't mean to get you all fired up."

She deflated in disappointment. "Where's Alex, what's happened to him?" The chief had stopped by to see the couple before he hired Alex and had already met Jenny.

"You gonna invite me in?" He was undecided about how blunt to be with her since he was unsure of how much she could handle. Nothing more upsetting than a hysterical woman.

"Of course, Chief. I'm sorry, come in." She held the door wide. He walked in and dropped onto the leather couch in the living room. He was a huge man with massive shoulders, and the room shrank with his presence.

"Nice room you got here," he said. "Good taste in furniture." In the country the amenities always came before business. He took off his hat and ran his hand through his thinning hair to smooth it. As he glanced around, he noticed that almost every light in the house was on. *Typical reaction,* he thought. *Keepin' away the bad things.*

"Alex. Where is he?" she prodded, standing over him and washing her hands in a helpless gesture. She sat down stiffly, but kept her eyes riveted on him.

"Fact is, we don't know. Found their car about twelve miles outside of town. Just parked. Seems to still run, work perfectly. Long way from any houses or buildings, but the important thing is, at this point, there ain't no evidence that anything's wrong. Just ain't there, is all."

"I don't understand. How could they simply be gone?" She jumped up and paced the room.

He shrugged, then massaged his aching temple. He'd been taking a nap on his couch when the station called him at home. He suffered from insomnia, and it was one of the few times in the last month he'd been sleeping soundly. "Your husband call you about anything during the day?"

"No. Well, to be honest, I don't know for sure. He might have called when I was outside. We haven't plugged in our answering machine yet. Maybe he called, I don't know." She sat opposite him again in an over-stuffed chair, unmindful of the dirt smudges on her face and arms. Her hands were clasped in front of her and she kneaded them continuously. "Could they just be having a beer somewhere?" she asked. "Of course not," she said, answering the question herself. "Why wouldn't they call in, and why would their car be sitting out there unoccupied. That's not something Alex would do."

"Ain't something Officer Warren would do either. He lives alone and keeps regular hours. Dependable as that clock," he said as he pointed to the antique ticking on the wall.

"What are you doing to find them?"

"First thing we did was search along the road. Then checked all the open bars in town." He glanced up at that. "Didn't expect them to be there, of course, but . . ." He shrugged. "Never know. Got two cars out patrolling the area trying to turn up anything." He stood, sighed, and pulled his weighted belt up on his hips. "Everything that can be done to locate them is being done. Can't tell you to relax 'cause I know you won't. All I can say is, when we find him, you'll be the first one we call."

Her lip quivered, her jaw set, then her shoulders straightened.

"Thanks," she said. "I guess that's all I can ask. Call me anytime. There isn't any way I can go to bed tonight . . . not until I know where he is."

"You want me to call someone to come sit with you, you being new in town and all?"

"Thanks, no. No point in another person being up half the night too." She smiled thinly.

"You sure? Ain't no shame in bein' scared, you know."

"I'm real sure."

"Okay. If that's the way you want it. I'll call you in a couple of hours regardless." He stood, walked to the door, opened it, and hesitated. "You try to not to think on it too much now."

She nodded in appreciation.

He looked back at her standing rigid, arms crossed. This pretty city woman had some starch in her backbone. Opening the door, he left without saying good-bye and walked to his truck.

Until he had an answer to some of her questions, talking was pointless.

Besides, if it was what he was afraid of . . .

He might never have any answers for her.

3

Alex returned to consciousness like a boat traveling at
full speed furrowing into a wet, sandy beach—abruptly
and painfully. His eyes burned with such intensity that
opening them seemed risky. Hot tendrils of agony
coursed through his head like molten lead, threatening to
burn out his nerve pathways. He coughed deep in his
chest, and the jolt to his system came close to driving
him back into oblivion.

"God help me, am I dead?" he heard himself say as he
tried to move his head. He took stock of his senses
without moving.

Taste: Disgusting, vile. His stomach still reeled from
ejecting its contents. His sinuses were inundated with the
sickening odor of exhaust fumes.

Smell: Taste and smell had melded almost into one.
The only odor that overlaid the disgusting taste of vomit
was the dank, thin stench of something burning,
medicine-like. It was almost as much a feeling as a scent.

Touch: Hard, unforgiving, cold—along the length of
his body. Muscles aching. Clothes gone except his pants.
The muscles of his stomach quivered, and he had to
swallow hard to keep his gorge down.

Hearing: Quiet, unnaturally still. Just the sound of a
distant fluttering. *Birds? Could it be?* But he had to be
inside. How could it be birds?

Sight: The last. He risked the effort and found that

opening his eyes was easier than expected. His lids trembled wide and instead of painful light, it was black. He turned his head to the side, and it fell of its own weight until it stopped against something hard and cold. High in the blackness, a square of dim light came into focus. It had no meaning at first, then he realized it was the moonlit sky. He was lying on a hard floor, maybe concrete, and the window was at least twenty feet in the air. He turned his head, and it flopped back the other way. In that direction, there was nothing but velvety darkness.

"Hello?" he muttered. "Is anybody there?" He drifted in and out of consciousness, listening for an answer, but it was deathly quiet except for a muffled skittering sound high above him. "Speak to me if you're there," he choked out, a bit louder this time. His vibrating voice made the pulse in his temples thump, and he had to close his eyes. No hangover was ever close to this. Afraid to risk movement, he lay motionless to avoid the pain.

A creaky voice out of the blackness finally spoke: "Shut up, go to sleep."

"Where am I?" Alex asked.

From the void someone said: "Shut up, bastard." Then something hard and sharp hit the side of his face.

He drifted away again, off into the soothing arms of the pain-relieving blackness.

Jenny drank tea and paced most of the evening. Around two in the morning, the chief called and told her the men were still missing. He talked for a long time and tried to comfort her. He told her not to worry, but Jenny knew it was just one of those statements people make and rarely expect anyone to listen to.

After he hung up, she sat in the living room for a few minutes and tried to relax, but the ticking of the clock annoyed her. She stood countless times, flipped on the outside light, went out onto the porch, and peered into the blackness of the West Virginia night. The crickets and bullfrogs continued as though nothing had happened in her life.

Something serious was wrong. Alex would call if he were anywhere near a phone—or was able to. The words "able to" chilled her. God, that possibility was unthinkable. Alex was her life, her reason for living. If anything happened to him—

The thought was frightening.

Somehow, him being in a dangerous profession had never really seemed tangible, especially since they were out of a high-crime city like Los Angeles. The concern was just something she'd filed away like an old insurance policy. Alex would always be there, and they would always be happy—she knew that. Before this, it had never occurred to her to worry about him.

At four-thirty in the morning, she called the station again. A sleepy woman's voice answered, a voice grated with too much coffee and too many cigarettes.

"Police Department."

Jenny hesitated for a moment, considering her other options. *What other options?* she thought.

"Jenny Gregory again." She was amazed at how businesslike her voice sounded.

"Morning, Mrs. Gregory, nothing yet. Sun'll be up in 'bout an hour and a half. . . . Chief said he'll have the dogs out scouting around where they found the car, I guess." The voice was bored, matter-of-fact, as though they did this every day.

"Where was the car found again?" Jenny asked. The woman disappeared off the line. Getting permission to give her information, Jenny figured. She was prepared to argue if the woman refused to tell her. The woman came back on. Her voice was sympathetic as she told Jenny where it had been found.

Jenny thanked her, hung up, then ran into the bedroom. She retrieved a local map from a nightstand drawer and unfolded it on the bedspread. She took a pen and made a circle at the location, then put her hand on it trying to sense whether Alex was there. She suddenly felt foolish, and hot, salty tears welled in her eyes.

"No!" she yelled. "I have to be strong. Alex needs me

if he is in trouble." She stood and took the map into the kitchen. As she tried to fold it, she had to resist the urge to rip it up when it buckled instead of folding. Her nerves were frayed to the breaking point. Reaching up into the top of her cupboard, she took down a thermos.

She put on water to heat. Strong tea would be just the ticket to keep her going through the morning. The house seemed foreign and empty as she worked in the kitchen. A few hours ago it had felt comfortable, like home. Now, she had the hollow sensation that she was in a strange house in a strange land, and nothing here belonged to her.

What the hell am I doing in the mountains anyway? she wondered.

She forced herself to eat two slices of toast with butter. She'd made the fresh-baked loaf of bread yesterday morning. Her stomach was not interested, but it would be many hours before she had a chance to eat again. Coming back without Alex was not something she wanted to consider. If they failed to find him, she'd have to do it herself.

What could have happened to Alex and Josh played and replayed in her mind. Nothing made any sense. According to the chief, the car was operational and the keys were in it. Alex and his partner were far from a house or building of any kind, and the search for tracks had been unsuccessful.

That left only a couple of possibilities. They had climbed out of a serviceable car and walked off the road looking for something, or they had left the area for some reason.

But that made no sense at all—

Unless—

They had been *forced* to leave.

Alex came awake with a start. Early morning light filtered into the building, and he was unaware of movement around him. Then he heard slow, shuffling sounds accompanied by a clanking coming from metal being dragged.

He blinked and looked up at the ceiling. Small birds by the hundreds preened themselves and flitted about the bulky cross-members in an open-framed building which appeared to be a oversized barn of some kind. The birds made small peeping sounds as they rustled, and from outside the building, a rooster crowed. The medicinal smell from last night took on a new character—the heavy odor of wet cereal—grain.

The slice of sky he'd gotten a glimpse of during the night was a large opening at one end of the peak of the building. The morning air wisped across his bare upper body. He shivered, then rolled his head to the left. The bottom fell out of his stomach. His head whirled for a moment, then righted. He closed his eyes and swallowed, the taste of fumes strong in his nose and throat. His mouth was sour.

A voice came from his left. "Gonna live, are you? Too fucking bad for you. You'd been better off dead, boy." It was a high voice with a New York accent and echoed in the open building. Alex squinted into the morning light, then turned toward the sound.

A small thin man sat up and leaned back against the unpainted timbers of a wall. He had a long, unkempt beard, and his hair was graying and matted. His garments were wrinkled, obviously handmade, and looked like pajamas. Dirty—filthy, in fact. Thongs hung on his bare feet. Alex judged him to be forty-five, give or take. Alex studied him, trying to focus his eyes. The man had a large nose and deep-set eyes that sparkled with life. His thin lips went up on one side as though smirking to himself.

Alex blinked. The memory of what had happened to Josh Warren started to come back with a chill. It was real, and it *had* happened.

He sighed, laid his head back on the hard surface, closed his eyes, and tried to focus on what had occurred.

Josh—my God! he thought. It came surging back in a flash.

As they drove nearer, the woman's head had turned toward them and she'd glared. . . .

They had braked to a stop behind the rust-stained Packard, climbed out, and walked to the woman who

stood by the car's yawning trunk. Josh took a handker-
chief out of his back pocket as he approached, wiped the
sweat from around his neck, and gave her his patented
good-old-boy smile.

She watched them with the same detached demeanor
exhibited by the men on the porch earlier. Her eyes had
similar deep-set characteristics, and her salt-and-pepper
hair framed a blank, skeletal face. Her thin lips were
bloodless; her cheeks wrinkled and sunken. She was
short and her faded floral dress hung straight down from
her sticklike frame.

"Evening, Mae, what's your problem? Got a flat?"
Josh asked. She nodded noncommittally and blinked
back, still expressionless.

Alex felt a chill go up his back. These people were
primitive and had an aura of seething violence about
them.

The teenaged girl on the rock to the right of them
giggled. When they glanced over, she raised both legs
and exposed her naked body under her dress. She leaned
her legs wide, intending for them to see.

Josh was shocked to inaction for a second, then said,
"Put your legs down, girl, you're getting too big to do
that." With her hand up to her mouth, the girl tittered,
then lowered her hand to touch herself.

Josh turned back to the woman while saying: "Damn,
Mae, tell your daughter to—"

He froze.

Mae had a sawed-off shotgun—

She'd taken it out of the trunk while they were turned
away.

Alex started to reach down—

"Don't," she threatened as she clicked the hammers
back with a loud clatching sound.

Josh said, "Leave your gun be, boy. That scattergun
would make a hand-sized hole in you."

Alex raised his hands. His spine tingled and perspiration peppered his forehead. *What the hell have I gotten
into?* he wondered.

The girl stood and shuffled to her mother's side, and said, "Worked just lack you said, Ma. They's peepin' on me, gettin' they eyes full whilst you drawed 'em down."

"What's goin' on, Mae? Best you be layin' that scattergun down 'fore it lights off," Josh warned.

Josh's accent became heavier when he talked to these mountain people. Alex remembered that they stressed in the academy how important it was to communicate in the vernacular where possible.

Mae glared back, and her meager mouth worked with tension.

"Shed them guns," she said to the daughter. "Sneak round back of 'em." The daughter giggled again, then edged out to their left and made a wide circle to come up behind.

"Ain't nothin' we can't solve if you back off now, Mae," Josh reasoned.

She blinked and waited.

Alex thought about grabbing the girl when she came near, but it would be a stupid play. The old woman could shoot faster than he could move.

Snickering under her breath and enjoying herself, the girl slipped their guns out of their holsters. She held them out like prizes as she padded barefoot back to the car, opened the rear door, and threw them on the floor.

In back of the woman, a small boy stuck his head out around the corner of a rusted fender. Spittle webbed from his mouth, and his one arm was atrophied and pulled up like a chicken wing. He had all the inbred features, only more accented. Smiling dumbly, he made small guttural noises.

"Take your brother and git in the car," Mae ordered.

"Aw, Mom, I wanna watch." The girl's voice was high and wheedling. Alex guessed her age at fourteen or fifteen.

"Which one you want?" Mae asked of the girl.

The girl's eyes brightened as she swayed over and pointed to Alex with one hand, the other up to her mouth sucking her fingers. "The pretty one with the cute blue eyes and the freckles. I'm partial to him," she said. "'Sides, he looks a mite stronger."

"Git in the car, hear me?" The woman's voice was strident and threatening. Both the daughter and the imbecilic son went to the car, grumbling, and climbed into the rear. They slammed the doors, then immediately pressed their hands and faces against the rear window and peered around the edge of the trunk lid to watch.

"The trunk—get in. Both of y'uns." Mae stepped away from the car and motioned to the yawning opening.

Josh said, "We can't do that, Mae. Why don't you back off now, we'll just forget what's happened, then—"

"Shut up. Don't chew my food more than once. Git in now. Finger's gettin' itchy."

Alex found his own voice and said, "My name's Alex Gregory." Smiling, he continued with the reasonable tone they'd taught him at the academy: "Certainly, there isn't anything that we can't—"

The explosion of the twelve-gauge rocked him back toward the car—

Ears ringing and heart pounding, Alex realized she'd shot above their heads.

"Last warnin'. In now. You first," she said, waving the smoking weapon at Alex. "Got another load o' thunder, just like that'n. Unless yer fixin' ta check out, best ya be movin' lively."

Looking into her unfeeling eyes, Alex had no doubt she meant what she said. He stepped up on the bumper and lowered his body into the trunk.

"All the way back." She motioned for him to scoot into the depths.

He inched back as he watched the waving barrel.

As Alex settled on the steel floor, he was aware of the smell of gasoline and rust, mixed with exhaust fumes.

"Now you," she said to Josh. Alex could hear him sigh, start to say something, then he too bent and lowered his body into the massive trunk. The springs on the old car squeaked and groaned. Josh pulled his body out flat, his head beside Alex's.

"You're buying a peck of trouble here, Mae," he warned without conviction. He turned his head and whispered to Alex, "Damn. Just hang fire, boy, our chance will come."

The woman hovered over them, the shotgun pointed down. Her thin mouth worked, then she said, "This is for you, copper—"

Alex looked up, trying to decide what she meant, when—

She jammed the barrel of the gun tight against Josh's chest—

The gun roared!

Pain seared Alex's ears.

Pinpoints of pressure slammed his body, eyes, and face—

Bam! The trunk lid came down.

It was black—

For long seconds, Alex was rocked. *I'm dead, she's killed me,* spiraled through his mind. *No! If I were dead, I wouldn't know it!*

He brought his hands up to his face and neck. They were wet with thick warm fluid. *Coppery smell—blood,* he realized. What had smashed into him were droplets of blood, bits of skin, and bone fragments from Josh.

Alex could feel Josh quiver as his life drained onto the floor of the trunk. Ominous rattling and liquid choking sounds came from his destroyed lungs.

"Oh, God no," Alex whispered. He cringed back. The blood was hot on his body and there was no way to get away from it. The space was too tight.

The engine of the car started, then rocked and grumbled. As the floor vibrated, acrid exhaust fumes filtered into the trunk around the edges and through the new hole beneath Josh where the shot had penetrated.

Alex reached out and felt the artery in Josh's neck. His fingertips could sense the man's heart flutter, then hesitate, stop, and start again—

Then it stopped—

For the last time.

In his cramped position there was nothing Alex could do. Josh sighed, vibrated along the length of Alex's body—then he was quiet.

Alex's hand shook when he pulled it back.

"I have to get out of here," he whispered as he reached across Josh's body and felt for the trunk's locking mechanism. *No use.* A solid layer of 1930s steel covered the lock.

The exhaust fumes were stronger.

And he was trapped in the poisonous blackness—

With a dead man!

4

Alex opened his eyes again, and he was in a huge open barn. He focused where a man sat, studying him. Alex tried to speak, but his voice rasped. He coughed to clear his throat.

"Where am I?" he managed to say.

The small, thin man chuckled, then stood. A long chain clinked when he moved. It was secured to a manacle circling his left wrist. Alex frowned and raised his head to follow the links to see where it was secured. The end went to a small ring of steel imbedded in a large concrete block about twenty feet away.

Alex rolled up on his elbow, testing his strength. Other than nausea and stiffness from lying on what was a cold, hard-packed dirt floor, he was all right, everything worked. The carbon monoxide from the trunk of the car had left him with a sick feeling and a granddaddy of all headaches.

Of his clothing, only his pants remained. Metal clanked and his arm hurt him. He was shocked when he looked down. His own left wrist was manacled, and a similar chain was attached to it. He studied the unforgiving steel. The end snaked behind the block of concrete.

It has to be attached to something, another block maybe? he thought.

"What the hell is this?" he asked, holding up the chain. He jerked it, but it was solid.

The other man looked over and smiled, then said, "Welcome to the club."

"What club? What are you talking about?" Alex tugged again at the manacle. Pain flashed through his wrist because it was so tight. Whoever had put it on had wanted to make sure it stayed in place.

"Figure of speech," the thin man muttered and looked away.

Alex suddenly remembered Josh. "Where's the other guy? Josh?" Beyond the bearded man another man snored, turned away from them on his side. *Couldn't be Josh,* he realized. *Josh is dead.*

The thin man ignored Alex's question and walked across to a far wall. The chain scraped behind him in the dirt. He picked up the lid of a large clay pot and set it on the floor. Standing over the pot, he urinated into it, making a hollow sound, then put the lid back in place.

"Always put the cover on or it gets pretty ripe in here." He said it in a matter-of-fact tone, then returned and sat on his pallet. "Used to have mattresses out here, but the crawlies got so bad we had trouble sleeping. These are better." He scratched his side and indicated the wooden pallets. On the wall behind Alex, a similar one leaned against the timbers. Alex shook his head, then opened his eyes, and glanced around.

The building was an ancient barn. Small pinpoints of light sparkled through the decaying roof and hurt his eyes. The structure was immense. *A rectangle that must measure 150 by 200 feet,* he guessed.

Two birds flew in one opening at the peak and out the other. Outside a couple of dogs barked, then growled and snapped.

For the first time, Alex looked in the direction beyond his feet. In the middle were two metal pot devices, like oversized, pear-shaped copper stoves. Each had thin metal tubing projecting from the top leading to another wooden keg of some kind, then continuing to square boxes that were damp, the wood swollen. A small pipe with a spigot on the end projected from the bottom of these. Sticking from the side of each of the wet boxes were tubes that went along the back of the far wall and out through a hole cut near the floor. He could hear the tinkling of moving water. *Water lines of some kind,* he realized.

Off to the right were crates of empty glassware. To the left were huge stacks of bags and large cans of something, and a collection of open-topped, wood-sided vats. Beyond those was a wide doorway leading into a darkened room. In there, where the light filtered in from the barn, Alex could see bags and crates piled high.

"Stills?" he asked. The thin man laughed. Alex had never seen a still, but had studied pictures in the office so he'd be able to recognize them if he came on a setup in the woods. He'd never expected to because he'd thought illegal whiskey-making was something relegated to the distant past.

The man lying next to the thin man stirred, then went back to snoring.

"What's your name?" Alex asked. His head was clearer, more focused now, and he wanted more information.

"I'm the still man—the brains of this pathetic outfit— that guy there's the spigot man, not long for this world, and you, my friend, are the new mash man."

"What the hell are you talking about?"

"Personal names don't mean crapola in here. The only thing that keeps you alive is doing your job and not getting sick. Judging by how young and strong you are, you should last quite a while. Might even work your way up to still man if you last long enough, or I get unlucky along the way."

"I'm a police officer. Name's Alex Gregory. I asked what *your name* is."

"Police officer? I'm really impressed." The man chuckled louder this time. "Then why don't you go arrest someone and get us the hell out of here?"

Alex felt his temper rise, then his head throbbed from the rush of adrenaline. He reached up and brushed away his hair with his free hand in a helpless gesture.

"A cop? That really beats it. Just kiddin'. No harm in talkin' names, I guess." The man's voice was softer, more cooperative. "Names's Manny Lueger. Been here exactly fourteen months and six days. Don't keep track of hours, guess I should."

"Manny," Alex said in a testing manner. "Manny, what the hell are we doing here?"

"Making corn and sugar shine, boy. What do you think those are, popcorn poppers?" Manny motioned to the still pots.

"You been here fourteen months?" In Alex's condition, ingesting the information took some time. He rubbed his eyes and forehead.

"And six days."

"How'd you get here?"

"Salesman. The best damn salesman east of the Mississippi." Manny smiled with a sense of pride and looked up at the ceiling as though remembering. He fondled his beard as he continued: "Won a trip to Hawaii year before last as top producer. Got laid ten times in one week. Loved those mai tai's, yeah." He glanced back and cleared his throat. "Sold to reps up and down the Atlantic Coast. Taking a shortcut through these godforsaken hills to Charleston fourteen months ago. Had to piss so bad my back teeth were floating. Stopped alongside the road and walked back into the woods to drain the lizard and next thing I know, here's this snag-toothed old bitch pointing her blunderbuss at me. Marched me to that gangster car of hers and dumped me at this fucking barn. Cuffed me, and I been here ever since. Can you believe that shit?"

"She say how long she's going to keep us?"

Manny laughed hard this time. "You still got shit for brains like last night, don't you? There isn't any way out of here 'less you're planted against that far wall." He pointed off into the distance to the right wall still cloaked in shadows.

"How about the man I came with?"

Manny stretched and yawned, then gestured to the right side again as though getting bored with the conversation. Alex strained to see into the shade created by the hayloft. Two piles of dark clothing lay side by side. Projecting from one mound was what looked like a bare leg.

"He's lying over there with the guy you're replacing, the other mash man. They dumped your man there like a sack of potatoes in the middle of the night when they brought you in. The other poor bastard used to work at the job you're gonna do. Have to bury him today. He's starting to get choice. Poor mother got sick in his head and went bullshit two nights ago. Crazy! Biting his tongue, lashing out at everybody. Mae just up and blew his face off with that shotgun when she figured he wasn't going to get any better. Showed him about as much concern as she'd show a goddamned chicken." He sat on the pallet to the clanking of his chain and rubbed his arms as though he was suddenly chilly. "Got blood all over me." He looked up at Alex and his eyes appeared to be watery. "Nice guy. I liked him. Had a family. He was the mash man," he mumbled. His voice trailed to silence.

Alex could tell by his diverted eyes and the emotion in his voice, Manny was thinking about his own uncertain future. He talked tough, but it was obvious he was frightened.

"Who's he?" Alex asked as he motioned to the sleeping man who was snoring louder now.

Manny glanced over, then shook his head and said, "Name's Landry. Been here longer than me. His mind's checked out and gone south. Drinks sugar shine all the time. Coughs and pees blood. Don't get too attached to him. He's a short-timer who'll be feeding the worms in another few weeks at the most, then we'll have a new spigot man." Landry just continued to snore.

"My God!" Alex collapsed back and looked up at the roof. Two more birds fluttered out the opening.

He was a prisoner here, and Jenny, poor Jenny—she had to be scared to death with worry. Then there was Josh. Alex reflected on the conversations he'd had with him the few days they'd worked together. He knew very little about him except he lived alone in a walk-up apartment in Picksburg and spent most of his time scouting for new women. *His scouting days are over now,* Alex thought.

Staring at the sky through the opening, he judged the time to be five-thirty or six in the morning. His watch was gone along with his clothes. Jenny'd be up making breakfast now—that's if she could eat. She'd be calling the station and her mother in Charleston, everybody she could reach. *Poor kid.* God, he loved her. She was like a cat, stretching, then bounding to the floor when she woke in the morning. Her instant enthusiasm for the new day amazed him. It always took him minutes to find his feet.

If I could only talk to her, tell her that I'm all right, he thought. He glanced back at the bodies and figured that being okay could be a temporary condition. He felt the manacle, then shivered. He jerked it again to pull his wrist loose, but it was so tight it restricted his circulation.

"I have to get out of here! Now!" Alex stood and grunted through his clenched teeth as he strained against the chain.

The door at the front of the barn squeaked, then swung wide. Alex hesitated and glanced up.

"Sooee! Sooee!" the young girl called in a high-pitched voice.

"That's her idea of funny," Manny mumbled under his breath to Alex. "Does the same thing every morning. Thinks it's hilarious to call us like pigs."

The girl came through the door and kicked it closed with her foot. The door drifted open again as she walked forward. A powerful black dog came and looked into the cavernous barn, hesitated, then stopped. He sat framed in the opening, his massive head at an angle as though testing the air.

The girl carried a tray with three bowls on it and smiled as she picked her way forward. When she stepped into the light filtering down from the openings, Alex could see she wore the same clothes as when he'd first seen her last night.

She could be attractive if she used makeup and did something with her long stringy hair, he thought. His mind started to work, thinking about what to say to her to get her to let him go. Then he remembered Josh lying in the shadows like a bag of discarded laundry. Negotiating had failed for the other men, so it was naive to think it would work for him.

"Come on, piggies, it's time for breakfast." The girl's voice was thick with country twang.

She stopped and set the tray on the ground about ten feet away. Each bowl had a spoon in its dark contents. Alex stared at her as he swayed from weakness. She took two steps backwards, turned, and watched him almost shyly, her hands entwined in front of her. Her eyes took in his bare chest as she moistened her lips.

A clinking came from his left. Manny picked up a bowl and walked back to his pallet. He sat and began wolfing down the breakfast.

"What's your name?" Alex asked the girl. He knew he could save the preliminary attempts to get her to free him because she'd probably been through that many times. He thought of using an authoritative tone and insisting she release him right now, then realized how ridiculous that would be, too.

The girl smiled, revealing gray, stained teeth. "Wacha wanna know for?"

"We're going to have a hard time talking if I don't know what to call you." Alex said it in a conversational tone and tried to smile, but his face failed to cooperate.

"I ain't 'lowed to talk to y'uns. Ma says you're the devil, full o' mischief and evil." He took one tentative step toward her. She moved back a step to match his.

"I won't hurt you."

"That's for sure. You'd be dead's mashed taters if'n you did." She giggled. "Sarah. That's my name." She turned and ran toward the door. The huge dog chuffed and pranced back for her to pass. When the girl closed the door, Alex listened for the sound of a lock being clicked into place, but there was none.

"She doesn't lock the door?"

Manny smiled as he spooned in the last of his cereal. "Ha!" he said. "Doesn't need to." He wiped his sleeve across his mouth. "No need at all." Alex waited for him to continue, but he just belched and leaned back against the wall and closed his eyes.

"Why not?" Alex demanded. Irritation crept into his voice.

Manny shook his head, then shuddered, as though remembering something painful. "Hitler. That's what I call him. Son of a bitch weighs in at about one hundred twenty-five pounds. Him and two other dogs patrol the fenced-in area around the barn. Killers! All of them. That's assuming you can figure some way to get out of these chains and get out to where they are." He held his wrist up and rattled the links.

"You're kidding," Alex said, but knew he was serious. He asked as an afterthought, "What keeps them outside? That black dog you call Hitler stopped at the doorway."

"Trained. Won't step across the line into the barn unless they're ordered to, but you go outside—wham!— your ass is dog food."

Alex shook his head and walked over to the bowls. He wavered, then squatted and picked one up. He carried it back to his pallet. The bowl was warm and the cooked grain aroma made his stomach turn. He guessed it would have smelled good if his stomach were settled.

"What is it?" Alex studied the contents of the bowl.

Manny shrugged. "What difference does it make? It's the only thing you'll get. Eat it."

Alex pulled the spoon out of the sticky porridge and licked it. It was unrecognizable. He dipped up a spoonful and took a small bite. The gruel tasted grainy and pasty as he shivered, then chewed and swallowed.

At least it takes away the bad taste. Besides, I have to build up my strength if I'm going to escape, he thought. He was on his third spoonful when he crunched on something hard. He spit it into his hand and focused on it. It had legs.

"My God!" He spit the remaining cereal on the ground. "This stuff has bugs in it!"

Manny laughed hard. "Sure thing. Every morning. Relax, it's good protein."

"Uggh!" Alex grunted and laid the bowl at the end of the pallet.

"Can I have that if you're not going to eat it?" Manny asked. Alex nodded. Manny crawled over, picked it up, and carried it back. Alex watched him as he shoveled it in and his stomach roiled, undecided whether to revolt. Manny set down the empty bowl and belched again.

"How the hell can you do that?" Alex asked.

"You just ain't hungry enough yet, boy." Manny reached out with his foot and kicked the sleeping man on his haunches, rocking him back and forth. "Breakfast time, move your ass." The man stopped snoring, snuffled, then stirred. He rolled over onto his back, sat up, and smacked his thick lips. Alex guessed him to be fifty, closer to sixty. His breathing was labored as he picked up a fruit jar of clear fluid, sloshed in a mouthful, then coughed. Alex assumed it was moonshine.

The man's hair was thin, and his beard was wiry and flecked with white. When he stood, he ignored them. Alex watched as he wavered, then stumbled over to the last bowl. He picked it up and returned to his pallet. After he squatted, he made short work of the gruel or whatever it was. He ate it without hesitation and Alex's stomach churned again at the thought of the bugs it contained.

"Lean back and rest your eyes, boy," Manny said to Alex. "After the princess comes and gets the bowls, we'll have to start work. You've got some digging to do."

"They can't make me work for them if I don't want to," Alex said.

Manny just roared with laughter, harder this time. "That's funny, real funny."

5

Jenny turned off her lights as she drove along the dirt road. The hills in the background were black regimental silhouettes against the bright morning sky. When she left home, the air had been comfortable, but the wind coming through her open car window was warmer now and laden with humidity. It felt good even though the hair on her neck was starting to get wet. *Warm and getting warmer,* she thought. It would be stifling hot within two or three hours if it ran true to form.

As she drove, she tried to remain calm, to not think about why she was out here on this deserted road. She'd dressed in practical Levi's and hiking boots. Her hair was pulled back, and she had passed on the makeup ritual this morning. That nonsense was unimportant. Nothing mattered until she had Alex back again.

Up ahead, above the trees, she could see the blinking of colored lights coloring the sky. The gravel sprayed hard against the undercarriage of the car, making a hissing and crackling sound much like burning underbrush. Jenny rounded the last curve and could see two patrol cars and a pickup truck in the distance where a collection of men stood alongside the road. Three dogs strained at leashes being held by a heavyset man in civilian clothing. Jenny rolled up and stopped behind the last car and climbed out.

"Mrs. Gregory," the chief called. All the men turned

and watched as she approached. "We just got here," he
said to her unasked question. He walked over to the men
with the dogs and said, "Clarence, get them scented, and
let's get to it." The heavyset man untied the dogs, and
they danced around him in excitement.

The chief went to his car, brought back a jacket, and
gave it to the man, who then held it down to each of the
dogs. Jenny was shocked when she realized it was Alex's
coat. The dogs became more agitated and ran in ever-
widening circles, sniffing the ground and testing the air
with their sensitive noses.

She clasped her hands in front of her and they ached
from the tension. Two of the dogs ran to the edge of the
field into the undergrowth and disappeared. She could
see the tops of weeds move, then here and there a flash
of black as one of the dogs passed. She walked over near
the chief.

"They smell something, don't they?" she asked.

He shook his head. "You'll know when they do . . .
they'll take off baying in that direction." Jenny turned
her attention to the field again, where the man yelled
something to the dogs and the movement of the weeds
came toward him. Jenny walked back to the front of her
car after a couple of minutes of watching. The longer the
dogs ran around the area without picking up a scent, the
more upset she became. She knew she was close to tears
and wanted to be away from people if she started to cry.
What am I going to do? she wondered.

She allowed her mind to drift as she leaned back
against the side-view mirror of her Volvo. She remembered the first time she'd seen Alex. Tall and slim with a
shock of unruly blond hair, he'd come breezing into the
library and sat at the computer across from her. The
computers sat back-to-back.

She'd felt her heart jump when she glanced up from
her screen and he was looking at her. When their eyes
met, he grinned, as though afraid to commit to a
complete smile for fear of rejection.

She forced her eyes back to the blinking green monitor

and read and reread what it said with no understanding. What she had been searching for in the computer had lost any importance to her.

She was unable to ignore him as he just sat at his machine with his arms folded. She finally said, "It's impolite to stare, you know." Her heart picked up, and her face felt flushed. She wondered if he noticed.

"Can't help it." He ventured a full smile.

She glanced back up, and when she met the warmth of his smile, she could feel the corners of her own mouth being tugged upwards. Other than his teeth being a bit irregular, he was perfect to her. Freckles and blue eyes that burned through her; dimples that were disarming. When she hugged her pillow each night, the face she always imagined was similar to this man's.

"I can't work if you're going to sit and stare at me," she said.

"Great idea, let's go get some lunch—my treat."

She shifted with discomfort and looked around. No one was paying any attention to them. "I don't know you."

"No problem. I'm Alex Gregory. Twenty-four, unmarried. College-educated with a three point four average, no bad habits, and I think I've been searching for you all my life. So, now you do—know me, that is." As he talked, he stood, walked around, and sat in the computer chair next to her. She nervously glanced around the room again.

"We haven't been introduced. I don't know who you are," she heard herself say, but she knew it was just a space-filler. Inside, she struggled with how to react to this handsome man. Everything she thought of saying sounded stupid just when she wanted to seem sophisticated.

A short pudgy boy of about twelve came walking by carrying a book. Alex reached out and stopped him with his hand.

"Hi, guy," he said. "Would you do me a quick favor?" The boy nodded as his jaw worked on a piece of gum.

"My name is Alex," he said to the boy. "And your name is?" he asked her.

She squeaked out, "Jenny."

"Great. Introduce us," he said to the boy. The boy frowned, then looked around, uncertain what to do or say. "Just introduce us, like they taught you in school—me and her—it'll only take you a second." The boy smiled, thinking he was being kidded and showed his oversized teeth. "Go on," Alex urged.

The boy slumped his shoulders, sighed as though put upon, then said, "Alex this is Jenny, Jenny—Alex." He smiled as though he'd passed a test. Alex whipped out a dollar and handed it to him. "Have a Coke on me." Jenny let a giggle escape because the poor little boy looked so uncomfortable.

"Thanks," Alex said. The boy shook his head, pocketed the dollar, and skipped away to the counter with the book he carried. Alex turned back to her. "Okay. Now that we've been formally introduced, and you know all about me, how about that lunch?" He stood as though it was a done deal.

She glanced up into his eyes.

He was right. It was.

The sound of dogs barking and men yelling stirred Jenny to look back at the field. The man was leashing his dogs again. He had finished walking them up the road in both directions, and the dogs had just sniffed and barked instead of baying as she had hoped. Jenny felt her heart sink.

The men and dogs had only been here about forty-five minutes, and they were going to give up. The chief talked to the man with the dogs, shook his head, turned, and walked toward her. In back of him, the sound of engines coughing to life signaled the end of the search at this location.

The chief approached with his thumb of his left hand hooked in his pants loop. He waved to one of the cars that went by spraying gravel, then turned to her and said, "Gonna keep looking, got some other ideas."

"What other ideas?" Jenny asked.

"Mrs. Gregory. Why don't you let us do our job? I understand your worry, and I don't blame you, but we can't have you followin' us around. We got questions to ask and things to say we don't want to be heard." He hitched up his belt again. He was a muscular man except for his bulging stomach. His narrow hips offered marginal support to anything above them. "Y'all go home now, and I'll call you in a couple of hours, or as soon's we find 'em."

"You think somebody's hurt them?" She was thinking *killed,* but avoided saying the word.

"Now, you think on it," he said with a touch of annoyance. "Why in tarnation would anybody want to do that?"

"Chief, I'm not ignorant. Common sense tells me that another person had something to do with their disappearance, and they wouldn't have gone wherever they went without some kind of resistance." She crossed her arms and tried to look in control when she felt the tears coming again.

"Might be true as you say. But it sure ain't going to help us none to have you raggin' on my men and me. Every minute I spend talkin' to you is a minute I can't spend hunting." The logic of the statement was beyond argument.

"How about the state police or something? Shouldn't you call them in right away?"

"Give it some time, missy. We don't want to find these boys out in a house somewhere, doin' something they shouldn'ta, then look stupid to strangers."

"Alex wouldn't do something wrong, if you're talking about another woman. I know he's in serious trouble or he'd have called. And if he's in trouble, so's the other man. They could be dead right now." She winced when she said the word.

"I wouldn't dig no holes for them right now, little lady. Likely as not those boys can take care of themselves all right." He sauntered away to his car in a John Wayne rolling gait while shouting over his shoulder, "Try to relax some. I'll call you before noon. Don't you be thinking on diggin' no holes for them just yet. . . ."

"Git to work now. This here's where I want you to dig," the old lady ordered. She pointed to a rectangle she'd outlined on the ground with her scuffed heel. It was wide enough for both of the dead men. She held her shotgun with one hand to enforce her authority.

The young girl stood behind her, hugging two rusted shovels in her arms. She stepped forward, dropped them into the dirt, and they banged together. Alex jumped at the loud sound.

The woman and the girl moved away a few steps and Mae motioned to the ground again with the shotgun. Alex looked back at Manny and the other man, who sat on the pallets, watching with casual interest.

"They's not gonna help none. New men allus buries them what's dead," the old woman said.

"Why'd you kill Josh?" Alex asked, risking her wrath.

Her mouth worked, and the gun came up a couple of inches as she struggled with her temper. "Din't need 'im," she said. "Matter of fact, don't need you either. Two men's more'n nuff to run that shine, but totin' them hunert-pound sugar bags and fetching them five-gallon buckets to an' fro is more'n them two pissants can handle day out. Don't cost me nothin' cep'n some throw-out food ta keep an extra body 'round."

"If you didn't need him, then why wouldn't you pick up somebody who was by himself, instead of killing Josh for no reason?"

Mae looked at him without understanding. "Din't cost but one shell, and you's gon' have to dig this hole anyhows." His morals had no meaning to her. "Git to diggin'." The conversation was over.

Alex picked up the shovel and glared. She had what he guessed was a classic sociopathic personality—killing with no remorse or feeling, merely as a convenience. Mae smiled, showing her stained, snaggled teeth, then nodded again at the ground. Her plain, flowered sack dress hung on her work-worn body. Alex guessed her age to be sixty, give or take, then thought of the children's ages and wondered how it was possible.

"Whilst you're diggin', think on this." She took care to point the shotgun at his chest. "You hurt or hinder me or mine in any way, you'll be lookin' at dirt for eternity." She glanced at the open doorway where the huge black dog watched. "Even if you could get us all some'ows, ain't no way you can get outten them chains." She warmed to the threat. "Sure as winter'll come, you'd be crow bait 'fore you git loose."

Alex turned each shovel of dirt with exaggerated care as he continued to watch her. *If I could get close enough,* he thought.

"Even figurin' you do, them dogs'd have you 'fore you made the fence. Ain't trained to do but one thing. Second grave from the wall—man name o' Reeves. After two years of studyin' on it, he made it through the door, dogs downed him and had his arm off clean as a whistle 'fore you could say Jack Robinson. Bled him dry as a stuck pig." She chuckled as her eyes followed Alex's slow movements with the shovel. He shivered from a chill and had to concentrate to keep from throwing up again.

He wondered about the designation *sociopath*, and guessed she was simply insane. He looked beyond her at the girl, who was leaning against the wall and watching his every motion. One hand massaged the nipple of her breast. He noticed her chest rising and falling in shallow movements and filed that away. She was more developed, or older than he'd thought.

"Come on, girl, we got chores to do in the house while this boy digs. He's slow as molasses in January." Mae flashed the girl a glance, and she turned and ran out the door. Mae walked over to the opening and watched Alex for a moment while he worked. She grinned.

"We'll be back in an hour. Best you have those boys planted and done with by then." She disappeared, and

Alex could hear the door slam when she went into the adjacent house.

Alex took a couple more shovelfuls, then stopped and leaned on the handle. He looked at Manny.

"I don't know about you, but I'm getting the hell out of here—*now.*" He smiled.

"Sure, an' I'm the Queen of the May," Manny said as he sat up straighter. He stood and brushed his pants, then asked in a lower voice: "How you plan on doing that, boy?"

Scowling, Alex looked around, then threw the shovel down and walked over to Josh's body. He glanced up at Manny. "It'll work, I know it."

"What'll work?" Manny moved closer.

Alex stage-whispered, "She hesitates when she comes through the door, makes sure she can see all of us before she comes in, right?"

Manny gave him a "so what" shrug.

Alex continued whispering in an excited tone. "See, we take Josh and put him here." He pointed to his pallet. In back of them, Landry still snored as they talked. "You stay where you are. When she comes in, she sees three people over here and walks in."

"And then?"

"Then I leap out from where I'm hiding behind this door and grab her." Alex looked a bit disappointed with Manny's lack of enthusiasm.

"Great! We've got her and her gun, then what?"

"Then you jump up, run over, and jam this door shut and wedge something against it, maybe your pallet, so those dogs can't get in."

"Great idea, Sherlock. So then we're still in here chained up and those fucking dogs are out there licking their chops, waiting for us to waltz through the door."

"So, we have the gun. We'll blow Hitler away if we have to. Kill two of them. That's a double-barreled gun. That'd leave only one dog between us and the town. How tough can he be to handle? If we can find the keys to the antique car in the yard, we could be drinking wine and eating dinner at my house tonight.''

"And the chains?"

"God, don't be such a putz. Let's take this one thing at a time. Once we've got her and the gun, we can make all the noise we need breaking those chains loose from the concrete. Who's going to stop us? That girl or the kid can't do squat about it. The girl doesn't use a gun, does she?"

Manny grinned for the first time and walked over to where Alex was standing by Josh. "What are we waiting for?" He reached down and took hold of Josh's ankles. With Alex's help they dragged the body quickly to the pallet and rolled it over with the face away from the door.

"Jesus. He's got blood all over his back," Alex said. Manny held his hand up for Alex to wait, then ran into the storage room. He came out with two empty sugar sacks.

"We'll lay these over him. To look like you were cold, used 'em to cover yourself." He spread them over Josh's shoulders and stood back to look, then nodded. "That'll do it."

Alex picked up long lengths of his chain and trailed it out near the wall of the barn, then threw handfuls of dirt over the links to cover them. He worked his way to the corner where it was still shaded, then to the door. He held the door out just enough to hide behind.

Manny settled on his pallet and stared at Alex. They were too far away from each other to talk now, so Alex just motioned for him to look away and lay down. He smiled and circled his finger and thumb in an "everything's great" signal.

Alex looked back at the door. "Yeah," he mumbled softly as he hunched down to wait. "Everything's wonderful. Couldn't be better."

6

Jenny was sitting on the chair in the living room holding the telephone to her ear and listening to a number ringing. She wrapped and unwrapped the cord around her wrist in agitation. She felt completely frustrated because she was getting nothing from the police and had no idea what to do next; she only knew she had to talk to someone. Every time she'd called the police station, they'd simply said, "Nothing yet." *Come on, Mom, pick it up,* she thought.

"Mom!" she said when her mother answered on the tenth ring. Jenny choked back a sob, then told her mother everything she knew without hardly taking a breath. When she finished, her mother hesitated a long time before answering. Jenny thought they'd been disconnected and asked, "Mom? Are you there?"

"Yes, of course. My goodness. I'm just trying to figure out what to do, that's all."

"Mom, I don't want you to do anything. I just wanted your opinion about what *I* should be doing."

"Can't tell your father. Whatever you do, don't tell him until he has that bypass." Her voice was lowered. In her mind's eye, Jenny could see her mother looking around to see if he was within earshot.

"Mom, I know that. I wouldn't even consider it. I just wanted to know what you thought I should do." Jenny glanced around the room in frustration. This was accom-

plishing nothing—she had just upset her mother need-
lessly when her mother had enough problems taking care
of her dad, trying to build up his strength for cardiac
surgery in a couple of months.

"You haven't . . . found . . . well . . . you know . . ."
Her mother's voice broke.

"Found what, Mom?"

"Notes . . . telephone numbers . . . lipstick . . . things
like that?"

"God, no, Mom. Never. Nothing. That's not possible!"

"I'm sorry," her mother whispered. "I had to ask."

"Look, Mom. We're *both* sorry. I'm sorry I bothered
you. I know this is something that will work itself out
quickly, I shouldn't have called you—"

"Nonsense! Of course you should have called me. I
want to know everything that happens. I just feel bad I
can't leave the house right now, or that I can't do
anything for you." She heard her mother shift the phone
to her other ear. "You should let the authorities handle it,
you know, that's what you should do." She had changed
to her *"Mother knows best"* tone.

"Mom, they haven't done a damned thing." Jenny
could feel the tears welling again, and she blinked them
back.

Her mother was quiet for a long time, then said,
"Wesley."

"Wesley?" Jenny scowled in confusion at the receiver.

"Your uncle, Wesley. You remember him. Lives about
forty miles from you over in Beckley now. Haven't
talked to him in years, but he was in that special services
thing over in Vietnam, you remember?" Her mother had
never discussed him with Jenny at any length. "The ones
who wore those funny hats like those Frenchmen wear.
He should know about problems like this. Him and your
dad had a falling out about ten years ago and we lost
track of him, but I'm pretty sure he still lives there."

"You have his number or address?"

"Not anymore. You could likely find it in the phone
book, though."

"How's Dad doing?"

"You know him. Never complains. He's sleeping right now."

"Mom, I'll call you later and let you know what going on," Jenny said, then added, "Love you," and hung up.

She walked into the kitchen and pulled out her mixing bowl and jerked canisters from the cupboard, then started mixing dough for more bread. She stopped and stared at her white-dusted hands, then choked back a cry of anguish. To her left were six loaves of freshly baked bread.

What the hell am I doing? she wondered. *I don't need more bread—what I need is to be doing something constructive.*

She picked up the phone and dialed long-distance information. She'd only met her uncle once as a small child. She'd walked into the room and remembered him as a monstrous, shadowy figure without a face or voice.

"Wesley Ryan. If you're still alive, I'm going to find you, you old fart," she said. "Then we'll find out if blood is really thicker."

In the barn, Alex's legs were starting to cramp when he heard the door to the house thump in the distance. His heart jumped and speeded up. This was it. He'd only get one chance.

Alex glanced up and Manny stared back, his eyes wide and frightened. Alex urgently waved him to look away, then Manny rolled over and lay still.

Outside the cicadas hummed like electric lines buzzing on a sizzling day. Sweat tickled down Alex's spine. The soft crunch of her footsteps came closer and he could hear the snuffling of the dogs as they followed along behind. *Those damned dogs,* he thought. His body felt weak and the muscle in his left leg quivered from a cramp as he straightened and tried to be motionless. One chance. If he failed, they'd probably die.

The light on the ground in front of the door darkened.

He knew she was standing in the opening studying the pallets where the men lay.

Time creaked to a stop as he could almost hear her counting them—hear her mind working—

His heart hammered as he leaned forward and peeked around the door. From her shadow, he could tell she was still too far away.

"What the hell are you doing?" she screeched. Out of the corner of his eye he could see her step into the barn. "Get you lazy asses up—"

She moved forward, her back to him—

He leaped from behind the door and slid his forearm around her neck—

And jerked the shotgun from her with the other hand—

She screamed, "Bastards, bastards, bastards!"

She flailed in front of him like a small child, her thin arms pounding on him uselessly. Her body was slight, like a furry kitten—all fur—with tiny bones.

He released her and raised the gun.

She stepped away, rubbing her neck.

"Slam it shut, now!" he yelled to Manny who jumped to his feet and turned to leap toward the door—

Mae smiled, then held her fingers up to her mouth and released a penetrating whistle. Alex cringed—

The dogs were through the door and standing in front of the stills before Manny made it halfway to the door.

They both froze—

"So much for Plan A," Alex whispered as he whipped the shotgun toward the dogs. Manny glanced at him, then stared at the vicious, pacing animals that waited for further instructions.

"Get them out of here or I'll shoot you," Alex threatened as he turned the gun back toward Mae. The dogs snarled at the motion. Mae held her hand up, and they backed off slightly.

"Feel free to let 'er go, both barrels," Mae said, then chuckled.

"I'm not kidding," Alex said. He was shocked, not expecting her to call his bluff.

"Neither am I." Mae rubbed her neck where he'd held her and stopped smiling. "If'n I point my finger at you, an' say k-i-l-l"—she spelled out the word—"them dogs won't stop till you're in iddy-biddy pieces."

"You won't know that if you're dead," Alex said.

"How you gonna do that with no shells?" A smirk appeared.

"You're bluffing." Alex glanced down at the gun.

"Pull the trigger. 'At's the only way you'll know. Go on—"

"I don't want to kill you unless I have to."

"Shoot her!" Manny yelled. The dogs snarled.

Click— Click—

The hammers fell on empty chambers—

"Screwed," Alex whispered.

"Jesus," Manny wheezed out.

Mae smiled wide and strolled over in front of the dogs, where she turned and crossed her spindly arms in defiance.

"Figured on this long time ago. Never load it 'less I 'tend to use it. Been cartin' it empty all along."

Should have knocked her out, Alex thought as he lowered the useless gun. *Too late now.* The dogs pranced back and forth, slavering with fury.

"Like it or not, I won't be able to control 'em much longer. You boys ready to do as you're told?" She showed her snaggled brown teeth when she grinned.

Alex nodded and held the gun stock out to her. She snatched it away and stepped back, then waved the dogs out the door. The animals took one last lunge at them, barked, then were gone through the opening.

Mae motioned Alex back to the graves.

"Bring 'im," she said, gesturing down at Josh. Alex bent and pulled him across the floor by his arm, next to the other body. He retrieved his shovel and went to where he had been digging and started again. In the distance,

Manny dropped on his pallet and held his head in his hands, resigned to the worst. Mae stood farther away, nearer the door.

Alex was beaten for now.

As he worked, she said, "Only gonna let you live 'cause don't wanna bother gettin' a new man right now. I figured on lettin' you get by with one try, you being a cop. Next time, I'll kill you sure, you understand?" Alex nodded and concentrated on shoveling the dirt.

"'At's deep enough," Mae said when he turned the last shovelful. It had banged hard against the random rocks as he dug. The fresh loam smelled sour and gave off a heat of its own. The hole was up to his waist, about four feet deep, and extra wide because he'd dug it to accommodate the two bodies.

On the other side of the barn, Manny watched and the other man still snored. He wondered at that, amazed at what the human mind can become accustomed to. He flashed on the German death camps and wondered if it had been the same. Alex walked over to the two dead men, about thirty feet away. God! His stomach felt weak with the trauma and the sickness. This was the last thing he wanted to do. The woman hobbled behind, keeping a buffer of fifteen feet or more between them. Alex stood over the bodies for a long moment, reluctant to touch them.

"Get a move on, playtime's over. We got shine to run."

Alex rubbed his sweating arms and chest. They itched from the dirt and felt hot and irritated. He glanced at her and measured the distance. *I'd have to hit her in the head or I'd be back in the same soup,* he thought.

"You have a shirt or something I can wear?" Alex asked. Touching those cold bodies against his bare skin was revolting. The smell from the first man hit him and he cringed away. Bile rose in his throat. In his excitement it had failed to bother him before.

"You're lookin' at it." The woman motioned to the body of the man who'd worked there. Alex tried not to glance at his destroyed face. He knew he was being forced to handle these dead men as a warning of what could happen to him. If she was trying to upset him, it was working. He was amazed his stomach was still under control considering what he'd been through. He gripped the shovel. *Just a couple feet closer and I can flatten her,* he thought.

In back of Mae, the young girl came into the barn and stood in the shadows, watching Alex work.

Alex turned to Mae and asked, "You don't expect me to wear his clothes, do you?" The cloying stench rising from the corpse was so thick it seemed to coat his skin. In another twenty-four hours, the barn would reek.

"Don't care. It's up to you. It's them or nothin'."

"Jesus," he exclaimed. Knowing it might be the difference between surviving or not, he bent and unbuttoned the man's shirt, trying to breathe through his mouth all the while. That close to the body, the odor was almost unbearable. He threw the shovel over by the hole. *Have to try to get her when I cover them,* he reasoned.

He managed to pull the stiff arm from the shirtsleeve, then pulled the shirt under its body and off the other arm. The shirt was warm from where it had been pressed against the ground, the decomposition heating it to the touch.

His hands shook as he stood, then he carried the shirt several feet away and hung it on a nail projecting from the wall. He knew it would be a few days until he could put it on—no matter how much he wanted to.

"Hurry it up. Drag 'em over there," she shouted. Anger was quickly replacing her amusement. He went back to the bodies, removed the man's sneakers, and threw them in the general direction of the shirt. He took the man's cold wrist and lifted it up. The bones snapped and popped as the dead muscles resisted. It was sickening. That was it. Alex stumbled to the wall and heaved and heaved until his stomach was empty.

"Ewwww!" he heard the young girl exclaim in the distance. He wondered at that. Killing was okay, but his throwing up bothered her.

Finally, his throat still burning, he glanced around. The woman watched him, her mouth working like a cow chewing its cud. He had to get this over with as soon as possible. He walked back, leaned, grabbed the man by both wrists, and looking over his shoulder as he moved, dragged him across the barn floor. His mind turned off at the horror of what he was doing.

He dropped the body into the hole, and it tumbled facedown so the gore faced the dirt. The man's back was bruised—purple where the blood had settled. He repeated it with Josh. Everything of value had been stripped from Josh's body, and his blood-soaked shirt was unwearable. Alex had stains on his pants too, but the thought of stripping the pants from Josh or from the first corpse was unthinkable. He'd live or die with what he had.

After he dropped Josh in beside the other corpse, he picked up the shovel and stood for a long moment looking down on him. He choked and tears welled into the corners of his eyes. This was the part he dreaded. Covering him with dirt. This final act acknowledged he was forever dead.

Josh's accusing eyes stared up as Alex threw each shovelful in on top of his blood-spattered chest. Alex tried not to look, but his gaze was drawn back to that face—a face that would disintegrate after a few days in the warm, loamy earth. Alex glanced over at Mae. Almost as though she knew what he was thinking, she had backed up several paces, clearly out of reach. Throwing the shovel at her, or a frontal assault, would have been suicide from this distance. *Bitch. I'll get you,* he thought. He looked back to Josh.

Warm tears ran down his cheeks as he tossed shovelfuls of dirt onto Josh's face. Four, five, six—and just a lock of hair projected from the dark loam. Seven, and it was gone.

Finishing, he tamped the soft soil with his feet, conscious he was pressing the dirt down into those accusing, staring eyes.

"Rest in peace," he whispered. Although he belonged to no organized religion, he crossed himself and choked out another soft sob. He looked along the wall where the earth lay in many disturbed piles. He'd count them later. If each grave contained more than one body, like this one, there could be a dozen or more bodies here. He shivered.

The old lady nodded in satisfaction at the finished job, then motioned for the girl to pick up the shovels and take them away. Grinning, the girl watched him as she dipped and retrieved them.

"Git off with you," Mae said to the girl. She scurried through the door.

"That mash is ready, and hit's past time to run some shine." She hesitated at the door and added, "You made a good decision, boy, not tryin' anything with that shovel. You mind your manners from now on, you might live to see your next birthday."

One of us will be dead before my next birthday, Alex thought.

And it isn't going to be me.

7

Atlanta was muggy. The Thistledown Motel-Hotel sat off Route Eight near the intersection of Parson's Lane. One of the largest motels in the area, it contained 350 rooms, a piano lounge, and two pools. Heavy, billowy clouds drifted across the slate-blue sky above it, and the wind was freshening, promising rain.

It was three-thirty in the afternoon when Harley Burris filled the doorway of the lounge. He looked around the air-conditioned room with an expression indicating he smelled something bad, then lumbered over to the end of the bar and lowered his huge frame onto a leather-padded stool. Out of his element, his rough appearance gave away that searching for comfort was not his top priority. At six feet five, 280 pounds, he had the aura of a man who felt a lot more comfortable living and hunting in the deep woods. His ragged beard was unwashed, and his curly, dark hair stuck out at right angles from under his Atlanta Braves baseball cap. An open-sleeved hunter's vest covered his filthy T-shirt. Dungarees and well-worn cowboy boots completed his outfit. His bare arms were as thick as elder trunks; his shoulders were wide and ominous.

He hunched over the oak bar like a child sitting at a doll table and stared at the bartender, who was washing glasses in the sink.

"Boy, you gon' screw with them all day, or you gon'

fetch a man a drink?" he rumbled in a deep voice. The bartender glanced up from what he was doing, and his eyes widened when he took in Harley's bulk. He smiled and set a glass down. Wiping his hands on his towel, he shuffled over and looked up at Harley.

"Sorry, didn't see you come in. What'll you have?" He was a short, thin man with gray hair slicked straight back from his hawkish face.

"Bring me a bottle of sippin' whiskey," Harley grumbled. "An getcher self some glasses, boy. If'n you cain't see me, you're in piss-poor shape."

The bartender ignored the comment and asked, "A bottle? Sorry, I can't do that. We only serve liquor in glasses—shot glasses usually."

"Them iddy-biddy things? Bullshit. Gimme a man's glass." Harley seethed inside. He wanted to hurt somebody, but decided he'd have to try to hold on to his temper for now. Getting arrested in this town was too risky with the warrants outstanding against him, or he'd 've just reached out and smashed this little man. Resistance from anybody annoyed the hell out of him.

"Sure, glad to." The bartender edged away and stopped to fill a couple of orders for the young mini-dressed waitress before getting Harley's drink. Showin' me who's the boss here, Harley thought. The heat in his neck rose. Occasionally people treated him like trash, and when they did, he made them sorry. He felt under his jacket and patted the scabbard of his hunting knife.

"Single or double?" the bartender asked as he finally set the highball glass in front of Harley. "Seagram's okay?"

"Fill it to here." Harley held his sausage-sized finger at three-quarters the way up the glass.

"That's a lot of liquor. I'm not sure that I can—"

His voice jerked to a halt as Harley reached out and gripped the bartender's upper arm with his meaty fist. Light pressure brought the frail man to his tiptoes. Harley could feel the flaccid muscles collapse around the thin bone, and knew he could have easily have snapped his arm in two with a bit more pressure, but smiled instead of squeezing harder. The man swallowed and stared back into Harley's flashing eyes.

"No problem," the bartender squeaked in a strained falsetto, and began pouring the drink from his awkward position. When he hit the imaginary finger-line, Harley released his arm, and the man lowered back to his heels, then expelled air like a punctured balloon.

"Now, see how much easier it is when you're friendly?" Harley said evenly. He cradled the glass, and only the top of it showed above his giant fist.

The bartender cleared his throat. "That'll be ten dollars, sir."

"I'll pay when I'm done," Harley said with finality, and pinpointed the little man in the crosshairs of his eyes.

"That would be fine too." The bartender walked back to the sink, glad to be away from him again, then started to wash the glasses. Before sticking his hands in the water, he grimaced, lifted his hand, and unconsciously rubbed his arm. Harley smiled. People were so much more pleasant to be around when they knew his rules and realized he was in charge.

Scanning the room, Harley took in the small crowd of business people and noticed the men with disdain. They were wearing ties. *Christ, they all look ridiculous and uncomfortable,* he thought.

A soft murmur of conversation was background for a listless piano player who rolled out a selection of tired show tunes. Atlanta was one of the hubs of the South, and major industry all over the country sent salespeople to crack the market.

The outside door opened, and a red-haired woman walked in. She stood for a moment in the entry, surveying the crowd with the light silhouetting her hourglass body. A form-fitting red dress hugged her hips like a body stocking. Her heavy breasts strained to break out of the low-cut front and her large nipples pressed belligerently against the fabric. Her padded hips and huge breasts further accented an already tiny waist. Harley chuckled. *She's got these neckties by the balls,* he figured.

Her made-up eyes drifted to Harley, then scanned the selection of men at the surrounding tables like a hunter surveying prey. Conversation in the room stopped, and the male heads followed her, visually ravaging her body as she jiggled across the room, weaving a pattern of perfume. She sat at a hatbox-sized table within earshot of Harley. He grinned and took in a couple fingers of his drink.

Harley let his gaze swing around the room and watched as the agitated men stared to see what this bundle of sex was going to do next. Stupid. Where he was from, if a man saw a woman he wanted to screw, he just mosied up and let her know he was buyin' if she was sellin'. These neckties had a whole different set of rules to their game. Prissy and scared, and probably married— the most of them—they'd dance around half the night, smellin' and sniffin'. He leaned back and took a big swig of his fire-hot liquid and sighed.

This is gonna be interesting, he thought.

After Mae came into the barn and signaled to begin, Alex and the men worked steadily at the stills. Alex made no attempt to talk to Mae because the futility of trying to negotiate was evident. If he was going to escape from here, the first thing he had to do was find out what the hell was going on—who the players were—and what the lay of the land was.

Mae leaned against the wall of the barn and glowered at Alex's progress; her heavy shotgun leaned against her knee. He knew the answer to the question of whether it was loaded. After bluffing them before, she'd be carrying a full load in it from now on.

At first, it was quite a struggle for him to be near the vats because of the heavy fumes bubbling to the surface—heavy, yeasty smells belching up and drifting off through the openings at each end of the barn. He worked at a slow pace, then, after a while, began to sweat.

As he did, the dizziness receded and he felt a bit better.

For what seemed like an hour, Alex labored with a mash stick—a long stick with shorter sticks nailed to the end of it—breaking apart the clumps of fermenting grain and malt in the vats. Then Manny took him over and showed him the two vats ready for processing. Manny had been working on the stills, cleaning out the copper pots, copper lines, and what Manny called a thumper tub, preparing them to run the mash.

"How do you feel, boy? You gonna make it?" Manny asked him.

Alex glanced at Mae, who still watched his every move, then wiped the sweat from his arms and chest. "Feel a hell of a lot better if she'd stop watching me like a bug in a bottle."

"Relax. She's only worried she's goin' to have to deep-six you, boy, or deep-four you. Afraid she'll have to go and fetch on home another mash man. Kind of amusing to realize you're only being kept alive because your dying would create a minor inconvenience, isn't it?" Manny chuckled at his attempt at macabre humor. Alex winced at his strange mixture of country slang and a heavy New York accent.

"How the hell can you think that's funny?" Alex asked, wondering if this man was more screwed up than she was. The memory of Josh's face staring up at him as Alex covered him with dirt still burned.

"Get those two five-gallon buckets there, boy," Manny said. Alex glared at him, then walked over and grabbed the thick-sided wooden buckets. He returned and waited for more instructions.

"I'll work because I have to right now, but don't call me boy." Practically everyone had called Alex "boy" since he'd arrived in West Virginia and it was wearing thin.

"Git yer ass to workin' and quit jawin'," Mae screeched from across the barn. "Tote them buckets lively!"

"You heard the lady," Manny said. "Tote them buckets lively." He said it under his breath and laughed a trifle louder this time. As they ambled to the first vat, he whispered, his beard barely moving, "Boy, if you want to survive for any length of time here, you've got to laugh at everything a little, especially yourself. Only thing keeps me alive is that, someday, I know somebody's going to walk in that door wearing a badge, and by God, I'm going to be alive and standing tall, smilin' my shit-eatin' grin, ready to march back home."

Manny showed him how to fill the buckets, to just take the beer, the liquid, and leave the thick residue of mash behind.

"This here liquid's between six- to nine-percent alcohol. What we gotta do on that still is to get rid of the water in the distilling process and end up at the spigot at about fifty-percent alcohol or more. Anyway, that's the game plan. You could get a right nice buzz drinking this beer—if you can stand the sour taste, that is." Manny stuck his finger in, licked it, and smiled. "Mmmmmm," he said, "Flavored with bird shit. Secret is to know when the damn stuff is ready to run. Has to ferment about three days, give or take. Too soon, there's not enough alcohol. Too late, the damn stuff starts to turn to vinegar on you. If that happens, your ass is grass with the old lady!"

Manny dipped in the first bucket and carried it over to the still. It made a hollow, thundering sound as he poured it in the opening at the top.

"How much does that copper pot hold?" Alex asked.

"About three hundred gallons total."

"Sixty buckets, then," Alex said to himself without hesitation.

"You ain't as dumb as you look, boy. You can keep the books around here from now on."

"So, you simply boil this damn stuff, the steam rises through the lines, then it comes out the other end into the curled-up pipe you call a worm, where it condenses. Is that all there is to it?" Alex's inquisitive mind had beaten back his anxiety.

The other quiet man stuffed kindling wood under each of the stills, and a small fire crackled under the one they worked on. Clay bricks surrounded each copper pot and directed the heat around the sides, then up a chimney. Wood was shoved into and burned in an open space underneath each pot. *Backwoods technology,* thought Alex.

Reading his mind, Manny said, "You're like every other guy who's come in here. You think this is stupid hillbilly work. Fact is, making good liquor is really an art. You make this crap wrong and it's nothing but high-grade poison. The important part is getting the heat just right and working the still just so."

Mae yelled from across the room, "Pick it up, dammit! There's goin' ta be a pickup tomorry!" She was red-faced, but kept her distance.

"Sure, Mae! I'm working on it!" Manny shouted back, an edge of irritation in his own voice. "Bitch," he said under his breath to Alex. He talked with the confidence of a man who knew he'd be hard to replace.

"Why's the heat so important?" Alex snapped. It looked simple to him.

"Numbers don't mean crap to us because we don't have thermometers and no setup to measure it if we did, but the principle is important, okay? Alcohol boils at one hundred seventy-two degrees, water at two hundred twelve degrees. Since it's the alcohol we want, the secret is to get the temperature of the beer a tad above one hundred seventy-two degrees where the alcohol will vaporize, but keep it below the two hundred twelve degrees so only a small amount of the water will. You get it boiling too violent, it'll swell up and puke through the lines, and then you'll spend at least an hour cleaning everything out again. You don't want to know what that old woman will say or do then!"

"If you can't measure the temperature, how the hell you going to know that?"

"I'll show you how," Manny said with pride. "You just gotta know what you're doing." He smiled. "You just tap this collector on top of the pot, and the sound tells you when it's right." He glanced over at Mae, then back.

"We'd better get our ass moving right now. Once we get the still filled and perking, I'll show you how to tell by the tone."

"How the hell does she make any money on this still anyway?" Alex asked. "I didn't think there was any profit in bootlegging anymore."

Manny kept working while he talked. "There isn't. Unless you've got slave labor like us, and can buy your corn from the local farmers at pennies on the dollar. Only thing they pay market price for around here is the sugar, and it's my guess they steal half of that. I seen some of these cloth bags stamped with the name of some of the big chains around here. Probably ripped off a warehouse or two."

"Who would want it, though, when you can buy such good stuff in the stores?" Alex asked. "This shine. I tasted it earlier. Damn stuff would gag a horse."

"Alcoholics don't care what the hell they drink, just so it's cheap. I've got some ideas on that, too, but they don't exactly consult me on their marketing decisions around here."

"We're going to have to talk more later, when she's gone."

"About what?" Manny asked.

"What else? Making another go at getting the hell out of here."

"You got any other great ideas, you can count me out, cowboy. We're just damned lucky we're still alive. I wasn't exactly impressed with your planning the first time."

Alex stopped working and looked at him. "You don't mean that. You're not giving up, are you?"

Manny stopped too. "Look, if I got a choice between dying now, or dying later . . . I'll take dying later, thank you. You want to try another harebrained stunt—go ahead. Me, I'm waiting for the cavalry to rescue me." He turned back to the still. "You'd better get to hauling again before she comes down on us, Howdy Doody."

Alex shook his head and smiled. It had been a lot of years since his mother had called him that. As a child, with his blond hair and freckles, she had always teased him about looking like Howdy Doody. He picked up his buckets and went back to work.

Alex carried the beer with one five-gallon pail, and as the poisons sweated out of his system, he was able to handle two pails at a time. He glanced over when he was lugging two pails, and Mae worked her mouth and nodded in satisfaction. It amazed him that she acted as though everything were back to normal.

He thought, *Maybe I'll survive myself, survive to see Jenny again.* At the image of Jenny, he picked up the pace a bit.

He'd have to wait. His chance would come. A chain, an old woman, a girl, a kid, and three dogs—no matter how vicious—could keep him prisoner for only a short period of time.

A very short time.

8

In the bar, Harley sloshed the remainder of his drink around in his glass, downed it, then ordered another from the bartender by motioning with his hand. The small man reappeared and refilled it to the finger-line. He said nothing about money this time. Harley knew he'd be happy if Harley just left without hurting him again.

To the side of his stool, the woman in the red dress ordered a gimlet from the bar girl, whatever that drink was. The bar girl asked short, clipped questions, only what was necessary, no more. Harley chuckled, knowing she resented the attention the red dress was getting from the men in the bar.

Out of the corner of his eye, Harley noticed two men—young men, both in those damnable suits and ties—approach the woman in red. The big move. Ha!

"May we buy you a drink?" the taller of the two men said as he smiled down at her.

You could buy her the whole fucking bar, and like as not she'd finish it 'fore the night was out, Harley thought.

"You boys are so kind to this simple country belle," the woman cooed in a Southern lilt. Harley came close to spitting his drink on the bar at that. This was great fun. He could see her posing in his peripheral vision, those monster breasts jutting forward like twin sex-seeking torpedoes.

"What's your name, honey?" the shorter of the men asked, almost salivating on his tie as he watched her bosom rise and fall.

"Y'all can call me Daisy if you want to, you know, like Daisy Mae in the funnies." The men chuckled as though they understood. Harley knew they were too young to have read those old comics. *Jesus, lady, those walking hard-ons don't give a shit what your name is, they just wanna jump you is all,* he mused.

The slim, tailored men sat on either side of her, pulled their chairs in closer, then began a long, convoluted conversation they hoped would lead to the bedroom.

After about thirty minutes of verbal fencing, Daisy said, "I'm gonna have to go home in an hour or so to fix supper for my poor crippled mama. You boys want it or not?"

"Want what?" the shorter of the two asked stupidly.

"Sugar, honey. Down here we call it sugar." She smiled a syrupy grin, then leaned forward and made sure her cleavage was as close to his face as possible. She whispered, "Up North, I understand y'all call it— 'fucking.' That right?" She finished with a shy smile, dimples showing. Harley was quiet now, listening with interest, a chuckle rising in his chest.

The man she leaned toward coughed, then said, "Yeah, well, I, aah, yeah." He loosened his tie.

"Well, yeah, what?" She blinked her eyes.

"Jesus, yes," the man choked out. "Let's go." As he started to stand, Daisy reached out, touched his arm, and he lowered back to his seat.

"You understand, sweetness, a simple country girl needs a little something to tide her over in these hard times," she whispered, accenting the word "hard" while she looked at his very interested lap. He stared at her for a moment, confused, then the lights came on.

"Sure, no problem. Exactly how much to tide you over, honey?" he asked, suddenly a bit more apprehensive. The man was hooked. As long as the jerk could meet the tab, Harley knew that sexy Daisy would score.

"Let's say, a hundred for you alone, a hundred fifty for the both of you together. I like both of you boys, and I do enjoy taking care of my . . . obligations . . . all at one time, if you know what I mean." She took both of her hands and rubbed the inside of the men's legs. "'Sides that, it feels really good," she whispered hoarsely. They glanced at each other, then the older and taller of the two nodded.

"Now?" Daisy asked urgently. They both grinned. They were beyond talking, too excited to form words. "What room, boys?"

Harley shook his head as the two men sat and stared at each other. *They're pathetic.*

"Ahh, I think . . ." The shorter man fumbled a key from his pocket and studied it in his shaking hand. "Three eighty-six. Room three-eight-six," he said in a voice that quavered.

"Tell you what," Daisy offered. "You good-lookin' boys scoot on up there and get yerselves ready for the time of your little lives, an' I'll finish my drinky-poo, then I'll be right up." She nodded to the other people in the room and grinned. "A girl has to worry about her reputation, you know."

The two men leaped up as though their chairs had been jolted with electricity and left the room, banging chairs and tables on the way.

Obviously already naked and screwing her brains out in their minds. *Smooth*, thought Harley.

The lady had the dignity to wait all of ten minutes. In that time two other men made moves on her, but she just batted her eyes and declined with a smile like the genteel lady she was. When she left, the same swaying heads that had followed her in followed her out. Only this time, she headed for the motel lobby and elevators.

After several minutes of waiting, Harley too stood and walked toward the lobby of the motel. As he did, the piano man labored through "Moon River" for the fifth time since he'd gotten there.

The bartender made a point of not looking at Harley as

he swaggered by. Harley grinned to himself. He'd known before he left that the little man would ignore the twenty dollars Harley owed. Asking would take more nerve than he had.

Harley had left a dollar tip to show his appreciation.

The elevator doors on the third floor of the hotel slid open. Harley Burris stepped out, looked at the room-number directional arrows on the wall, then lumbered down the hall. A man in 375 opened his door and laid an empty food tray on the floor for pickup. He slammed his door when he glanced up at the scowling, dark figure walking toward him.

Harley smirked. He was used to that reaction.

Three eighty-two, three eighty-four, three eighty-six. Room three eighty-six. *That's where them boys is. They's well dressed, really slickered up,* he thought. *Betcha each of them monkey suits alone cost several hundred dollars.* He patted his knife scabbard again for assurance.

He stood for a long moment in front of the door, as though trying to decide what to do. Reaching down, he turned the handle and nudged the door with his knee. It pivoted without a sound, and a piece of cardboard dropped to the floor from the door latch.

Sticking his head inside, he could see the room was shaded but not dark. Perfect, no light will show from the dim hall, he realized.

From the other side of a wall came the fevered moans of the woman interspersed with urgent words: "Oh, you boys are too much . . . this is too much . . . oh, God!"

One of the men groaned and the squeaking springs increased in tempo. The wall contained a sink and mirror and shielded the door from their view. He smiled, stepped into the room, and shut the door behind him. The soft click of the lock would be lost in the sound of their sex play.

Shit, this is just too good, too good, he thought.

"Oh, baby! Do it faster! Do it faster!" Her breath came in gasps and the room reeked of hot sex. Harley was rock-hard himself with the excitement of listening to the thrashing and moaning coming from the other side of the wall. His heart pounded and his mouth was dry as he fingered the hunting knife under his jacket.

"Oh, God, that was so good!" the woman shrieked. "Now let's change places." The springs squeaked and groaned from their gyrations.

"Jesus," one of the young men said between gasps. The bed complained again as he lowered his feet to the floor. Harley took off his hunting jacket and laid it on the sink, then reached down and withdrew the long, razor-sharp knife and studied the tip as he listened for more movement.

"Where y'all goin', honey? . . . We ain't done yet," the woman whined.

"God, just a second, okay? I have to get a glass of water. I'm too hot."

Harley gripped the knife in his left hand and drew back with his right fist as he heard the feet padding toward him. In an instant, the man appeared in the opening.

The man's eyes sprung wide.

Harley got a quick glimpse of his pale, sweat-soaked body as he swung his hammer of a fist.

The blow cracked like a gunshot when it connected with the man's forehead—

The man was lifted off his feet and flew back against the wall—

The woman screeched.

The other man said, "What the—"

The first man hit the wall and slid into an unconscious heap and knocked over the wastebasket and lamp with a crash.

Harley sprang around the wall and dove onto the bed. He slap-grabbed at the hot, sweat-slick bodies as the woman squealed and crab-crawled back against the headboard.

The man made a dive to get past him while yelling—

Harley's fence-post of an arm came up and clothes-lined him back to the bed like a errant child. Harley knew the man on the floor was unconscious and presented no threat.

"Where the hell you goin', boy? The party's just startin'," Harley grumbled, finishing with a chuckle. *Sheeit! This is fun!* he thought.

The woman cringed back and tried to cover her bulbous breasts with her thin arms as Harley pinioned the man like a butterfly with his free hand.

"Please don't hurt me," the sweaty man choked from under the huge paw gripping his neck like a vise. "I'll give you anything you want! You want the girl? There— take her—you can have her." He stared wide-eyed at the knife in Harley's other hand.

"You ain't much of a man, are you, boy? You can't give me something I already mean to take, now can you?" Harley raised up by the side of the bed like a hairy bear standing on its hind legs and pulled the thin man with him by his neck. Harley outweighed him by over a hundred pounds of solid muscle, and Harley knew that even though the man's hands were free, he would be submissive. This boy was too smart to slap a bear and make it mad.

Harley bashed him hard against the wall next to the headboard and buried the hunting knife into the drywall next to his face.

The man squeaked in fear.

Harley pulled him forward, hesitated and smiled, then smashed the man's head into the wall. When it crashed through the wallboard, his eyes rolled back into his head. Harley released him, and he slid down into a limp heap at his feet.

"Sheeit! These boys wasn't no challenge at all." He turned and pointed a threatening finger the woman. She scrunched lower. "Don't move, girl, I'll get back to you."

"Please, let me go, I ain't done nothin'. I'll just be on my way—this ain't no business o' mine—I won't tell no one."

Harley chuckled deep in his chest. "Bitch, you're a

caution, you are. You even twitch that soft little ass while I'm workin', I'll have to hurt you some too."

He reached down and picked up the man by his hair. The pain would have been excruciating, but he was unconscious. Harley roughly threw his naked body onto one of the wrought-iron chairs at a sitting table by the bed. He did the same with the other man, who was also still out of it, then went into the dressing area and withdrew several precut lengths of cord from the side pocket of his hunting jacket.

Walking back, he tied their hands and feet. His baseball cap bobbed up and down as he worked. He then turned the chairs out so they faced the bed.

The man he'd hit first groaned as he came back to consciousness. The second man's eyes flickered open, but he remained silent, too frightened to say anything.

As Harley finished the last knot, out of the corner of his eye he saw the naked woman creeping up behind him, the knife held over her head. He smirked, then turned as she was about to thrust, and slapped her hard with his open hand. She fell back on the bed, and the knife rattled to the floor.

"Sheeit, lady. You're plumb stupid," he said. He was blue-steel hard as he hovered above her. He unzipped his pants and dropped them.

"Oh, God, no! I'm sorry, Mr. Mountain Man. I didn't mean it . . . please don't hurt me." She cried, holding one hand to her mouth where a thin trickle of blood showed. The two men were wide-awake now, eyes wide, gaze darting back and forth.

He jumped on her and bit her shoulders, her neck, then worked his way to her breasts. She groaned from the almost unbearable pain as he chewed on her firm nipple. Then he jerked her legs apart and entered her, jamming into her like a fevered stallion. Hard, cruel thrusts slammed her head back into the headboard. Slow, then faster and faster.

She cried and grunted with each lunge. He was like a crazed animal, with no thought of her torment—only interested in his own out-of-control lust. Finally, he smashed her hard against the headboard and held her firm against it as he gripped her red hair with both hands. He came in waves of pleasure. She moaned in agony and choked out a thin cry. They both fell away, soaked with sweat.

After a minute of rest, Harley rose, pulled in, and zipped his pants. He then strode around the room, casually going through the men's clothes and suitcases. He took all their money and valuables and laid them on the dresser top. Everything else, he threw on the floor in a growing pile. Finished, he walked over, retrieved the deadly hunting knife, and approached the men.

He grabbed the first man by the hair and jerked his head back. "You make a sound, boy, I'll slit your throat! You understand?" The man nodded as best he could. His stretched scalp opened his eyes even wider in fear. "Good," said Harley.

He ran the razor-sharp tip of the knife across the man's chest two times. The man gasped and made choking sounds, but remained quiet. Harley made a perfect "X" across his breastbone. He went to the other man, repeated the threat, and made the same marks on *his* chest.

The men breathed fast and grimaced, struggling to keep from crying out. They both stared as he sheathed his knife, then sighed in relief as he walked away into the entry and slipped on his jacket.

When he came back in, still buckling his belt, he told the woman, "You get your clothes on too, woman. You're going with me." Without a word, she jumped up, went into the bathroom, and started dressing.

Harley walked to the two men. The one on the left quivered under his gaze. That amused Harley. He smiled and said, "You boys look a mite used up." Reaching out with his finger, he poked the bloody X on the chest of the man on the right. The man cringed.

"When you figure on how to get loose, you both look in that mirror in there." He motioned to the dressing area. "'Fore you call the law, you think on how it'd feel to have that hunting knife o' mine stuck right where them two lines come together." He jabbed his finger hard at the intersection of the two cuts. The man groaned, then cried softly. "Reckon after you study on it, you'll decide ta just pack what's left and get your skinny little asses on up north."

Harley took one small suitcase and packed all the valuables into it. None of the clothes would fit him, but he took everything else he wanted. When he finished, he snapped it closed. Daisy came out and stood by the door, ready to leave. He started to walk through the door, then set down the case and walked over to the two men, who looked up at him apprehensively. The one still snuffled softly.

"Cain't abide a coward of a man nohow." He smashed each of them once more with the sledgehammer at the end of his right arm, and the men slumped unconscious in their chairs. He slapped Daisy on the butt and pushed her through the door, then followed.

"Sheeit," he mumbled.

The door clicked on the quiet room.

"Where'd you come up with that Daisy Mae bullshit?" Harley frowned at the woman in the red dress on the seat beside him.

"Seen it in a comic book over at Eldridge's house," she said. "Liked the sound of it."

"Stick with the name I tell you in the future, Ellie," Harley said. He stared out across the hood of the heavy truck and concentrated on the bouncing headlights as they flickered on the narrow road. The windshield wipers clicked, clearing the light rain that had been falling since they left the motel. "Thought for a minute you forgot to put that cardboard in the door lock like you's s'posed to."

"Not likely," she answered. "They's dumb as door-knobs, and was so all-fired hot and bothered to get at me, I coulda thunked 'em with a shoe and they wouldn'ta noticed." She bit her lip. "Think them boys'll call the law?"

"Soon's they get untied they'll make skid marks all the way back to New York City." He laughed.

She smiled, then frowned, and turned to him. "Next time, ain't no need to hit me so hard, neither."

"Shut up. You love it and you know it."

"Yeah, well, it ain't going to help our lovemakin' if'n my lip swells." She took out her pocket mirror, flipped on the interior light, and checked the swelling lip in the dim interior. "Can't see why you always gotta be so rough!"

"When I was a boy, back in Chattanooga, my pa would get all liquored up, two, sometimes three nights a week, an' beat the shit out of me an' my brother. No reason, just so we'd know who was in charge. Not like you would a kid, but with his fists, tryin' to hurt. Still have some of them scars where I'd hit something when I fell. Never said a word or cried. Only waited. Come my fourteenth birthday, I was big as him, 'cept all muscle. He came down on me on a Saturday night for his last time. Yeah, the last time! I turned and beat him so bad he pert near lost an eye, broke an arm."

"You never tol' me that before. You beat your own daddy?" She flipped off the light and settled back.

"You betcha."

"Jesus, dincha feel bad?"

"Bad? I loved every minute of it! Fuck him! Son of bitch said 'How high?' when I tol' him to jump after that. Then, next few years, I'd whup his ass every once in a while, sort of to let him know who's boss now. Learned me that folks don't give you no shit if you hit 'em first an' tell 'em after." He chuckled deep in his throat. "Hit 'em first, tell 'em after, and they listen good."

Ellie shook her head and wiped the sweat from her neck. "How much cash we got?"

"Five hundred and change, plus the usual credit cards we can sell to Willie." He pushed out his foot and tapped the lights to high beams.

"What time we got to be there?"

"S'posed to have a load of shine to run tomorrow. Like

as not she'll be late an' we can sleep in." He honked his horn and swore at a driver who was going too slow. "Hear tell from Jake that Mae Skaggit up and killed one of her still-hands. If'n she ain't got a new one yet, them boys she has'll be draggin' ass an' be way behind."

"Killed him?" She jerked upright. "Why'd she do that? You tol' me they was men chained in there, but you didn't tell me nothin' about no killin'."

"So now I did. Don't worry your pretty little head. This ain't none of your business. You ain't been there before, so's I'll tell you. In this liquor trade, folks sometimes have to hurt other folks. The less you ask, the better off you are, understand?"

She leaned back and yawned.

He continued: "Reckon we might be there a couple days, likely. It ain't the Hilton, but you'll be with me." He then squeezed her leg hard.

She pulled away from the pain and smiled. "Don't make me no nevermind. I could sure use the sleep. Mostly 'cause I ain't been sleepin' when I been in bed lately." She wiggled around in the seat and straightened her red dress. Changing her happy expression to an almost shy grin, she whispered, "That was fun." She leaned back and tucked and smoothed the bustline of her dress. "Sure like this dress, Harley. It gets a load of attention." He smirked.

She cuddled in next to him, closed her eyes, and fell asleep.

9

It took Jenny over an hour to drive to Beckley. Part of the road on the way was under construction. Before she left, she found Wesley Ryan's address and telephone number in the telephone book. When she called the number, she got the recording that said the line was disconnected. Information had no new number.

She stopped in a Texaco station on the main drag for directions to the street. A man came out wearing a greasy jumpsuit and an equally dirty baseball cap. He pumped her gas, then took her money.

While he handed her the change from a twenty, she said, "I'm looking for Benson Street. Can you help me, please?"

The man grinned, revealing three random teeth, all with brown spots on them. Feeling threatened, she reached down and tapped her automatic lock button.

"You ain't gonna wanna go there, little lady."

"Why's that?" She sighed, tired of problems.

"That's a bad area. They's negras and junkies and whores and such all over that street. Cute missy like you shouldn't even get out of her car down there, less'n you're planning on workin', that is." He chuckled. "An' if'n you are, I can give you some business right here. Save you the trip." He snickered.

Too stunned to speak for a moment, she recovered and shouted, "Stuff it, you disgusting pimple-brained jerk!"

She rolled her window up, then jammed the Volvo into drive and burned rubber out onto the street. She could hear him cackling as she drove away.

After a couple of blocks, she slowed down, then giggled while kneading the steering wheel. "Pimple-brained jerk," she repeated, then laughed harder because she'd never called anyone that before. Abruptly, her laughter changed to tears, and she broke into uncontrollable sobbing. She pulled over to the curb.

It was overcast and darkening, even though the sun was still somewhere behind the clouds. An occasional drop of rain peppered the windshield.

After ten minutes, she stopped crying and just snuffled softly. Drained of energy, she sat with her head resting on the backs of her hands that held the steering wheel. The engine was idling evenly when someone rapped on the passenger-side window.

"Wha—?" She glanced up.

A boy—a young black boy—thirteen to fourteen maybe.

Saying something through the window.

"What?" she asked, but his speech was still muffled as he signaled frantically.

I'll just roll it down a few inches so I can hear him, she thought. He looked too young to be any problem for her.

She fingered the button. The window whirred open about a half a foot. The boy was strangely silent as he stared in at her, just stood in the gathering dusk wearing a thin grin.

"What did you want?" she asked finally.

The boy smiled wide and said, "Got somethin' for you, lady. Here!" He raised his arms and dropped two large black objects through the window onto the seat.

She blinked her eyes and looked down.

Two huge sewer rats squealed—

One leaped onto the floor at her feet—

The other went over the back of the seat—

She choked, then screamed, then banged into the door, grabbing, clawing for the handle.

The door opened.

Still shrieking, she tumbled into the street and crawled away on her hands and knees.

About fifteen feet away, she leaped up and turned—

Just in time to see the boy jump in the car and slam the door.

"What . . . get out . . . that's my car!"

He smiled wide, dropped it in gear.

Then the car roared off into the dark and was gone.

"Get out . . . you can't do that . . . that's my. . . ." Her voice trailed away and she stood stunned for a long moment, long after the car had turned the corner and the evening had swallowed up the sound of the engine. "You bastard! You can't do that!" she screamed into the night, then stamped her feet on the wet pavement in frustration.

Finally, becoming fully aware of what had happened and where she was, she looked around. Her face was wet from the steady patter of small raindrops. In the distance, the dark street was quiet, completely deserted, and wind tumbled papers across the shiny asphalt.

From the darkness a man's voice asked, "Yo, mama. You needs a ride?"

Jenny looked into the shadows of the building on the corner. A man stepped out and repeated, "I asked, you needs a lift, mama?"

Frightened, she glanced around quickly. It was an older business section and most of the stores were dark except for a lit-up restaurant on the next block. She felt like crying, but was too shocked and nervous to allow herself the luxury.

Her car was gone and she felt absolutely stupid standing in the light rain. She shivered as the warm wind cut through her sweater and slacks.

"No, no, thanks," she mumbled as she brushed off the dirt from her knees and sidestepped toward the lights. The man laughed.

He'd obviously seen what had happened . . . maybe actually set it up, she realized. No point in asking him for help.

As she walked, she glanced back over her shoulder occasionally. Laughter echoed over the cold, wet pavement, but no one followed.

Jenny counted eight people standing against the side of the building by the restaurant. As she approached, conversation stopped. They all turned their heads and studied her. She avoided their eyes and walked past, into the old building. She expected catcalls and laughter, but they went back to their own conversations.

The high-ceilinged restaurant was smoky and lit by plastic-shaded lamps that hung from the ceiling. It originally had been a store of some kind, but had been converted. The lights were dim and the air was stale and smoky. The five scattered black couples sitting at the booths and tables ignored her. Two older men sat at a counter that ran most of one wall. They looked straight ahead as they ate with the beaten look many old men put on with their drab clothes in the morning.

She sat at the end of the counter, as far away from anyone as possible. A heavyset black waitress approached carrying a coffee carafe.

"Hi, sugar. I know you didn't come in for the ambience, so you must be hungry." She giggled at her sense of humor and laid a hand-printed menu on the counter. With the other hand, the waitress poured coffee into Jenny's cup. "Don't see many folks in here wearing clothes from Nordstrom."

The woman's voice was refined and she spoke with a West Coast patois. It was so unusual in West Virginia that Jenny was taken aback.

"Anne Klein blouse, Bruno Magli shoes?" the waitress asked. Jenny's head snapped up and she nodded yes, wondering how she knew that. "Goodness. Don't look so surprised, I'm from civilization too, honey. This black face is just a disguise. I used to practically live in the South Coast Plaza in Costa Mesa." She chuckled, reached out, and patted Jenny's hand. Jenny smiled and breathed a sigh of relief at finding a friendly face.

"I'm sorry, I didn't mean that . . . it's just that I didn't expect anyone in here to . . . you know."

"Don't give it a thought, honey. I'm not sensitive, and if I was in your place, I wouldn't expect it here in Crackersville, that's a fact."

"You have a phone? Some boy stole my car," Jenny said evenly, amazed her voice was steady.

"Lord have mercy, those little bastards are back." The black woman frowned and set the carafe on the counter. "They've arrested them two times for doing that down on the corner, and those boys bounce out of jail like bad pennies." She shook her head. "Throw them filthy rats in your car?"

Jenny nodded, then shivered. It would be a long time before she'd forget that feeling of utter revulsion.

"There's a phone in the hall there." The woman gestured. Jenny stood and took a sip of the hot black coffee. It tasted good. "If you're going to call the police, that's fine, but you better be calling home too."

"Why's that?"

"Honey, think about it. They have your car, probably all your keys, and they know where you live and have a big head start." She paused for effect.

As it sunk in, Jenny felt a chill.

"If they do like they usually do, they'll strip your car and the police'll find it in the morning likely. Next thing, they'll call your house. If there isn't anybody there, they just might stop on by and help themselves. You understand? Your family home?"

All Jenny could manage was a shake of her head. She reached in her pocket and winced because she had no money. It was all in the car along with her keys and purse.

Realizing what was wrong, the black woman went to the register and came back with ten dollars in change. She also laid a ten-dollar bill on the counter.

"Name's Julia," she said. "Send me a check care of the Rockette Diner when you get this sorted out. We city folk have to stick together." She winked and walked away.

"Thanks, Julia. My name's Jenny, Jenny Gregory," she called as she picked up the change. "I don't know how to thank you."

Julia waved it off and stopped at the order window and picked up an order of a hamburger and fries. From the front, by the window, the jukebox came to life and throbbed out an MC Hammer rap song. Jenny shook her head, wondering if anybody really understood the words.

She called the local police, and after they switched her to three different people, they promised to send a car to the restaurant immediately. She then dialed the Picksburg police, identified herself, and told them what had happened. They said they'd drive by her house frequently to check it.

"Better call Carole and ask her to stop by the house," she whispered. She realized it had been a day since she'd talked to her and wondered at that. Carole always called daily unless she was out of town. She answered on the third ring.

"Still haven't found Alex," Jenny said before she asked. "I'm over in Beckley, in a seedy section of town. Someone stole my car and I wanted to ask you for a favor."

Carole hesitated, then said, "Gee, I don't know, Jenny." Her voice sounded strained.

"What do you mean, you don't know? I haven't asked you anything yet."

"I mean, I don't know whether I can."

"God, Carole. All I want you to do is stop by my place and make sure I locked all of the windows. I'm afraid these kids who stole my car might try to break in before I can get back. It would take you just ten minutes."

"I know, but I can't, I'm sorry."

Jenny suddenly became worried. "Oh, no. You're not sick, are you?"

"No, I'm fine." Carole's voice was still colorless.

"What's going on. You sound weird. You having some kind of problem you haven't told me about?"

"In a way."

"Carole. This is a pay phone, and I'm running out of change. You want to tell me what's wrong before I become a basket case?"

"I can't see you anymore . . . at least . . . right now."

"What the hell are you talking about?" Jenny was getting frustrated.

"It's Don. He's upset."

"Upset? Upset about what?"

"This . . . thing . . . that's happening . . . you know, Alex missing and all, and nobody knowing what it's about—"

"Why is it I don't have any idea what you're talking about?" Jenny ran her hand through her hair, then rubbed her forehead. A headache was on the way.

"Don's running for Congress, you know. He's worried this might affect his chances somehow. Said maybe those men were involved in something they shouldn't have been." She hesitated for a long moment, then said, "There's been gossip in town, you know. About that Officer Warren. Something about drugs or something. I'm sorry."

Jenny collapsed against the wall, too shocked to be angry, then managed to say: "You think Alex was doing something illegal and since Don's running for a political office you can't check my windows?"

"It's not that simple, you know. I have to do what he says." Carole's voice was stronger, more determined now.

"My God, Carole. I had no idea you were this shallow and insensitive. Alex is missing, could be dead, and all you care about is . . . is . . ."

She choked and sobbed, too upset to be angry now.

Carole was silent at the other end.

10

Jenny gently hung up the phone and went into the small bathroom. She leaned over the dirty sink, splashed cold water from the tap on her swollen eyes, and concentrated, trying to get a grip on her emotions. Having Carole talk to her that way was a crushing humiliation.

After she was able to control her crying, she brushed her hair with her fingers. She touched a skinned mark on her face where she'd hit the pavement. In her emotional turmoil, she had been unaware of any scrapes or pain.

Julia greeted her at the counter with a smile and stared at her with concern, then poured more coffee.

"Problems?" she asked. Jenny nodded and sipped the comforting coffee. This strange woman in a strange town was showing her more warmth and compassion than a woman she'd thought was her friend.

The door banged and she looked up. The police were at the entrance. All of the black faces in the restaurant glanced up, then looked away with an *"oh no"* expression. The blue uniforms meant trouble.

It took twenty minutes for the police to take the information about her car. Jenny couldn't identify the boy, she'd been so frightened. They gave her little hope her car would be found in one piece, then left when she refused their offer of a ride to the station. She planned on calling the credit card companies tomorrow. She cringed when she thought of her license and other items in her purse.

"What you going to do now, honey?" Julia asked.

"You've been kind," Jenny said. "I don't want to cause you any more trouble. I'll catch a cab to where I'm going."

"I'm off in ten minutes. I'll give you a ride. Besides, girl, you don't have enough money left to go anywhere, cabs cost serious money."

Jenny was too grateful to turn the offer down. She just smiled and blinked back the tears that kept trying to fight their way from the corners of her eyes. She nibbled an oatmeal cookie with her coffee while she waited.

When they had settled in Julia's Toyota, the waitress started the engine, turned to Jenny, and asked, "You have the address?"

"Forty-six twenty-five Benson, here in Beckley. I have no idea where it is. They stole my car when I stopped for a moment. I was going to have to ask someone for directions."

"You're kidding. Near as I remember, there isn't a house on that block of Benson, just old factories and buildings. You sure about that?"

"Got it out of the phone book. It has to be right."

"Why didn't you just call from the restaurant?"

"His phone's been disconnected." She felt stupid and incompetent all of a sudden. "I know it sounds crazy, but it's the only alternative I have right now. I don't have anyone else to call." Jenny considered telling her why she was there, then thought better of it. Julia shrugged her shoulders in resignation, dropped the car into drive, and pulled out onto the dark street.

"You have to do what you have to do, girl. But that area of town makes what you've just seen look like a summer camp." Jenny was silent as they moved through the dark streets, each looking a little more shabby as they drove.

"This is Benson," Julia finally said. She pulled onto a darkened street. Most of the street lights were broken. Jenny could see cars huddled silently at the curbs and shadowed forms moving along the sidewalks. The wide avenue had old railroad tracks running down the center of it. "Drug city. You want to buy it, you get it here."

"Jesus," Jenny said in a gasp.

"You won't be finding him down here, honey." Julia glanced over. "The address you're looking for is two blocks ahead. You sure you want to stop along here? I could take you somewhere to catch a bus or something."

"I have to." Telling her the whole story about Alex was out of the question. She read *4400* on the side of a building in one light that was still working. Julia shook her head as they quietly drove the last two blocks. Few lights were on in this area and the streets were empty.

"Least the scum don't work this area," Julia said.

"Stop. Here it is." Jenny pointed to a dark building with corrugated metal siding. It had dimly lit clerestory windows along the roofline, and one caged red light shone on a faded sign above two chained and locked entrance doors. A chain-link fence with long sections collapsed and missing surrounded the building.

Conner's Aircraft, Inc., Jenny read. "An aircraft factory?"

"Honey, you got the wrong address. There can't be anyone living here."

"There's a light around the back. I have to go in." Jenny looked ahead through the windshield. Julia turned off the wipers because the rain had stopped. About four blocks away she could see a well-lighted thoroughfare crossing Benson. "What's that street?"

"That's Jackson. Turn to the right and it goes into town. It's about a mile, I guess. Why?"

"You leave, I'm going inside. If I can't raise anyone, I'll walk up to Jackson. The rain has stopped. You've done all you can, and I'll remember it."

"You're crazy, girl. Use the brains God gave you, and come with me."

Jenny opened the door and stepped out.

Julia is right. This is crazy. I should get back in, shut the door, and leave with her. But I can't, she thought.

She bent and looked into the car window, the interior lit by the overhead dome light.

"Julia, I'll send your money. I'd just about lost hope I'd find anyone I liked in this damned state. You've restored my faith."

"Come with me, girl."

"Nope, but thanks for asking. See you again."

"I'll wait, then," Julia insisted.

"No. I'm sure this is the right address. If no one is here, I can walk up to the street in about ten minutes. Go. Don't worry about me."

Jenny shut the door and waved as Julia drove away slowly, as though expecting Jenny to change her mind and call out. Her tires splashed on the wet pavement—

Jenny was alone.

She turned and looked at the building. The wind picked up and cut through her sweater. She shivered even though the air was still warm. She brushed her damp hair back.

The dark building stared down on her like a huge, hungry monolith, waiting for her to approach. She looked around the side of the large structure where a dim light in the back shone out onto the concrete. The front doors were locked, with no sign of life.

It was darker along the side of the building and she had trouble seeing where she stepped. She tripped on a pipe and it echoed hollowly, then clanked and rolled.

When she got around the side, she noticed the building was much higher and extended back several hundred feet.

In the rear of the structure was a large open area with two dark machines huddled with canvas tarps covering them. They looked like helicopters. The tarps crackled in the stiffening wind. Small security lights burned around the shapes. It looked eerie.

Damn, what the hell am I doing? she thought. This was light-years away from doing anybody any good, especially Alex, wherever he was.

Lightning flashed and lit up the landscape. Debris lay

everywhere, debris she couldn't see in the dark. Her blood went cold. *No one could be living in this abandoned building, this was ridiculous!*

The rain started in tiny drops, then came down faster and heavier and finally thundered on the tarmac—as though someone had turned on a spigot in the sky. She ran toward the lighted door on the side. No cover anywhere. In the back, closed hangar doors were between her and the end of the building.

She tried the door. Light leaked out around the edges, but it was locked. She pounded on it, but it was quiet inside.

To her right, in the darkness, a pipe clanged on the ground and rolled.

She froze.

Listening, she could hear nothing but the rain and the grumbling thunder. In the blackness, she imagined she saw movement, but there was no way to be sure. Her heart pounded as hard as the rain as she pulled her wet hair away from her eyes.

Her body and clothes were soaked. To the left was one small window. Reaching over, she banged on it, then tugged hard. It was tight—

Dammit! What am I going to do? she wondered.

In back of her, another sound—

She started to turn—

Heard two hurried steps—

Something huge crashed into her—

Seized her around the neck—

She was jerked off her feet by powerful hands—unyielding—

Then she screamed—

And fainted from the terror and pain.

Jenny jerked awake to a sizzling sound and a strong odor. Bacon, frying. She struggled to move, but found herself tangled in cloth. She looked down. She was wrapped in a warm sleeping bag and it was zipped to her neck. Glancing up in fear, she saw a black man standing with his back to her, cooking bacon in a skillet on a portable electric stove. She slowly unzipped the bag from the inside. She was still clothed and her clothes were soaked, but warm.

The man turned, then smiled.

"Want a bacon sandwich? Always picks me up a bit when I get wet." He spoke with an English accent. He was tall, wide-shouldered, and in his fifties. The room was about twenty feet by twenty feet and had pictures of aircraft and helicopters on all the walls, interspersed with flags of several countries.

She shook her head no, dumbly, afraid to try her voice. She reached up and felt her neck. It was still sore from being manhandled.

An interior door to the right banged open. A bearlike white man came in. He had a gray beard and wore camouflaged army fatigues. He was in his fifties too, and a handmade cigarette dangled from his lips. Jenny smelled the unmistakable odor of marijuana.

"Sorry about that, girl," he said. "Thought you was one of the kids who've been breaking in around here. Good way to get yourself killed. How's your neck? Guess you just passed out."

"Who are you?" Jenny asked. She was afraid to try to get out of the bag, so she just lay and watched them. The black man ate the sandwich he'd made with gusto, then sat at a small dinette table where he had poured himself a cup of coffee.

"You try to break into our place, then you want to know who *we* are? Think you've got it bass-ackwards, love," the black man said while chewing. His Cockney accent sounded out of place.

"I'm looking for Wesley Ryan, he's my uncle."

"Coo, you're funnin' me now, ain't you, love?"

"Knock it off, George. Who are you, girl?" The fatigue-clad giant of a man stepped forward and towered above her in a menacing stance.

"Jenny Gregory. Who are you?" Her voice choked with fear as she shivered in the bag.

The huge man bent, took a big drag on the cigarette, and let the smoke drift up across his grizzled face as he studied her features closely.

"Jenny Gregory, huh? You married?"

She nodded.

"What's your maiden name, kid?"

"Ryan."

He laughed and said, "Jenny! You skinny little pissant! It's you! Goddamned almighty, George, this here's my niece I was tellin' you about. Last time I seen her, she was—what? Seven?" He stood, then slapped his leg. "Dammit, girl, I'm your Uncle Wesley. Don't you remember bouncin' on my knee?"

Jenny's lip quivered, then she started crying and huddled tighter into the bag. Her sobbing came in deep shuddering explosions as the tension of the last two days poured out. She felt completely alone and hopeless. Before she knew it, he was sitting on the floor next to her, his huge arms around her shoulders, her head leaning on his chest. He just cooed and whispered to her like a child until her body slowly stopped quaking.

She snuffled. He rose and got some Kleenex tissues from a shelf and sat back beside her. He lit another joint, took a puff, and asked:

"You want to tell me about it?"

George went to bed long before she finished her story. Wesley moved around and faced her. He sat back and let her story and emotions wash over him while he finished yet another hand-rolled joint.

Jenny thought, *He looks like an aging revolutionary mountain fighter, a good-looking Castro.*

Finally, she asked, "What do you think I should do? I guess that seems dumb, huh? I couldn't ask Dad because he's so sick, then I thought of you."

"Your dad sick, is he?"

"Yeah. Heart. He's going to have an operation. Mom claims he's going to be fine, though."

"That's good. He's a damned good man even though

he never took a shine to me." He cleared his throat. "Now, back to you. Seems to me, the first thing you have to do, little lady, is get home and out of those clothes before you get damned sick."

"Don't worry about me, I'm pretty sturdy."

"Let's go out into the hangar and get you some transportation first, then maybe we can talk about it." She crawled out of the bag, stood, and straightened her clothes. She was still damp, and her skin itched.

He led her through another door, and they walked out into the dark hangar. Stopping at a huge electrical panel, he pulled a switch and the interior of the building crackled and hummed, then lit up in fluorescent light.

The scene stunned Jenny.

The huge hangar was forty to fifty feet high and had an ancient Beechcraft aircraft in the middle, with camouflaged military trucks and jeeps sitting around the perimeter.

"What the dickens is all this for?" Jenny asked.

"My toys—tools of the trade." He laughed, walked over to a huge four-wheeled vehicle, and climbed into the cab and tapped the gas gauge. "Plenty of gas, and it's got a brand-new engine. Overhauled it myself," he said with pride. He jumped to the floor.

"Those helicopters parked outside. Do those belong to you too?" She walked over and looked up at the cab of the truck and wondered how she'd climb up there.

"You betcha."

"What do you use them for?" she asked, then added, "I'm sorry, I guess that's none of my business, is it."

"You was anyone else, that's just what I'd tell you." He looked at the floor and ran his fingers thoughtfully through his beard. "Let's just say, there's folks around here that has things they want moved around—to other places—and they want to do it so's other folks don't know when and where they move it. That's what I do." He seemed to like the sound of that, and added, "I'm a mover. Yeah. The Bekin's Man, that's me."

Jenny thought of the marijuana he smoked, then

realized that's what he was talking about. These hills were alive with marijuana farmers. She'd heard about it from Alex, but it had to be Wesley's business, so she'd not ask any more questions.

"Best you be going back home now, girl. It'll take you the best part of two hours, 'specially if the rain keeps up."

"How am I going to get the truck back to you?"

"I've got a couple fellows work up your way. You just call when you're done with it. Let me know where it is. I'll have it picked up."

"About Alex. You never answered. What do you think I should do?"

"You climb in this truck, I'll show you how to shift the gears. It's simple." She scrambled into the driver's seat and looked around. The truck was equipped with radio equipment she had never seen before. He jumped in on the passenger's side and showed her the shifting pattern. It was simple, with seven speeds instead of the usual four or five.

"You take it off the road and want to get hold of me, you just pick up that mike there, flip this button, and give me a call. Don't touch nothin' else. Don't have to say nothin' fancy, just: *Wesley, you there?* or somethin' like that. If I don't answer right off, you try back in about a half hour, I'll answer."

"Why don't I just call you on the phone?"

"Don't use phone lines. They're too impersonal— other people can listen in."

"How about this? Other people could hear this too."

"Maybe yes, maybe no. Anyway, there ain't nothin' we got to say that would interest anybody else, now is there?"

"Anyway, about Alex, what do you think—"

"Start her up, I want to be sure she's running right." He reached over and turned the ignition. The powerful engine growled to life. It echoed in the big hangar and poured blue smoke out the side stacks as it started. Then the smoke cleared. "Let me get the outside door for you—" He opened the truck door and jumped to the ground. He pushed a button on the wall and the hangar door started to grind up. He then walked around to the driver's side.

She rolled down the window and shouted above the idling engine. "You didn't answer me. What do you think I should do about Alex?"

He worried his beard again, then yelled back, "Go home, girl. Let the police handle it. Ain't nothing you can do. 'Sides, since the war, I don't ever give nobody no advice on nothing. Absolutely nothing." He signaled her to drive out. "Made some decisions over there that got a lot of people killed—

"Now, somebody asks me something,

"I just smile—have a toke—

"And mind my own business."

11

"God, this stuff is making me sicker than hell," Alex said to Manny as they passed each other in the barn. Manny shrugged his shoulders and continued to work. It was dark out now, and the birds had repopulated the eaves hours ago in a wave of fluttering and chirping.

Alex wondered how the birds could stand the fumes drifting up from the vats. *Used to it,* he thought. As they settled in, the droppings rained down on everything. When that happened, Alex glanced over at Mae, who sat on a stool by the door and watched the men work. She gave no sign that she was aware that the droppings littered everything, including the open fermenting vats. Incredible.

Four Coleman kerosene lanterns lit the barn. They hissed and sputtered at eye level from where they dangled from the ends of wires that stretched up into the superstructure. The uncertain light they emitted wavered and flared and was absorbed into the dark corners. Some flickering light came from the crackling fires under the stills where the green wood popped occasionally.

Alex looked around. Hundreds of mosquitoes and bugs flitted around each light, creating a surreal sight—a thin animated fog, constantly in motion. After the first hour of darkness, Alex stopped slapping the mosquitoes. A uniform rash from their bites covered his arms and shoulders.

Each still now produced a pencil-thin stream of moonshine, and the crates of filled gallon and half-gallon jugs grew, to the right of each spigot area. Alex found out why Manny called the small barrel a thumper tub. It pounded, hissed, and thumped from the surging hot steam that built up pressure, then released it as the liquid condensed and vaporized again, further distilling the whiskey.

Alex watched Landry, the spigot man, carefully, wondering what kept him going. As the night wore on, Landry stumbled and moved slower as he worked. Constantly sampling the moonshine, he had found his personal escape from this living hell.

Alex shook his head. This shell of a man who was still mute worked as though he were the only one in the room. He wondered if Landry's mind was going too. Landry had no interest in anything except filling jugs and drinking the shine and sleeping.

Alex's head was spinning. He stopped what he was doing at the vat and walked toward Mae, who watched him approach indifferently. He held his hands up so she would feel safe. She fingered the shotgun on her lap, loaded this time, he knew. Her recessed, watery eyes followed him, and her moving jaw slowed.

"Git to work," she ordered with malevolence when he came within twenty feet.

"I need ten to fifteen minutes of fresh air," Alex said. "The fumes from those vats is making me sicker."

"Ain't no summer camp, you're lucky to be alive the way it is," she said without emotion.

"But I think I might accidently throw up into one of the vats. You wouldn't want that, would you?" Appealing to her on any other basis except her own self-interest would be a waste of time.

"Don't matter nohow," she mumbled.

"You're kidding."

"Time that alkyhol scalds an' steams through them pipes, ain't nothin' coming with it. Any bugs what does cain't live in that shine anyways. You can shit in them

vats for all I care." She chewed faster. Alex thought of
the birds that did so on a regular basis.

"Why don't you fix the exhaust on your car?" Alex
asked. It was a stupid question, but it was all he could
think of to say at the moment. "I know you don't care
about us, but you could kill your kids someday."

"Costs money," she said simply. "Keep the winders
open is all." He shook his head as he looked at her.
Trying to reason with her was a waste of time. Alex
wondered if she ever spent any of the considerable
amount of money she made producing this damned
moonshine. The clothes she and her children wore gave
no indication material things were of any importance to
her.

He was about to turn and walk back to the vats when
she said, "Ten minutes—tha's all. Stick yer haid out
there. You get another gander at that fence and them
dogs, it'll show you for sure there ain't no way outta
here, an' maybe you'll smarten up."

She motioned to the door twenty feet away. The dog
stood in the opening. Coming from beyond the dog, Alex
could hear the night sounds from the woods. Mae waved
her hand, and the animal reluctantly backed into the
blackness, growling deep in his throat. She nodded and
motioned to Alex that it was okay. The fact that she had
so little anger about what had happened earlier confused
him.

He dragged his chain to the door and leaned his head
out. Hitler had disappeared, but Alex was tense, expecting the dogs to charge him from the darkness of the yard
at any moment. In spite of himself, he had to admire the
way all three dogs were trained. He could hear the
unhurried trotting sounds in the dark as they patrolled
the perimeter of the chain-link fence about eighty to a
hundred feet from the barn.

He'd studied the fence earlier, before they'd begun to
work, up till Hitler saw him and came galloping toward
the door. The fence rose to an average height of about
twelve feet and circled the entire barn and house. The

only way through it was out a now-locked gate. Tire tracks showed the opening was used to bring in vehicles delivering supplies for the stills.

On the back side of the barn, a gradual, tree-sheltered grade stepped farther up into the hills. Although it was too dark to see, off to the side, beyond the fenced area, he could hear a stream bubbling its way over rocks toward the lowlands. Alex guessed that's where the water came from that was piped into the worm boxes. It kept the curly copper pipes cool and caused the alcohol to condense when it steamed through.

"Step beyond that doorway, and you're on your own," Mae said without turning. Her voice was low and relaxed now, no longer worried about Alex trying to escape immediately. Alex had no intention of trying to, right now anyway. Besides, unless he could get loose from the chain, he could only go another twenty or thirty feet into the yard. "Yonder, other side the fence, thar's kin and dogs in them woods." She'd apparently added that to punctuate what she knew he was thinking.

The air was clean and crisp. Trees around the barn were gone, so the black sky was open above.

Alex glanced up at the crystal-clear heavens and drank in the clean air. Stars glistened and shimmered across the expanse, and he felt a sudden lurch of sadness. Jenny could be looking at those same stars at this moment, worrying whether he was alive or dead. He thought of the chief and wondered what he was doing to find Josh and him.

Josh. There'll be time to think about him later. Have to work on how to get out of here now, he thought. Above the barn, Alex heard the velvet-soft murmur of wings. An owl, out hunting for supper—or would that be breakfast to him?

In the last few hours, Alex's belief in the inherent goodness of man had taken a real pounding. He had always realized there were a lot of very bad people out there, but inside he'd felt every person had a God-given conscience, and even though they occasionally did wrong things, down deep they were good. He'd mentioned many times that even Adolf Hitler had loved kids and dogs, but he had trouble seeing any light of humanity in Mae Skaggit's eyes. They were cold and flat like a killer shark's, with not a hint of warmth or mercy.

When Alex was six, his mother and father had divorced. As a consequence, he saw his father only three or four times a month. His dad had a twenty-four-foot Sea Ray and they spent almost all those visits on the water somewhere, either fishing or taking short pleasure trips.

When they fished, they did a lot of talking. What his father told him about his life on the police force had stayed with Alex to adulthood. To a young man, it had been exciting but frightening at the same time. The violence associated with it seemed heroic to his young mind, but Alex had trouble visualizing doing those things himself. He'd have much preferred to write about them than to live them.

When Alex was close to finishing college, he reluctantly agreed to join the L.A. police force after constant prodding by his father. It was met by instant enthusiasm from his dad against the objections of his mother. They were long divorced and it was another cause for friction between them.

"Alex, you have such great potential to be so many things. Do something you're more suited for," his mother had said. "After a few years on the streets, you'll become hard, like your father did. It'll change you, you'll become bitter and pessimistic."

Now, standing in this doorway in West Virginia, he realized he should have followed what his original instincts had told him to do. Spend his life writing. A few days on the force and his professional law-enforcement career could be over before it really got started.

His thoughts drifted to Jenny and how happy they'd been the first two weeks as they had worked around the old house. He always marveled at how she never complained, always tackling any job with enthusiasm. He wondered what she was doing right now—

"Hey, cop," said Mae Skaggit from behind Alex. "Time to move yourself." Alex took one last look at the panoramic night sky, turned, and walked back to the still. He avoided glancing at Mae. The image of Jenny was vivid in his mind, and he wanted to keep it to himself for a while, untarnished by her scowling face.

He was tired, so tired all of a sudden. The adrenaline that had kept him moving in spite of the way he felt was beginning to lose its ability to whip his body. As he stumbled back to work, he found his legs moving slower and slower. The buckets seemed heavier, and some of the resolve he'd built up earlier was breaking down under the constant grind of working below the hissing lanterns.

He needed sleep desperately, and more important, he needed time to recover from the carbon monoxide poisoning. Although he was still sick to his stomach, sleep was what he needed, what he craved. His eyelids were burdened by six-ounce weights, then one-pound weights, heavier and heavier as the hours ticked away.

Toward morning, he was bumping into and tripping over firewood and buckets in the room, unaware that his eyes were actually closed while he was walking. Twice he'd come awake, startled, when he had burned his hand on the side of the still-pot.

The young girl had brought in a bowl of beans and a piece of unidentifiable meat for each of them. A small side bowl contained what Manny described as mixed greens, an unsavory mixture of poke, dandelion, and sour dock—weeds to Alex—all seasoned with vinegar and oil. Alex ignored it, and Manny finished it for him as before.

"Keep awake, boy," Manny had admonished him through the night. "Watch what you're doing."

As time passed, Manny settled into his job, tired himself, and stopped prodding Alex with his voice.

When light appeared in the opening at the top of the barn, Alex was losing touch with reality and had the vague feeling he was floating into the rafters with the birds, sitting on a cross-beam, where he looked down upon the slow-moving automatons working under the eerie warm lights. He'd read about out-of-body experiences and wondered if they were anything like this. The birds. God, how he envied the birds. Only an occasional flutter, but otherwise they were quiet. They slept undisturbed even with the noise the men made, their heads folded under their wings for the night.

Just a half hour, that's all I need, he thought.

His eyes blinked, but he kept moving. He was having trouble feeling his hands as he forced one foot in front of the other. Left foot, right foot, left foot.

"Alex, what the hell are you doing?" Alex shook his head and concentrated, but the voice was alien, from somewhere far off. "Alex, where are you going? Alex . . . where . . . are . . ."

The hell with it, he decided.

. The lights and the smells receded, and he drifted again. *The hell with the stills and the buckets and the woman and . . .*

They were all gone as he stumbled dumbly into the darkness . . . and his heavy eyelids closed—

The ground came up to meet him. The pain of impact was mild, and he settled into a fetal position to sleep. Off in the distance Jenny's face came through the fog toward him, her arms outstretched—

Bam!

A thunderous explosion jarred his body. He awoke screaming, lying on his stomach stretched out—

Fire burned his buttocks and legs—

The image of Jenny evaporated in the agony—

He ran his hands over his backside where small tatters of cloth were ripped away from his pants. His yelling turned to painful groaning.

"Got another vat to run 'fore noon! Git up!" Mae screeched. Alex blinked his eyes through the morning haze and could see her standing twenty feet away with the shotgun pointed at him. "Git up, you ain't dead!"

Alex brought his hands to his now wide-awake eyes. Droplets of blood smeared his fingers. He was confused about what had happened. If she'd have shot him with buckshot, he'd be bleeding profusely from the wound.

"Jist something to git your 'tention. Light load of rock salt. If Woody was still here, it'd be mor'n rock salt, you can bet!" She smiled. "You ain't gonna die."

"Are you crazy?" Alex yelled. He wobbled to his knees, then stood. "I'm still sick from that exhaust. I need to recover." He stopped moaning, not wanting to give her the satisfaction of enjoying his suffering.

"You can sleep all you want when you're finished in about six more hours." She pulled back the hammer on the other round in the double-barreled shotgun.

"Six hours? I don't know whether I can make another half hour the way I feel," he complained. His legs shook from the insult to his system. In the background, the two other men continued to work, but their heads were up, watching what was going on.

"I got a shell to light your fire every time you feel lack restin'." Mae backed off a bit to make way, then waved the gun toward the vats and the buckets he'd set down. Alex stared at her as he passed within ten feet. He knew he could withstand the full force of another rock-salt blast—if that's what she had in the gun—then she'd be defenseless. He could tackle her, get her on the ground, and grind her into the dirt floor—

He could choke her until her tongue popped out, strangle her, for him and Josh. He'd smash his fists into her face until it was a pulpy mass.

"Relax, Alex," Manny warned in a low voice. "Don't do it." Manny could obviously read the hatred in his eyes. Alex blinked and swallowed deeply. The urge overwhelmed him. Mae had to see it too, but she remained calm, just held the gun on him as he walked by.

When he stood over the buckets, he shook inside with the realization he'd thought about killing her so violently, with pleasure, actual pleasure. The pain, sickness, and sleep deprivation were stripping away his humanity.

He glanced back at Mae and considered saying something else, but decided he needed to save what little energy he had. Only a fool argues when there's no alternative. His time would come. Now, if he could stay awake . . .

Alex picked up the full buckets, carried them to the open still, and poured them in. He set them down and went to the worm box—the wooden box filled with the cold stream water—and splashed handfuls of it onto his face as Manny watched.

"Why the hell didn't you warn me?" Alex asked Manny under his breath. He winced as the burning from his butt and legs came in waves.

"Wouldn't have made any difference. You were too far out of it, I could see that." Alex picked up the buckets, and ignoring him, walked back to the vats.

He's right. I probably wouldn't have believed it anyway, he thought.

"Who's this Woody she's talking about?"

"Not now." Manny gestured to the buckets. "Get to work."

As Alex filled his buckets again, he thought about his dad. For some reason, some ludicrous reason, the memory of what his father had said to him long ago came back to him. He was going to apply for a job at McDonald's for the summer when he was a sophomore in high school.

"Now, whatever you do, don't ask them about breaks and time off and stuff like that," his father had said. "If they think you're interested in getting away from your job all the time, they'll hire someone else." Alex nodded he understood. The interview went well, and he was one of the lucky high-school kids to have a summer job that year.

The money had gone for his first motorcycle, and his last one as it had turned out. The engine blew up after a couple of weeks and repairing it was a low priority.

His dad had been right. Not asking had been the correct thing to do. "Act as though you really want to work." Through his pain, he chuckled at the irony of those words.

He had avoided asking about breaks here—and he'd gotten this job too.

12

Wesley Ryan's complete lack of interest in her problem had shocked Jenny at first. After thinking about it for a while as she drove the huge truck through the darkness, she realized it had been a foolish fantasy to think it would have been any other way. Hell, he hardly even knew she existed. What had she ever done to earn his devotion besides ignore him? She'd been so absorbed in her situation, she'd made the assumption it would concern other people in her family too.

Besides, she thought, *he's still living his sixties rebel fantasy, back in the days of Vietnam, protests, and pot smoking.*

As she had settled into the drive, she realized with certainty that he smuggled marijuana out of the hills with his equipment. She looked around the spacious interior of the truck, then down at the glowing lights on the dash and shook her head.

"What the hell are those kids going to do with a Volvo here in West Virginia? Who are they going to sell the parts to if they strip it?" she mumbled. The roads of West Virginia were empty of almost anything except pickup trucks and older, American-made muscle cars, not crowded with Japanese and German cars like California.

It took her almost two hours to drive the lumbering truck through the drizzling night to her house.

It was four-thirty in the morning when she bounced to

108

a stop under the tree in front. The branches scraped the roof.

"Darn," she grumbled. She'd forgotten about how high the truck was. It was dark and quiet when she turned off the noisy engine. Exhausted, she closed her eyes. It was tempting to just fall over on the wide seat and sleep right there.

She forced her eyes open and dropped to the ground. It was windy in Picksburg, but there was no evidence it had rained during the night. She was unsteady on her feet. The ride in the jostling, noisy truck had left her with a mild motion sickness, not unlike on a boat at sea.

At the house, the door lock stuck, then she kicked it open in frustration.

She clicked on the light.

And froze.

The floor was littered with papers—

Most of the furniture was gone.

Alex guessed it was about nine in the morning when they were through processing the last vat of mash through the stills. They'd actually finished over an hour earlier, but before they could rest, they had to prepare three more vats to ferment. Prior to filling them with water, they covered the bottom of each vat with cornmeal from forty-pound bags. The hard part was hand-carrying the hot waste water left in the still pots. Alex labored to the vats with the large wooden buckets, then sloshed the steaming liquid onto the cornmeal and mixed it in.

"To scald it good to get it cookin'," as Manny had said. They added a couple hundred pounds of sugar. "A day to cook, then tomorrow we add some malt and yeast and let it boil and bubble for a couple of days, stirring it occasionally, and breaking up the clumps that form."

Manny's words floated in and out of Alex's consciousness. Past giving a damn about the process, all he cared about was sleep. The burning in his backside and legs no longer bothered him. The only thing that kept him marching down the tunnel of exhaustion was the promise of sleep at the other end. He was even too far gone to hear the hundreds of birds flutter out in chittering waves in the morning.

After they pumped the water into the last vat with a squeaking rusty hand pump, Alex stumbled over and collapsed onto his pallet. His head bounced on the flexible boards, then his eyes closed.

He was sound asleep before his body settled.

"I gotta pee," Ellie whined. She'd awakened as the small moving van approached the turnoff to White Sulphur Springs. She'd slept through the night with her head on Harley's lap.

"Hold your water, girl," Harley gruffed. "Get up, you're makin' me sweat." They had driven out of the rain squall hours ago. Even though he had the window open, the air swirling around the cab was warm and laden with moisture, making him even hotter instead of cooler. "It's goin' ta be a hot one today. Costner's is just ahead a piece."

He glanced at her. She straightened, took her brush from her purse, and tried to resurrect her flaming-red hairdo. In the light of early morning, her makeup was smeared, and her hair lay in moist clumps from where she had sweated on his lap.

Small damp spots had darkened the dress under her arms and near her neck. Her bulging breasts that had looked so tantalizing in the dark piano bar were now covered with bright red heat splotches along her wet cleavage. He chuckled deep in his throat and wondered if them boys from last night could get it up if they could see her in the light of day.

"I need a bath real bad, and need to change clothes," she complained. The heat had warmed her body and the odor of the sexual orgy was strong in the cab of the truck. When Harley first noticed the smell, he smirked, thinking back on the pleasure of beating those men, then taking her.

God, that was great, he thought. It was an act they had

repeated many times and it always excited him. Simply
screwing her without beating the other men was boring.
Getting charged up on their fear made it really exciting,
especially if they had to sit and watch him fucking up a
storm.

It was hilarious.

Them tied tight as Thanksgiving turkeys and not
knowing what he was going to do when he finished with
her. By God, the picture of that'd make any man's pecker
hard.

The closed van rumbled into the lot of Costner's Diner.
Weeping willow trees draped around the perimeter of the
dirt parking lot, and in back of the diner, the murky New
River swelled and boiled between its overgrown, weed-
choked banks. Two cars waited for their owners and had
all but disappeared under the branches of one tree.

Harley's olive-green moving van was ideal for driving
through the backwoods, the color blending in with the
foliage. Harley thought it was even better than those
hokey brown-and-green colors they painted army trucks
for camouflage. "Ever park it in them trees and walk
away, we'll never find the damned thing again," he'd
laughed.

Costner's was hot inside as they slammed the screen
door behind them, then shuffled down the long line of
stools. Grease-coated floor fans at either end of the diner
whirred constantly, giving customers the impression it
was cooler inside, but with the open grill facing the
counter, it was actually hotter. The smell of burned
grease hung in the air.

"I'm goin' in back," Ellie said. Harley knew she was
headed for the bathroom. Considering the condition of
her makeup, he knew she'd be in there a while.

"Harley," J. D. Costner said, and nodded as Harley
spun a stool in front of him and sat. "Ain't seen you in a
coon's age." Wearing a used-to-be-white T-shirt and a
gray apron, he was thin and gaunt, his smile revealing
uneven teeth too large for his mouth.

"Ain't likely ta see me again if you don't clean up this

fucking pigsty," Harley grumbled without a glint of humor. It was just too damned hot to be neighborly. He was across from J.D., and laid his Atlanta Braves baseball cap on the stained, crumb-covered counter. He slicked his wet curly hair back. This heat riled him sure as hell.

J.D. grinned again, then turned back to the hot plate and hovered his spatula above four strips of sizzling bacon. Like everyone in these parts, he knew better than to act offended by anything Harley said. Harley had beaten the hell out of somebody in virtually every eating and drinking spot within a hundred miles, and Costner's was no exception.

A few months ago Harley had been driving through, running a load, and stopped for some coffee. After he had finished his coffee, he took the time to adjust the attitudes of two Yankee college boys. They were making altogether too much noise to his thinking, playing their damned radio and laughing in back of him. They shouldn'ta answered him back when he told them to shut up.

He'd left them unconscious on the floor, scattered among four or five of their teeth and mop-up amounts of blood. One boy had a concussion and was carted off to Beckley for a spell with a sugar-dispenser-shaped dent in his forehead.

When the state police came nosing about in their funny hats, nobody knew who the huge curly-headed stranger was, as usual. The state police figured who he was, but what the hell. Them college boys was simply smart-assed Yankees, and God knows, they must have deserved it. Wasn't worth pitching a fit about, they allowed, then forgot it and went on home and off-duty. They'd dropped in Perlie's for a couple of cold ones and talked about it some.

"Two cheeseburgers and fries," Harley said. "To go. Too damned hot to eat in here, boy."

"Comin' up," J.D. said without turning. Harley tapped his hat and glared at the noisy fan at the end of the counter. J.D. worked fast, concerned about pleasing Harley.

Down at the end of the counter, two men sat eating their food, talking quietly. Both wore cowboy hats. Harley shook his head and thought, *Stupid bastards*. He really hated those pretend cowboys and wished they were making too much noise or something so he could go stomp 'em good.

Ellie came out after a full twenty minutes. By then, the paid-for box of cheeseburgers and fries sat on the counter, grease soaking through the sides. Standing by the door, Harley was ready to get the hell out of there and on down the road. He grabbed the box of food and was out the door without a word. It banged shut behind him. She opened the door and followed into the humid morning. Not a wisp of wind disturbed the willow trees as he pulled the van out onto the main road.

They drove along in silence for another fifteen minutes. He was still unsettled even though the wind coming into the cab made him feel tolerably better.

He opened the box and devoured a cheeseburger in four bites, a signal for her that it was all right to eat. They finished the food and threw the grease-soaked debris out into the hot, swirling air.

"You ain't talkin' to me?" she asked finally.

"Shut up and go back to sleep."

"Ain't sleepy now."

"Then just shut up."

Ten minutes later, when the road narrowed to a two-lane blacktop, Harley slowed at the sight of something in the shimmering heat of the distance.

"What'sa matter?"

He reached out and backhanded her hard across the bridge of her nose, and said, "You ain't good on listenin' today!" She held her hand to her nose and cried softly.

As he came closer, Harley could see a fat man hunched over a motorcycle, working on the engine. He'd pushed the dead cycle back under the shade of a tree. The man's dusty coat lay across the seat, and he was sweating dark spots on his black T-shirt. He looked up in exasperation when Harley pulled the small moving van behind the motorcycle. A choking cloud of dust kicked up from the shoulder of the road and engulfed him, causing him to blink and spit. Harley smiled as the man stood and rubbed his eyes.

"Jesus Christ! What the hell are you doing, you asshole!" the man screamed at the truck. Harley stepped down from the cab and sauntered to the irate heavyset man. As Harley approached, he could see the man's eyes sizing him up and questioning his choice of words. "Got dust in my oil here," the man said weakly, his voice lowered in explanation.

"Callin' a man an asshole—'specially a man you don't know—is downright stupid," Harley said. "Reckon a man could take offense and hurt you real bad." He grinned as he picked his front teeth with a toothpick from the diner.

"Sorry," the man apologized, doing an about-face. "Didn't mean no offense. This damned thing broke down for the fifth time. Been on the road for two days now." He kicked the tire as though punishing the machine for its intransigence. Harley took in the man's well-fed figure. Two hundred seventy to two hundred ninety pounds, he guessed, but soft. Over six feet, big in the middle with heavy arms, he showed no evidence of hard work.

"What's your name, boy?" Harley asked, smiling softly. *This is gonna be fun,* he thought.

"Ti." He pronounced it like tie in necktie. A thin smile broke his lips too, happy to see Harley grinning.

Twenty-two or twenty-three years old, I'd say, thought Harley.

"What's your name?" Ti asked.

"Ti? That's a ridiculous fuckin' name," Harley said in a scoffing tone, and snorted, ignoring the big man's question. Ti's eyes narrowed and the remnant of his smile disappeared from his fleshy lips.

Ti studied Harley closer, then appeared to decide he was in trouble if he said the wrong thing. Harley had seen

the same thoughts travel across many a face. The fat man
lowered himself to the machine, picked up a wrench, and
started working again. "I ain't lookin' for no trouble,
mister. I just wanna get this fixed and get on my way."

"Well, let me help you, then." Harley's tone of voice
was convivial. He laughed, stepped forward, grabbed the
handlebars of the machine, and pushed it at a trot to the
edge of the road. When he released it, the fat man froze
in place, his mouth wide at this madness.

The motorcycle crunched over the edge and smashed
down through the brush, bouncing and picking up speed,
thirty or forty feet into a patch of undergrowth. Except
for a thin path that would close shortly, it had disappeared.

Harley glared at him with a challenging smile. Ti
stared back with an open mouth, his crescent wrench
gripped defensively.

"You're crazy," Ti whispered as he glanced at where
the motorcycle had been swallowed up. It was said more
in wonderment at what Harley had done than in anger.

Harley lumbered forward. "You're just makin' a lot of
poor word choices today, fat man."

Ti stepped backwards and raised the crescent wrench.
"I don't want to have to hurt you, stay back!"

Harley was amused that Ti was huffing, and his only
exercise had been watching Harley run the bike off the
hill. "You're goin' with me, but you oughta think real
hard on hittin' me with that wrench, boy. Makin' me mad
could go real hard on you."

"I ain't goin' nowheres with nobody."

"Mistake number three."

Harley smiled, and as he walked toward Ti, he
thought: *This is gonna be good.*

Alex came awake and blinked his eyes. His body was
sore, but his mind was functioning closer to normal now,
unlike yesterday when he had been a virtual zombie,
stumbling back and forth in a mental fog from being
gassed in the trunk.

He raised on one elbow and looked around. The fires in the stills were banked, but the odor of burning wood still hung in the air. Most of the smoke from last night had gone out the crudely made metal chimneys, but the system was old and inefficient. It allowed a lot of the smoke to escape into the barn.

The sun crept across the floor from the opening near the roofline, and a haze drifted through it. Flying insects flitted in and out of the rays of light, and outside, the steady buzz of cicadas came from the trees where the heat lay like a suffocating blanket.

Sweat soaked Alex's pants even though he was lying on a pallet without moving. He coughed and rubbed his arms and shoulders, which were irritated into a raised rash by the hundreds of mosquito bites he'd gotten during the night. He wondered how anyone ever got used to that. Being out of it had partially insulated him from the constant torture.

After tonight, I'll have bites on my bites, he thought.

The other two men lay on their sides on their pallets with their backs turned to him. They both were snoring lightly.

God, what I'd give for fifteen minutes in a bath.

He remembered how he'd complained to Jenny about the ancient shower at home when the water temperature fluctuated constantly. Right now that would be great, no problem at all.

He labored to his feet. The hated chain clanked and clinked behind him as he walked to the worm box. Reaching in, he cupped his hands, cradled the liquid, and let the refreshing water pour over his head.

Wonderful! The cold felt good to his hot, sweating skin. Stripping off his pants, he poured handful after handful on his body and rubbed in the soothing water like an emollient. The almost icy-cold bath cleared his head even more. He shuddered lightly. It felt good to be too cold for a change.

It was time to start thinking—thinking about how to get the hell out of here. All things considered, escaping was a surmountable problem, and yet, by the meager evidence so far, no one had ever managed to do it.

He first walked to the concrete block his chain was attached to. It was a heavy, maybe two-hundred-to-three-hundred-pound block of concrete with a ring projecting from the top. The links were affixed to the ring. Technically, he assumed he could lift it, but carry it to freedom? No way. It would even be tough to make it to the fence with that much weight.

Next, he looked at the links of the chain. Solid steel, with no separations anywhere. Impossible to pry apart. They were attached to a metal ring on the manacle at his wrist. The manacle was wide—four to five inches—and had been kept latched by a heavy-duty Schlage lock. He wondered about that. Did having a lock instead of something more permanent mean they removed the chain occasionally to take the men somewhere else? To do some other kind of work? Other portions of the manacle were spot-welded.

Spot-welded. That means there's a welding torch around here somewhere, he realized. His eyes lit up. If it had been welded at one time, the manacle could be cut off with the same torch.

He glanced around the expansive barn. The shadows clung to the corners and it was graveyard-dark in the supply room in the back. Wherever the torch was, it sure as hell would be out of reach of the prisoners, that's for sure. *Probably in the house somewhere.*

He marveled at how well all the metalwork was crafted. *Must be the same guy who made the copper still-pots and hardware,* he speculated.

And why would a man on the outside make something like this, knowing what they were intended for? But did he know? It was difficult to believe so many people could be involved in something this horrific and keep the secret for years. And the tough part to accept was, how could he be that wrong about human nature?

"Mama don't 'low y'uns to walk 'round buck-naked." Alex jumped. It was Sarah's voice from the dark under the loft storage area. He focused his eyes on the shadows and could see her leaning against a supporting post.

He felt his face flush, thought of covering himself, then said, "The hell with it." They'd forced him into this position, so it was their problem, not his. "You wouldn't have to worry about it if you didn't sneak around without making any noise."

She stepped out into the light, but kept her eyes diverted from his body.

He straightened, tired of their attempts to intimidate him.

"Ma says I have to check up regular-like." Her voice was low, almost apologetic. She looked at the concrete block his chain was attached to. "If y'uns thinkin' on gettin' loose, better fergit it. Ma'll punish you somethin' fierce."

"There isn't a whole lot she can do to me that she hasn't done already." The girl scuffed the dirt in front of her with the point of her shoe. Alex frantically tried to think of some way to reason with this girl. "I'm sorry," he said. "I don't want to create any additional problems for you, especially with your mom." He picked up his pants, slipped them on, and zipped them. The girl seemed reluctant to leave, so he walked back to her, staying some ten feet away so she'd feel comfortable.

"Who's Woody?" Alex asked, remembering what Mae said after she had shot him with the bird shot. The girl's head snapped up, then her eyes clouded. She turned, ran to the door, and banged through it without looking back.

"Shit!" He'd spooked her, and that was exactly what he was trying to avoid. "Stupid!" he muttered, confused.

"Good try, no cigar." It was Manny's voice behind him. Alex walked back to his pallet and sat. Manny stood, relieved himself in the pot, and returned. "Woody was the girl's father. Never met him, but every once in a while the old lady gets liquored up and drones on and on about him. Son of a bitch got shot at a raid somewhere around here. Killed dead as a shithouse mouse by government people."

"Jesus, I really put my foot in it, didn't I?"

"Yeah, you did. Don't ever mention his name again, especially around Mae. She gets crazy in the head when she talks about him—killing crazy. Last time she got on the subject she went off the deep end. I thought she was going to shoot us all, but Harley came in just before she blew us away and stopped her. Came that close." He held out his thumb and forefinger. Alex shook his head. The list of rules was getting longer.

"Who's Harley?"

"Don't get your hopes up, boy. He stopped her because he didn't want anything to interfere with the liquor run we were finishing right then. Would have cost him money. He didn't give a rat's ass about whether we lived or died."

"What's his part in this picture?"

"Big, sadistic bastard. Comes by regular, six or seven times a month. Picks up the shine we make and runs it into the big city somewhere. If we don't have a big enough load, sometimes he hangs around for a few days until we do." This was getting more complicated by the minute. Alex scratched the bites on his shoulder again.

"Where is this guy right now?"

"Hear that sound in the distance?" Alex nodded he did. The whine of a vehicle grinding through the woods could barely be heard above the cicadas. Alex assumed, by its slow progress, it was coming up the grade to the barn. "Ten to one that's Harley. You think the old lady is bad, you ain't seen nothin' yet, boy. And whatever you do, keep your mouth shut, okay? Don't antagonize him."

Manny stood with an effort and walked over to the door. The drone of truck was louder now.

"Unless you want to get us all killed, the best thing to do from here on is to simply listen and do what you're told. I'll tell you everything I know as time goes by, but don't be asking questions of these people. You never know what'll set them off. Okay? You know, things could be a whole lot worse."

Alex nodded again, then followed him to the opening,

where he stood next to Manny looking out into the sizzling morning heat. By the fence, the heads of the three dogs popped up. They watched the men from where they lay in the shade, apparently not wanting to expend any more energy than necessary. The penetrating low-gear protest from the truck was close now.

Alex tried to imagine how things could get a whole lot worse.

13

The small green moving van rocked to a halt in front of the tall gate. Harley leaned out the window, yelled something, and blew the horn two times. Sarah ran out, opened the lock, and swung the gate wide. He raced the truck's engine while he waited, then, when the fence was open, pulled over in front of the steps of the old house.

Alex and Manny leaned out the door of the barn to watch. Neither of them could see the front of the house, because it could only be viewed from the yard. All three dogs surrounded the truck, sniffing the tires, barking and dancing excitedly.

Sarah stood back, smiling, while Harley and a woman in red stepped down from the moving van. Sarah's expression changed when she saw the woman. Then she studied her closely. It was obvious to Alex, even from a distance, that the girl felt uncomfortable. Alex strained to listen.

"Don't mind the dogs," Harley said to Ellie. "Long as me or one of the family's around, they's tame as pussycats." He reached down and scratched Hitler behind the ears. Alex shook his head at that.

Ellie held up her purse, intimidated by the inspection she was getting by the waist-high dogs as they smelled her over, paying particular attention to her crotch.

In the barn, Manny said, "Jesus! Look at the body on that broad, will ya?"

"You haven't seen her before?" Alex asked in a low voice.

"Hell, no. Harley's always come up here by himself before. God damn! Look at those tits, will ya?" Alex thought she resembled a Sunset Boulevard hooker, but Manny had been here for more than a year. Any woman with teeth or without tobacco in her mouth had to look good to him.

Harley and the two women disappeared up the steps. The door banged shut, followed by muffled talking and laughing.

"Jesus," Manny said under his breath. "It's been so long since I've had a woman. I think I just creamed my jeans. You see the way her ass rolled when she walked?"

"Let's talk about how to get the hell out of here, okay? When we do, you can go back to your wife."

"Wife? Hell, I ain't married." Manny sounded offended. "Never been. No crumb-crunchers for me."

"Well, in case you missed it, that Harley guy looks like he could unscrew your head with one hand. You're not thinking of doing anything stupid, are you?"

"Jesus! I'm always thinkin' of doin' something stupid. I just don't do it, is all." He went and sat on his pallet. "God, what tits! I can just taste 'em."

"Tell me about the other men that were here, the ones before me." Alex glanced over at Landry. He was snoring lightly, sleeping off the shine from the night before.

"Last guy I already told you about. He was a lot like Landry in a way. Drank that rotgut crap night and day. His mind went south, started pissin' himself, mind drifting, and stuff like that. Finally went bullshit, like I said. *Blam!* One blast of that cannon, and the fucker was dead before he hit the dirt. Still see some blood over there." He pointed.

"How about the guy before him?"

"Mae told you about him. Name was Jack Reeves. He was the smartest one that's been here, by far. Musta been twenty-two to twenty-three years old. Talked a lot with him. Pretty athletic. Planned on trying out for the

Cleveland Indians' farm club. Day before he took off, he told me he was leaving the next day. I didn't believe him. Hell, guys are always havin' wet dreams about that in here."

"How'd he get out of his manacle?"

"Damned if I know. He spent a lot of time in the back room, rummaging around, doing stuff that night before I bedded down. Whatever it was he used to break out with, it wasn't there when I went in and checked the next day. Mae came in and picked the place clean that night."

"Dogs got him?"

"Hell, yeah. That was the worst, the fucking worst. I sometimes still lay awake at night hearing that poor bastard scream. Took him almost an hour to die after Mae called off the dogs. He made it partway up the fence, but Hitler nailed his leg and jerked him to the ground. Christ! It was awful. I was lying awake listening 'cause he came and tapped me on the shoulder before he left. Told me he'd have the cops out here soon as he got back. Had to lay there in the dark and hear him scream. Put my hands over my ears, but I could still hear him. Mae could have put him out of his misery, but she let him suffer and yell. Figured it would be a lesson to us, me and Landry."

"Who was here before Landry?"

"Beats me. Landry don't talk hardly at all about anything. Use to, no more. He was here, dead drunk, the day she brought me in and chained me up."

"And before you? The guy you buried?"

"Don't know. Tried not to look at his face before I buried him. Only thing I recall is, he smelled really bad."

"Anybody else you remember?"

"Yeah. The guy before the guy you replaced. He was an old guy. Name was Parker, or something like that. Had to beat him off a couple of times right after I got here. Guy would screw a lizard if you'd hold its head for him."

"How'd he die?"

"He tried to feel up Mae's daughter when she came in doing a head count while we were running a batch. Head count . . . that's funny. It was the middle of the night and he had his pants down, going to give her the old one-hole punch, you know what I mean? I'm over at the vats, working my ass off. No way I'm going to have anything to do with *that*. I'm not the brightest guy, but it sure seemed like a good way to kiss your ass good-bye to me. Not that I'm so pure and all, and not that I didn't think about it a little, especially if she was willing. You know, after a year in here, I'm startin' to feel like a priest or something. Jesus, how do those guys do it? Anyway, the kid, Sarah, she was game for it too, if you can believe that shit. Surprised the hell out of me. Gettin' ready to strip down herself, breathin' like a filly in heat."

"You're kidding. Then Mae walked in?"

"Never even heard her. Coulda been there all the time for all I know. That scattergun tore out half his back. Son of a bitch died with a hard-on, I'll give him that."

"I counted eight graves. There were two in the last one I dug. That makes ten guys at least. You figure there's more than that?"

Manny shrugged.

All things considered, what the hell difference does it make? Alex thought. *I'm impressed with ten.*

"One thing that's bothering me," Alex said as he rubbed his fingers across his stubble. "Why does she have these damned manacles on our wrists? Why wouldn't she have shackles for our ankles to leave both of our hands free so we could work easier?"

"You gonna ask? I sure ain't. We're not talking college graduates here. Who knows? Maybe she picked these up in an S&M store someplace." The sun had crept up the far wall and changed to a warmer color.

"You really a cop?" Manny asked. "You don't look very old."

"Had a whole three days' experience," Alex said, and smiled thinly. He ran his hands through his thick hair, then down across his chin. His stubble was scratchy already.

"Why the hell would this lady pick up a couple of

cops, for Christ's sake?" Manny asked. "Wouldn't she be afraid of the ton of shit that would bring down?"

Alex continued rubbing his chin. That question had occurred to him also.

Why *would* she chance abducting two cops?

A couple of hours later, as he lay on his pallet, Alex was still wondering why she'd kidnap a couple of cops. He looked up. Mae and Harley had been in the house for a long time when he heard the front door slam and the sound of talking in the yard.

He stood and walked to the barn door. The other two men were taking a nap before going back to work. Manny had told Alex earlier that it was only because Harley had arrived that they'd been spared having to go to work immediately.

When Alex reached the door, Harley was at the rear doors of the green truck, unlatching the locking mechanism. Alex was stunned at Harley's size. The woman in red and Mae stood back and watched.

"Git on down from there, boy," Alex could hear Harley say to someone in the truck.

From the darkness of the moving van, a voice answered. "God, I thought you'd gone off and left me. Don't hurt me anymore, okay? I need some water real bad, it's been like an oven in here."

A fat man climbed down to the ground and leaned against the hydraulic hoist to keep from falling. His black shirt was soaked with sweat, and his skin glistened. He had been bleeding from his nose and his chin was caked with dried blood.

"Git on into that door over there," Harley ordered, and pushed his shoulder. The man grunted and stumbled toward the door where Alex stood. Alex backed away and scuttled across the floor and shook Manny.

"Wake up, they're coming this way."

"Ask me if I give a shit," Manny grumbled and pushed his hand away.

"Along with the woman in the red dress."

"Jesus, why didn't you say so!" Manny sat up and rubbed his eyes in expectation.

"Git your ass in there!" came Harley's rough voice from the door. The fat man stumbled through the opening in a cloud of dust and fell onto the ground. He whimpered and held his hand up to fend off more blows.

"God," whispered Alex. Harley came in the door, followed by the woman in the red dress, then Mae.

"Wow," Manny exclaimed under his breath as he stared at the voluptuous redheaded woman. Since she was Harley's girlfriend, he knew better than to say it loud enough for him to hear. Harley and the two women stood in the doorway for a moment, looking around, trying to adjust their eyes to the dim interior.

Harley's eyes stopped on Alex, then he swaggered over and stared down.

"So this is what a cop looks like without his gun and fancy uniform." Alex was bare to the waist with his arms wrapped around his legs as he glared at the towering man.

Although Alex weighed around two hundred pounds, it was obvious this man was much larger and stronger. The man Harley'd thrown in the door with ease outweighed Alex by sixty or seventy pounds. Harley obviously enjoyed inflicting pain. "Still got his queer cop pants on," Harley said to Mae. Mae smiled, chewed faster, and fingered her shotgun. When she came in, she walked a little unsteady, and Alex wondered if they had been drinking.

"Please, can I have some water?" the fat man cried from the ground.

"Shut up! I can't stand a cowardly man!" Harley walked over and offered to kick him, and the man drew away in fear.

"What the hell we gonna do with him?" Mae asked. "Cost an arm and leg to keep him in vittles."

"Yeah, but if you work some of that baby fat off, big as he is, he's bound to be stronger than most of them men."

Ellie sauntered over to the stills as they talked, rolling her hips as she moved. She touched the pipes with feigned interest, then posed with her breasts jutted out. Turning nonchalantly, she first checked out the other men, then her eyes settled on Alex.

To see if we're watching, Alex knew. He looked back at Harley and Mae, who were talking near the door. The fat man lay on the ground in front of them, still sniffling. Alex wanted to avoid any contact with that woman. He knew trouble—serious trouble—when he saw it.

"You're really good-lookin' for a cop, 'specially any that might be 'round these parts," Ellie said to Alex. She was standing right in front of him now, so avoiding her was impossible. Alex glanced up indifferently, trying to keep his gaze neutral.

In spite of his resolve, he answered, "Thank you." To be quiet was more of an affront than to answer noncommittally.

"Bet you know how to treat a woman," she said huskily. She bent forward and put her hands on her knees so more of her cleavage would show.

"You're right. I treat my wife good. She's a great woman."

"And I'm not?" she said a little louder as she straightened.

Oh no. This thing is escalating as she probably wants it to, he thought. "Look lady. I don't know you. How could I have an opinion about you?" In the distance, Harley and Mae continued to argue about the fat man. Alex was thankful this exchange was out of their hearing range.

"Well, now that you do, what do you think?" Alex knew a yawning trap when he heard it. It was important to select the right words. Since they had one extra man, any one of them could be dispensable. All she had to do was turn and yell that she'd been insulted and his life would only be worth a shotgun shell, just like Josh's had been. "Well?" she asked, tired of waiting.

"I think you're a very attractive woman. I know almost

any man would think so. Wouldn't you say so, Manny?" He hoped bringing him in would defuse what she was trying to do. He could imagine she'd started many a fight in country beer bars.

"Sure . . . like you say . . . really pretty," Manny sputtered. Caught off-guard, he was embarrassed about being talked to while checking out her body.

Her face lit up. Relaxing, she breathed deeply. They'd said what she was fishing to hear. Alex knew she made her way through life with her face and body, and it was the only thing of any importance to her.

"Go on now, I bet you say that to all the girls."

Alex studied her carefully.

"What's your name, sugar?" she asked Alex.

"Alex Gregory." She nodded and smiled, then batted her eyes and posed her body to flirt. To Alex, it made as much sense as petting a chicken before you cut its head off.

I'm a prisoner they can kill at their discretion, and this stupid woman is flirting with me like we're on a Sunday picnic. Damn. What insanity!

"Ellie! What the hell you doin'!" Harley screamed from across the barn. She jerked around as though stung by a bee.

"Just visitin'," she whined, and pranced back to where they were standing.

"Git your ass in that house!" he ordered, and pointed toward the barn door.

"Fergittin' the dogs?" Mae asked in a slurred voice.

She has been drinking, observed Alex.

"I'll walk her in. You take care o' business," Mae finished.

A chill crawled up Alex's back. *God, he must be going to kill one of us.*

The two women walked to the door. Ellie stopped at the sunlit opening and looked back one last time and smiled. Then they were gone.

Harley walked over and stood in front of the pallets,

his hands on his hips. The fat man's chest still heaved from stifled sobs.

"So you limp-dicked little boys want to play with my Ellie?" None of them moved or answered. A yes, no, or maybe answer would get them a good beating at the minimum. Landry still lay on his side, sleeping softly. *It pays to be drunk.* Alex shook his head.

"Already told that fat peckerwood about how the dogs love to eat people," Harley said without looking back at him, then laughed. "He won't go for the door."

Alex relaxed a little. Apparently his first question about playing with the woman was just rhetorical, and they could avoid a confrontation.

"Talked with Mae. She said she don't want four men, so it 'peers we got a problem, don't it?" Harley continued.

"Mister, let me go, I won't tell nobody—nobody at all," the fat man said in a weak voice. "I don't care what you're doin' here. This ain't none o' my business."

Harley walked back to where he lay and kicked him hard in the ribs. The man folded over, gasping, and was quiet except for his shuddering chest.

Alex shook in frustration, then thought, *God, if there was some way I could help him. Sitting and taking this is almost more than I can stand.* "Keep a grip on yourself," he said under his breath.

Harley walked back, smiled, and swayed in front of them. "I really hate bein' interrupted. That'd be something to remember. Now, as I was sayin', we got a problem—mostly, *you* got a problem." He stabbed his finger at the men. His voice was slurred too. He'd been drinking the shine. "'Peers we're goin' to have to get rid of one o' you boys, but Mae an' me wanna be fair." Alex almost laughed out loud at that. Manny and Alex glanced at each other with apprehension, then back at him, waiting for the other shoe to drop.

"Come with me." He crooked his finger at Manny.

"But you can't get rid of me, I'm the main still man here. Hell, these other guys don't know crapola about making shine!" Manny yelled. His voice was desperate.

"Don't be a shithead, I ain't gonna kill you. You boys is gonna decide that."

Manny stood reluctantly and followed him over to a supporting post near the door. Harley picked up Manny's chain and held it up. "Walk back that way about four steps," he said. Manny did and stopped. "Now don't move, just stay there."

Harley went outside the door and came back in. He had a large hammer and heavy pieces of metal with points on the end, shaped like *U*s.

Manny cringed at the sight of the hammer. Harley grinned again. He lifted the chain, captured a link, and pounded both ends of the metal into the old wood like a giant staple.

"Knew these things would come in handy someday."

He came and hovered over Alex, and said, "You next." Alex was furious and wanted to attack him, but he held it in check. If he lost control, this crazy bastard might kill them all.

Alex walked to the next heavy supporting timber about twenty feet from Manny. Harley had him walk until he was about six feet from Manny, then stop. Harley wanted them near each other but not able to touch for a reason known only to him. Harley picked up the chain and attached it to the timber.

Harley had to kick Landry a couple times to get his attention, then brought him stumbling, and attached his chain to a timber about twenty feet from Alex. Landry looked around, confused about what was going on, but remained quiet.

Above them, the first two birds came in the opening and flew up into the rafters. Alex thought they must have come in to get out of the raging heat.

Finally finished with what he intended to do, Harley called the big man from behind him and had him sit on the dirt floor adjacent to the three men.

"Well, it's time you knew what was goin' on, I guess," Harley said. "We got four men, we only need three." He glanced from face to face and his smile grew. Alex knew he was going to drag this out; he was having too much fun.

"Now, Mae and me, while we was a drinkin' in the house, come up with this plan. After you hear it, I'm thinkin' you'll feel it's a fair one yourself." He walked over and pulled a full half-gallon bottle of shine from one of the crates and opened it. After he took a healthy swig, he rubbed his mouth on his shirtsleeve.

"Fact is, the way we figured on it, it's the best damn idea we had since we started selling this lightning to the negras in Atlanta." He hesitated as though he wanted to take that back.

Alex recorded that for future reference. *If I have any future,* he thought.

Harley continued: "What we been doin' up till now is, when one still-hand dies or we have to kill him, we go out and get another man, simple as that." He opened the top of the still-pot and looked inside. "You best be cleaning this before you use it again, boy," he threatened Manny, who nodded weakly and shivered in spite of the searing heat. "Figure you boys need a taste of doing some of the dirty work yourselves. You get your hands dirty with killin', seems to us you won't be so all-fired anxious to run away and tell the law."

"What?" Alex asked, not able to keep quiet any longer. "This is crazy! None of us are killers. Besides, if you force someone to kill, they'd never be convicted, but *you* would!"

Harley looked daggers at Alex, then grinned. "Your notions are about as important as that bird shit in yer hair, boy." Frustrated, Alex felt for the soft white droppings and wiped it on his pants. Harley laughed out loud now. He pointed at the fat man on the ground, and said, "You're going to be my first killer, Porky."

"Me? No, it can't be me. I can't kill anybody, I can't." Harley stepped toward him, and he cringed into silence again.

Satisfied he was quiet, Harley walked back and raised

his voice. "Okay boys, here's the rules, listen up. I'm only gonna tell you once." In spite of themselves, the men all leaned forward in expectation. "Here's how it's gonna go. First, I'm goin' in that house and have me some dinner and take a nap." He blinked and checked his watch. "It's five minutes till four. At exactly six—a little over two hours from now—I'm comin' back through that door carryin' a shotgun. Two hours and five minutes. No more, no less." It was quiet in the barn. Even the birds had settled down. "You, Porky. You're gonna kill one of these men. Not injure or knock him unconscious, *but kill!* You got that?" The fat man quivered, afraid to move. "Now, the rules are: If one of these men ain't dead when I come back, there ain't goin' to be no conversation about it at all."

He hesitated for effect.

"If there ain't no dead man, then I'm goin' to blow your brains out, Porky, right after I walk in the door. You! You get what I'm sayin'?" The fat man nodded, apparently afraid to do anything else. "Oh, you might need this," Harley said. He walked outside the door and came back with a four-foot length of four-by-four lumber and handed it to him. "In case you don't like to get too close to your work."

Harley took another long swig of the shine, then threw the bottle against the wall in back of them. It crashed into small pieces. "Since ain't none of you boys got a watch, I'll lay this right here." He took off his watch and laid it face-up on the top of the still-pot. "Guess I won't have to worry about you boys stealin' it or anything!" He guffawed with delight.

Harley walked to the door, stopped, and turned back, his massive figure an outline against the brilliant, sunlit yard.

"Six o'clock, boy. You don't knock one of these boys' heads in—then that's all the time you got to live."

He laughed and was gone.

It was deathly quiet in the barn.

None of the men dared breathe—

It was as though all the oxygen had been sucked out of the air. They stared at the opening, still hearing his words.

"He was kidding, wasn't he?" the fat man choked out finally. "He didn't mean that. He's just trying to scare me, right?"

All of the men turned and looked at him—

Then at the timber.

The fat man whispered: "My God, he couldn't have meant that, could he?"

14

Jenny sat on the one chair left in her living room as the morning light streamed into the violated house. She just stared, not even aware of what the time was. Everything had been taken except this one chair, the dinette set, and the beds. Even the pictures on the walls and the clock that had annoyed her so much were gone.

After she called the police, they came by and took a report. When they left, she went in and lay down and slept fitfully for a few hours. The events of the evening and the burglary had left her emotionally and physically exhausted.

She got up and made a pot of tea and thought about her options. Wesley was out, of course, him and his drug problems. And poor Mom and Dad had their plate full with Dad's heart problems. Then there was Carole. Jenny was still numb over Carole's reaction to her plight, and shook her head when the conversation from last night came back. No matter what happened with Alex, she'd never be able to look Carole in the face again, not after that. The raw injustice of her stance was unforgivable and made Jenny wince. Unbelievable.

The only thing that seemed logical was to look for Alex herself, and the place to start would be along that damned road. She knew the police chief and his men had searched thoroughly, but she felt *someone* must have seen them park there. And perhaps that person had seen what had happened, and maybe who they went off with—if they had—or where they walked to. And just maybe there would be some little clue they had over-looked. She had the feeling her closeness to Alex would make any small clue leap out to her like a beacon, speaking only to her. She knew it was being unrealistic, but had to try if she was going to live with herself.

Drinking her tea in silence, she listened to the insistent sound of the cicadas coming through the door screen. *What a strange thing to have to put up with every day,* she thought idly.

She quickly dressed in hiking shoes, jeans, and a light jacket, put her hair up in a bandana, and felt ready for some serious searching, whatever the terrain.

"It's past time I called him." She stood decisively, pulled out her black book, and phoned Alex's father at his apartment in Los Angeles. She had planned on calling him only as a last resort and she imagined this was it.

His name was Lee Gregory. Sergeant Lee Gregory, more accurately. He was the stiff-backed type of man who always carried his law-enforcement persona around as though it were a part of him. His uniforms were immaculate, and his white hair was combed in a regula-tion style. Even in street clothes, he had a formal demeanor. He'd always looked at her with a barely controlled tolerance. But then he made her feel uncom-fortable, and maybe he translated her discomfort into hostility.

Could be my fault. Who knows? she thought. *Whatever.* She dismissed it. It was time to do something, and he was the only one left.

The telephone rang for the fourth time, then his answering machine picked it up. Not wanting to tell him what had happened second-hand, she just left her name and telephone number and punctuated the message with: "Important! Please call as soon as possible!"

She then called the station where Lee worked. He was in the field as expected. Leaving the same message without the urgency, she asked that he call her that evening since she knew she'd be out most of the afternoon.

As Jenny went out the door, she realized she'd have to get something a little less obtrusive to drive than the huge camouflaged army truck. She'd rent a car and keep the truck for a few days before she called Wesley to return it. She might need it to look off the road somewhere. She walked out, climbed up into the truck, and drove into the hot afternoon toward that lonely spot on the gravel road.

"I know you're alive," she said with tear-clouded vision.

"And I'm going to find you, dammit!"

The police department was on Liddell Street in downtown Picksburg. Like the rest of the streets, it was rough blacktop with a sprinkling of gravel. A cracked plastic sign reading *Police* was attached to the brick wall above the door. In a window, an air conditioner pumped water down the sides of the bricks, and it dribbled across the sidewalk and into the street.

A patrol car pulled up to the curb in the early afternoon and parked in one of the four restricted parking places in front. Two policemen climbed out, adjusted their gunbelts, and banged in the door.

"Jennings, Mason," the chief acknowledged when he looked up from his flyer-littered desk. Off to the side sat a table topped with dirty cups and a coffee urn with an orange light shining above the spigot. The two men walked over and poured coffee before sitting. As Mason finished, Jennings fingered a couple of notes on the message board.

"I'd give my left nut for a cold one right now," Officer Mason said as he sat in a chair with a sigh. His uniform showed sweat spots around his shoulders and armpits. He was thin and in his forties.

"Ninety-two fucking degrees out," Jennings offered as he poured his coffee and stirred in his sugar. "Another ninety-ninety day!" He meant ninety degrees and ninety-percent humidity. It was a common expression around Picksburg. Jennings had a paunch that rivaled Cody's. "When we gonna get a cold soft-drink machine in here, Cody?"

"Stop pissin' and moanin'. You run by the Talberts' house again? Catch them home?"

"Yeah. They been out of town, so naturally they don't know shit, either."

"Boys, we're startin' to look pretty stupid here. Either one of you dipsticks got any more ideas on where to search?" the chief asked.

Jennings said, "Cody, we ain't had but four hours' sleep in the last two days. Talked to everybody twice and more out on Gilbert Road." He took a swig of the coffee and cringed at the taste. "Ain't nothin' changed. It's like they was swallowed up. Just fuckin' evaporated!"

"One thing we ain't done so far," Mason said as he glanced at Cody.

"Spit it out!"

"Well, we ain't gone up to Cason's Ridge, that whole area. The Skaggits has been driftin' in and out of town the last few days. We could send a four-wheeler up there and ask around. They shouldn't get riled if we handle it right."

"'Less we have some hard evidence, I ain't sending nobody up there. You boys go up on that mountain without a reason, like as not I'll have four men missing. They sure as hell wouldn't take it kindly. No way you can ask without them thinkin' you was accusin' them of something. They'd take offense right off."

"Don't seem right not to ask," Mason said in a low voice.

"You ain't paid to think, Mason. You're paid to use the sense that God gave you. I won't have none of my men dead for no reason, you got that? Now, you got any facts, any evidence the Skaggits had anything to do with this? Yes or no?"

"No."

"Then I'd suggest you drink that taxpayers' coffee

quick-like, and get your ass haulin' on the list I gave you this morning. You sure as hell ain't goin' to find them boys in here."

"We're just about out of ideas. When we gonna bring the state police in on this, Cody?"

"When I say, not before."

"What about them rumors been floatin' about town? 'Bout Josh havin' some kind of drug contacts. Any truth to that?"

"Folks talk. Can't stop 'em. If I had any hard facts, he'd of been gone long 'fore now, you know that."

"Don't want to piss you off again, Cody," Mason said, "but you got any ideas yourself? Ideas about what could have happened?"

The chief squeaked back in his chair and folded his fingers over his stomach. "Well, to tell you the truth, I don't like to believe it, but I think that new man went crazy or something. He made me a mite nervous to begin with, with his slick city manners and all, but with his dad bein' on the force in L.A., I reckoned at the time it was worth the risk." The two men leaned forward and listened. "Figure them boys got in an argument somehow and he up and shot Josh or something. Then he got scared shitless and dumped Josh's body somewhere and flat-ass freaked out. Took off for parts unknown."

Mason scratched his head. "But if he done that, then how come them dogs didn't scent him in them fields?"

"Maybe the bastard stole a car or something, or even had another car parked there when he pulled up. There's those other car tracks we found. Problem is, those could have been made anytime before that happened. Maybe have nothing to do with it, but odds are they do. How the hell do I know. You asked me what I thought, I told you!"

"Sorry, Cody," Mason said. The two men set their coffee cups down and walked toward the door. They turned when Cody called to them.

"Remember what I'm tellin' you. Don't you be goin'

up on that mountain and fester up them Skaggits 'less I tell you.''

The sunlight coming through the opening in the barn had moved only a couple of inches up the wall since Harley had left them all sitting in stunned silence.

After what seemed like five minutes, Ti introduced himself to each of the men formally. He was embarrassed, standing back as though afraid to get too close, then directed most of his comments to Alex. Landry was silent as usual. He'd simply blinked and nodded when Ti gave his name.

Alex assumed Ti talked primarily to him because he was a police officer. Ti jabbered in short, explosive sentences that came out faster and faster. He started with Harley picking him up along the road, then backtracked to his home life in Tennessee, his mother, brothers, and where he went to school.

His mind hopscotched back and forth, as though desperately searching for something to fill the void left by the topic he was avoiding—the threat to his life. Alex's knowledge of psychology was limited, but he knew Ti was going through this free-association litany to try to touch on a subject that would release him from his horror.

The three manacled men had all lowered themselves to the ground and leaned against the huge timbers they were tacked to, like mice with their tails stapled to a wall. They could walk six to eight feet from their personal timber, then their chains jerked tight.

Ti sat on the floor in front of them, eyes unfocused, and fondled the length of lumber Harley had given him.

Alex looked at the other two men. When Harley limited the length of their chains, it had seemed nonsensical at first, but Alex now realized he did it to keep them from ganging up on Ti, or being able to help each other. The person Ti decided to attack would be on his own in trying to defend himself because the others were out of reach.

"Time's passing, what are you going to do?" Alex

asked, forcing the issue. Ti stared at him as though not comprehending what he was saying. "If you're going to try to escape, you should do it now, not wait until the last minute. Your chances would be a lot better."

"The dogs! You heard him! What he said about the dogs!" Ti shrilled.

"What he said is true." Alex tried to talk in a soft, even voice, hoping to calm him a bit. "But you're reasonably fresh and haven't been chained up for a long time like us. You'd have an excellent chance of making it to the fence before them. With only three dogs, maybe you could divert their attention—go around to the back and holler out a door or something to draw them back there, then run through this door for the fence before they realized what you were trying to do."

"And what? And what? And what if I couldn't?" Ti screeched in a voice that was close to out-of-control.

"When you beat them to the chain-link, you simply climb beyond their reach, crawl over the top, and drop down to the other side. Below in the foothills, the trees are thick and it's getting close to dark. You'd have a great chance to get away," Alex reasoned.

"That's ridiculous! I couldn't do that! I'll have to do something else. Besides, he was just trying to scare me. No way he's going to shoot me. People don't do that!"

"Ti, ask either of these other men about it. See those piles of dirt by the far wall there?" Alex pointed, but Ti ignored it and frowned. He turned the four-by-four faster and faster in his hands as he studied it.

Above them, a flurry of birds came through the opening and argued for their places on the beams.

The men jumped at the sound. It made them conscious of how tightly their nerves were strung. They were almost hypnotized by the big man rolling the timber over and over in his chubby hands. Ti's fingernails were bitten to the quick and his nail stubs were black.

"Ti, you can't let your time drift away and do nothing. Those are graves, those piles of dirt. At least ten men are buried there. Don't you see? One more killing doesn't mean anything to them. If you'd been there when Mae shot my partner Josh in the chest, you'd understand these people mean business. Hell, I buried him in that last grave with my own hands. He was *dead* for God's sake! I should know! That Harley means it when he says he'll kill you at six. Ask Manny here."

"He's right, you know," Manny said. "Harley'll kill you with that scattergun sure as hell. Your only chance is to try to get away over that fence." Alex could see that Manny was nervous about what was going to happen next because he was the smallest.

"Screw the fence, goddamn it!" Ti screamed. His voice quavered. He was emotionally disintegrating. They were forcing him to deal with this when all he wanted was to run off and hide somewhere.

"Ti, listen to me. You only have two choices here. Be logical. You can go for the fence, or you can do what I'd do—you can fight for your life when he comes back." It was silent in the barn.

Ti shuddered and slammed the timber to the floor in revulsion. It echoed in the large open structure. To Alex's left, Manny breathed out a lungful of air in relief.

Ti stood suddenly, trotted to the still-pot, and held the cheap leather-banded watch up to the light.

"My God! Now I've got less than an hour and a half!" he squeaked.

"Ti, listen. Bring me that timber. Maybe we can use it for a lever to tear loose these chains. We've got time. We might be able to get all of us loose. We could all wait for him and jump him when he comes in. How about that?" Alex asked.

"I give you that lumber, he'll be mad. Kill me for sure!" Ti screamed.

"He's going to kill you anyway, dammit!"

"I could still hit one of you guys," Ti sniffed.

"Come on, give me the lumber while we still have time."

"I have to think." Ti sat again and rocked while looking at the ground.

None of this was sane. Alex had to talk Ti into some course of action or he'd die. Who was more deserving of life was beyond their right to decide. Alex had to talk him into fighting or running because either one of those choices could lead to freedom for all of them.

The chains of the other men clanked when they shifted.

"I know you're not the kind of man—in fact, none of us are—who could kill someone in cold blood, even to save his own life," Alex continued as he scratched his itching arms and shoulders. It was either the bites or his inflamed nerves. "Let's talk about it, don't just sit there. How about the idea of going for the fence?"

"I can't! I can't!" Ti wailed. "I couldn't pull myself over the thing, can't you see that! I'm too goddamned heavy! And I'd rather be shot than have those dogs tear me up!"

Alex looked at the floor and shook his head. Given only those two choices, he'd take the shotgun blast himself. Dying under the ripping jaws of those vicious dogs would be too frightening for anyone.

"How about the other alternative—taking that timber and bashing Harley in the head when he comes in—how about that?"

"Great! Even if it worked—which I don't think it would—then what'll I do? Them dogs'll still be out there. What'll I do then, huh?" Ti stood and waddled over to the opening, looked into the late afternoon, and shivered at what it held for him.

Alex could hear the dogs growling as though they knew what he was thinking.

"Besides," Ti said, wheeling to face them, "he ain't goin' to just walk in big as you please like some idiot. Like as not he'll peek in first, then come in real cautious till he sees all of us. Hell, he could even come in a back door if there is one." Alex flashed on the storeroom door leading to the outside. That made it at least a fifty-fifty chance, unless there was a door upstairs, then the odds could be even lower. But right now, fifty-fifty was a whole lot better than zero.

"Ti, the reason none of us has ever attacked Mae or Harley is because we'd still be chained up with nothing to break loose with. You're not chained. When he brings that shotgun with him, you can disarm him after you stun him with that timber. Then you can take the gun and force him to let you through the gate." Alex watched his face for some response, but Ti's gaze bounced around the barn, searching for some escape from this madness. "Hell, you could even take his keys to the truck and drive out of here. Worse comes to worst, you could shoot those damned dogs. There wouldn't be anything to stop you then. Besides, you saw what happened when he walked you between those dogs. They won't attack as long as him or Mae is there . . . can't you see that? All you need is the gun."

"Yeah! Well, that's easy for you to say. He didn't beat on you like a drum. You don't know how strong that crazy man is. I'm not even sure hitting him, if I could get that close, would even knock him out or anything." Ti walked over and stood in front of Alex, then crumbled into a heap on the floor and sobbed like a child, rocking back and forth on his padded rump.

Alex glanced over at Manny, who shook his head in frustration. Time was ticking away, and Ti's courage was inadequate to try to save his own life, much less their lives.

And the subject that hung in the air was:

They had still avoided talking about the final alternative—

The alternative of killing one of them.

The men glared back and forth at each other as Ti swayed and sobbed. Alex wondered how long it would be before the fat man felt the pressure to consider that possibility.

And when he did—if he did—

Which man he'd select to kill.

15

As Jenny walked along the country road, she was struck with how hopeless what she was doing was. She had started out with enthusiasm, but faced with reality had wilted immediately. Thinking about and planning this course of action had seemed constructive; now it just seemed a waste of time. She had no idea what she was searching for, or even where to begin. The afternoon sun was hot on the right side of her face as a bead of sweat tickled her neck.

A battered stake-bed truck loaded with hay came rumbling over the road. Jenny picked her way off into the deep weeds, and the truck passed, trailing a concussion of heated air and flying gravel. She blinked away the dust and the tears. The driver looked straight ahead and passed without even glancing at her.

She stepped back onto the road and continued in the direction she'd been walking. What was she hoping to find that the chief and his men had missed? Tears welled up as she trudged along, kicking at the clumps of grass here and there, hoping against hope that some clue would be lying in them. In the distance, her truck waited by the tree where Alex's car had been found.

About a hundred yards away, she came upon an almost invisible dirt driveway in the weed-choked field, obviously used infrequently. She had to stand at the end of it to see the path it weaved back through the now-shadowed trees and up onto a hillock populated with thick-foliaged birches. Between the leaves here and there, she could pick out flashes of dull color. Color out of character for the woods.

A house, has to be.

She glanced back at the truck with apprehension, then thought of Alex, then plowed into the deep grass and followed the indentations in the ground left by the tires. A flock of birds rose on beating wings and startled her. She glanced around to see what had frightened them, but there was nothing. The grass was shoulder-high in some areas and whipped her forearms as she passed.

She carefully placed her footfalls and thought about what she was going to say or do when she got to the house.

Shuddering, she looked at the ground, watching for snakes as her feet separated the grass. This field had to be full of them—slithering, slimy, wanting-to-bite-her-ankles snakes. The smell of the underbrush and the earth was strong, and she imagined she could hear small animals scuttling through the deep undergrowth.

As she closed on the copse of trees, she had the unsettling feeling that someone, or something, was watching her. She glanced back toward the truck, but it had disappeared behind the trees and into the deepening shadows. She turned and walked toward the birch trees that obscured the house.

Nothing hidden in there could be any worse than living the rest of her life without Alex.

In the barn, time slowed down for Alex, and he had the feeling that hours had passed as the men watched Ti sob. After the crying jag, Ti became eerily quiet and sat with his head in his hands. While he was silent, Manny and Alex struggled to tear the chains loose, but it was impossible without a pry bar. They both worked for minutes, then collapsed and watched Ti.

This was a life-and-death decision Ti had to make on his own. Alex had already drawn the alternatives for him and could do nothing more except wait—wait like the other men—wait for Ti to make his decision.

Ti would probably die if he chose any alternative except killing one of them. His odds on escaping or waylaying Harley were almost nonexistent. Alex decided he should butt out at this point, even if Ti asked for a suggestion. What was going to happen was bad enough without being forced to lie to him.

Alex tried to estimate the time left, but it was impossible to do accurately. It could be anywhere from thirty minutes to a full hour until Harley came back in with his deadly shotgun.

A couple of times in the last few minutes, Alex had glanced over at Manny and been shocked to see how this confident, damn-the-torpedoes guy was reacting. It was obvious Manny expected to be selected. He was the shortest, at about five six, and the frailest, at about 135 pounds.

Manny's deep-set eyes stared at Ti like a mouse in a cage watches a snake, knowing it's going to be dinnertime shortly and it's the main course. His sallow skin glistened with moisture, and his loose-fitting clothing was stained with sweat. Alex jerked on his chain again, but there was no way to get loose.

"My mama wants me to live—she needs me!" Ti shouted. The three men jumped at his voice. Other than the flutter of an occasional bird and the random sounds from the woods, it had been quiet, each man working on his own thoughts.

"You think I should kill this Harley guy, that what you want?" Ti said in a shaky voice as he looked at Alex. Without waiting for an answer, he asked: "Who made you God?" His tone was aggressive. Alex knew that when Ti decided to kill one of them, he'd have to work up some rationale, some righteous indignation, to justify it in his mind. It was impossible for a normal person to kill without emotion.

"I didn't say you had to kill him," Alex answered in a measured tone. "You just have to do whatever you have to do to disarm him if you want to escape." He could hear the rustling of the chains of the other two men, disturbed by the rising tension.

"Well, if somebody has to die, why is *his* life so much less valuable than any of *yours*?" Alex could hear the pieces of Ti's case for murder slipping into place. Ti wanted to keep the exchange at a life for a life to make his point.

"He's a criminal, for starters. These two men and I are victims here. Can't you see the difference?"

"The Bible says, 'Thou shall not kill.' It's one of the Ten Commandments," Ti reasoned. "God wouldn't care more about *your* lives than he would that Harley guy's." Ti hoisted his bulk to his feet, and swayed for a moment, breathing deeply. His gaze flitted around the barn, then came back and settled on Alex. The chains clinked again as the other two men thought about defensive positions.

"If you kill one of us, it would be murder, regardless of what you decide to call it," Alex said.

"You told Harley that they couldn't convict me 'cause he made me do it. I heard you!" His voice was stronger now, deeper.

"You'd know it was murder! You mentioned the Bible. If you believe in it, then you know God will know it's murder too!"

"Shut up! You're trying to confuse me. You're the one who said I should kill Harley!"

"You know I didn't say to kill him—don't use that to justify what you want to do!"

Ti started to say something, then in his anger, he choked and coughed. He held one beefy hand up to his mouth as he glanced to where the watch lay ticking away one of their lives. Ignoring Alex, he jogged over and picked it up. His mouth contorted as he studied the dial. "Dear God! Forty minutes! That's all I got!" His penetrating, high-pitched voice echoed through the barn, causing the birds to shift in the eaves.

He dropped the watch to the ground as though it were hot, then turned and faced the men with fevered eyes. "I wanna live!" he wailed with intensity as he bent down and fumbled for the heavy piece of lumber. "I got a right!"

Alex knew that the discussion was over.

The decision had been made.

The only question now was—

Who would he select?

Under the shelter of the trees, the weeds were matted and retained the furrows left by the tires of the old pickup truck sitting by the tiny cabin. Two of the tires on the rusted hulk were flat, and the tailgate was missing.

Jenny studied the house before walking closer. It was hand-hewn by someone who had never built a house before. No attempt had been made at refinements. No porch, only a wooden stoop, sashed windows askew in their moldings, no fireplace that she could see. Flat boards covered the skeleton of the house and were unpainted and black, buckled and cracked with age. Tar paper on the roof, with ripped-off edges, was wrinkled up where it had been hammered into place.

A limp curtain rustled in one of the windows, then pulled open. A tired, battered face of a woman with blue bruises around her left eye looked back. She wore a haunted expression.

Jenny jumped when a man appeared at the side of the house and stood in a challenging pose, a heavy board in his hand. "This here's private property, din't you see the signs?" The threat was raw and angry. He was bulky and wore bib overalls. His bare arms were sinewy and his thick hair and beard grew in all directions. Jenny guessed he'd worn the clothes for weeks. *God, they must stink,* she thought.

"Please, I don't mean any harm. I'm just looking for my husband—"

"Your husband be damned. He ain't around here, woman!" When Jenny heard the hate in his voice, she knew where the bruises on the woman's face had come from.

Jenny held her ground. "My husband's a policeman. He and his partner disappeared from a car down on the road. I thought you might have seen something—"

"Told them stupid cops lack I'm tellin' you. Nothin'! Din't see nothin'. Now git!"

Jenny glanced up at the window, and the woman made a suppressed motion with her free hand. Jenny's brow wrinkled as she tried to determine what the woman was trying to tell her. Was she attempting to say, *"Help me,"* or was she signaling that she knew something about Alex?

"Maybe your wife? Maybe she saw something?" Jenny asked as she stared at the woman. The man followed her gaze to the glass.

He swung and smashed the heavy stick against the curled siding. The sound echoed like a gunshot through the trees—

Jenny jerked.

The woman leaped back and disappeared from the window.

The drapes swung back and forth where she had been.

You bastard! Jenny thought when she saw the raw fear in the woman's eyes.

The man turned to Jenny and spit on the ground in front of her feet. "She ain't seen nothin' neither." He spoke like a man who was used to being listened to.

"Can I ask her?" Jenny implored. Her stomach was quivering with fear, but she had to know more. "My husband is missing. It's important!" Her voice got higher in spite of her attempt to control it. The man took two steps toward Jenny and elevated the stick a bit.

"You got ten seconds to get your ass movin', lady!" Jenny started to say something, then realized it was hopeless. She wanted to tell him off, but she'd be flirting with serious injury. Back in these woods, he could do anything he wanted, and she knew he would.

She glared, half turned, and edged away. He stopped and watched as she worked her way between the trees.

Farther down into the field, the house and the man

faded behind the dense cover of leaves. Her breath came in deep gasps, and her heart pounded.

"You ugly bastard!" she allowed herself once she was out of hearing range. She was furious with the way he had treated her, and more importantly, for what he was doing to that poor woman. Her heart slowed. The handsome face of Alex with his square jaw and kind blue eyes came to her. *God, I loved him.* Love *him,* she corrected.

How could someone as nice as Alex be gone—just gone—and that animal be alive and well? And the woman. What about that poor woman? Did she know anything about Alex? What was she trying to say to me with her hand signals? What a terrible life she must lead.

The dilapidated truck gave mute evidence they had been stuck in those woods for weeks, months maybe. *How horrible!* A prisoner of someone that cruel.

What a dreadful life.

What could possibly be worse?

16

"You! I'm gonna hit you," Ti said as he glared at Manny. He avoided using the word *kill*. Ti's hands shook as he glanced down and rolled the four-by-four over and over, studying it as though trying to decide how to commit this awful act.

"No!" Manny shouted. "You can't kill me. I've got a wife and family! Six kids! If I don't get back to them they'll never make it!" He screamed from behind the timber he now used as a shield, "I've got a son who's crippled, needs braces! He'd be all alone. Kill Landry there . . . he's sick anyway . . . kill him!"

Ti looked up from his piece of timber and took the first tentative step forward—

"Don't do it, Ti!" Alex yelled. "You can still change your mind! Do the right thing. Try to get Harley!"

Ti continued walking. . . .

He seemed to be in a trancelike state, unaware of what Alex had said. Ti lumbered toward the beam Manny was crouched behind and blindly swung the four-foot-long timber with all his might—

He connected with the heavy support with a thunderous bang—

Manny shrieked—

The four-by-four timber went flying, jerked from Ti's hands by the force of the blow.

The birds covered them with droppings and feathers as they screeched out of the barn in a brown whirlwind of wings.

Dirt rained from the rafters.

"Goddamn it!" Ti yelled, and dropped to his knees and wrung his hands from the pain.

"Son of a bitch!" Manny screamed and ran behind the support timber. He reached for the four-by-four, but his chain was too short. Then he lay on his stomach and stretched, but it was still too far away.

Ti's groans changed into soft sobs as he rocked back and forth. Without warning, he leaned forward on his hands and knees and threw up in long wracking explosions, then shook.

The men knew they were safe.

Ti's conscience and his aversion to killing had won.

"Oh my God oh my God oh my God," Manny whimpered as he lay on the ground breathing like an overheated dog. Alex slid down his post feeling drained and helpless. Happiness or relief was inappropriate because Ti was going to be murdered in front of them any minute. It was almost time—it had to be.

"SHUT UP, GODDAMN IT!" It was Landry's surprisingly strong voice. The two men looked at him in shock, and Ti's head raised in awe at the power of it. "Stop that sniveling—I'll save your life, boy!" Ti hiccupped his tears back and gawked at the newly animated man. "Do what I say and you'll live!" Landry yelled. Ti stared back and waited. "Don't ask questions . . . do two things . . . NOW!" Ti nodded. Alex stood, amazed at the strength of the man's will when minutes before he'd been quiet.

"Get a gallon jug of that moonshine and bring it here, and pick up that damned watch." Ti blinked, trying to understand how that would save his life. "Do it now if you want to live! NOW!"

Ti jumped up, wavered, ran over, and picked up the watch first, put it in his pocket, then stumbled to the cases of moonshine. His hands shook, and he dropped the first jug. It broke at his feet and drenched his pants.

"Another one! Hurry!" Landry screamed. Ti wrestled a second jug from the case and cradled it in both hands. He carried it to Landry and set it down like an offering.

"Give me the watch—NOW!" Landry ordered. Ti fumbled through his pocket and grunted when he failed to come up with it the first time, then jerked it out along with the lining of his pocket. He pulled it loose and handed it to Landry.

Studying the watch, Landry said, "Twenty minutes. We have twenty minutes." His voice became calmer. "Plenty of time, boy, plenty of time." Ti stood in front of him, shaking. He was a child again, waiting to be told what to do. Landry unscrewed the top of the gallon jug of alcohol. Ti followed every movement with trusting innocence.

"You're weak, son. Just like my boy was. Isn't any sin, it's simply the way things are. He's dead now, killed in the Marine Corps ten years ago in one of them banana helicopters. Stupid! Died for nothing."

Landry lifted the jug to his lips and chugged the fire-hot liquid without taking a breath. Huge bubbles rose as he took it in. He set the jug down for a moment, coughed hard, then raised it again and continued drinking. Three more times, and all but a mouthful in the bottom of the clear jug was gone.

"What the hell are you doing? That'll kill you!" Alex shouted. Manny's eyes were wide as he watched in morbid fascination.

"Shut up and listen!" Landry shouted, then coughed again. "I'm a doctor—*was* a doctor, that is. Listen, boy. I been dyin' of cancer," he said to Ti, "but I'm a dead man, right now, this minute! You hear me! I know what I'm talking about. I'll be dead minutes from now." He belched, then grimaced. He gripped his stomach before continuing. "First I'll go unconscious, then my respiration will shut down or my heart will arrest—*stop*," he clarified. "If neither of those happens right away, I'll be gone in an hour or so from alcohol poisoning. No way I can be saved unless they could pump my stomach. You kill me, you're killing a man who only has minutes to live anyway, you understand?"

Ti answered with a nod and his lips trembled as he tried to form words and questions.

Landry hushed him with a wave of his hand. "Soon as I go unconscious, you fetch that board and hit me on the head as hard as you can—several times—you hear me? Make sure I'm dead." Ti nodded again, then whimpered. "Listen, boy," Landry said. He lowered his voice to a whisper. "I had one or two months to go anyway, you understand? When Mae picked me up months ago where my car broke down, I was already dying. Should be dead by now. I just been putting in my time waiting."

Alex shook his head. That explained why Landry drank the shine constantly—to mask the pain and to forget the inevitable. Landry's eyes glassed over and his head wavered.

"Bless you, son, bless you. I thought I was going to die in this awful place like an animal, for no reason, but now . . . *now* you give a . . . a meaning . . . a meaning to my dying. Thank you, God. My boy, he was a good boy . . . but weak . . . like you . . . but . . . he . . . was a . . . good . . . boy. . . ."

Landry stopped and swallowed, then took one last look around the room through his watery eyes. He coughed and closed his fluttering lids.

"Make sure . . . you hit me . . . really . . ."

His voice trailed off and his head flopped to the side. The post held him in a sitting position or he would have fallen. Alex watched for some small movement as his own heart pounded in his ears. The massive amount of alcohol had worked fast, really fast.

Landry was silent. Unconscious. His chest quivered in shallow, rapid breaths, and Alex knew his heart was careening out of control.

Ti sobbed. This time for Landry, Alex hoped.

"Get the board," Alex whispered. Ti's shoulders shook as he buried his face in his large hands. "Now," Alex ordered. "You don't have much time. If you're going to live, you have to do it *now*. Don't let him die for nothing. It's what he wanted." Ti rose, shoulders still shaking. He shuffled over and picked up the timber, then came back and stood in front of Landry, tears flowing down his round cheeks.

Alex looked up at the ceiling of the barn as two small brown birds came through the opening, then glided to a cross-beam where they landed and fluffed their feathers. Letting his mind drift would be so easy . . . it would be so easy to ignore what was happening.

He sensed Ti was frozen into inaction, afraid to do what had to be done to save his life. Alex knew what he had to say to activate him, but he had to avoid watching. If he did, he'd have nightmares about it for years to come. As he stared at the birds, he cleared his throat, then choked out the last three words—

"Do it now."

A long hesitation followed, then—

A swishing sound—

The dull, hollow impact echoed.

A bird's head popped from under its wing at the sudden noise. Alex moaned deep in his chest as he forced himself to keep looking at the birds. Alex studied their well-formed bills and pointed wings. They were beautiful. *Swallows of some kind,* he guessed. He'd spent so much time trying to solve his problems, noticing them before had been impossible.

Swish—thud!

Alex cringed.

A bird fluttered its wings—

Swish—thud!

Then more sickening reports came—

Thud, thud, whop, thud, whop!

Alex willed himself to concentrate on the birds, but it was difficult.

Hot tears streamed down his cheeks,
As he cried for the first time,
Since his wedding day.
Oh, Jenny! Oh God—
Please help us all.

17

Slauson Avenue in Los Angeles was crowded with the usual bumper-to-bumper traffic as Alex's father, Lee Gregory, drove his Camaro home from the station. The car was pointed due east, away from the nightly red-and-yellow Hollywood-style light show, the sun going down in flames out over the Pacific Ocean.

He inched toward Telegraph Road, where he'd turn south to the bedroom community of La Mirada and his small, wood-framed stucco house with his too-small yard and a thirty-year-old empty swimming pool with weeds growing through the plaster.

The sky was clear of clouds except for the smog that obscured the rim of mountains in the distance. On the few days of the year they could be seen, people who were used to the monotonous gray backdrop expressed shock when they realized there were actually mountains on the horizon. Veteran Angelinos were thrilled if they could just see the tips peeking out of the top of the inversion layer hovering like an invisible glass lid above the city, encasing the heat and exhaust from the millions of vehicles.

"Your son called?" asked Lieutenant Marsh Wheeler from the passenger's seat. Marsh lived in La Mirada too, and they took turns driving. Lee reached down and touched the blue Post-it slip he had pressed to the dash as a reminder.

"His wife, Jenny, not Alex," Lee said. "Makes me nervous as hell that she would call instead of him, especially at the station. She wouldn't do that unless there was something wrong." The traffic light at Western Avenue changed to amber. Lee shifted to second, dove to the inside lane, and accelerated across the intersection, the rear of the Camaro fishtailing from the power of the V-8 engine.

"How old did you say you are?" Marsh asked as he buckled his seat belt and laughed. He leaned back and relaxed as the traffic slowed and stopped. "You call her from the station?"

"Of course. No answer, just their damned machine. Going to try calling as soon as I get home." The traffic moved forward three feet, then stopped again.

"Didn't you say they're living in West Virginia? What's the name of the town?"

"Picksburg. Population of around a thousand, give or take."

"A thousand!" Marsh shook his head. "Why a burg like that? How could you have any fun at all? God, what a way to live."

They both shook their heads, trying to visualize that strange lifestyle. Lee looked back over his shoulder for an opening in the next lane. He darted in, cutting off a Volkswagen as a huge eighteen-wheeler in front of him downshifted with its engine cackling, and coughed black billows from its vertical pipes.

As he drove through the cloud of oily exhaust, he reached down and rolled up his window, then closed his exterior vents. He lit another cigarette, then thought about Alex and Jenny.

And the strange land where trees grow without being planted.

And they have mountains you can see all the time.

Ten minutes after the violent death of Landry, all three of the men sat silently, each staring in a different direction—none daring to look at Landry's crumpled, bleeding body.

Everything had been said and argued before. It was now time for sober reflection and sorrow. Ti walked to the right side of the stills, slid down to the dirt floor, and leaned against the ochre bricks. He let his head loll back, gazed up into the darkening rafters, and tried, not successfully, to choke back small sobs.

Hating Ti for not having the courage to try to escape or to confront Harley was impossible for Alex because the odds on either action being successful were pathetically poor. It was only Landry's strength of character in volunteering that had saved Ti. Without that, Ti would have been the one to die, no question about it.

Even though the killing had been done by Ti, Alex felt thrashed and used up. Before it happened, he'd had the raging urge to kill Mae and Harley, especially Harley, for putting them in the position where the choice had to be made, but now, all he felt was sadness. Overwhelming grief for Landry, and remorse that they had been turned into a pack of self-serving animals whose only thoughts were of survival. *Damn him for that!*

In Ti's place, he felt he would have tried to escape or fight, but it was difficult to be sure. To be positive. That uncertainty ate at him as he gazed out the door into the waning sunlight. The only way any man could know would be to face the decision himself. Alex walked over and lit the one lantern he could reach.

At exactly six o'clock, Harley swaggered from the shadows of the back room with the shotgun in one hand. It looked tiny in his bulky hands.

Harley had come in the back door. Alex thought if he'd had to choose, that's where he would have been waiting for Harley. The realization depressed him further.

"I'll be damned," Harley grunted as he looked down at the battered head of Landry whose thin hair was matted with still-oozing blood. He glanced over to where Ti was staring into the rafters and sniffling. "Figured you for a wimp, boy. Me an' Mae said they's no way you'd have the gumption. I ain't often wrong." In back of him, Mae sidled out of the dim light of the storage room. "This son of a bitch killed Landry," he said to her.

"You don't say, you don't say." She stepped up and glanced down at Landry. "Whomped him good, he did. Deader'n a doornail. Well, som'bitch wasn't gonna last much longer anyhows." She said it much as Alex would say, *Yeah, he killed that fly all right.*

She turned her back, walked to the vats, and ran her finger through the surface of the bubbling mash, then tasted it.

"Christ! Got snowballs big as yer fist poppin' up," she exclaimed, already uninterested in the subject of the death of Landry. She tested two more vats and announced they were ready for running. While she did that, Harley went into the back room and returned with a crowbar in his other hand.

Harley set the shotgun by the still, then went to each beam and pried out the steel *U*'s he'd driven in to shorten their chains. He hung each of them on his belt, intending to take them when he left.

"Ti, get yer ass over here," Harley ordered. Ti shook his head to clear it, then turned as though hearing him for the first time. "Drag this boy's body to there." He pointed with the crowbar to the last grave.

Ti stood and wobbled to maintain his balance. He lumbered over and without hesitation grabbed Landry by the legs and dragged his body next to the last mound of freshly turned earth. The chain attached to Landry's arm rattled and clinked along behind. Ti dropped Landry's legs, then still wavering, looked to Harley for further instructions.

God, he looks like a damned robot, or something, Alex thought. *Must be shock, has to be. In this state, he'll do anything Harley tells him.*

Mae walked to Ti and kneeled. Alex watched with interest. From a side pocket of her shapeless dress, she withdrew a ring of keys. After she tried two in the lock on Landry's manacle, the Schlage lock popped open and she pulled it off. She motioned for Ti to step forward. He did without hesitation and offered his left arm. Harley smirked when he saw his obedience. As Mae attempted to affix the unforgiving steel to his wrist, Ti studied what they were doing with the fascination of a child whose arm was being treated for a cut. Whatever fight and fire he'd had was gone after what Harley had forced him to do. At least temporarily.

The keys, Alex realized. *No way she was going to have them with her all the time. Must keep them in the house somewhere.*

The keys! All the lights clicked on in Alex's mind at the same time. The woman had the keys for their manacles, and the shotgun was leaning against the still. It was loaded if Harley was carrying it. This was probably as good a chance as he was ever going to get.

The gun! If I can get by Harley to the gun—

Harley and Mae were concentrating on Ti. They were having trouble getting the manacle closed and locked because his arm was so much bigger than Landry's. Alex tried to get Manny's attention, but he sat and stared at the ground in utter defeat. Alex knew he was reliving the shame of the string of lies he had spewed out to try to save his life.

No time to recruit Manny.

Have to act—

Have to get to the gun.

To get by Harley, he'd have to hit him first, then dive for it. His chain would rattle when he ran, but he'd simply have to move fast before Harley could react. If he could down Harley and grab the gun, Mae would be no challenge. He thought about Mae's promise to kill him if he tried to escape again, then dismissed it. They were all going to die anyway. . . .

Thirty feet away.

Harley's back was to him.

Alex pushed off from the dirt floor and ran at top speed, the chain clinking behind—

Harley turned, wearing a grin.

Alex swung at where Harley's head should have been—

Whiffed air—

Harley's massive fist smashed into the side of Alex's head like a pile driver.

Lights flashed and Alex felt the impact of his body against the dirt floor. Searing pain wracked his body as he writhed on the ground trying to regain contact with his arms and legs.

Through the haze covering his eyes and the whirling in his head came laughter. Someone was laughing.

Harley! You son of a bitch! Alex shook his head and the ground spun into focus. Without looking, he pushed his body up and lunged at where he'd last heard Harley's voice.

This time,

After the pain—

Came only blackness.

It was seven-thirty when Jenny's telephone rang. She'd been pacing around the house waiting for Alex's father to call earlier, until she remembered the difference in the time. Three hours. At six o'clock when she'd first started pacing, he was probably still at work in the field somewhere in Los Angeles.

After they finished with the hello, Jenny said, "Alex is missing." Not waiting for his response, she launched into the whole story. Lee was experienced enough to be quiet and ingest the information until she got to the part about what she had been doing that morning.

"That's crazy!" he exclaimed. "You shouldn't be out knocking on doors yourself."

"Lee, you haven't seen the law-enforcement people work in this town. The chief and the officers I've met are backwoods, way backwoods. You know—the *mañana* syndrome—everything happens when it happens, no hurry. I really get the feeling I'm getting the runaround every time I call."

"Look, I'll be there tomorrow. In the morning sometime if I can get a flight. In the meantime, I want you to keep a low profile. I don't want anything to happen to you too."

Jenny broke down and cried. Having anyone express concern for her dissolved her resolve to be strong.

Lee was quiet for a moment, then said, "Honey, listen to me. Think about this until I get there, okay? If someone wanted to kill two police officers, they sure as hell wouldn't kidnap them. There wouldn't be any reason. They'd just shoot them and leave their bodies alongside the road or in the car. The fact they're missing means they're probably still alive."

Jenny knew his logic had holes in it, but it was something to hang on to. If they'd been kidnapped for money, or even for some vague political reason, the kidnappers would have contacted someone by now and made their demands known.

"Have to go. I'll call the airlines, then I'll get back to you and tell you what time I'll be there, okay?"

They hung up. She went into the bathroom and washed her face with a warm cloth, holding it on her swollen eyes.

While she stood in the bathroom, letting the warmth of the cloth comfort her, she thought about the woman in the window that afternoon. The woman had tried to say something to her, but what? Was it simply that she wanted to get away from the man who was abusing her?

One of her first things to do after Lee got there would be to question that woman. Maybe go by sometime when the man was away. Even if she knew nothing about Alex, she felt the need to help her.

God, if she was powerless to help herself—

Maybe she could help that poor woman.

18

When Alex came back to consciousness, Manny was at the stills showing Ti how to stoke the fires and explaining the operation of the equipment. Alex rolled over on his back and stared up at the ceiling and groaned. The last blow had caught him on the temple. Pain flashed through his eyes as he tried to focus. His brain felt loose in his skull.

"Great," he whispered to himself. "So much for the direct-assault method." He'd never been hit that hard in his life except for one time he'd been knocked out playing football. This Harley guy was an animal with the strength of three men and no moral restraints on using it.

At least he didn't hit me with that damned crowbar, he thought. After considering it, he wondered how it could have been a whole lot worse.

The interior of the barn was getting dark. Just a small amount of warm reflected light from the setting sun came in the opening, and the birds flitted around trying to find a place for the evening. White droppings fell as usual.

"Manny, come here a minute," Alex groaned out. Manny glanced over, then walked to him and looked down. "Where'd they go?"

"House," Manny said. "They'll be back in a few minutes, I think. Incidentally, I'm pretty sure you made his day. He was expecting you to try that and was ready. First time I've seen that bastard really smile."

"Feels like he hit me with a sledge," Alex reached up and rubbed the lump on his temple and sat up.

"I can't see any way anybody could come up against him one-on-one and win. The man ain't human," Manny said. "If I were you, I wouldn't try that again, because next time he'll probably kill you. I figure he didn't hit you with that crowbar because he didn't want to seriously injure you. If he did, they'd have to bother getting another man."

"I kind of knew it wasn't because he liked me."

"If you can stand, you'd better bring that mash to still number one now. Don't want the pot to get too hot before we start filling it. It'll scorch the grain and the shine'll taste burned."

"You're beginning to sound like a company man." Alex wobbled to his feet, then ran his hands through his hair. He was dizzy, but his head was clearing.

"Yeah, well, you don't see me lying on my ass with a goose egg on *my* head the size of a doorknob."

Manny walked back to the idle still and began cleaning the lines.

Alex glanced over into the dark at the line of graves. Landry lay in the shadows in a rumpled heap. They'd have to finish the current run of shine before they'd let Ti bury him. That would mean working all night again.

As he walked to get his buckets, he thought about Landry and what a class thing he'd done to save Ti's life. The tragedy was, unless one of them survived, nobody would ever know. Underneath all of Landry's silent pain and his alcoholic veil had been a real man.

Alex detoured and grabbed the shirt that he'd hung up to air out on a nail. Without bothering to smell it, he slipped it around his shoulders and buttoned it in the front. The manacle stopped him from pulling it on his one arm. He'd have to talk her into taking off the chain later so he could put that arm into the sleeve.

He sniffed the shirt, then thought, *The hell with it.* The voracious mosquitoes would be swarming soon and he hated them more than he hated where the shirt had been.

Alex labored filling the still, hoping that working up a sweat and using his muscles would make him feel better, as it had before.

As he struggled with the buckets, he watched the other men to his right. Manny said only what was necessary to Ti, who was shuffling around in a trance.

Alex remembered his first day here and the surreal feeling he had had during the whole time, as though moving through a dream. Considering what Ti had been forced to do as his first act in the barn, it was amazing he was able to function at all. Even if they all got out of here somehow, there was no way any of them could ever forget what had happened. It was fodder for years of nightmares.

As Alex expected, working and sweating helped. His headache dissipated as he carried the buckets in a rhythm. Filling, emptying, filling, emptying. The men worked silently, expecting Harley to come in at any moment. What had happened to Landry had had a sobering effect on all of them, not just Ti.

Alex guessed the time to be two or three o'clock in the morning when Mae came in and stood off in the shadows and watched as they worked. The lanterns burned and hissed and sputtered as the usual cloud of insects swirled around.

Alex observed her from of the corner of his eye. She was drunk, judging by the way she moved. Finally, she settled on a stool by the growing cases of shine and stared, her head wavering back and forth as she glanced from man to man. The hated shotgun was gone.

"Ain't none of you worth your salt!" she snapped. All the men kept working and avoided looking at her. Responding to a drunk who had the power of life and death over you would be suicidal. "Now Woody— there's a man for you!" Alex could tell they were in for a harangue, but kept moving. He was emptying the still on the left, preparatory to refilling it with mash.

"Woody'd work in 'is hyere barn day to night, with only a boy to tote, and could turn out twicet the shine as you pot-likkers, and t'were twicet as good. Shit! Still got a teedum barrel o' his coolin' in the crick. Smooth's apple cider. . . ." Her voice trailed off at the memory.

As Alex poured a bucket into the opening of the still-pot, he glanced over, and her deep-set eyes were wet.

I don't believe this. She actually expects us to feel sorry for Woody after what she's done to us, he thought.

Alex remembered what Manny had said earlier, about how she'd threatened to shoot them all when she talked about Woody. He wondered if he should try to deflect the conversation with a question of some kind, then decided against it. *Let her talk herself out, maybe that's better.*

Mae sat for a long time and watched them work, then continued in a low voice. She told them Woody had gone to help a neighbor with his still. They'd worked three days on a run and had been drinking large amounts of shine when they were raided by government people. All the other men ran, but Woody stayed to defend the still with a couple of shotguns. In drunken indignation, Alex guessed. He held them off for two hours, wounding two men. Finally, when he refused to give up, a sharpshooter put one bullet through his heart.

"Sum'bitches shot him dead!" Her voice raised in anger. "Stop it! Quit workin' whilst I'm talkin'!" Manny and Alex halted and looked back at her. The last dribbles on the second still were being finished, so Ti shut off the spigot and stood at attention, obedient as usual. He stared and waited for instructions. His black shirt was soaked with sweat and his arms glistened in the warm, sputtering light.

"Sit on them pallets," she demanded.

The three men walked over and lowered themselves onto the pallets with resignation. Alex was worried how this was going to play out. Would she get violent as she told her drunken stories? Stories about a man she remembered as a saint, but who was probably a vicious killer in his own right.

Mae got up, picked up her stool, carried it over and sat in front of a still. In back of her, the fire crackled under the pot. To let it burn unattended with the pressure unrelieved would be a sure way for it to foul all the lines, not that Alex really gave a damn.

When she finally finished with her stories, they'd spend at least an hour cleaning the still before they could start running again. The irony was, she'd blame the delay on *their* incompetence.

"Woody was the best damned man in them woods," she began. "Warn't nothin' he couldn't do better'n anybody else if'n he put his mind to it."

For an hour, she harangued them with stories of the fights he'd won, and a long convoluted story about a turkey shoot he'd won hands down every year. The still hissed and thumped and sputtered in the background.

The fires were getting low under the pots and the embers were falling in on themselves when she told her last story—the story of the wolf. In back of her, from the shadows, Harley came in and pulled out a half-gallon bottle of shine. Obviously drunk too, he sat on the floor and listened along with the men.

"Hit come late autumn, and Woody's running the trapline, lack he allus did—'fore some o' the critters bedded down fer winter an' hit got too cold." She hiccuped, then frowned and wiped her mouth. "Come on a jaw trap, big as you please."

"What was onna ground 'round the jaw trap, Mae?" Harley asked. He weaved and smiled. It was a story he'd obviously heard many times, and his part was to ask the questions at the proper places. It took on the aura of a ceremony. *Probably every time they were drunk,* Alex realized.

"Blood, ev'ywheres!" she said as she made a wide circle around her stool with her hand. A trace of a smile showed on her pallid lips. "He knowed anythin' got in that trap couldn'ta got out. It was a full eight-inch, nine-pound trap, staked with a heavy iron drag."

"What'd he find when he follered, Mae?" Mae got up and staggered over and jiggled out another jar of shine. She unscrewed the top and took a drink before lowering herself to the stool with exaggerated care. Harley no longer bothered to keep an eye on Alex, satisfied he was no match for him physically. Alex bristled when he realized that, but Harley was right. Beating him in a fair fight was impossible. Besides, the shotgun was gone, and Mae must have hidden the keys somewhere inside the house by now. Even if he tried again and won, it would accomplish nothing. He'd still be a prisoner.

"You's first 'posed to ask, 'What'd he find?'" she said in a thick-tongued murmur.

Harley laughed, as though at a party of good friends, then asked, "What'd he find inna trap, Mae?" He roared again as though that in itself were funny. The three men watched the exchange stern-faced, their frowns deepened by the flickering light. Alex was sure it would be years before he could laugh.

"A front leg of a gray wolf, all covered wi' blood," she said. "Blood a-drippin' and leadin' off through the light snow."

"What'd he find when he follered, Mae?" Harley chuckled that he was back in synch with the story.

"Any other man'd a-given up, but Woody follered that critter fer four miles back inta the narrows. Finally got 'im cornered twixt some rocks."

"How big 'uz 'e?" Harley's accent grew heavier the drunker he got. Alex reached up and rubbed the knob on his temple. He knew his eyes would be rapidly turning black-and-blue. Mae took another long swig of shine before continuing.

"Over a hunert pounds, easy. Biggest damned wolf he ever seed! Standin' tall, ready ta fight on only three legs. Damned critter was so desperate ta git outten that jaw, chewed off his left front leg clean a whistle!"

"Chewin' off his leg? That's what I'd call real desperate! Pelt had ta be worth a bounty."

"Woody drawed down on 'im sure as hell!"

"An' killed 'im, right?"

"The critter pulled hisself up an' growled fer a fight, like 'e's gonna take on Woody an' ever'body."

"An' then wha' happened, Mae?"

"Woody lowered his bead an' uncocked that Winchester. Figured any critter with 'at much spunk was deservin' ta live."

"Shit! You don't say." Harley chuckled deep in his throat, took another draught from his jar, and wiped his mouth with his shirtsleeve. "Then wha' happened?"

"As he's workin' his way back through them boulders, 'at wolf let out a howl, like one hunter salutin' another." She was somber now. "Woody said it chilled him some fer days after. Said it was like 'at critter was jawin' at 'im from off yonder in the ghost world."

"Ever see that wolf again, Mae?"

"Seed him once. On a full moon 'bout six months later. Moving like a cat on them three legs twixt trees on the ridge. Howled at Woody a time or two, just lack he knowed Woody was still out there." Mae's eyes were heavy as she stood. Without another word, she wobbled toward the door and disappeared into the night. The bugs snapped against the lanterns in the heavy silence that followed. Finally, Harley stood up, turned, and looked at the three men.

"Best you get up, clean that still, and finish that last vat. Another day or two and I'll be out of here." He walked over to Alex and smiled down at him. Alex tensed.

"You figure on chewin' your way to freedom lack that wolf?" Harley laughed.

"It's not a bad idea. If I had some way to do it, I'd consider it."

"Ain't none of you city boys got the balls to do anything like that. Hell, y'all lay here like slugs and die one after the other without a peep." His smile changed to a sneer. "Once in a great while, one'll get the fire to make a try at me, but they ain't none of you man enough ta handle that."

"You talk about *our* courage. It doesn't take a hell of a lot of courage to intimidate smaller men you keep chained and feed slop to," Alex said.

Harley started to lunge, then stopped and grinned, this time with a cold malevolence behind it.

"Ain't gonna kill you now, boy. We got some shine to run. Git up and have at it." He stepped back and drained more of his jug. "Go on!" he yelled. He stumbled as he stepped back. Even though he was drunk, Alex knew he was still formidable.

The men rose with effort, walked over under the flickering lanterns, and began disassembling the still to clean the lines that had clogged while they were on the pallets.

Harley stood back in the shadows watching them. Alex wondered what he was thinking, and whether Harley would still attack him for what he had said. Harley's mind was working slower, and it might take him longer to take offense. It was quiet with just the sound of crickets and an occasional bullfrog croak coming through the barn door.

Thunk!

They jumped back as something hit the heavy beam above the stills. Their heads jerked up.

A long hunting knife quivered from the force of the throw. The men apprehensively glanced back at Harley as he moved into the light.

"You's puttin' me down. Le's see how much guts *you* got, boy." The men remained motionless, not understanding what he was talking about. "Ever' time I come in here, I wanna see that knife on that beam—if it ain't, there'll be hell to pay. But, when I ain't here, ya'll are free to git up there, fetch it down, and make like that wolf." He laughed deep in his chest and walked toward the door, wobbling as he went.

Stopping, he glanced back and said, "All you have to do is cut off your hand ta git loose, that's all! Put your money where your mouth is, cop, an' go fer it!" He leaned on the door and chuckled. "That done, all you got to do is git by them dogs, then climb that fence with one hand, make it down through them woods and by our kin's dogs. 'Course, by that time, with all the ruckus, we'd be huntin' fer you with our own dogs an' all." He stopped laughing and scowled at them as he weaved. The men froze.

Harley finished in a conversational tone, "Now, you can't say you din't have no chance. If'n you din't bleed out, like as not you'd have one chance in . . . let's say twenty, of gettin' away. Yeah, that sounds good. One chance in twenty. I'd say that would take a lot of courage, wouldn't you?"

After he disappeared into the night, the hissing of the lanterns and the snapping of the bugs against the glass seemed louder. The front door to the house slammed as Harley went in to sleep off the shine.

The three men stirred.

Then turned—

And stared up at the knife.

19

It was dark in the small cabin an hour after Mae and Harley'd left the barn, and Mae was up and moving around because sleep was impossible. Still drunk, she moved unsteadily. She first unlocked and looked into the bedroom where Harley and Ellie lay. Harley snored, and she could see by the moonlight coming through the window that he was curled up with his heavy arm around that tramp.

That no-count tramp he brung up here had sashayed around the house, defiled it—stinkin' of perfume, sex, and sweat. The whore!

Mae sniffed and clicked the door closed.

At one time, I'd have burned this house down rather than have a woman like that in it. Harley's a man and subject to the ways of a man, but Woody wouldn'ta stood for it. Not Woody.

She went into the small enclosed porch to check on Sarah and Lester, her pitiful, wordless son. She shook her head as she watched him sleep.

Lester would stay.

He'd stay on this land that had passed down through her family beyond remembering. Lester's days of sufferin' were short. She'd made up her mind he would remain along with the rest of them when she and Sarah left. It'd be a kindness—what Woody would have wanted.

She picked up her small flashlight from the kitchen and went to the second room. The door was secured with two thick metal latches and heavy-duty combination locks to make sure it stayed closed. She removed the first lock and dropped it in her pocket, then dialed the combination and the second lock clicked open. She looked around in the dark and the house was silent except for snoring.

Sliding off the second lock, she slipped it into her side pocket, lifted both of the latches, then pulled the heavy door outward. She smiled when it opened soundlessly because of the oil she had applied to the hinges. Closing the door after she stepped inside, she took in the comforting aroma of oiled wood. More a storage room, it was twice the size of the other bedroom.

She reached up to a shelf by the door and took down a coal-oil lantern, then laid the flashlight in its place. The light illuminated what she was doing. Lifting the glass, she turned the wick up, then struck a match that lay next to it. The light flickered to life as she adjusted the knob for brightness. She set the lantern back on the shelf and clicked off the flashlight.

Looking around the room at the ceiling-high stores of unopened boxes and luxury furniture that were in black-and-white contrast in the light of the lantern, she breathed in a deep sign of satisfaction. She came in this room every day, and always reacted the same way.

This was the room of "things," as Woody had called it. It was his dream, his things—things they were going to need when they moved from this cabin, out of this area, and into the outskirts of Martinton where they'd have electricity and indoor plumbing just like they'd always planned. Almost enough money now, Woody. Soon.

First the calendar. She walked to the wall and lifted the page of the coming month. Toward the middle, a date was circled, and next to it the word *Leeve* was crudely lettered. She counted back to the current day and whispered, "Eighteen days, Woody. Fifty to sixty more batches, that's all."

She straightened and gazed about the room, then walked around each wall, caressing each box, each piece of new furniture that he'd lovingly stored in this room over the years. A box containing a big-screen Mitsubishi television, unopened from the factory, and a Panasonic VCR box were mute evidence they had no electricity. Waterford crystal, each piece hand-wrapped and boxed. On prior visits, she'd opened one of these and inspected the treasure in the light of the lantern, but not tonight— she was too tired and unsteady. Tonight, it was enough to touch the boxes. She wiggled the toes of her bare feet through the luxury of the Karastan wool rug that was partially unrolled.

Against the far wall was a rolltop desk. She picked up the lantern and carried it over to the desk. Placing it on a piece of newspaper left there for that purpose, she scraped back the chair, and sat. Rolling the cover back, she removed a pile of loose one-hundred-dollar bills, put there earlier in the day when Harley had first arrived from his run. She counted them with concentration, rubber-banded the pile, then stacked it with the rest of her money that almost filled the filing-cabinet drawer.

Finished, she withdrew a small notebook and pencil from the middle drawer and recorded the count in a labored scrawl with the chewed-off stub of a pencil. Her tongue out, she totaled $235,425, and drew two heavy lines under it.

Satisfied, she slid everything into the drawers, took the lantern back to the shelf, and turned the wick down until it went out. She fumbled for the flashlight and turned it on, then left as she had come. She checked the locks twice before she went in to sleep on the overstuffed chair in the living room.

Time was getting short, very short.

20

The bags were unpacked and Alex and Jenny rested on the bed for a few minutes before going down into the formal dining room for dinner. They were on the third floor of the Del Coronado Hotel in San Diego. The old turn-of-the-century hotel was a multistoried landmark that had seen every great or near great grace its rooms in its time. It sat above the Pacific Ocean. The evening breeze puffed the drapes away from the open windows on either side of the bed. Alex could feel his eyelids getting heavy.

They'd kissed long and urgently after they'd stood holding each other, gazing through the window, then had lain down and rolled away on their backs, too excited and tired to do anything but stare at the ceiling. They'd planned this honeymoon for so long, it was impossible to believe they were actually here.

Below them, the tennis courts were lit and the sidewalk cafes were crowded with hundreds of guests and passersby. The happy sounds of conversation mixed with music drifted up the hotel's red-colored, wooden siding to them, along with the rhythmic cadence of the surf from the distance.

Out over the ocean, the sun was setting and the shrill call of lonely seagulls floated in on the breeze. Alex smiled as he allowed his mind to slip into the velvety silence of sleep.

He awakened from his reverie to pleasure—unbelievable pleasure. Jenny, it had to be Jenny. Sucking, stroking—slowly, languorously, back and forth across the length of his erection, bringing him closer and closer to ecstasy and release. He soared and moved his hips as he worked along with the pleasure-giving warmth of the moist mouth, enjoying it, luxuriating in it, reluctant to open his eyes. The lips were soft, so soft. If he kept his eyelids closed, maybe she'd keep going, keep—

The smell of grain!

His eyes fluttered open.

His chain rattled on his arm—

He was in the barn!

Revulsion flashed through him! Was it Manny or Ti? He withdrew from the mouth with a popping sound.

"Honey, don't you fret yourself," a woman's liquid voice comforted. "Let me finish." A hand touched him again and he jumped back. His eyes focused on the figure crouched next to him in the blackness.

"Who the hell?" he shouted as he reached down and zipped his fly back up. Normally he would have awakened at someone's touch, but he was exhausted.

The woman took his right hand and guided it to the tip of her smooth, bulbous breast. The erect nipple rubbed the back of his hand as he pulled it away again.

"You're in deep shit if Harley comes out here," he whispered urgently.

Manny stirred on the pallet next to him. "What the—" he said, then yawned.

The woman whispered to Alex: "Honey, you're just too groggy right now. You don't know what you're a-missin'. Let me show you." She stood, flicked on a flashlight, and sashayed across the dirt floor to the stills. Although the light shone away from her, Alex could see by the reflected light she wore nothing but panties and high heels. She laid the flashlight on the copper still-pot.

This is insane. Harley is within earshot of what's going on here.

The match whooshed, and it illuminated a ten-foot

diameter around her. In the circle of light, she looked like a cartoon of something he'd seen on the back of a playing card. Skin shiny; breasts huge, bare, and shadowed in the light; hips generous, but rounded.

Alex could hear the shocked intake of air from Manny to the left of him. The woman stretched up and turned on the Coleman lantern, and it began its familiar hiss. When she lit it, the light reached out and soaked up the blackness.

She stepped in front of the stills so the light would play on the front of her body. It made long shadows from her breasts and nipples, followed the contour of her chest and stomach, and disappeared into the apex of her crotch. Her heavy thatch of pubic hair showed through the thin white bikini panties. She wore four-inch spiked heels, but stood in them with the assurance of familiarity.

"Jesus," Ti exclaimed. Alex and Manny glanced his way, surprised he was awake. He eagerly sat up and rubbed his eyes to clear his vision.

She smiled and began to sway back and forth, a half beat behind her swinging breasts, which moved in a counter-rotating motion that, in this forgiving light, was the most erotic thing Alex had ever seen. She did a slow, petulant kiss with her lips while making a *shoosh, shoosh ka shoosh* sound, imitating a slow brush stroke on a snare drum. She looked like a mannequin with her heavy makeup in the harsh warm light as she turned from face to face, lipstick staining her front tooth.

She changed the rhythm and ran her hands in tight circles over the nipples of her breasts while making the drum sound louder and more urgent. Her fingertips were tiny red dancers, gliding feather-light across them. Her shoulders shivered and her stomach contracted with waves of pleasure. The men's heat rose as they followed her undulating hips and breasts under the haunting light.

Alex glanced toward the door trying to break the spell of the hypnotic motion, and six eyes gleamed in the darkness beyond the opening.

The dogs were watching too.

Something about that bothered him.

She stopped the sound and moaned as she continued to move. Slipping her one hand into the front of her panties, she held her heavy breasts up with her other forearm and the fingers plucked the closest nipple in time with the undulations of her hips. The hand in her panties made a wet sound as she rubbed herself with her long fingers.

"Holy shit," Manny muttered in a voice choked with desire.

"Think about it before you do anything," Alex whispered. Manny was too enraptured to answer.

Then, she stopped the sound and just quivered and pulsated in the light, her eyes closed with the ecstasy of what she was feeling. Alex realized her shiny body must be covered with mosquito repellent. Otherwise she'd be slapping at them instead of fondling herself.

The ticking of the bugs against the lantern was the only sound in the huge barn except for the heavy breathing coming from her and the men. Her eyes fluttered open as she continued to writhe, even slower now, grinding into her hand.

"Who's going to be first? " she mumbled. "I want to be fucked now. Fucked hard!" Her voice was husky with her own pent-up desire.

"Me! Me!" Ti squealed. "I want to!"

"Not you. I want a big, hot dick, not some tub of jello!" She looked at Alex and smiled. "See anythin' you like?" she asked.

Alex heard himself say, "Thanks, but I'll still pass." His voice echoed in the room. *This is a setup. I know it.*

She stared at him for a long time as though confused about what he had said, stunned that he'd refuse.

"You too fuckin' good for me?" she hissed.

"Think what you want."

"Fuck you, you bastard!" Her face turned hard in the harsh light.

"That leaves me," Manny said.

She pivoted to him. Hesitating for a long moment,

trying to decide what to do, she then made a dismissive grunt and smiled.

"Consider what you're doing," Alex warned.

"Already have. If I can fuck her, I'll die a happy man. Come on, I'm ready."

She shrugged her shoulders, and her bare breasts jiggled with the motion. "What the hell. Why not." She glared at Alex. "You probably like boys anyway. Maybe when you see how much fun he's havin', cop, you'll be sorry an' change your mind about wettin' your wick, only then it might be too late. I just might say no."

She swayed over the hard-packed dirt to Manny's pallet, motioned for him to scoot to the side, and dropped on her back without ceremony. Manny had his pants down and was on her like a trapdoor spider snatching its prey. The panties stayed in place; Manny just pushed them aside. Alex moved off into the shadows, and shook his head. Being close was like participating.

In the flickering light of the lantern, Manny's skinny ass pumped like a piston trying to get the job finished before someone took this juicy piece of candy away from him—a dog gulping his food.

"Manny! The dogs! The dogs let her in," Alex shouted. "Someone from the house has to be with her!" It dawned on him why seeing the dogs' eyes in the dark had bothered him.

Manny screamed with childish pleasure as he pounded into her. He was beyond reason until he finished. She had her legs wrapped around his sweating rear, flexing in time with his machine-gun thrusts, helping him drive harder and faster. The pallet bounced and slapped the ground with each lunge and their shallow gasps were in synch was they both sweated harder and faster toward orgasm—

Booooom!

An ear-splitting explosion rocked the barn, echoing and reechoing.

The men were treated to another shower of bird shit and flurry of feathers. The thundering and simultaneous flash of flight came from their left, out of the shadows of the storage room.

Their heads jerked up.

Harley stood smiling on the edge of the circle of light, aiming the smoking shotgun into the rafters.

"Jesus Christ! You limp-dicks did want to fuck my girl!" he shouted, still grinning. Alex worked his jaw to get his ears to stop ringing. He looked back at Manny and the woman. Manny had leaped up, pulled up his pants, and was fluttering with his too-large belt trying to get it cinched.

She struggled to her feet, suddenly having trouble standing on the high heels. If Alex were Catholic, he'd have crossed himself because bad things were going to happen for sure.

"What's your name, girl?" Harley asked.

"Please don't hurt me, mountain man. My name's Marybelle," she whined in a tiny voice as she walked over to the stills, wavering on her heels. Her makeup was smeared.

"What's your name?" What the hell is this? Alex wondered.

"You been bad, girl. I'm gonna have to punish you somethin' awful."

Ellie, a.k.a. Marybelle, began to cry. It sounded sincere.

My God, this is some kind of perverted game. What sickos! Is the end of this game going to be death for one of us?

Having secured his belt, Manny shook in fear, thoughts of sex long gone.

"I wouldn't have done it if she hadn't have asked," Manny whispered. "She came out here . . . and danced naked . . . and—"

"Shut up! You callin' my Marybelle a tramp?"

Jesus, don't answer that one! thought Alex.

"No." Manny's voice was barely audible. He was in deep shit no matter what he did or said. Harley walked over and Manny wavered in front of him like a child standing on the track of an approaching train—unable to move—waiting for the worst.

It came in a split second.

The butt of the shotgun flashed—

Hit Manny in the chest—

Lifted him into the air—

Manny slammed into the ground with a grunt amid the rattling of chains.

Alex made a lunge, then stopped when Harley raised the barrel of the shotgun and smiled. "Do it, cop. I'd love to splatter you on them boards."

Alex took a step backwards. He was about thirty feet away. *He doesn't bluff,* Alex reminded himself.

Harley laid the shotgun by his feet, then lifted Manny up and hit him hard in the chin. Manny's teeth clacked together and two of them snapped off. He dropped Manny's unconscious figure like a discarded doll, and it fell into a heap, toppled over, and lay still.

"Jesus H. Christ! This is like whuppin' up on a bunch o' kids," Harley growled with annoyance. He took one last glimpse at Alex, then picked up his gun, turned, and looked at Ellie, who, with a terrified look, leaned on one of the still-pot walls for support. Harley jerked toward Ti and grinned.

"What you got to say for yourself, fat boy?"

"I din't do nothin'."

"'I din't do nothin','" Harley mocked. "How come you *din't* screw Marybelle there, boy?" He waved the shotgun under his nose. Ti's eyes followed the barrel and his lips trembled.

"I don't know."

"'Cause you're a pig an' she wouldn't have you! Right?!" he thundered. "Say it if you want to live, boy!"

"Cause, I'm . . . a . . . pig . . ." He looked down at his pants leg where a long dark stain grew. Harley's eyes followed his.

Harley grunted.

He slashed the butt of the gun across Ti's face.

Ti crumpled alongside Manny. *Fell with no noise at all.*

Manny moved and groaned.

"Can you believe that shit?" Harley grumbled as he walked over to Ellie. "That fat piece of shit pissed himself. I do hate a cowardly man!"

Alex watched as Harley jerked Ellie around to the other side of the still. He turned her back to him, then pushed her forward, forcing her to lean on the bricks with both hands. She cried in snuffling sobs. Harley kept staring at Alex. Making sure he was watching, or watching him, it was hard for Alex to be sure.

"Please don't, Mr. Mountain Man. That way hurts somethin' awful," she said in a weak voice. He ripped her panties down, then opened his fly. Without hesitation he jammed himself into her, then jerked up hard, lifting her feet off the ground. She screamed with the pain, but kept her hands on the warm bricks of the still wall. Alex cringed.

Impaled, she bounced up and down on the tips of her high heels, crying and screaming with each thrust. Harley grabbed her hair once again and pulled back, dangling her out in front of him—writhing and shrieking in agony like an animal pinioned to a fence post—while he grimaced with pleasure.

All the time, his furtive eyes watched Alex, who was still back in the shadows. Alex had wondered why Harley opted not to attack him too, and now he knew. He was to be the spectator Harley wanted—had to have. Both Harley and the woman needed an audience for this bizarre ritualistic sex. Alex found himself standing in awe, his mouth open. It was like viewing a barbaric mating rite of prehistoric animals, animals that snapped and clawed and could kill each other in the process.

Alex looked at the gun, but from forty feet, he would only take two or three steps before Harley'd dive and pick it up. *Not a chance.*

Finally, after a shuddering orgasm, Harley turned his head from Alex and threw the woman back against the still, finished with her like a used condom. He smiled, pulled in, and buttoned his pants.

"Git!" he shouted to Ellie. He picked up the gun with one hand and pushed the abused woman in front of him. She wobbled on her high heels like a girl going to her first prom. Even in the lantern light, Alex could see the red marks all over her back and legs. She and Harley disappeared from the circle of light and were gone out the door.

Alex stared into the blackness for a long moment, his heart pounding in his ears.

Manny moaned.

Alex went to help him—

If he could.

The morning light streamed in the east side of the barn as Sarah walked through the door carrying the morning's food. Alex's stomach ached with hunger. As soon as he saw her, his mouth salivated. After she laid the tray down and stepped back, he ran over and picked up a bowl. Overly hungry, he ate it where he stood. She watched him for a moment as he gobbled the food, then turned and slipped through the door.

It was the same gruel he'd been rejecting the last two mornings, but he ate it with gusto today, trying not to chew it before he swallowed. Any lumps were unimportant. This morning, nothing could bother him. He was ravenous. Ti had recovered and hunched over his bowl, finishing the gruel at his pallet. He made small groaning sounds as he ate.

"It's late," Alex said to Manny, who'd been up and moving around the barn, as though out for a casual morning walk. Last night, Alex had held a rag soaked in cold water from the worm box on Manny's battered face until Manny had mercifully gone to sleep. Ti awoke in pain once during the night. He lay on his pallet and cried for a long time, then he too drifted off. All things considered, they were damned lucky not to have permanent injuries.

"You figure they left during the night?" Alex asked. Manny shrugged his shoulders. His face was swollen and two of his front teeth were jagged where they had snapped off. He walked over to Alex, started to say something, then backed away, appearing to change his mind. He was very troubled. Manny went to his pallet and sat down. His eyes were unfocused as he gazed at the far wall above the stills.

"You thinking about Landry, or what happened with the woman?" Alex prompted. Manny shook his head and stared. Alex continued, "If we're going to get out of here, we'll need each other."

Manny sounded beaten when he spoke. "We ain't getting out of here, *ever*. This is where we're gonna die." He reached up and touched his injured chin and mouth. "This is where we're gonna die."

"We have to keep trying. We'll come up with something if we work on it together." Alex attempted to add a touch of energy to his voice, but failed.

"When we getting more food?" Ti asked from his pallet. He belched. Both men looked up as though realizing he was there for the first time.

"Jesus. How can you think about food?" Manny asked. His breakfast was untouched.

"Late this afternoon," Alex said to Ti. "They feed us twice a day."

"You're kidding. How the hell are we going to survive on one meal and this bowl of awful stuff?"

"Whether we survive doesn't bother anybody around here in case you haven't noticed," Alex answered. He glanced up at the hunting knife. It shimmered in the light coming in the opening at the top of the barn. Manny followed his gaze and cringed.

"That damned thing is still there," Manny said. "I figured they'd sober up and come out and get it before morning. I'm amazed that Harley didn't take it after he came back last night." He hunched down onto his pallet and stared up at it. "We'd all be better off if we'd just get the damned thing down and cut our throats. Wouldn't that rain on their fucking parade." He managed a wry smile through his broken mouth. His swollen eyes were already black-and-blue.

"Yeah, for about two days," Alex said. "That's how long it would take to replace us."

"You guys are sick!" Ti yelled. "Stop talking about that sick stuff!"

"We're talking facts, the real world," Manny said.

"Well, if we do what they say, don't make any trouble, work hard and stuff like that, won't they let us go eventually?" Ti asked. Both the other men looked at him with disbelief. Manny shook his head in disgust.

This guy doesn't want to accept the truth, Alex realized.

"I can't believe you're serious," Alex answered. "This isn't a comic book, for God's sake. You killed Landry, in case you've forgotten. They would be tried for that. And how about the other people who have died? No way they're going to let us go. The only way we're getting away from here is if we escape or die. And sitting around waiting for someone to rescue us doesn't make any sense considering how long this damned still has been operating." Alex watched Ti for a reaction.

"You gonna eat your breakfast?" Ti asked of Manny.

Manny glanced at him, said "Jesus" under his breath, and nodded yes, he was going to eat it. Manny was going to be a long time warming up to this man who had made a feeble attempt to kill him. He looked back at the far wall and tried to ignore Ti. Finally, he turned to Alex. "I don't have six kids, I made that crap up." He was subdued.

"You were trying to save your life. Anybody'd have done the same thing. Don't let it bother you."

"And I shouldn't of said he should kill Landry."

"Don't worry about it."

"Yeah, well, it made me sound like a coward."

"Cut yourself some slack, will you? We're all doing stupid things." Alex reached up and rubbed the painful knob on his temple. *Really stupid.*

"When you gonna eat that?" Ti asked.

"For Christ's sake, forget my breakfast already!"

As the two men glowered, Alex glanced back up at the hunting knife buried in the timber, taunting him from eight feet above the floor.

He reached down and rubbed his manacled wrist and shivered.

Desperate, could we get that desperate?

He knew that after last night—

They were close.

Damned close.

21

"Hey! Here I am." Jenny held her purse in the air to get Lee's attention as he walked down the terminal ramp in Charleston at ten A.M. He smiled, but his steely blue eyes showed concern. Jenny was struck with how much he looked like Alex, just older, a lot grayer, a little shorter, but with the same lean build.

He greeted her with a quick hug, a peck on the cheek, and they hurried toward the glass doors. They were both aware they had things to do, places to go, and people to talk to. As they walked fast, Jenny had to skip every once in a while to keep up.

"Any news?" he asked.

"Nothing."

"You call the police station this morning?"

"At seven. Same thing, no details. The chief wasn't in yet, but he hasn't been cooperative with dispensing information. He won't even tell me what he's checked or anything. When I ask, he gives me the *'Now don't you worry, little lady'* routine. Down here, women aren't supposed to ask questions, I guess."

"Jesus! I can't believe that bullshit! What an asshole!"

Lee threw his case in the trunk of the Mustang Jenny had rented earlier. He slammed the lid, then turned and said, "Sorry." She smiled that it was okay. They checked out through the parking-lot turnstile, paid, then drove onto the freeway with the morning light in their faces.

"What happened to your Volvo?" he asked.

"You won't believe it." She gripped the steering wheel, still upset about what had happened in Beckley. She'd saved telling him about that adventure until he arrived.

"Try me."

She hesitated for a long moment, then related to him what had happened. The rats, the car, the theft. Everything.

In the passenger's seat, Lee whistled, then stared straight ahead, his mouth set in a grim line. Traffic was light because it was Saturday morning. Jenny pushed the car up to sixty-five and held it there. Off in the distance, the Appalachians were black against the light morning sky.

"You should get out of this pigsty, come back to California."

"Maybe. You have trouble getting away?" she asked, wanting to change the subject.

"I've got vacation time coming out my ears. Don't worry about it. I'll be here as long as this takes. One way or the other, if these hicks can't find him, I will." Glancing over and obviously realizing that "one way or the other" was a poor choice of words, he added: "Don't worry. We'll find him. He's going to be fine. Alex can take care of himself, always could."

God, let him be right, she thought.

As they drove through the warming humid air, Jenny told him what had happened at the cabin off Gilbert Road. About the man, and the woman signaling something to her. Now that she retold it, it sounded pathetically unimportant, or maybe just paranoid. A frightened woman looking for something out of nothing. In the light of day it seemed a long stretch to hope it would lead to finding Alex.

Jenny's elbow rested on the open window and her hair whipped around her face as she talked. She gestured with her right hand. He nodded and listened.

"Can't you get more information from the chief than me, you being a cop?" she asked.

"Only if he's cooperative. My badge doesn't buy me anything here. I'm just a citizen like you. He doesn't have to tell me squat."

"That's not very encouraging."

"Unless he has something he's keeping under wraps, there isn't any reason why he wouldn't work with me. Forgetting that Alex is my son, day-to-day cooperation on something like this between departments is normally a given—a question of courtesy."

They rolled along the highway in silence for a few minutes. The mountains grew larger in the windshield and took on their rolling characteristics. The hot wind swirled around the interior of the car and promised an uncomfortable day.

"I ever tell you about his adventure when he was twelve?"

"Does it involve another woman?" she asked.

"Yeah, in a way. Mother Nature. Alex was in the Boy Scouts and they were camped out in the Angeles National Forest. First week was fine, then like most kids, Alex got a bug and wandered off with another boy, confident they knew where they were and could find their way back."

"Got lost, right?"

"Three days. Both boys had nothing but their clothes and Alex's hunting knife."

"God! I'll bet they were scared to death."

"Hell no. Just a whole lot hungry is all. Little jerks were having a great time. Big adventure. I could have warmed his pants if I hadn't have been so relieved. They never even considered the possibility they could be in any serious danger. Alex was able to locate water. Finally, on the third morning, after we'd all been without sleep for two nights, the sheriff's chopper located them twelve miles away from where they had camped." Lee's smile disappeared. "Freaked out me and his mom. Lots of people have died in those forests. They just never find

them. The animals eat their bodies, I guess." Jenny
clouded up and bit her lip. He glanced over and shook his
head. "Sorry, that was stupid. Last thing you needed right
now was a comment like that."

"You want to go home and take a shower or eat or
something?" she asked, not wanting to talk about herself.

"Hell no. Let's go right to the police station. Time's
wasting."

She nodded and blinked back her tears.

Picksburg was quiet as they drove the main drag, but
maybe it was her imagination. She remembered showing
visitors around her home in Torrance, and recalled how
she'd had a tendency to see the town through their eyes,
knowing they were scrutinizing everything. She remembered noticing the lawns, brown from the drought, the
wilted palms, and the thick smog. Things that, as a
resident on a day-to-day basis, she would never have
seen. Although Lee was quiet, she could sense his awe at
the small size of the town and the innate poverty
reflected in its tired buildings and homes.

"Damned place looks like a movie set from *The Last
Picture Show* or something," he grumbled. "Except
maybe not as prosperous-looking, or as big."

"Come on, it's not that bad," Jenny said defensively.

Instead of answering, he stared out the windshield as
she pulled into a parking spot next to the portable air
conditioner projecting from the window of the chief's
office. Now, sensitized, she noticed the rust stains on the
wall and the missing mortar between the aging red bricks.

The place does look terrible, she thought.

They got out and walked through the door, Lee leading
the way. At the vinyl-topped counter inside, Becky, the
secretary, greeted him with her slight stutter, then said
hello when she recognized Jenny. Becky was heavyset
and wore an outsized floral dress and comfortable flat
shoes. Her hair was short, drawn back over her ears in a
no-nonsense, shoulder-length style with a just-in-case
pencil showing next to her barrette.

Jenny could see Lee's experienced eyes take in the unkempt office and the scarred furniture. She'd never been to his station, but she knew it was different than this. L.A. had to have the some of the finest equipment in the country and the offices had to be buzzing with activity. Becky was alone in the outer office.

"Chief in?" Lee asked. "Want to talk to him about my son." She disappeared into the inner office, then returned and crooked her finger from the door for them to come in. The chief stood behind his desk with a cigarette in his hand when they entered.

Hellos were exchanged and Jenny introduced Lee. The chief offered some coffee to Jenny and, almost as an afterthought, to Lee. They both refused politely.

"Do you have any information on my son?" Lee asked, anxious to get on with it. The chief leaned back, picked a piece of tobacco from his tongue, and studied it before answering. Jenny leaned forward in anticipation.

"Right now, we got some leads we're followin' up."

"What kind of leads?" Lee pressed.

The chief's eyebrows came together as he shifted forward in his seat a bit and thumbed out his cigarette in a half-full ashtray, with overly intense concentration.

"We ain't got fancy high-tech ways here, but we do our job," the chief said.

"Chief, forget the fact that I'm in law enforcement. Right now I'm only a father who's damned worried about his son and wants to know what's going on. That's not unreasonable, is it?"

"People in this town trust me to do my job, that's why they hired me."

Lee glanced at Jenny and back, then shifted in his chair. Jenny could tell he was straining to maintain control.

"I don't understand," Lee said in an even tone through his clenched teeth. "The question I asked is normal, understandable. The kind of question anyone would ask. I flew over two thousand miles last night to get here because I'm worried."

The chief lit another cigarette and pulled in the smoke before answering. Jenny wanted to scream at him, but managed to hold it in. This was all nonsense. All she wanted was Alex, to see him again and go on with their lives.

"We're a patient people, we knock on doors, then we go back again and again until we get the answers we want. We don't send in some fancy SWAT team at the first sign of trouble." His resistance confused Jenny. Since the second morning, he'd been acting strange, almost hostile.

"What the hell are we talking about here? Every police force in the country works the same way. Ninety percent of it's legwork. Hell, fancy equipment doesn't solve most crimes, you know that. What are we talking about here? You going to tell me anything or not?"

"Got your phone number. Tell you the same thing I told the little lady here. When we have something, we'll call you right off." The chief's voice rose, angered by Lee's persistence.

"I don't believe this shit! You mean you're not going to tell me anything?" Lee stood up, and Jenny could see the veins bulging on his neck.

"Not right now, Mr. L.A. Policeman." The chief stood too.

"Shut up!" Jenny screamed. "You're both puffing up like a couple of roosters and my Alex is missing! I don't give a damn about jurisdiction or who's got the shiniest badge! My Alex is missing!"

She leaped up and ran through the outer office and to her car, where she leaned against the door, crying. She felt helpless. Waiting for Lee had seemed to be a solution of sorts. Something was going to happen when he arrived, but now she could see nothing had changed.

Lee jogged out the door and looked relieved when he saw she was still there. When he walked over, she leaned into him and cried harder.

"I didn't mean that . . . I . . . I'm just so upset . . ."

"Shhh. I know." He cleared his throat as he held her uncomfortably.

Taking the keys from her hand, he helped her into the passenger side of the car. He walked around, climbed in, and started it.

He sat glaring at the window air conditioner on the wall, then said, "Alex is okay. If he were dead, I'd know it. I'd be able to feel it in my bones. Wherever he is, I'll find him, so help me God. With or without help from these redneck bastards!"

"Let's go and talk to that woman," Jenny said as they got nearer her house. "I'm sorry about the way I acted back there. I don't blame you for anything, it's that damned chief. He has me upset."

"It's forgotten. How about if I take a quick shower first, then change into something that's fresh." She nodded. They drove in silence until her house was in sight. He pulled under the big tree in front next to the huge army truck and stopped, then turned to her. "Can I explain something to you?"

"Of course."

"Don't go reading a conspiracy into the way that chief acted. It's easy to let your imagination carry you away. Hell, in L.A., we have petty and major jealousies among divisions, not just problems between cities. Between cities, now that's a whole different bag of worms. Here, we're in an entirely new state, a state where attitudes and methods are twenty years behind the rest of the country. You have to remember, these clowns have a natural resentment to anyone from California or up north. Can't change that, it's just the way it is."

He rubbed his hand across the back of his sweating neck. "Everybody thinks that all the guys in blue are one big happy family, but that isn't the way the real world works," he continued. "Fact is, we're competing against each other all the time. It's like a bunch of little fiefdoms—each chief guarding his authority and the information he has on individual cases."

"That's ridiculous! How can you ever get anything done?"

"It works in spite of the system, not because of it." He climbed out of the Mustang and jerked his bag from the trunk. "Jesus! How can you stand this damned heat?" he asked as they walked up the steps.

Gilbert Road was deserted. Only one car had passed them coming the other way since they'd left the blacktop marking the city limits. Lee shook his head as they slowed when the gravel sprayed the undercarriage of the car. The warm air blowing in the open windows was hotter as waves of heat shimmered up from the road ahead and from the fields in the distance.

"Really makes you want to sell everything and move here," he muttered under his breath as he mopped his brow with the back of his hand. "Jesus, what a shithole!"

"It isn't always like this."

"This is the good part, right? It gets worse——"

"Very funny. See that huge tree alongside the road in the distance? Slow down about two hundred yards this side of it and I'll watch for the driveway that leads to the house."

Finding the driveway the second time was easy because she followed a line of sight from the copse of trees where the house was hidden, down to the road. They parked and locked the car, walked down to the field, then into the deep grass and toward the trees. Lee had to step carefully because his Italian loafers kept finding burrows and indentations.

"Damn!" he exclaimed as he tripped again. "Paid over a hundred fifty for these shoes." Jenny smiled. This was different than city blacktop. Amused by his discomfort, she'd forgotten to worry about the snakes this time.

"Hold on," he said. They stopped about twenty-five yards short of the trees. "We have to plan something here. I don't want to go through this, then walk away empty-handed. This jerk met you at the front door, you say?"

"Yeah. He came from around the side of the house. Must have been working in back or came through a side door."

"Hate to play games, but I don't want to leave with a zero." He rubbed his chin while looking at the trees. "I'll go around to the left here, sneak up behind the house. You go straight to the front door like before. Make all kinds of noise as you're walking. If he's home, we want him to hear you coming, okay?"

"What am I going to say to him?"

"Wing it. Just fake like you want to ask him something, anything. Don't even mention his wife. That's what set him off the last time."

"God, this is spooky."

"Don't worry. If the guy goes for you, you belt out at the top of your lungs. I'll drop what I'm doing and come to your rescue, got it?"

"Screaming I can remember." She turned to go.

"Wait." He put a restraining hand on her arm. "Give me ten minutes before you approach the house. It'll take me at least that long to do a circle to come around back." He stared in her eyes. "Can you handle this?"

"Sure, I do this kind of thing all the time." She tried to smile, but her lip quivered instead. He patted her arm, ran off to the left, and disappeared between the trees.

Jenny felt as though she were coordinating an invasion. She watched the red second hand on her watch as it crept around the dial. In the fields, the cicadas buzzed in the unmoving air, and cold sweat tickled down her shoulder blades. She'd never felt this alone before, and swallowed as the pulsing red hand crept toward twelve.

Launch the boats, she thought.

She hurried toward the trees with a feeling of déjà vu, then pushed the leaves aside as she worked her way between the low branches and into the opening in front of the house.

A voice from her right asked, "Where's that man!"

She jerked around.

The man stood in his usual arrogant stance, this time

with a cut-off baseball bat in his hand. He wore the same
filthy pants, but today, in deference to the heat, he wore
no shirt. Thick black hair covered his chest and shoulders.

"What man?" she whispered.

"The man I seed you leave that car down by the road
with. I come back up here ta wait, and only you showed
up. Where is he?"

"He went back to the car." She realized that he'd seen
Lee and that lying was pointless.

"Why'd he do that?"

"He didn't have the shoes to walk in that brush." *Not
too far from the truth.*

"Whataya want?"

Jenny glanced up at the house, hoping to see the
woman's face in the window, but the window was empty.
She looked back, so as not to draw his attention. "I just
wanted to ask you a question. I don't want to bother your
wife."

As she was talking, the man had moved to block the
path she'd taken through the trees. He continued to pat
his palm on the bat.

"Go on. . . ."

In the back of the cabin, Lee pushed on as quietly
through the brush as he could. He worked his way closer,
then peeked around the side. Jenny's voice coming from
the front of the house was normal, but muffled.

Along the side of the house, ten feet from the rear, was
a door. A rusted washer and a dryer sat on the ground
under a window, and a profusion of electric wires went in
under a partially opened sash. *UL-approved,* he thought.
Stupid shit-kickers!

Lee stepped around the appliances and reached the
door in three long strides. The side screen door stood
ajar. He opened it carefully, then squeezed into the dark
interior.

After the brilliant sun, his eyes took seconds to adjust.
The smell of rotting food came from the sink about four

feet away, so he breathed through his mouth to minimize the effect of the odor.

"Meow!" A large gray cat touched his leg and rubbed it. He jumped, then glanced around to look for movement. Nothing.

All this bullshit and the lady will be off to the market or something, he thought.

He stepped into the small front room and looked out the left front window, where he could see the figures of Jenny and the bare-shouldered man. Inside the house, their voices were unclear, but he could see Jenny gesturing to make a point.

Ballsy lady. Maybe she's not the whiner I thought.

He knew he had just a couple of minutes at the most. If the good chief caught him at this, he'd be spending his first full day in this armpit of a town in the slammer.

God, I can hear my captain.

Through the great room and into the bedroom. Nothing there, then onto a small, screened-in porch. He shook his head. One last peek into the bedroom as he was leaving and—

The closet.

It had a hasp on the outside of the door with a screwdriver securing the latch to keep it locked.

Locked? From whom or what?

Anybody on the outside could pull out the screwdriver and open it. He took two quick steps to the door and removed the screwdriver in one smooth motion.

The door swung wide—

Two swollen eyes blinked back at the bright light.

"Lady, that's the biggest crock of bullshit I ever heard," the man said, still tapping the bat. "Ain't seen nothin' like that round heres. I think you're funnin' me."

"Well, it's true. If you haven't seen him, I'll leave now. Sorry I bothered you." This time, searching for something to say, she'd blurted out a story about losing her dog when she had been here the prior day. A black-and-white terrier. After she'd said it, she felt stupid, but had

had to continue describing the dog in detail until the man had blown up. Hell, it had sounded lame to her as she told it, but once committed, she'd had to keep going.

She took a deep breath and edged past him, nervous to be within hitting distance of the bat. His eyes followed her, but he took one grudging step back and let her pass. She tried not to wrinkle her nose at the stench from his body.

"Don't you be comin' back, y' hear?"

"You've got it," she answered as she picked up her pace between the trees. She was frustrated that she'd failed to stall him any longer, but he was the kind of man who talked in shorthand sentences. He was a yes, no, or hitting kind of guy.

Back at the spot where she and Lee had separated, she stopped and looked around. Not wanting to draw the man away from the trees and toward her, she turned and headed back to the car. She'd wait for Lee if she got there first.

At the Mustang, she started the engine. She knew she should be ready to go, to get the hell out of here when Lee showed up. She felt a chill. If he was caught in the house, he might not show up.

Damn, it's hot!

She reached over and banged the air-conditioning button.

Wouldn't you know I'd get a car with an air conditioner that doesn't work. Really stupid, she thought, then rapped it again.

"Lee, where the hell are you?" she said, pounding the steering wheel. In the distance, by the tree, she saw movement in the deep weeds—the deep weeds that the dogs had disappeared into when they'd tried to scent Alex the other morning.

It's Lee!

With the woman—

What?

She dropped the car into drive and spun the wheels in the gravel trying to get to them quicker. Lee limped, but hurried along at a trot with one arm around the woman's wrist, steadying her.

Jenny slid to a stop in a cloud of dust. Lee opened the back door and helped the woman in. She was sobbing.

"What?" Jenny asked.

"Get moving, we can talk about it on the way!" He motioned ahead. The Mustang threw gravel as she fishtailed into the center of the road, then headed for town with the engine screaming.

"Slow down," he warned. "Bastard doesn't have a car according to her! We're safe." In the backseat, the woman wailed from what Jenny assumed was the emotional release of escaping. "She saw Alex and that other officer. Says she'll tell us as soon as we get to safety."

"Ask her now! I want to know now!" Jenny's hands shook on the wheel. "Is he alive?"

"According to her, 'yes, possibly,' whatever that means. Let's get her to your house. There'll be plenty of time to question her there."

Jenny's head popped up when she heard a siren.

In the rearview mirror.

A police car with its lights flashing.

"Damn!" she swore as she slowed.

22

Alex rested on his pallet, eating his dinner of under-cooked black-eyed peas and a small amount of rice. He noticed with some satisfaction there were no bugs in this batch and wondered how that had happened. *Certainly not concern for our welfare,* he thought.

The men ate in silence. In spite of what had happened to him, Manny had handled his injuries well, and had washed his bruised face with the water from the worm box only once. *Tough little guy.* Alex really liked him.

Ti returned his bowl to the tray within five minutes, and complained he was starving to death until the men told him to shut up. Ti was a boy in a man's body. He'd be a nonentity as long as he was there, slavishly doing what he was told by Harley or Mae—no more, no less.

They'd finished running the three batches of mash and prepared another three for fermenting in the same vats just processed. After working hard all day, the men were ahead of the cycle a few hours and had only cleanup work to do until tomorrow morning at the earliest. Being able to rest when finished had motivated them to work faster, so they'd worked the last batch efficiently.

Of the nine vats total, three were being run as the other six were fermenting. Since it took two and a half to three days for a batch to mature—if they kept them all going on a cycle—three new batches were ready to run every day. *Job security,* thought Alex as he ate. Close to the myth about the poor guy in Hell who had to roll a rock up a hill, only to have it tumble down again, over and over throughout eternity.

Earlier, Mae had come in and prodded them to work faster. She spent a lot of time counting and recounting the stacks of finished shine. Alex guessed they had six to seven hundred gallons filled, and the pile was growing hourly.

Alex wondered why she ignored the hunting knife hovering above them on the beam. Surely Harley had discussed it with her, for her own safety if nothing else. It was becoming clear that Harley was really in charge, his brute strength and vicious personality overruling any seniority Mae might have in the pecking order.

She stalked back and forth, glowering and mumbling to herself. Finally satisfied with the progress, she went into the house, and the men worked in silence for another hour or two.

Sarah came in and out of the barn frequently and when she did, she looked over her shoulder as though checking to see if Mae was watching. She wanted to talk to or get near Alex, but was reluctant to approach.

"Better not," Manny had said when she left the last time. "All kinds of bad things could happen if you start talking to that little bitch."

"But I have to try," Alex answered. "We've got nothing to lose."

Manny grunted and continued with what he was doing. "It's your ass," he mumbled as he walked away.

Finally, Sarah came in to collect their food bowls. Alex's was sitting on the floor by his pallet. Mae had told him several times to put it on his tray, but he ignored the order, wanting to see if the girl would come close enough to pick it up.

Sarah edged over to him and looked at the bowl from ten feet off, trying to decide how to handle the situation. Alex was surprised when he noticed she had changed her clothes. Her hair shone as though just washed and combed. Cleaned up, the freshness of her youth partially canceled out the small eyes and thin face.

"I needs to take that," she insisted to Alex as she pointed to the bowl and spoon.

"So take it." Alex picked it up and held it out.

"Ain't s'posed to get that close."

"You look nice today."

She put her hand to her hair and flushed. "Ain't s'posed to talk to y'uns." She moved a couple of steps closer while looking at the bowl.

"Sarah, think about it. Why would I harm you? If I hurt you in any way, your mother would punish or shoot me. You don't have to be afraid."

"She only shoots them what has the devil in 'em. An eye fer an eye 'cause o' Pa, lack the Bible says."

"If she shot me, how would that be an eye for an eye, since I didn't even know your daddy? When he died years ago, I was living in California."

Her gaze bounced up from the bowl when he said the word *California*. "That where them movie stars live?" she asked. She moved closer to hear his response. About six feet away now, she was close enough that he could jump and grab her if he wanted to.

"Yeah, that's right. That's where most of them live. In Hollywood. That's only a few miles from where I worked in L.A." He smiled. *At last, a little progress.*

She cracked a grudging smile herself, showing her bad teeth, then hesitated a couple of beats as though thinking.

"That Clark Gable. You ever seed him?"

"Sure, several times," he lied. "Used to eat lunch at the same restaurant I did. Snooty one on Hollywood Boulevard, saw him every day. He always drove up in a fancy car—shiny, long, and black—with a chauffeur and everything."

Alex figured the fact Clark Gable had died when he was a boy would escape her. She was probably illiterate, but even if she could read, where would she get anything to read here? If he could do it without embarrassing her, he would have liked to ask her a few questions, like what the year was, and the name of the current president. *No matter. She probably never even gets out of these woods,* he thought. He could see her working on what he had said. And entertainment? If she was as interested in boys as Manny said, considering what had happened with Parker, where would she find them? He flinched when he imagined the selection she'd have to choose from back in these woods. Real mouth-breathers with room-temperature IQs. Guys who were more genetically screwed up than she was.

Her eyes had brightened at his comment about Gable. Ti groaned in the background when he made that statement. Alex hoped he would be smart enough to not call him on it in front of her. Ti was a dim bulb who would only understand what Alex was doing if he sat down and carefully explained it.

She walked forward, snatched the bowl in a quick movement, then stepped away a couple of paces. He smiled and tried to look friendly. He felt crummy about lying, but under the circumstances, feeling guilty about anything they had to do to escape was stupid.

"He have perty ladies with him?" She ran her fingers through her hair, still flushed with his compliment.

"Always."

"What was they a-wearin'?" Her eyes sparkled brighter with heightened interest. Movie stars were her hot button.

He explained that the women wore the finest gowns, even at lunch, and always ate exotic foods. The menu he described was lavish, with fruits, shellfish, and French-sounding entrées—entrées he'd only heard of, never eaten, not on a student's income anyway. His stomach panged as he described each dish in detail as well as he could. His fabrications were elaborate lies designed to fire the imagination of a young girl. He was a fisherman reeling in a big one.

Ti chuckled in the background again. Alex turned and glared at him. Ti recognized the threat, quieted, then rolled his bulk over onto the pallet with his back toward them, shutting them out as usual.

"You got a girlfriend?" she asked, staring at the tray on the ground. Alex started to speak, then hesitated and choked on his answer. If he told this young girl about his wife, it would end any chance of using her to escape. He knew she was attracted to him by the way she watched his movements. He sighed and lied again. "No, I don't have a girlfriend. I never met anyone I liked, I guess." He hated this. Denying Jenny was the final degradation. *Dammit!* In spite of the urgency to escape, it still bothered him. Using this young, impressionable girl was sleazy—almost as bad as having sex with her. "Your hair looks real pretty today, you just wash it?" He wanted to keep asking questions, keep her talking.

In the background, Ti chuckled. *What a stupe!* Alex was going to have to straighten out Ti's priorities as soon as they were alone.

"Shut up, Ti!" Manny interjected.

Sarah's head popped up and she glared at Manny, then glanced over at Alex. As though awakening from a trance, she said, "Yer tryin' to sweet-talk me, I know." She bent, grabbed the tray, and studied him.

"Sorry you feel that way. I just think you're special, that's all. Gets pretty lonely out here." He turned away and rolled back on the pallet with his hands cradling his head as though offended. He sighed and closed his eyes.

Have to be patient, he thought.

Her feet padded away, then the snuffling dogs greeted her in the yard as she walked toward the house.

He tried to imagine the conflicts she was going through. Young, but exposed to a life of more violence than any child ever sees, she had to have constant battles with decisions of right and wrong, between what her mother said and what she saw with her own eyes. Then there were her emerging sexual instincts. Those had to be tearing her apart too.

Even if he could gain her confidence, her tides of emotionalism would make her undependable, much like any young girl. But with her, it could mean death to him if he guessed wrong or got caught trying to escape with her. A "pass" from Mae for another escape attempt would be unlikely.

"Good idea," Manny whispered, "but dangerous as hell."

"I know." Alex stared at the ceiling, his brow wrinkled. "But doing nothing is a hell of a lot more dangerous."

"Don't forget what happened with the last guy who toyed with her. He was gonna play hide the weenie with that little bitch, and instead, he's hidin' his whole fucking body along with his weenie under that dirt over there."

Alex sat up and hugged his knees and stared into the shadows at the graves. Landry lay unmoving like a discarded pile of clothing.

"We ought to bury Landry," Alex said. In the oppressive heat the body would start to stink soon, and the thought of having to deal with that odor again was unthinkable.

"Sooner or later, she's going to want to cozy up, play kissy-face or more. What are you going to do then?"

"I don't know." And that was the truth. "Guess I'll do whatever it takes to get out of here."

"You'd better work it out here, my friend." Manny tapped his forehead. "Your life and ours could depend on what you decide."

The blue, red, and white lights atop the patrol car blinked as the chief climbed out and walked toward the Mustang.

"Damn," Jenny mumbled as she peered into the rearview mirror. "It's that chief of police. How did he get here so quickly?"

"Couldn't have responded to a call from that Neanderthal husband of hers. He didn't have time, even if they had a phone, which I doubt," Lee said as he climbed out to meet him.

"Who you got in there?" the chief asked. He stood in a challenging stance at the rear bumper, one thumb over his leather belt. Lee bristled and beat back the instinct to tell him to mind his own business. The chief had been spying from the distance—that was why he had stopped them. Lee had been a cop too long to believe in coincidences.

"Woman from a house back there. Says she has some information about Alex and the other patrolman."

"And you was headed for the station, right?" The chief's voice was tinged with acid. "Goin' to do yer civic duty." He walked over to the side window. "She say anything yet?"

"No. The beating she took from that bastard of a husband traumatized her too much."

"Name's Cleary," the chief said, catching a quick glimpse of the woman through the side window. "Rod and Ida's their names. Been out there a couple times to keep 'em apart when he gets a might feisty from dippin' into his squeezin's."

"From the look of her, I'd say feisty is a mild word. He beat the shit out of her, then locked her in a closet like an animal. That guy's one mean son of a bitch."

Jenny left the car and stood next to Lee, listening. The sobbing continued unabated from the Mustang.

The chief scratched his chin and asked, "Now how would you be knowin' he locked her up anywhere if she ain't talked to you yet?"

Lee mentally cringed. Anything he said from this point could only dig him in deeper. Breaking and entering popped into his mind, and with a bit of imagination and a twist to the telling, this country bumpkin could make a far-fetched case for kidnapping too.

"Call it creative intuition."

"Look, what does it matter?" Jenny piped in. "She has important information. She saw something. Maybe the people who picked up Alex and the other officer—that's what matters!"

"I'll be deciding what really matters here." The chief walked over, opened the door, and leaned in. "Ida, climb on out, you're coming with me." His uncompromising voice boomed in the interior.

Ida looked up from the Kleenex tissue she'd been cradling and nodded, but continued to whimper as she slid across the seat toward him.

"Ask her now," Jenny insisted. "We want to know now what happened to them. We have a right."

"An' I got a right to conduct this investigation without a bunch o' Californians stickin' their highbrow noses up my ass all the time!"

Lee fumed. "Shit! What kind of a lawman are you? This woman's husband is missing, for Christ's sake!"

"I'm the kind of lawman who'll have yer candy ass in my jail if you don't get in that car right now and shut up!" While the chief talked, he led Ida to his car. He opened the rear door, helped her in, and slammed it behind her.

"We're going to follow you," Lee said. "When you finish questioning her we want to know what she said."

"It's a free country. You can do as you like. After I finish with her, you'll be told what I decide to tell you, but not till I'm done. And it could be quite a while. Be just as easy for me call to you at home." He tossed the last comment over his shoulder as he opened the front door of his cruiser.

"We'll follow," Lee persisted. He walked to the driver's side and motioned for Jenny to go to the other door. "'What I decide to tell you,'" he muttered under his breath as he cranked the engine with almost enough anger to snap off the key.

They rode in silence most of the way back to the police station. Ahead of them the chief only slowed a bit for the few stop signs in Picksburg instead of stopping. *Divine right of kings. Prick!* Lee thought.

"So, what do you think of the chief now?" Jenny asked.

"I'm going to find out what that woman knows if I have to kidnap her from his goddamned jail."

"Great. Then you'll be locked up and I'll be on my own again."

He reached over, patted her hand, and smiled. "As far as the chief's concerned, that redneck must have actually followed us, can you believe that?"

"Did you see him behind us?"

"No. Wasn't looking, wouldn't have occurred to me that he would. But how else could he have known to stop us? Probable cause doesn't mean crap around here." They were quiet as they pulled into a parking lot in front of the police station.

"What do you think she saw?" Jenny asked.

He looked over at Jenny, and his face showed more worry than he wanted it to. "I want to know, and I don't want to know, babe. I'm working on that one word, *probably*. When she said that, it really screwed up my brain, no point in pretending. I can't imagine what she could have meant."

They got out and banged through the door into the station.

To wait.

To just sit and wait.

23

The light streamed through the entrance window of the police station. It had turned golden again as the rays lengthened and shone on the far wall, highlighting the mess of the coffee machine and unwashed cups. Lee and Jenny sat in silence, having exhausted small talk long ago.

Earlier, they'd gone out for a late lunch at the dinette next to Hercholt's Barber Shop. The Dixie Belle served hamburgers and fries, heavy on the grease, with all the gravy they could handle for the fries. These people would put gravy on pie, Lee had said. Conversation had been subdued. Asking questions before they had the answers was a waste of time.

"What could they be talking about this long?" she'd asked while stirring her coffee. He shrugged his shoulders. Ten minutes later they repeated the same question and response.

As they waited on the bench, Lee folded his arms in growing indignation, and she balanced her chin on the palms of her hands with her elbows resting on her knees. They both glared at the closed door to the chief's inner office—willing it to open.

Instead, the front door flew wide and Patrolman Mason walked in. Behind him, moving sullenly, was the woman's husband, now wearing a wrinkled, unbuttoned shirt and heavy untied boots, his hair askew. His body stench followed him as though trying to catch up.

The man hesitated when he saw Jenny, then followed Mason into the interior office. He glanced over his shoulder and glared at Jenny and Lee with hate before he went through the door. It banged shut with finality.

"What's he doing here?" Jenny whispered.

"He's her husband, it's that simple. This is where the shit hits the fan for us."

"But shouldn't he be in jail—arrested?"

Lee shook his head and bit his lip. "I imagine around here women are treated differently than they are in California." In Los Angeles, there were organizations that dealt with the economic and emotional problems of battered women. It was imperfect, but it was getting better.

"Certainly he can't beat her and keep her locked in a closet like a dog and get away with it?" Even as Jenny asked the question, she knew the answer.

"Want to bet? In this backwater, my guess would be the law is pretty much what the chief says it is, and in that shit-kicker's house, he makes the rules."

Jenny frowned and glanced at the door again.

"The question probably being decided in there right now . . ."

He hesitated for effect.

"Is he going to throw me in jail for rescuing her?"

Waiting was getting to be a major part of Alex's life. Waiting for meals, to start work, for work to be done, for the birds to leave or to come back. His life had developed into a rhythm of small events punctuated by major ones. Unfortunately, the major ones now included the death of someone, and he could see the possibility of that occurring over and over unless he did something to get away. And the sooner the better. This kind of existence could sap him of his will to resist and his desire to try to escape. The only thing left would be a pathetic attempt to subsist a day at a time.

He tried to imagine what he would do if faced with the same dilemma as Ti. Would Harley give *him* the part of predator next time? Given enough time, Harley would create the problem again. He had to—he'd enjoyed the dilemma too much not to repeat it. Alex shivered. Killing someone to save his own life was out of the question. No way. He'd have to opt to try to escape or get Harley.

Earlier, Mae had had the girl bring in the shovels, and Ti had dug a hole adjacent to the last one and buried Landry. After he'd finished and they'd left, Ti came over, lay down, and cried for a long time. It was a sound Alex was getting used to.

What a night, thought Alex. He reflected on the death of Landry and the perverted sexual tableau. It was amazing to him that there were actually people who got pleasure from something like that. Even Ellie. In a twisted way, she appeared to love the pain. Actually seemed to enjoy the whole thing as much as Harley.

"Waiting," he muttered under his breath. He was never very good at it. He chuckled without mirth. Right now, even as the light leached from the sky, the person he waited for was Sarah, the young girl who might hold the keys to this prison.

What he was going to do about her had been decided in a raging internal battle hours ago. And that was: whatever was necessary to save his and these men's lives. His conscience would be ignored until they were free.

And they had to do something soon. Waiting was like a ticking time bomb for all of them. Not only would they become demoralized and weaker, but there was always the possibility of injury or illness.

Even a minor injury or illness—something that they'd recover from given enough time on the outside—could end up being fatal. Even a goddamned toothache could end their life. A toothache! The odds were that anything that interfered with your ability to work would be a death sentence. No way they'd spend the time and energy to nurse one of the men back to health, or take him to a doctor or dentist. Forget it. Not a chance. Too easy to just stuff him in a hole and get a replacement. A new bug to play with.

Outside, above the insistent humming of the cicadas, the Packard's engine grumbled to life. Alex rolled over and pulled himself up on one elbow to listen. Then came a metallic complaint as the gate squeaked open. Voices exchanged a few mumbled words over the rumbling exhaust, and the ancient car creaked and bounced down the dirt path, the sound of its going absorbed by the thick woods. Alex sat up and concentrated on the diminishing thumping and clunking.

Must be Mae. But where could she be going this time of evening? And did she take Sarah with her? If she did, that ends any attempt at escape this evening.

"You think they left?" Manny whispered from his pallet.

"I'm not sure, but my guess would be it was Mae who left."

"You got a minute?" Manny asked.

Alex had to chuckle. "No, I'm really busy right now." He smiled at Manny so he'd understand he was kidding. "Have to get dressed in black tie, get ready for dinner out, then it's on to the theatah."

Manny's swollen mouth cracked into a thin grin showing his broken teeth. Alex glanced over at Ti, who had his back to them as usual, his chest rising and falling in deep sleep.

"We ought to think about doin' it," Manny said.

"Doing what?"

"The wolf thing." Manny's gaze flicked up to the knife.

"Hell, no! Are you crazy? That has to be a last resort." Alex grimaced at the image of cutting off his hand.

"Seems we're close. You got any better ideas?"

"I thought you were the one who said there was no use in trying to escape and had given up."

"Changed my mind."

"How come?" Alex asked.

"Screwin' that broad made me realize what I been

missing on the outside. Jesus, that was great, even with the penalty!" He blinked his discolored eyelids, then sat up and hugged his knees to his thin chest. "Ain't only that. I wanta smell some free air again before I die. Take a walk in the woods, go fishing or something. You know. All by myself, out on the water, just drifting, drinking a brew, farting and scratching, not caring if I caught anything or not. You know what I mean?"

"Yeah, I know."

"Ideas?" Manny repeated.

"Yeah. The girl."

Manny shook his head. "How you gonna do it?"

"She likes me, I can tell. Besides that, I sense she wants to get the hell out of here herself."

"Yeah, but balancin' that, she doesn't let on, but she's scared shitless of the old lady and that crazy man."

"I know. She simply has to be convinced she'll be safe if she leaves with me. I think I can talk her into unlocking this"—Alex held up the manacle—"then helping me by the dogs and through the woods."

Manny rocked and looked at the ceiling where the birds were rustling around, settling in. "I don't care if I never see another fuckin' bird in my whole life. This gives a whole new meaning to the term 'gettin' shit on.'"

They both laughed. The light was disappearing, and the stills were difficult to see in the shadows.

Manny asked, "You think the princess is gonna come out here tonight?"

"Wish I knew. She seems itchy to do something, but I'm not sure. The thing that bothers me about this plan is, I have no idea how long it'll take to get her to help. Could be tonight, or it could take days or weeks."

"If that doesn't work soon, with her, how about the knife? You think one of us should go for it?"

"I have to be honest with you, Manny. I like to think I'm pretty brave, but I don't know whether I could do it or not." They sat in silence for a moment.

"Yeah, I thought about that too. I tried to imagine

doing it, but down deep, I know I couldn't cut my own wrist in two, either."

"Guess that kind of settles it. It's a given that Ti there won't."

Manny's eyes sparkled. "Hey, one guy could do the other one. How's that sound? Maybe that would be easier? Sharp as that pig sticker looks, shouldn't take more than a minute of sawing."

"Jesus." Alex thumbed his wrist again. "How would a man stand the pain?" *I can't believe we're talking about this.*

"We got an anesthetic," Manny said, and motioned to the mountain of jars of water-clear moonshine. Alex rubbed his chin. His whiskers had grown about a quarter of an inch.

"Even if we do it—and I'm not convinced we should—and the man drinks enough crap to knock the edge off the pain, how the hell is he going to negotiate that twelve-foot fence and get away in his condition? One hand gone."

"Damn good question. I hadn't considered that. Shit!" Manny sat for a long moment, then added with assurance, "He could drink just enough to zap the pain, no more."

"How about the blood?" Alex asked. "Wouldn't do any good to make it over the fence, then fall over from loss of blood a mile or so away."

"Cauterize the stump," Manny said, then pointed to the red-hot coals that peeked through the pile of burned wood at the bottom of the stills. "Already thought about that. Afterwards, we could wrap it real tight. The same way they did in the old cowboy movies."

"My God. Burning the stump could be more painful than the amputation." Alex shivered at the image and felt his stomach get weak and flip over. "Only for conversation, assuming we decided to do this thing as a last resort—"

"Who?" Manny filled in.

"Yeah. Who?" Their smiles were gone, and they stared at the floor, not wanting to look at each other.

"I was thinkin' maybe you'd want to volunteer," Manny said.

"Funny, I was thinking the same thing."

"You would?" Manny asked, surprised.

"No. What I thought was the same thing you were thinking—that maybe *you'd* want to offer to do it." They both chuckled and stopped short. Then they turned to the sleeping form of Ti.

"Forget it. He couldn't make the fence with two hands, remember?" Alex said.

"Don't seem fair."

"Life usually isn't."

"Has to be me or you, then."

"If we do it."

"How we gonna decide?" Manny persisted.

"How about . . . the guy with the longest beard?"

"Not funny. Seriously now."

"The oldest, or the worst-looking teeth?"

"This situation ain't amusing."

"I know . . . that's why I'm joking."

"I don't believe this!" Lee said as he glared around the office of the station. He stood. The clock on the wall showed fifteen minutes after seven.

Jenny had trouble just sitting. She had risen several times in the last couple of hours, then taken short walks up and down the sidewalk in front of the office. The tension of waiting in the oppressive heat was getting to her. She came in the door from her current walk as Lee approached the counter.

"That's it. I want to see the chief *now*," Lee announced to Becky, who was getting her things ready to leave for the evening. Becky nodded and went in the interior door for the fourth time. The other three times she'd come out and said the chief was still talking.

Becky stuck her head out and crooked her finger from the doorway. Lee took Jenny by the arm and guided her into the inner office. Inside, they were shocked to find the chief sitting behind his desk alone. The man, woman, and the officer were gone.

"Sit and listen," the chief said quietly, and pointed to two wooden chairs in front of his desk.

"Where are the man and woman?" Lee asked.

"Sent 'em home."

Jenny wore a confused expression as she lowered herself into one of the seats. Lee remained standing. He glanced toward the back hall and noticed a side door, and realized that was the way they'd left.

"Why?" was all Lee could choke out. He was furious that the chief had let them sit for hours, especially when he knew how concerned they were about Alex.

"Sit and listen," the chief persisted.

"How long they been gone?" Jenny asked.

"About an hour. *Sit!*" he demanded.

Lee was on the verge of attacking this man for the way he was treating them, but realized he'd better back off. Locked in one of these cells, he'd be no help to anyone. Lee worked his fists to dissipate his anger.

"That's a mite better." The chief lit a cigarette from the one he was smoking, then continued. "Had Mason take them folks on home for now. Knowed you was upset, and didn't want you badgering them, considering what a pissy mood her husband Rod was in. Didn't want no fights in here an' have to lock y'all up. Give 'em time to get home and settle down, you know."

No, I don't know, you bastard! Lee thought.

They waited as the chief took another casual drag. "Ida, that's her name, you know. She was in the lower field by the road picking blackberries the night them boys disappeared." He coughed, then sucked on his cigarette again. Lee worked his fingers faster. "A truck was parked there by that tree. 'Peered there wasn't nobody in it."

"What kind of truck?" Lee asked.

"Go a lot faster if you'd just let me tell it."

Yeah, and I'll be a hell of lot older, you jerk, Lee thought.

Jenny reached out, laid her hand on Lee's arm, and he realized he was rigid with tension. He leaned against the chair, tried to relax, then nodded for the chief to continue.

"Was a white truck, enclosed van of some kind. Twenty-five or thirty feet long was her guess. The two men pulled in behind and went out and inspected the empty truck. Wasn't that interesting to her, so she went back to pickin'."

"That's it?" Jenny said in a frustrated tone.

"'Cording to her, they's two men come up out of the field on the other side of the road 'bout that time. When she heard voices, she looked over. When they got to the two officers, they whipped out these guns. Voices gets louder, then one of the men takes the cops' guns from 'em and opens the rear door and points. They climb in since it didn't seem they had any choice."

"Can she I.D. them?" Lee asked.

"One's tall and heavyset, the other's short with a beard. Too far away to recognize them or see their faces clear-like."

Jenny slumped back and looked at the floor.

"What kind of guns?" Lee asked.

"Handguns of some kind. Didn't know whether they was automatics or revolvers. Guess she doesn't know handguns very well."

"What happened then?"

"They put Josh and Alex in the truck and locked the door. Pulled out and drove away. Left the cruiser where we found it."

"She get a license plate?"

"White with red letters and some kind of figure on it looked like a horse and cowboy according to her. I make it to be a Wyoming plate. Only one it could be. Didn't get no numbers."

"That's it? That's all she knows. Why didn't she go find a telephone and call your office?"

"You don't know much about people round here, do you?"

"No, guess I don't." *Not sure I want to if they're that stupid and indifferent,* Lee thought.

"Your boy know anybody from Wyoming?"

"Christ, we've never even been in the state, and I haven't even met anyone from there in my life, it's just a wide spot on the map. And I doubt if Alex ever has, either." He stood and paced in a tight pattern. "What else did she say?"

"That's pretty much it."

"That's it? We waited over five hours. She *had* to say something else."

"Sure. We talked a lot. Just not something to do with this case, or that would be of interest to you."

"Why couldn't I have sat in on this?"

The chief groaned and leaned forward on his elbows. "Let me give you some advice. First, we're workin' on this as fast as we can. We got an A.P.B. out on the truck for starters." Lee wondered when *that* had happened. "If you'd go home and check in occasionally, we'd be able to work a damned sight quicker and easier. You're wastin' my time right now when I could be workin'."

"That's all you're going to tell us? That man imprisoned the woman in a closet like a goddamned animal. What are you going to do about *that*?"

"If I locked up every man around here who had a set-to with his wife about something, I'd have to build an addition back there." He motioned toward the cells. "'Sides, had to talk some to keep him from pressin' charges against you and the little lady here. Breakin' into houses is a jailing offense in these parts, same as California, I reckon." He ground out his cigarette. "I'm sure we're a mite primitive by your standards, but we respect folks' rights too." There it was again, the old "*them* and *us*" attitude, the same as Lee'd seen in small towns all over California.

"Let's go," Lee said to Jenny. He had to get out into the fresh air to clear his head and decide what he was going to do. She stood, followed him to the door, then stopped and looked back.

"Why should they want Alex?" she asked, voice quivering. "He never did anything to anyone."

The chief stood and straightened his belt, self-conscious under her gaze. "Don't know, but we'll find out soon. And another thing—" He directed this to Lee. "You won't be gettin' off free next time you break in somewheres. We got everything we're gonna get from those people, so I want you to stay away from them now. Call it more than advice. Folks around here all have guns, and it don't take a lot to rile them."

"I'll remember that." Lee stomped through the outer office and out the front door. Jenny followed. They stood for a long time in front of her car before getting in. Lee scanned the streets in both directions. The heat shimmered up from the narrow pavement in the distance, then the road disappeared into the trees. It was like someone drew a line—*this is country, this is town.* He shook his head and wiped his brow again. He had forgotten how hot it was.

"You really like this place?" he asked.

"I do—or did."

He shook his head. "If you like this place, I think I need a puff on whatever it is you're smoking." He and Jenny climbed into the Mustang and pulled out onto the street. As they cruised along, Lee was trying to decide what to do before continuing. The urge to go to the house and try to question the woman was strong, but he guessed the officer would be out there somewhere, watching to check if he did. *If only they put that much effort into trying to find their two men.*

"What do you think happened?" Jenny asked as her eyes teared up again.

He glanced at her, then reached over and patted her folded hands. "I don't have a clue. But one thing I do know, there's something going on here that doesn't ring true." He picked up the speed a bit and headed for her house. "Doesn't make any sense. What would those men have been doing in the field? And if they did force them into the truck, what was the reason? Christ! We haven't heard a word about any demands or anything. This whole thing is too far off center."

He had expected the lady to say something that would have resolved where Alex was. Now everything was blurred and muddied even more.

Accepting the story was difficult, but whatever the truth—

Alex was in deep trouble.

24

"Where's that fool girl Sarah?" Harley asked Ellie. It was dark and they'd made a quick search of the house. The only one there was the boy, Lester, sitting on the porch playing with a toy on the floor.

"She's 'round here somewheres, but I ain't seen her for half hour or so." Ellie wore a halter top and shorts that had the effect of dividing her in two. She'd had to lay on the bed that morning to pull them on.

"Damnedest thing. Ain't never seen Mae take off when I was here before. And 'specially to be gone overnight. Just left and said when she'd be back. Wouldn't tell me nothin'."

He went out to his truck, then carried a small tool case into the house and laid it on the hall floor. "Couldn't be better for me, though. Give me a chance to find out what Mae's got hid in this room. Always gave me a nevermind when I asked." He withdrew a long, rubber-handled screwdriver, then went to work on the latches in earnest. "Woman's got the brain of a blowfly. Puts these heavy-duty hinges on here with them Fort Knox locks on 'em, an' has the screws on the outside so's you can just turn 'em out."

Ellie giggled. "You're so clever, Harley, honey."

He looked up from the screws he was turning. "Ain't hard to be clever when the people what's around you is so fuckin' stupid." She giggled again, as though afraid not to. "'Stead of standin' there with your finger in your pretty little ass, go to the front door and make sure and keep that girl out till I'm done."

"What'll I tell her if'n she comes?"

"Don't give a shit! Don't waste no energy on workin' up a story. Tell her to stay the hell out for a while, that's all. She gives you any crap, take her across the mouth. That's the way you learn people to listen." He glanced down the hall to check the darkening yard. Even from where he stood, he could hear the constant pacing of the dogs along the perimeter of the fence. From beyond that came the night sounds from the woods.

Within five minutes the latches were off and lay on the floor with their locks still in place. Harley chuckled to himself thinking about the amount of thought and effort Mae had put into securing the door. *Stupid bitch!* He opened it and walked in.

The room was black inside, but he could make out the outline of boxes and a desk. He glanced to his left and noticed the lantern. Picking it up, he ran his hand along the shelving and found the matches. He lit the lantern and blinked his eyes as spots danced on the walls for a moment.

"Hold shit! What we got here?" He walked around the room and touched each box as he passed. At a couple of them, he bent and held the light next to the lettering so he could read it. He made several whistling sounds under his breath as he inspected each one. These were useless in his life, but he knew they cost a lot of money. He'd always wondered what she was doing with the thousands of dollars he'd been bringing to her like a trained puppy at the end of each trip.

He'd made a lot of money himself, but he always spent it faster than he earned it. Now Mae there, she never gave any indication she ever spent a dime on anything. It had always been a source of wonderment. It was like blowing air into a balloon, and the damned thing never getting any bigger.

He reached the desk, opened the middle drawer, found

the ledger, and opened it. *$235,425.00* jumped off the page.

Gasping, he held the lantern closer. "Mae, you wrinkled-up old piece of dog shit, you!" He slapped it closed and rifled the drawers of the desk. The only thing he found in the ones on the right were spiders and two keys ringed together.

He jerked open the letter drawer and froze. It was filled with stacks, deep stacks of one-hundred-dollar bills. All rubber-banded in what looked like five-thousand-dollar bundles. The drawer was close to three-fourths full. He leaned back and smiled from ear to ear. *Shee-it! Don't that jerk you off,* he thought.

He heard steps and Ellie said from the doorway, "Better hurry. She's gotta come in soon."

"Ellie, get your ass over here right now." His voice was excited, but low. She minced across the room, arms up. "Now you look in that drawer an' tell me what you see." He smiled, stepped back, and held the lantern over it.

Her eyes grew wide. "Oh! Oh! Oh! I ain't never seen . . . Oh, oh, my God!"

He slapped her hard on her skintight shorts. "Whatcha think, baby?"

She leaped and squealed, then covered her mouth while smiling and pumping her legs up and down in barely contained joy.

"Git on back to that door and keep watch," he said, still grinning.

"We gonna take it?" Her eyes wide and dancing with excitement in the lantern light.

"Does a bear shit in the woods?" He chuckled and pointed to the door. "Go on!" She unfroze, ran into the hall, and padded to the living room on bare feet.

"Are we gonna take it?" he muttered to himself as he chuckled. "Sheeit!" He rubbed his chin in thought. "No hurry. Gotta figure on this first." He left the money in the drawer and closed the desk, then put everything back the way it was. He sauntered around the room, taking one last look while shaking his head. He passed the calendar, then stopped, and went back.

"Looky here. . . ." Where the corner of the current month was peeled away caught his eye, so he held the lantern closer to look. He lifted the sheet. The word *Leeve* circled the fifteenth of the next month.

"I'll be gone to hell. She's leavin'." Frowning, he flipped the two pages back and forth. "But leavin' for where?" he whispered. "I'll be damned. She din't tell me nothin'." He straightened and took one last look around the room. "An' who's gonna run the business?"

It was clear in a flash of insight. *Nobody* was going to run the business. It was gonna be closed down. And when she did, she'd try to punch his clock sure as he was standing here. Hell, he was the only one who could tie her into everything. Murders. Fourteen, by his count.

"Son of a bitch, can't trust nobody these days." He smirked and blew out the lantern, then replaced the latches on the door. After inspecting them with a flashlight, he nodded. It was perfect. She'd never know.

All these years of working together, first with Woody, then with her, and now he was gonna have to get rid of her before he left. The girl and the idiot too. No loss. Neat and clean. He grinned. This was gonna be fun.

Burn the place down and take the money. *Jesus, the money. I can go anywhere in the country I want. Party every night. Dump Ellie and get a real woman.* The excitement of that image made him start to get hard. He threw the tool case on the floor of his room.

Standing in the bedroom door, he yelled, "Ellie, I'm done. Get your ass in here an' outta them shorts right now!"

"Mama, help me, Mama," Ti whimpered from his pallet. Light lingered in the sky, but the inside of the barn was dark. The men lay on their pallets. Manny and Alex stared at the black ceiling and listened to Ti.

"For the tenth time, shut up!" Manny said.

"Let him be," Alex said. "Couple of times, in the

middle of the night, I've felt pretty damned scared myself." He turned to Ti. "Don't let it get to you, Ti. We'll get out of here yet."

"You gonna turn into a bird and fly out in the morning?" Ti choked through his hiccups. He snuffled his nose.

"Don't tell him nothin'," Manny warned Alex. "We're all scared, but you don't see us blubbering about it."

Alex turned back to Manny. "If we have to do the wolf thing, how do you propose to keep it from him? There's going to be too much blood and pain to ignore. Besides, he has to know what's going on or he might accidentally let on."

"Wolf thing? Blood? What are you guys talking about?" Ti's voice changed from self-pity to fear. He raised to a sitting position, and his pallet creaked in the darkness.

"Relax, Ti," Alex answered. "Whatever we do, it isn't going to involve you. We have a couple of plans. If the first one doesn't work, we're going to consider cutting one of us loose to try to escape."

"You're crazy! Cut yourself loose. How? How you gonna cut these chains?" He rattled them in the darkness for emphasis.

"We'll tell you, when and if the time comes. Right now, it's important you understand you have to be quiet about *anything* we're doing. Especially when I'm talking to Sarah."

"It's not right to lie to that girl," Ti said.

Manny shook his head in exasperation. "Boy, you got shit for brains?" Manny yelled through clenched teeth. "We're all gonna die in here if we don't do something fast. Ain't you figured that out yet? You could be the next one gets hit over the head with a board!" He jumped up and walked a couple of steps trying to put distance between himself and Ti. He snapped over his shoulder, "Nobody could be that stupid!"

"You call me stupid again, I'm gonna have to hurt you!" Ti threatened.

"Shut up, both of you," Alex said. "Nobody's going to hurt anybody. Give it a rest. We've got enough trouble without arguing among ourselves. Ti, you have to know everything that's going on, so you can help us when the time comes." Manny stood off in the darkness, unmollified. Alex explained his plan to get the girl to help him escape. When he was finished, he told him what he and Manny had discussed, about what they called "the wolf thing." Alex could hear Ti's breath accelerate in the dark. Ti tried to interrupt a couple of times, but Alex shushed him, then continued. His resistance disappeared when Alex made it plain he was too heavy to be considered as a candidate for the escape attempt.

Manny came over and lay back on his pallet. They were tired, and it was quiet for a couple of minutes before Ti spoke. "How you gonna decide who tries to escape?"

Neither of them had made reference to how it was going to be accomplished since the original discussion. It was one of those things too horrible to dwell on or to repeat. Henceforth, Alex guessed, it would be called just "the escape" or "the wolf thing."

They were quiet for long minutes thinking about it. It was almost dark in the barn now and the birds were asleep. The banked fire under the stills popped, and outside, the crickets and frogs once again drowned out the humming of the cicadas.

"Straws, I guess," Alex added while yawning. "That's the way it's done, isn't it?"

"We ain't got no straw," Ti complained.

"Who cares," Manny said, his voice becoming thick with approaching sleep.

"Who the hell cares. . . ."

Jenny and Lee sat at the dinette set in the kitchen, reflecting on what had happened during the day. It was past eleven and they were exhausted.

"What are we going to do now?" she asked. "It doesn't

seem productive to just sit around and wait for something to happen. What do you think?"

He took a sip of his tea, then stood and paced. "I want you to take me over and I'll rent a car in the morning. Then I'm going to that Cleary woman's house. Try to talk to her myself. To hell with this hick cop."

"Great, I'll go with you."

"No. It's a one-person job. Besides, we can't afford to have both of us locked up right now. He catches me, there's a strong chance that's what'll happen."

"You think you should, considering that?"

"I don't intend to sit around like a jerk and wait for him to call me. After that, I'm going to find out where this Josh lives and check into his background. Odds are high this might have something to do with him, and Alex might have simply been in the wrong place."

"You don't believe the story about the truck, then?"

"Fifty-fifty at best. The way the chief handled the woman and man, it was as though he was *afraid* we'd talk to them. I know it's not my imagination. Somebody's pulling my chain, and I'm going to find out who."

"I've been thinking, about what to do myself . . . and I've decided," Jenny answered.

"What's that?"

"Alex is always talking about how powerful the pen is, compared to the sword."

"So?"

"I'm going into Charleston in the morning. I'm going to get the papers and the television stations involved in this. That chief won't be able to play games with those people on his back."

"You don't have any papers here?"

"Be serious."

"Stupid question. Well, it sounds like a place to start. Me, I'm going to the Clearys'."

"Let's get to bed, then. Tomorrow's going to be a busy day."

Alex awakened knowing something was wrong, a feeling like the one he'd had when he was six or seven years old

and he'd gotten up many times in the middle of the night.
Frightened, he had turned on his light, positive there was
something with hungry jaws staring at him from his
closet. This was similar, yet not so ominous—a presence
near him—

Movement in the blackness. Then a scraping—

*Not mice and rats, but something else, something
bigger.*

He raised his head and listened. The other men snored
in unison.

"Shhhh, don't jump now." Sarah's voice.

As his eyes adjusted to the dim light coming from the
coals of the fires, he could make out her figure above his
had. "Foller me." She disappeared into the darkness in
the direction of the storage room. He stood and tiptoed
out without answering, trying to keep the chain from
making too much noise. The men continued their cadence of snoring.

Inside the supply room, it was even darker. A light
flicked on in the corner. A flashlight held to the floor to
minimize the illumination.

"Sit down." She motioned with the light to a pile of
cornmeal bags. He sat about three feet away. "You stay
there, you hear?" Satisfied, she sat and flicked off the
flashlight.

"Talk quiet-like so's they cain't hear."

He nodded, then realized how fruitless nodding was in
the blackness.

"Ma's gone."

"Where?"

"Other side o' Martinton. Buyin' a house an' barn an'
horses, I 'spect. Said somethin' about dickerin' an' papers
and such. Back tomorry night."

"That's nice. What's she going to do with it?"

"Live in it, what else?"

Alex waited, hoping she'd add more, but she was
silent. He imagined what was going to happen to the barn
and to them, chilled at what it probably meant. "When?"

"Less'n a month." She hesitated for a long moment,

then said, "I ain't goin'. Been planning on leavin' fer months now."

"What are you going to do?" *Keep it casual, don't spook her this time.*

"Gotta git. Tired o' gettin' whupped and takin' care of Lester. He ain't never gonna get no better. 'Sides, Harley's on me alla time, 'cept'n now this woman's hyere. She goes, it'll be the same again."

"He hits you too?"

She shuffled her feet. "That too, but he's allus on me—you know—doin' *it* to me."

Alex grunted "Oh," then felt stupid because he'd missed the meaning. "Your mama doesn't stop him?"

"Don' care none. Says 'ats the way they is—men. Cain't stop him anyways, even if she wanted. He hurts me somethin' fierce an' he's so rough with me while he's a doin' it, then afterwards he slaps me around lack he's mad. Lotsa times, everythin' gets black."

My God. What a terrible life for a kid. It had to be a never-ending nightmare, he thought.

They both sat in the dark, thinking and listening to the snoring from the barn.

"You wanna do it to me?" Her voice was tentative. "It's okay, jus' so's you don' hurt me like Harley."

"No."

She absorbed his unexpected response for another few seconds. His eyes had adjusted well enough to tell she was staring at the floor. Alex wanted to ask more about this impending move of Mae's that could have ominous overtones for them, but knew it would change the subject. Sarah'd come out here for a reason, and he wanted to hear her out without sidetracking the conversation.

"How come?" Still looking at the ground.

"Sarah, grown men don't do things like that with young girls where I come from."

"Even if'n the girl says it's okay?"

"Even then."

"Oh." With sex out of the way, she looked up at him

now. "I ain't had no schoolin', but I can work real hard."

"When are you going to leave, Sarah?"

"Tonight."

Alex's heart skipped. "Where you going?"

"California. Hollywood. Made up my mind. Been thinkin' on it some, even 'fore you told me 'bout Clark Gable and all. Reckon they got palm trees, big houses, an' sunshine alla time . . . so I hear."

"That's true. That plus Disneyland and a lot more."

"Have to go while Ma's gone. 'S'my only chance, likely. Got me some money."

"I could find you a place and show you around, get you settled, if I were free to go with you." *Settled in a foster home of some kind after I clean up this mess here,* he thought. Wherever her new home would be, it would have to be better.

"But you work right in Picksburg, don't you?"

"I've been thinking about going back to California anyway. Not sure I like West Virginia at all." And *that* was the truth. "Why don't we go to California together?"

"I been thinkin' on that too. Maybe we could get a house together or somethin'."

"Why not, we could have a lot of fun. I'll take you to Knotts Berry Farm, Magic Mountain—all the fun spots." He could make out her smile in the dark.

"Even though I gotta leave, I don't want no harm to come to my kin." Her smile disappeared.

"Once I'm out of here, I intend to forget this place. No hard feelings as far as I'm concerned."

"And you won't tell no one about this place? Promise?"

"I promise." He thought about the other men, then realized releasing them when he left was impossible. Not now. She might believe he'd keep quiet because she wanted to, but accepting that *they* would, would be too much for her to swallow.

"Swear to God? You ain't just a-sayin' that?"

He crossed his fingers. *I'll work this out later.* "I swear to God." He could take the keys once he was loose, and let the other men go, but if he did that, she'd revolt, and he needed her help to get away.

"You know, you cain't git past them dogs and outen them woods without me. It's a far piece—fifteen, twenty miles maybe."

"Can you get the key to the truck?" He'd have to bring someone back to rescue Manny and Ti.

"Harley keeps it on a chain 'round 'is neck."

"The guns. Can you get a gun?"

"Keeps 'em in his room. Door's allus locked. 'Sides, if'n you ain't gonna harm no one lack you said, ain't no need of guns."

"Well, we'll have to do without. You going to get your stuff?"

"Ain't takin' nothin' but money." She patted her pocket in the darkness.

"You have the key?" He held up his manacle in the dark, and the chain clinked.

She inched closer and reached down—

He could hear the tink of metal as she shuffled through the side pocket of her dress—

Jingling.

At last.

The keys—

The wonderful keys!

25

It was dark and quiet in the house except for the deep snoring sounds coming from the hall. Lester stirred, then got up and went out to the outhouse. After he finished, he stumbled back to bed, making low grunting noises. When he passed the cot where Sarah always slept, he stopped.

She was gone.

He pulled the covers down and rummaged through them as though expecting to find her tangled in the bottom of the bedding. Nothing.

He made a whimpering sound, then ran down the hall and into the living room. His low, questioning moans got louder when he discovered Mae was missing from her chair too. He hobbled to the storage room and jiggled the locks. They were secure.

Ma and Sarah were gone—abandoned him—in the middle of the night. He panicked, ran, and burst out into yard. The night air was still warm. The dogs along the fence barked deep in their chests. They rushed to greet him, then trotted along as he ran to the barn as fast as he could. At the door, he stopped and looked in. It was dark inside, and he could hear the snoring of the men.

Grunting louder, almost squealing, he was losing control. Sensing his panic, the dogs whined and loped along behind as he raced back to the house. Breathing hard, he banged open the front door and scuttled to the bedroom where Harley and Ellie slept. Inside, snoring sounds.

He turned and listened for his mother and sister, but could only hear Ellie and Harley inside the room. This had never happened before. *Scared.* He glanced around, trying to think of where else to search. *Panic.* He shook his head, grunted, and tapped on the locked door with his frail fist. The snoring continued, so he rapped harder.

Man—woman—they must know!

He leaned back, then smashed his thin body into the door as hard as he could. He held his ear against it and smiled when the snoring stopped and—he grinned.

Someone coming to answer.

"Damn it!" Alex said as he stumbled over an exposed root of a tree. He fell to a knee, then pulled himself up and kept moving, trailing behind Sarah as best he could in the darkness. Most of the time, he had followed her sound instead of her actual movement. Low branches had whipped his face as he scrambled between the trees, forcing him to protect his eyes with his hands. It was inky black in the forest, with a half-moon peeking through the drifting clouds giving Alex and her just enough light to make out large objects. They passed two cabins.

Three rail-thin coon dogs barked and came into the woods to investigate. Sarah called the dogs by name, and they followed along, tails wagging, for about a quarter of a mile. Then losing interest, they drifted off back to their cabin.

So far, this was a whole lot easier than Alex had anticipated. Getting the manacle unlocked had been difficult, but once it was undone, they'd hurried out the door of the barn to the gate without a problem.

Before he left the storage room, he slipped the three keys on a ring between two of the bags of cornmeal near the floor. She was walking away from him as he hid them. *Couldn't hurt—just in case,* he thought. They'd be there for the other men to find, or God forbid, if he got caught, he could use them himself at a later date. Not likely to happen. He had to make it, because if Harley caught him this time, the odds were he'd kill him.

The barking dogs, with Hitler leading the way, came up to them in the yard. When they recognized Sarah, they wagged their tails. Two of the dogs pressed against Alex as he walked to the gate, smelling him as though wondering how he would taste. Sarah being with Alex was obviously a disappointment to them. His skin crawled and it was hard to relax, even after the gate was closed and locked behind them.

The dogs on the other side chuffed and paced back and forth as he and Sarah disappeared into the woods. Sarah leading, they loped along the narrow road the truck had taken for about twenty minutes, then veered off to the left into the deep woods.

Sarah said the road was too risky because it went right along next to many cabins, then through a populated hollow. Down there the dogs would attack them because she had never played there as a child and was a stranger to the dogs. The ruckus raised by the other dogs would bring someone to investigate. Mountain people would shoot into the night if they thought someone was prowling around their homes.

Moving away from the road made Alex nervous because walking in the forest would take much longer to get to the main road or town. The weaving switchbacks made for slow progress. Back in the woods, working their way over rocks and up and down steep banks, it was not only much slower, it could be very painful. Like when he'd just stumbled over that root.

"How long you think it will take to get to a road to town?" Alex asked, his toe still aching from when he'd tripped. They stopped and leaned against a couple of trees to rest for a moment. The woods were alive with the sound of the incessant cicadas, crickets, frogs, the distant bark of a dog, and what he guessed were coyotes.

Bears, he thought. *There are black bears in these woods somewhere.*

"Reckon it'll be some time. Never walked it all the way before. If'n we could stay on the path, it'd take the better part of 'bout seven hours. Where we is, maybe two, three hours mor'n that."

Ten hours? Alex shook his head. That would take them to daylight. Harley'd be up and realize they were gone long before they reached the road. With his truck, it could be pretty close whether they'd beat Harley to the road or town.

Son of a bitch! Should have disabled that damned truck! Really not thinking. Just letting the air out of a couple of tires would have done it. Damn!

The few times he'd gotten a glance between the trees at the moonlit hills in the distance, it overwhelmed him. They rolled on forever with no sign of where the town was. No idea. He was helpless, at the mercy of the instincts and knowledge of this young girl.

If he had to strike out on his own, it would be tough to find his way in the dark. Going downhill seemed to be a simple solution at first, but in the time they'd been traveling, they'd been up so many hills and down into so many valleys he'd lost all sense of where he was in relation to the town. It made him realize even more why no one had ever escaped from the barn. These hills made the barn as inaccessible as Alcatraz is from the mainland of San Francisco.

"We'd better be moving," Alex said. He rubbed his itching arm where the manacle had been.

"Shoulda brought somethin' to eat, I'm gettin' hungry already," she said as she turned and began pushing through the woods again.

"I'll eat when I get home." He'd eat some of the homemade bread Jenny had baked—heated and covered with mounds of butter. *Have to remember not to mention Jenny—at least until I get out of here.* It was going to be tough, especially when he found his thoughts shifting to Jenny the closer he got.

After what he guessed was another hour, they stopped and sat under the overhang of a cliff. They were panting and sweating from the effort. Not a hint of breeze stirred the night air. They had just finished an arduous climb to another small ridge before they'd plunged several hundred feet down into this narrow valley. They'd waded across an ice-cold creek, stopping long enough to wet their clothes with the refreshing water that Alex assumed was spring water. Ahead lay another ridge to climb.

"You ever kill anybody?" Sarah asked.

"No. Never had to." He could almost hear her thinking in the dark.

She sighed. "Gets down to it, Harley'll take some doin' ta kill."

"We make the town, I'm hoping I'll never see his ugly face again," he said. Behind them, the creek gurgled over the stones. It was tempting for Alex to sit and relax. Away from the barn he felt free, but he knew their time was ticking away. If Harley turned Hitler and those other killers loose in the woods, they'd find them in no time unless they could put some serious distance between them and the dogs. He was more afraid of the animals than he was of Harley. Even with Sarah with him, he had a feeling they'd attack once they were hunting.

"Harley'll kill both us if'n he catches up."

"I don't plan on that happening." He shook his head and blinked his eyelids, heavy from lack of sleep. Sleeping on that uncomfortable wooden pallet, he'd gotten only about four hours of rest each night.

"Tell me some more 'bout the movie stars."

"When we get out of here, I'll tell you everything I know. I won't leave anything out." In the moonlight, he could see her smile widen.

"Can't wait. Soon's I get me to Hollywood, I'm gon' buy me some new clothes, then I'll get me a job, then I'll . . ." Her voice drifted away from Alex as he leaned back and watched the clouds moving across the moon. . . .

He thought of Jenny again. Beautiful Jenny.

After they'd napped on the bed at the hotel during their honeymoon night, Alex and Jenny showered separately, then dressed. They avoided showering together because they'd be late for their dinner reservation at the hotel if they did.

The dining room was crowded. When they finished, they had left early and went back to their room because the couple sitting next to them had gotten into a loud ongoing argument. The attractive blond woman was with a Mediterranean-looking man with a beard. The man was embarrassed and tried everything to keep her quiet. She was drunk and kept repeating over and over, "But you said I was your baby." The man leaned over and kept whispering to her, but nothing worked. She finally became so loud the maître d' asked them to quiet down, but the peace lasted only a couple of minutes before she started badgering him again.

Back in the room, Alex and Jenny both showered for the second time because of the heat, and climbed into the luxurious king-sized bed and lay for a while before touching. Alex sighed at the feel of the crisp, cool percale sheets. It was a special moment on a special night, and they wanted to make it last as long as possible.

The chattering of the crowd outside on the boardwalk had diminished, and the screeching gulls had gone inland for the night. The only other sound was the rhythmic rolling of the surf in and out, in and out. A cool evening breeze washed into the room from the open windows and teased the draperies on either side of the bed.

"Tell me we won't ever argue like that," Jenny whispered with a choke in her voice. Alex could tell she was crying. He felt love and compassion rise in his chest.

"It's not possible," he promised as he moved to her. Her warm body shocked him as she blended against him. Her arms wrapped around his chest and pulled against his back. She clasped his right thigh between her firm upper legs, and his skin burned where it pressed against her pubic bone. Her breasts were firm against his chest as her urgent lips sought his ear. He shivered as she explored his lobe.

"I love you," she whispered. Her voice broke with the deeply felt emotion.

"As long as we live," he answered. He rolled over and entered her in a smooth, choreographed movement. He pressed deep into her, and they lay rigid, feeling their throbbing desire climb. She moaned with restrained pleasure before they began—

"Hey, you listenin'?"

Alex shook his head and looked around.

"You sick or somethin', mister?" Sarah asked as Alex jerked his head up, his attention back in the forest.

"Sorry. I was dreaming."

"I hear somethin'." He came alert at the urgency in her voice, then stood and cocked his head to listen in the direction they had come from—back across the stream.

"Baying. Dogs!" He turned to her and asked, "Someone out hunting?"

"They's huntin', that's a fact."

"Us?"

She nodded.

"Let's get moving, then." He grabbed her by the arm, but she resisted. He stopped and asked, "What's wrong? Come on!"

"Ain't no point."

"What do you mean? We have to try!" His heart raced at the primal sound of the dogs howling and echoing in the hills.

"Cain't outrun them dogs nohow," she said. "Harley'll find us in an hour or less."

"Well, I'm leaving. You can stay here if you want to."

"Only one way to git away," she said. "One chance."

"What? Quick, what is it?" He quivered from the need to get moving.

"Them dogs is farther away than they sounds 'cause of them hills. We need to go this way. Foller me an' I'll show you how we can get away." She took off through the woods at a right angle to the direction they had been going, seeming not to care whether he followed or not.

He stood for seconds in the darkness, fighting indecision, then crashed between the branches after her. The die was cast, he had to trust her. He had no choice at all.

They came upon and followed a long narrow trail leading between an outcropping of rocks and a steep cliff on the other side, then wound down to a small valley. In the dark distance, Alex could make out the outline of a cabin, outbuildings, and cleared fields. Beyond that, the forests took over again, and the land rose to another shallow ridge.

It took them about twenty minutes to make it down to the edge of the clearing. They kneeled on the edge of the field and looked across at the first of the outbuildings. Fences lined the area between the structures, cutting the clearing into many little squares.

"Granny Emmy lives here," Sarah choked out between explosions of breath.

"Have dogs?"

"Dogs is gone since her husband took sick and died couple years ago." In back of them, wailing down from the hills, lashing their nerves, came the penetrating baying. It chilled Alex's spine. In his mind, he could see Hitler salivating with the anticipation of tearing into his flesh.

"They's closer now," she whispered.

No shit! "What're we doing here?" he asked, and looked down at her, trying to hurry her along. Seconds could make a difference now.

"Follow me." She took off running toward the buildings across the clearing. The clouds were gone, and ahead, her dress flapped in the moonlit field. He sighed and followed with no idea of what she had in mind, his life hanging on what she had decided.

She came to the fencing, stopped, and looked around. Inside the fenced-in areas, Alex heard grunting and the sound of restless movement.

"Pigs?" he asked.

Instead of answering, she continued along the railing until she came to a building. She opened the door and went in. The pigs charged from the fenced-in area into the building, then across to the door where she stood. She leaped back and slammed the door. He looked into the dark trees, expecting to see the dogs in the clearing, but they were still in the woods.

"We cain't go in there, they's too dangerous," she said. "Wait here." She ran to the other side of the fencing and ran back carrying a large bucket.

"Gonna go out inna open pen, feed 'em this. The last o' the feed. When I yell *now*, you run into the buildin' and close and latch that inside door leadin' to the pen."

Alex nodded.

She ran to the open pen, then yelled *now* as she dumped the feed into the trough. The pigs crowded and fought for the feed. Alex ran into the building and closed and latched the inside door. The building floor was wet, soft and spungy, and the stink from their droppings was rank. His feet sunk in where he stepped, and he cringed when he realized what he was walking in.

Sarah ran back to the door and into the building.

"God, it stinks in here," he complained.

"That's the idea," she said.

"What? What are we doing here?"

She answered by flopping down on her back and rolling around in the soggy filth. She stopped long enough to say, "Spread it all over lack I'm doin'. Do it real good and them dogs cain't smell you no more."

"Jesus!" He watched her for another split second, then spurred by the sound of the dogs in the distance, dropped to his hands and knees. The smell was gagging terrible. The floor was inches deep in droppings.

"Hurry! Ain't got much time."

He rolled on his back and began spreading the wet, sticky goo over his clothes. "Faster," she urged. "Face, hair and everthin'." He held his breath and grabbed handfuls and spread it over his face and hair. When he had to breathe in, hot bile rose in his throat from the stench. He worked fast. If he threw up, the hell with it. Being sick beat the hell out of being dead.

Finally, both of them black with pig shit and mud, they

made their way out the door. The yelping was near the
clearing now. Harley and the dogs were just minutes
behind and closing. Alex followed Sarah along the last
fence, then past the cabin and across into the woods.
They went about thirty yards into the brush where Sarah
stopped.

"Far enough," she said.

"What are we going to do?" Alex felt really stupid,
having to ask her constantly what she was doing. He
never felt more like a city boy than right now. In the
humid, warm night, Alex had to keep breathing through
his mouth to avoid throwing up.

"Backtrack." She hurried along the trail they'd made
to the edge of the clearing. On the opposite side of the
field, the unmuffled sound of the baying dogs indicated
they had broken out of the woods. "Hurry," she whispered, then took off toward the cabin. As they trotted
across the moonlit field, Alex was relieved to see she
kept the cabin between them and the approaching dogs
on the other side of the pigpens. When they reached the
cabin, she kneeled down, breathing hard.

"What now?" Alex asked, still feeling foolish.

"Under here. Used to play here." She went around to
the side of the house and crawled under an opening in the
foundation. It was about sixteen inches high. Alex had to
get down on his stomach to follow her. As soon as he
crawled under, it was so black he had to inch along by
feel.

Spiderwebs clung to his hair and face as he pulled
himself through the dirt until he got to where she lay,
breathing hard.

"Can't your grandmother hear us?" he asked in a
whisper.

"Deaf—almost," she answered.

"What do we do now?"

"Wait."

"For what?"

"For them ta get tired o' lookin' 'round here and ta go
into the woods. They's pig scent all round and them

dogs'll go crazy lookin' for us, but we should be safe fer a few hours or more. When they's gone for sure, we'll git into the woods in a different direction."

"Your granny got a gun?"

"Reckon."

"Think you can get it?"

"Reckon."

Outside, the urgent sound of the dogs baying around the pigpen was loud and penetrating, and he could hear Harley cursing. No chance to get the gun now. He guessed with a little luck, the dogs would follow the pig scent into the trees, get confused when it disappeared, then keep on going. But *would* the dogs follow the pig scent, and why would they know to?

Now, they had to be quiet and pray the dogs would miss their smell underneath the layer of filth. Sarah slid over and curled up against Alex in the darkness. His slimy hands patted her shoulder, and he could feel her shivering with fear. Outside, the dogs no longer bayed, but barked randomly. Alex could tell by the erratic sounds, they were searching—

Searching to kill them.

26

At the barn, it was a long time after Harley and the baying dogs left the fenced-in area before Manny and Ti considered exploring the yard. They'd both awakened when Harley ran in, lit one of the lanterns, and went into the supply room to check the end of Alex's chain. He swore, the chain clinked, and then he came back to where they lay.

"How'd he get loose?" was his first question. Both men shrugged their shoulders and rubbed their eyes in confusion. "That girl in here?" He walked over to Alex's pallet and picked up his discarded shirt.

"We been sleeping. Didn't even know they were gone," Manny said.

"Don't have time now, but we'll talk more when I get back." Harley went out the door, taking Alex's shirt with him.

Come and take it out on us, more than likely, thought Manny. "Son of a bitch did it," Manny whispered in suppressed excitement to Ti. "He got the girl to release him and escaped. Son of a bitch did it," he repeated.

"Why didn't he unlock us too?"

"Probably figured he couldn't. He needs the girl's help to get down the mountain. He makes it, he'll be back with the cavalry and get us the hell out of here." In the distance, the dogs yelped and bayed in the hills. Manny crossed his fingers in the dark, not wanting Ti to see.

"You reckon he can get away?" Ti asked.

"You'd better hope—it's the only chance we got right now." They stood and walked to the door. Conditioned to not going any farther, they stopped and looked around the yard first. When they edged out into the night, they realized the dogs were gone, and found their chains reached almost to the fence.

"Bein' out here almost makes me feel free," Ti said as he looked up at the sky.

"You religious?"

"Some. When I was a boy, mostly. Baptists. You know, lots of singin', clappin', and yellin'."

"Now'd be a good time to say a few words for Alex and us if you want to."

They went back inside the barn and Ti did.

Alex was exhausted as he lay in the dark under the cabin, holding Sarah close to him, reeking of sour pig shit and listening to the sounds outside. Resting or sleep was impossible. The first half hour after they'd crawled under the cabin went slowly. Expecting to be discovered any second, adrenaline boiled through his blood.

The dogs had barked and snuffled around the cabin. When the sound got louder, then diminished to the perimeter of the clearing, he realized the dogs were confused about their trail. He smiled. Sarah's plan had worked, at least temporarily. He wondered how long the pig scent would cover their own. *Maybe until our bodies heat up in the confined space.*

With all the barking and yelling going on outside, he kept listening for the sound of the old woman in the cabin above, but heard nothing. *She has to be some kind of sleeper,* he mused.

After what Alex guessed was over a half hour, the barking disappeared into the woods in the direction Alex assumed the town lay.

"What should we do now?" Alex asked in a hushed voice. It sounded eerie in the confined space.

Sarah jerked and said, "Huh?" She'd been sleeping.

Concerned about his own exhaustion, he'd forgotten about how physically and mentally tired she must be. *Sleeping? How could she do it, with their lives on the line?*

"You think we ought to be on our way?" he asked.

"Don't know, don't think so." Her voice was heavy with sleep. She coughed. The penetrating fumes of the pig shit were getting stronger as their bodies warmed in the confined space.

"You said the woman has a gun. Have you seen it?"

"No, but most folks does."

"You think we could wake her and borrow it?"

"Likely, but her bein' deaf, wakin' her'd be a chore, less'n you could shake 'er or somethin'."

"Yeah. Sure as hell don't want to beat on the door. Sound would carry a long way." He moved to try to get comfortable. His arm was asleep where her head lay.

"I could try a window," she offered.

"Let's do it." He listened for a moment. The dogs seemed to be gone. Outside, they might still be able to hear the dogs, but they had to be quite a distance off.

He moved first, wiggling his body through the spider-webs toward the wedge of moonlight at his feet. The odor of the moist earth combined with the pit shit was overpowering. He willed himself not to think about it. If the dogs came this way, the vomit might draw them to where they had been hiding.

Out in the moonlight, he stretched his cramped legs and back, then bent and helped Sarah slide out the last couple of feet. They walked around to the rear of the small cabin and found two wooden windows. Alex tried the first one. It was stuck, painted shut he guessed. He walked over to the second window. It was wedged open about a foot, a stick propped in the narrow crack to keep it that way.

"Best I go in, so's I can say somethin loud if'n she comes awake," she suggested.

"You know where the gun is?"

She shrugged.

He said, "You stay here. If she can't hear like you say, doesn't make any difference who goes in first. Huddle down and stay still." She nodded and hunched against the house. When he lifted the window, it made a loud scraping noise. He grimaced and listened, but heard nothing from inside.

He jumped up, gripped the sides, and pulled himself to the window. His wet body lubricated the sill as he slid through and thumped onto the bare wood floor.

Damn! That had to wake her.

He lay for another long moment listening for movement. Nothing.

This lady really is deaf.

The house was quiet. The door to the room was closed. An ancient treadle sewing machine sat next to the window; several boxes were stacked on the adjacent wall. He rose as soundlessly as possible, tiptoed to the door, and nudged it open. It creaked.

The new stench stunned him backwards.

In the blackness, he was confused at first, then realized what it was. When he was going to the academy in L.A., part of the indoctrination program was to go to the morgue.

The cloying odor of death was unmistakable.

A decaying body. Recently dead. Few days maybe. *Jesus. No wonder she's been so quiet during all of this.*

He went back to the window and asked Sarah for the flashlight she'd been carrying in her deep side pocket. She handed it up without standing or speaking. Telling her about the dead woman right now would serve no purpose. After they escaped, there would be plenty of time and opportunity. She was upset the way it was.

Breathing through his mouth, he walked down the dark hall of the cabin. In the living room, he let the light roam along the walls.

No gun here. Shit!

Two overstuffed chairs with doilies covering the arms and backs filled most of the room. Three walls were lined with shelving containing hundreds of plastic and creamic figurines, the kind you'd get at the five-and-dime. No television because of the lack of electricity. This was an old woman's home. A poor woman. Now a poor, dead woman.

He walked into the kitchen. The remnants of her last meal still sat on the countertop. A mouse scurried when his light hit it. He jumped. Nothing in the kitchen—no gun.

A pattering sound. He froze and ran the light along the floor. Two eyes reflected back the weak beam as the cat meowed and cringed. He walked toward her. She ran to the front door and meowed again. Walking over, he turned the latch, and creaked it open. The cat raced into the night, its claws scraping the floor and porch in its hurry. Then he closed the door and relocked it. The cat was better able to take care of herself out there than he was.

"Good luck, kid," he said under his breath. A couple of days in that barn allowed him to know how that trapped cat felt.

He looked around. The cabin was tiny. It had only two small bedrooms in the back, and that was where the woman would be lying, in the other bedroom. Unfortunately, that was where the gun would be if she had one.

Damn! I don't want to do this.

He walked to the woman's door and pushed it. The sweet-foul stench was so oppressive it formed an almost impenetrable wall at the opening. Gagging, he forced his way in and avoided shining the light on the bed where the horror moldered. Not looking was almost as bad because he could see the vision of the bloated, rotting corpse in his mind.

His head swam as he panted, trying to limit the amount of the disgusting air he took in. The light bounced around the edge of the room, and as it did, it yellowed and dimmed even more. The batteries were going.

Quickly. Don't want to be stuck in here in total darkness.

No gun, anywhere. *The closet.* On the floor were work shoes, good shoes, an old bucket. The old woman's clothing brushed his face as he rummaged through her

few work-worn dresses and a cloth coat. Behind the
clothing—something wooden—the stock of a gun.

All right!

He bent and pulled it out. A shotgun, single-barrel,
filthy, caked with mud, unused in years. He pushed the
lever on the top and cracked open the breech. *Empty!
Dammit! Have to find some shells—they have to be here.*

Closing it and leaning it against the wall, he began a
hurried hunt of the floor. No shells anywhere, not even
loose ones.

The shelves? Shoe boxes were stacked two-high on
one side. Rummaging through them, he found sewing
needles and thread in one, old faded pictures in another.

As he worked in the hot room, sweat coursed down his
bare chest and back, making tiny rivers in the filth on his
body. No question about his body scent sneaking out
now.

Have to find shells, dammit!

Working his way through the boxes across the shelf,
he came to the last box. He took it down. A junk box. As
he dug in the balls of string, pieces of wire, buttons, and
pliers—he saw them.

Four red cylinders. Shotgun shells. He picked them up.
Twelve-gauge. They were green with age and the sheen
was gone from the copper ends. His stomach relaxed a
notch.

That's four. But will they fire?

One for Harley and one for each dog if necessary.

But with Sarah with him, he might be able to avoid
shooting the dogs. That'd leave four for Harley. Face,
chest, stomach, and leg. The thought gave him pleasure,
a lot of pleasure. He visualized the gun exploding and
Harley's huge bearded head flying out from under his
baseball cap as the round hit him in the chest. *Yeah!*

Reflecting on the lack of shells and a good gun, he
thought, *God, I thought all these hill people were
hunters.*

Four shells would have to do it. Not able to stand the
odor any longer, he grabbed the gun, hurried out the door,

and shut it. He went into the spare bedroom and closed that door too. Sticking his head and shoulders through the window, he sucked in the clean air several times, then said "Hi" to Sarah, who still huddled on the ground.

"Them dogs," she whispered. He cocked his head and listened. Barking echoed from the woods.

No mistake—

That bastard Harley was coming back—

Screw you Harley!

This time—

I'll have a surprise.

Something crashed in the house and Lee Gregory jerked out of his dream. A metallic sound. His heart pounded as he sat up and looked around.

Alex. I'm at Alex's house.

He glanced at the clock.

Two-thirty in the morning.

After he slipped on his pants and shirt, he padded down the hall toward the light coming from the kitchen.

Jenny was kneading dough on a breadboard. She looked over as he leaned against the doorjamb. She smiled. Flour dusted the side of her cheek and her hair was askew.

"Sorry. I wake you? Oven handle slipped out of my hand."

"No, I wasn't sleeping anyway," he lied. "What's happening?"

"Bread. We like to bake it fresh a couple times a week. Alex loves it. When he was here, we took turns. We can't get enough of fresh wheat bread with honey. He's pretty good at baking, too, you know." Lee could feel the heat radiating from the oven from where he stood. The smell of bread baking was comforting, reminding him of his own home and mother. He smiled back. He noticed she already had six loaves sitting on the counter. She was dealing with this the only way she knew how. Business as usual.

"Can I ask you a question?" he asked.

"Is it going to make me cry?"

"God, I hope not."

She nodded and stopped what she was doing.

"You sorry Alex became a cop?"

As she returned to pounding the dough, her eyes narrowed, working on the question. "Hard to say *no*, considering what's happened."

"If this hadn't happened? How about then?"

"Either way, I'd want him to do what he wants."

"That isn't an answer." He straightened and crossed his arms as he studied her.

"You won't say anything to him when we find him?"

"Of course not."

"I hate it—everything about it—always have." She stared at the dough as she talked. "But I'd never say anything to him. I knew what the rules were when I signed on. If he ever decides to quit and go to writing full-time, I want him to feel he made the decision without any pressure from me."

"You're kind of special, you know that?" Lee said. The memory of the many arguments he'd had with Alex's mother over his job came flashing back. Late nights punctuated with a few drinks to relieve the tension when he was finished.

"Thanks, but it's not so complicated. I just love him." She choked on the last word, bit her lip, and kneaded faster.

"Sorry. Didn't mean to upset you."

"That's okay," she said, then grinned as a tear fell into the batter she was working.

"You going to have enough energy to go to Charleston without sleep?"

"Sleep's not important right now."

He nodded. They were both talked out. Tomorrow would be devoted to action.

"'Night," he said, and turned toward the bedroom. Behind him, he could hear the rhythmic slapping as she worked the dough with excessive energy.

He wondered how long it would be—

Before sleep was important to her again.

27

"What the hell is he doing out there?" Alex whispered to Sarah as they squatted in the dark. He had pulled her into the room and closed the window except for a thin crack. It had been quiet for a long time as they listened to the dogs. The ominous sound of their barking ebbed and flowed in the distance. The dogs were obviously still searching for their scent. Each time the noise receded, Alex hoped Harley'd keep going and disappear—maybe give up and return to the barn.

Too much to hope for, he realized.

Through the window the white beam of Harley's flashlight flickered in the brush when he passed in back of the cabin. Alex knew without seeing him that he'd be carrying that deadly shotgun of his.

"What's that awful smell?" Sarah asked. For the first time, Alex realized the odor had penetrated the closed room—not as strong as the death room, but potent nonetheless. She had to have smelled it when she first came in, but had just listened to the dogs, like him, not wanting to talk.

"Your granny is dead. I'm sorry. She's in the other bedroom."

She huddled closer and shuddered. "Ain't my blood granny. Just what ever'body called her is all," she mumbled in a frail voice. "Liked her a lot—used to give me stuff."

Outside, the barking of the dogs came nearer the front of the house. Alex tensed. He'd been wondering when Harley would decide to investigate the cabin, and why he'd passed it up the first time. When he did, what would they do then? From the way they'd sweated and scraped along under the house, he felt sure the dogs would be able to follow their scent now. If he jumped out the back window and made for the woods, the dogs would be on their trail, if not right away, certainly in plenty of time to catch them before they could reach the road or town.

Bang! Bang!

They jumped as Harley's pounding on the front door thundered through the frame of the structure. In the living room, something fell. *Probably those damned figurines,* Alex realized.

"Granny! Inside the house. I wanna talk to you!" Harley bellowed.

"What we gonna do?" Sarah's soft voice had an edge of panic. He could feel her eyes on him in the dark, questioning.

The thought of going in and ripping open the door and blazing away with his shotgun was tempting, but considering the age and condition of the weapon, the odds were too high it would misfire. In the daylight, he could have inspected it, but in this dark he'd just picked it up. *Only God knows the age of these shells. As green as they are, they could be older than me. No. Our best chance is to avoid a confrontation.*

"What'll we do, mister?" she asked again. She'd never used his name, not once.

Ambush Harley from the kitchen or living room, or try to hide, hoping he'll go away? he wondered.

His mind worked fast, trying to decide.

Go for the woods?

He liked that one least of all with the dogs out there. At best, he could get one of the dogs with his shotgun before they downed him. Took too damned long to load this single-barrel. With the pig smell covering them, the dogs would have trouble recognizing Sarah. Yes, relying on the animals knowing her was risky.

"We're going to hide," he whispered.

"Granny! Open this door or I'll break it down, damn it!" Harley shouted. His voice boomed through the porous old cabin. *Damn him!*

"Where we gonna hide he won't find us?" Her voice shook.

From outside: "You got one minute an' I'm comin' in!"

"Quick, follow me," Alex whispered. He straightened and went to the door. She followed so close she bumped his back when he stopped. He creaked the door open just wide enough to get in, then tiptoed across the hall to the woman's door.

He breathed through his mouth, then opened the door and walked in with Sarah still tailgating. She choked as she took in the room's foul air. He stopped and comforted her for a moment with one arm, cradling the shotgun in the other.

"Oh . . . dear God." She gagged.

"Try to breathe through your mouth," he whispered in her ear.

Crash!

Harley smashed into the front door hard. Alex could hear boards splinter, but it held.

"Son of a bitch!" Harley yelled in frustration.

Alex pulled out the small flashlight he'd slid into his rear pocket. It was slick with pig droppings, and he almost dropped it. He flicked it on and held the beam to the floor around the bottom of the bed.

Thank God!

The big quilt met the floor all around the edge. He laid the gun on the boards. Out of his peripheral vision he could see the body on the bed, but he concentrated on not looking at it.

Crash!

This time the door gave way with a rending and cracking of boards—

The floor of the cabin vibrated as the door slammed to the floor—

A smashing sound racketed from the living room as the shelves gave way, dumping the hundreds of figurines.

In the front yard, the dogs were in a frenzy, snarling and snapping in anticipation of a kill. Alex flicked off the weak light and slid it back into his pocket.

"Under here," he directed Sarah as he bent and held up the edge of the quilt.

As she pulled herself under the bed, she said, "I'm gonna be sick."

"Shhh," he warned as he got down on his hands and knees to follow. Heavy thumping and crunching glass vibrated the living room floor, and the clear, deep-throated barking penetrated the now-open front door. As he crawled under the cover, his head bumped something. *The dead woman's foot. It's hanging over the edge!*

Alex shivered and slid all the way to the middle of the bed, then reached out and drew the shotgun next to him as quietly as he could. He aimed it at the door side of the bed. He'd have one chance if Harley looked under the quilt.

After Alex made sure the blanket covered to the floor, he took his free hand and cradled Sarah's head to his bare chest to comfort and quiet her. It was inky black, and the stomach-wrenching stench from the corpse and the pig shit was thick enough to cut. His hands were slick with the slime where he touched her.

He felt Sarah's chest contract, and before he could react, the warm contents of her stomach exploded onto his chest and dribbled the floor. She tried to pull away but he held her firm.

Perfect, goddamn it!

As Harley's heavy footsteps approached in the hall, Alex reflected:

A decaying, maggot-ridden corpse pressing down on the springs above my face—

Slimy pig droppings covering my body and hair.

Warm, sour vomit dripping off my chest onto the floor.

Dogs threatening to rip my body to shreds.

And a crazed mountain man who loves to inflict pain, seconds away from finding us.

He flashed on the commercial where two men were sitting on the edge of a riverbank drinking beer.

One turned to the other and said:

"It doesn't get any better than this."

"What're we doing?" Manny asked in a disgusted voice. The two men were still standing in the yard, looking around at the sky.

"What?" Ti was confused.

"Everybody's gone, including the fucking dogs, and we're standing out here with our mouths open, hay sticking from our ears like a couple of ignorant dirt farmers visiting the big city. Jesus! This is a one-in-a-thousand chance!" Manny walked to the door, turned, and motioned for him to follow.

Ti stood for a moment, then trailed him inside. "Why is it I never understand what's going on around here?" Ti asked as he moved along behind.

Manny bit his tongue to avoid saying what he was thinking as he detached one of the burning lanterns from its line. He held the light away from his body and said in a low, serious voice: "Alex is gone—unlocked his chain?" He waited for Ti to understand. No response. "With a key?" Manny prompted.

"So?" Ti said with a note of irritation. "Just tell me, I don't know what you mean."

"If he opened it with a key, then the key must be . . ." Manny paused, waiting for him to fill it in.

Ti looked flummoxed. "What? I don't know what the key might be—copper—long—what? Tell me!" He was angry now.

"It's not a what! It's a where! I don't believe you!"

Ti face clouded. His fists clenched and unclenched.

No way he's going to get it, thought Manny. "Listen. If he unlocked his chains with a key, it's possible he might have left the damned thing around here somewhere, got it? So let's look, okay?" Manny turned and followed Alex's chain lying on the floor, into the supply room. When he entered the room, his light flickered on the mounds of supplies and made eerie shadows.

"Why didn't you just say that?" Ti muttered as he stormed in after him.

Manny made his way along the stacks of sugar, bags of malt and cornmeal, and a small stack of yeast. He checked the surface of any protruding bag, half expecting to find it lying there, ready to pick up. After he made one complete circuit around the edge of the room with Ti standing in the middle watching his progress, he returned to the cornmeal sacks where Alex's open manacle lay on the ground.

"Let's rethink this," Manny said. "If he left in a hurry, maybe he put the damned key near the pallets when he went, under his or mine." Manny charged out of the room, swinging the lantern.

Ti yelled, "Hey!" from the dark after Manny had left.

At the pallets, Manny laid the lantern on the floor and made a thorough search. He turned over each one, then worked across the floor on his hands and knees, poking at loose dirt clods here and there. "Wish I had my metal detector," he mumbled.

Ti wandered up next to him as Manny finished.

"Nothing!" Still on his hands and knees, Manny rocked back on his heels and glanced around the barn in frustration. He wiped his forehead. "Hate this fucking heat!"

"Why would he come in here?" Ti asked. "They musta been sittin' on them cornmeal bags, 'cause that's where the end of the chain was. If it's here, why wouldn't he simply have stuck it down between one of them?"

Manny looked at him, then grabbed the lantern and ran into the storage room. It took them one minute of fumbling between the cracks of the bags to find the three keys on the ring. Ti screamed in jubilation.

"Me first!" shouted Ti. He juggled the keys and dropped them.

"Here, let me do it." They both sat on the ground facing each other. Manny picked up the keys and tried each one in the lock on Ti's manacle with tongue-out concentration. The lock popped open.

Ti removed his manacle, then took the keys from Manny. His face was shiny with sweat in the light of the lantern as he worked on the rusty lock on Manny's manacle.

Click—

And he was free too!

The sound of Manny's lock snapping open hypnotized them. It fell to the ground along with the manacle, and Manny rubbed his raw wrist where the steel had scraped off the skin. They both stared at each other, not saying a word. Giggling, they gave each other a high five, two times, then collapsed on the ground and laughed with relief.

"Let's get the fuck out of here," Manny said as he stood and grabbed up the lantern.

"What's the hell's goin' on?"

The two men turned.

It was Mae.

Standing in the doorway with a handgun.

"Look's like I got back just in time. Where the hell *is* ever'body?"

"Fuck!" the men exclaimed in unison.

Alex listened to Harley working his way through the cabin, room by room, searching for them. Harley had to be able to smell the dead woman from the front of the house and must know by now she was in this room. Like Alex, he'd search there last.

Haley was checking behind every door and piece of furniture. Outside, the dogs continued to bark and snap. Trained not to enter buildings, they waited impatiently at the opening.

After what seemed like a half hour—but was probably a couple of minutes—Harley thumped down the hall and passed their partially opened door. The quilt glowed at

Alex's feet as the moving light wavered by the doorway, then it grew dark again. Harley thumped to the other bedroom with heavy steps. The second door creaked.

Alex had loaded the gun and the hammer was cocked, ready to fire. If Harley peeked under the bed, Alex was going to take off his head with a blast if the shotgun worked. Harley would kill them without mercy if he found them. *Have to time it perfectly.* Alex's heart hammered as Sarah quivered against his side.

Three steps in the hall, then the door to their bedroom groaned full open. The floor lit up again as Harley edged into the room and stopped.

"Holy Jesus!" Harley swore as he choked on the concentrated stench. Harley took three quick steps to the closet. Alex shifted his shotgun in that direction, being careful not to hit the floor with the barrel, the long gun awkward under the bed.

Alex could hear a rustling and the jingling of hangers as Harley jerked the clothes to the side.

The light turned toward the bed. Harley had to be shining it on the corpse.

"Mother of God!" Harley spat in revulsion, then thumped out of the room and slammed the door.

Alex and Sarah jumped.

Alex was silent, his body tense, as he strained to listen for Harley's retreating steps. Sarah took in a huge lungful of air, then gasped and choked. She had been holding her breath while Harley was in the room.

"Relax," he whispered into her hair. "He's going to leave. He couldn't handle the stink."

She nodded and continued to breathe with her mouth wide, trying to make as little noise as possible.

From the front room came the sound of Harley kicking the broken door, then the dogs greeting him in the front yard. The timbre of the barking changed as they moved off toward the trees again.

"He's leaving," Sarah whispered with a tremulous chuckle. "Sorry." She pulled away from where she'd thrown up.

"Let's get out from under here," Alex said.

Sarah needed no coaxing, and scurried out from under the other side of the bed and was through the door before he struggled to his feet. He shut the door tightly. Barely breathing, they both tiptoed down the hallway and into the kitchen.

Through the window above the sink, Harley's light flickered in the distance as he entered the trees with the barking dogs.

They both smiled with satisfaction.

"Let's wait a few minutes, then we'll take off at an angle over that way," Alex whispered, and motioned to the left. Right now, how long it took them to get to town was of no importance. *The hell with it!* He just wanted to be sure they were far from Harley and those damned dogs.

"I have to clean myself." Alex grabbed the pump handle and pushed it up and down. A thin ribbon of water dribbled, then gushed faster with each thrust. He took the stopper and put it in the drain with his free hand. The well water was ice-cold and smelled of dark caverns.

When the sink was full, Alex began the impossible task of cleaning his face, hair, and body. Unmindful of the mess, he allowed the water to splash onto the kitchen floor as he scrubbed with a clean dish towel he found on the countertop.

"God, that feels good!" He had to get rid of the stink, at least most of it. If his scent was exposed, he'd have to live with the consequences. Besides, now they had a weapon if the dogs came for them. He rinsed his shirt and put it back on wet. His pants were hopeless, so he just rubbed the worst of it off.

After he finished, he walked into the living room, sat on the floor, and leaned back against the wall. He hugged the gun against his side as he waited for Sarah to wash. She hummed a disconnected song as he felt his muscles relax. The baying had faded into the blackness, and the night sounds returned.

His body was cool for the first time in days as the

water evaporated from his arms and chest in the fetid, foul air. He allowed his eyelids to close, thinking: *As long as I listen for the dogs, I don't have to worry about him sneaking up on us. I'll leave as soon as she's through, but right now, I have to rest.*

He smiled at the image of Jenny walking toward him with her arms outstretched—

As he fell asleep.

28

A noise jarred Alex awake and he jumped to his feet. His heart jerked, then hammered as he gripped the shotgun and looked around the cabin, trying to get oriented. Sarah glanced up from the floor, frightened. She had been lying next to him, asleep too. Another tinkling sound came from his left.

"Those damned figurines," he mumbled, then chuckled with relief. He sighed as another one slid and smashed to the floor.

It was still dark in the room as he ambled to the kitchen window and peered out into the night in the direction Harley had disappeared. The sky was lighter and the black outline of the hills was visible on the horizon.

"Must be around five o'clock," he whispered. Sarah came to the window. She pushed the handle of the pump, then bent and drank the cold well water.

"Have to use the outhouse," Sarah said.

"Wait, let me check first." He walked to the open front door and peeked out into the morning. From across the open space, the pigs grunted at the movement and sound. He knew they'd been starving since the old woman died, then dismissed it. *Enough to worry about right now. I'll tell somebody in town,* he thought.

Seeing no threat outside, he stepped into the yard. The morning air was warm and calm. Glad to be out of the cabin, he took in huge breaths to clear the odor from his lungs. More crowding and snuffling came from the pens as the pigs responded to his footsteps.

He motioned to her at the door. "Come·on, make it quick. I'll stay here. I want to get moving before it gets any lighter."

She disappeared around the side of the house, and he could hear the door to the outhouse creak open and slam.

Alex fingered the shotgun and patted his pockets to check for the other three shells. *All there.* As soon as it was light enough, he intended to break the gun down and give it a thorough going-over, mostly to make sure the firing pin worked. If it was defective, all he was carrying was a heavy walking stick.

He squinted at the skyline and tried to guess the distance to the road or town. "Six or seven miles at most. Maybe as little as two or three miles, depending." As they'd moved among the trees, it had been impossible to assess their progress.

Sarah screamed!

Alex hunched, ran to the edge of the cabin, and glanced back at the outhouse silhouetted in shadows of the rear yard.

Two figures struggling—

"Bitch!"

Harley's voice!

A loud smacking sound and the smaller figure slammed to the ground. Harley's arms flashed above his head and smashed the butt of his gun into Sarah. A hollow impact echoed, then she groaned and lay still.

Alex aimed the shotgun at Harley's massive outline—

Click—

The shotgun misfired.

"Damn!" Alex whispered. No way to tell whether the gun had not worked or the shell was defective—

Harley was thirty yards away. He jerked up from the still figure and strode in Alex's direction—

Shit! Alex turned and bolted for the pigpen.

The house was between the two men as Alex sprinted across the open yard—

As Alex ducked behind the whelping building, Harley's gun exploded and a shot tore into the boards by his head—

The pigs squealed from the noise, and crashed into the fences of the pen. Alex leaped through the door into the building. In the open pen, the huge sows ran back and forth in confusion as the piglets scurried in small packs trying to keep up.

Just seconds before Harley got there, Alex moved stealthily across to the door to the open pens and made sure it was still latched. Afraid to go into the yard because of the frantic, aggressive sows, Alex knelt in blackness and fumbled in his pocket for another shell. He held his breath. If the huge sows knew he was in there, they'd charge the door and attack.

He cracked the breech, discarded the shell, and pushed in the new one just as Harley banged in the outside door into the dark interior.

Harley hesitated, then inched forward. "Where are you, cop? You can't hide." Harley was enjoying the hunt.

Alex resisted the temptation to give away his position by aiming and shooting, still not sure whether the gun would work. He stayed motionless, knowing Harley's eyes would have to adjust before he could see him in the shadows.

Harley's footsteps moved toward Alex—

If he flicks on his light, I have to fire.

Alex clicked back the hammer—

If his gun failed to fire this time, he was dead.

Behind the door, the sows screamed.

Harley's wet, sucking footsteps came closer—

Boom! An explosion of light from the barrel—

The blast blew out the wall next to Alex's shoulder.

Alex jerked open the door to the pen.

A heavy sow squealed a challenge and pounded by into the building—

"Son of a—" Harley yelled as he tried to sidestep the

thundering pig, but the four-hundred-pound animal caught his leg and pinwheeled him through the air.

The furious sow screeched and shook its head, slashing at Harley's legs as he crawled toward the door he'd come in. Alex jumped up—Harley scrambled through the door.

The sow slammed into the frame; the building shook. She was unable to follow because the space was too narrow.

Harley's lost his gun, flashed through Alex's consciousness.

Alex jogged outside to the edge of the pigpen, dodging other sows as he ran, and vaulted the low fence. Harley was at the door, hefting up a long piece of lumber ready to hit the sow's head sticking out the doorway.

Alex charged up to him. "'Morning," Alex yelled as he slid to a halt and leveled his shotgun at Harley's chest. The sow was still snapping and snorting its anger. It was lighter and Alex could see better. "Don't move, asshole."

Harley's face distorted in rage and frustration, then he screamed, "Fuck you!" He was rubbing his upper leg where the crazed animal had shredded his pants. He'd lost his baseball cap and his hair was wild.

"Don't piss me off, big man," Alex warned. "It wouldn't take much for me to kill you."

"You're bluffin'. I heard that damned thing click. It won't fire!" Harley took one halting step toward him. Alex raised the gun higher and Harley hesitated.

"That was a bad shell. I have a good one in the chamber now. I'd demonstrate, but I'd have to reload, wouldn't I? You want to chance I'm bluffing, take one more step. Killing you would give me a lot of pleasure."

Harley chuckled and stared into the barrel with uncertainty.

"Make a decision, you've got thirty seconds, then I'll make it for you."

Alex's heart raced. Would this gun fire? If Harley refused to surrender, Alex *had* to pull the trigger. He had no choice.

Harley cleared his throat. The seconds clicked away, then Harley slammed the two-by-four to the ground and grunted in contempt. "I'll kill you soon enough. I can wait a mite longer." He turned and kicked the sow in the face. Trying to get to him, the animal squealed and crashed hard against the door frame.

"Move," Alex ordered, waving the shotgun.

"Where."

"To the outhouse. I want to see how Sarah is."

"Wastin' your time. Little bitch is dead. Felt her skull mash like a melon."

Alex threatened him again and Harley grumbled, but held up his hands and trudged ahead. Alex hung back to keep out of Harley's reach because the man was a long way from helpless and probably still had a knife. The barrel of the shotgun was too long to hold on Harley while Alex searched him.

Sarah lay unmoving. Her face was peaceful in the morning light as Alex bent over her. He had Harley sit on the ground about fifteen feet away with his hands behind his head. Harley smirked as he watched Alex check her crushed skull.

Sarah was dead. Her eyes were rolled back and a pool of blood grew larger around her head. No pulse beat in her neck.

I should kill him now. Who'd know here in the woods? I could say it happened when he attacked us—here's the evidence, he thought. *But I can't risk firing and have it fail again. Hand to hand, I wouldn't have a chance.*

Alex closed Sarah's eyelids. "Sorry I lied to you, kid," he whispered, then turned to Harley. "You're lucky I'm a cop, or you'd be dead now." As he said it, he knew that killing someone in cold blood was impossible.

"Stupid is more like it," Harley spat. "You don't kill me, you're dead for sure."

Bastard! He's right. I should kill him.

Alex held up the gun and aimed at Harley's head.

Harley smiled and glared into the maw of the twelve-gauge.

He's a lot of things, but he's not a coward, Alex thought as he lowered the gun.

"Come on, let's go into the house." Shooting Harley was out of the question unless he was threatened. He thought of taking Harley with him to the road, but dismissed it. Trying to control him over miles of unpredictable terrain was risky. One misstep would be all it would take. Anything could happen. Harley chuckled when he realized Alex was struggling with what to do.

The two men walked to the front door. It was light enough now to see inside the cabin.

He had Harley lay on the kitchen floor facedown, his hands stretched straight out. Harley resisted at first and Alex poked him with the barrel of the shotgun. Alex retrieved a length of clothesline he'd seen hanging on the kitchen wall. Harley watched him from the corners of his eyes as Alex tied his ankles first. Then he had Harley hold his hands behind his back. Harley smiled while Alex worked.

"You're weak, cop. Weak people don't cut the mustard here in the woods."

"You're confusing weakness with principles."

"Principles! Sheeit!" Harley spat in disgust.

Alex tied the ropes at his ankles and wrists together and cinched the knots. Satisfied he was secure, Alex searched him and withdrew a ten-inch knife from inside his coat. As Alex slid it behind his belt, Harley glared.

"That's a man's knife, boy."

"It is now."

"These ropes is too damned tight!"

"Ask me if I care. What'd you do with the dogs?" Alex asked. "Kill them too?"

"Dogs is safe. Closed 'em in a corncrib by that ridge yonder. Figur'd you was hidin' some'eres 'round here, so I parked 'em and come back on my own. My bad luck that little bitch come out that door as I was sneakin' up on the house."

"Why'd you leave the first time, then return?"

"Reckoned you'd made it off through the woods an'

we'd pick up your scent if I worked back and forth. When didn't find nothin', I knowed you was still here some'eres."

"You didn't have to kill her, you bastard!" Alex choked.

Harley laughed. "Gonna do that anyways 'fore I left. Her an' that crazy ma o' hers."

"Why?"

"Fuck you! Figure it out yourself!"

"When I come back with the law, you're going to pay for that."

Harley chortled. "Must be somethin', not to have the stomach to do yer own killin'."

"You'll die, you animal, but I won't be the one to kill you. You'll die of old age in prison or somebody there will kill you. Too damned bad they don't have capital punishment in this state!"

Alex picked up his gun and took one last look at Harley, who smirked and nodded good-bye. He thought again about shooting Harley, then shook his head and went out the door before he changed his mind.

Outside, the sun had broken over the ridge. The position of the sunrise would give him a guidepost for his trek to the road.

He went to the pigpen. The animals had settled a bit, but the sow was still agitated and paced inside the building. She snorted and charged him when he stuck his head in the door. Alex wanted to get Harley's gun, but he'd have to coax or force the angry sow to leave somehow.

I'll scare her.

He stood in front of the snorting animal, held his shotgun into the air, and pulled the trigger.

Click—

"Shit!" He opened the breech and checked the firing pin. The end was broken off. *Damn!* He threw the useless shotgun to the ground and smiled. It was going to be a pleasure telling Harley that when he came back to get him.

*He'll have a lot of years in prison to think about it
before he dies.*

Alex trudged down the walkway to the open area. At
the fence, he called to the sow. She came flying from the
building and charged the fence.

"Good mama," he whispered, then ran to the door at
the side of the building again. When he started to step in,
the sow dashed inside and smashed against the outer
doorjamb again, trying to get at him. This pissed-off sow
had a one-track mind. If he had no feed to lure her away,
she was damned well going to eat *him*. No way he could
retrieve the gun with her in there.

"Damn! Okay, mama. It's all yours." Alex walked by
the cabin toward the woods. Getting moving was more
important than spending more time trying to get the gun.

He stopped and looked back at the quiet form lying in
the dirt by the outhouse. Shaking his head, he jogged
across the field toward the next ridge.

"Hang on, Jenny, I'm on my way. . . ."

Jenny and Lee were up early. He came out, nodded, and
sat at the dinette table. She poured him a steaming cup of
black coffee. Neither of them spoke, just smiled good
morning. It was strange to have a man in the house with
Alex gone.

"Eggs and bacon?" she asked. She snugged her robe
tighter around her body.

"Whatever you got," he said. "Don't feel hungry, but
I'd better stoke the furnace. I have a feeling this is going
to be a long day, one way or the other. I'll either find out
something or I'll end up with my butt in jail for sure."
He'd been finishing his shower when she went to the
kitchen and made coffee.

"Don't say that."

"It's a fact. Anything happens to me, you keep on
working with the newspaper and television people.
Seems that's the best approach. Less likely to get hurt
that way, too." He finished the cup, rose, and filled it

again. "From what I've seen, there are plenty of people around these hills you've got a right to be careful of."

"To hell with them," she spat out. "The hell with this town, the hell with these hills . . . the hell with the chief—the hell with them all!"

She broke four eggs into the skillet and bit back her anger.

29

Alex guessed it to be eight-thirty or nine in the morning when he heard the rumble of traffic over the next ridge. It was difficult to tell how far it was because sound echoed and reechoed in these hills. It could be one mile or ten.

He'd skirted a couple of cabins on the way, not wanting to make contact with anyone if he could avoid it. Finding the direction to town had been simple. Once he had cleared the first ridge after he left Harley, he could see the flatlands in the valley between the peaks. That removed any doubt. Besides, the rising sun was a perfect compass.

"Wonder what Harley's thinking right now. Whether he's finally getting a bit worried. Animal!" Harley'd be there when he got back, no question about it. He was tied too tight to get loose.

Alex stopped for a moment, bent, and drank from a mountain spring bubbling between black rocks on the side of a hill. Water spiders nervously flitted across the surface of the small pond below it. After wiping his hands on his bare chest, he moved down a gradual grade, through a thin stand of sycamores, then into the clear again. At his approach, a white-tailed deer hesitated, then gracefully bounded across the brush and into the shelter of the trees.

In the distance, the sun flashed off the windshield of a

moving car that was switching down a hill. He followed what he could see of the road for a long moment, but the car disappeared into the dense foliage.

A mile at the most—thank God.

As Alex studied where the car had disappeared, he heard a sound in back of him that froze his blood—

Dogs—baying!

Alex's mind raced, trying to think of how it could be possible. It was either someone else, or one of the mountain people must have found Harley and untied him.

Somebody who heard the shooting maybe—that had to be it! Should have figured some way to get his gun out of that pigpen. Gave up too easy, should have kept trying until I got the damned thing.

Alex ran down the hill toward the road—

Toward freedom.

After five minutes of thrashing through the brush, he stopped and listened. His body was cut and bleeding where the branches had lashed his body.

He ran and leaped a ravine to a shale shelf, and the splintered sheets of rock gave way under his foot. He landed hard on his back. Pain flashed across his shoulder blades. He could feel warmth on his shoulder.

Blood. Had to be. No time to check the damage.

Scrambling and sliding, he pulled himself to the top of the shallow ravine and jogged between the trees.

The dogs are near now, much nearer. Three or four hundred yards away—

What to do? His mind bounced from idea to idea, rejecting each. His one chance was to reach the road before they caught him.

Fingering the knife, he shook his head. The knife would only buy a couple of minutes when the dogs caught him.

It will be close—

Ahead lay a gradual downgrade, a stand of trees, then a drop-off into a deep hollow. He withdrew the long knife from his belt and held it in his hand, afraid if he fell he'd jam it into his leg. The road was somewhere ahead, but unless he could stop a car, the conclusion would be simple. The dogs would kill him in the road instead of in the fields.

Alex entered the stand of trees, then leaned against a trunk and looked back up the grade. His back was burning and his energy was flagging.

As he stared across the field, the dogs broke into the open followed by Harley and a second rangy man.

That figures. That would be the man who cut the bastard loose. Dammit!

The dogs were about a quarter of the way across when Alex got his wind and started running. As he moved, he held the knife in front to fend off the branches.

Alex came to another clearing, and ahead he could see a road winding down the hills and disappearing where the land dropped away. He ran to the edge and hesitated.

Two or three hundred feet below was a road, but sheets of loose shale lined the almost vertical bank leading to it. He scanned the trees on the other side of the clearing, and the barking dogs were closing now, ready to break into the last clearing.

He looked up the road where a truck approached in the distance.

The dogs scrambled into the opening behind him—

They saw Alex and lowered their heads at a full gallop—

No trees to climb.

The red four-wheeler rounded the last curve and headed toward him—

Lights on top of it!

"A police unit!" yelled Alex.

A glance at the men who stumbled behind the dogs—

One hundred yards away and closing.

One man stopped and raised his rifle.

"Yeehaw!" Alex screamed as he dropped off the side of the cliff as the rifle roared—

He skipped off the first ledge, then rolled and frantically tried to grab something—smashing from shelf to shelf—slashing pain—out of control—

Rocks and shale tumbling all around him.

He hit and bounced from a final ledge to a bank of solid rock, then scrambling and finding no purchase, fell the rest of the way—over and over—

Alex's head cracked into a rock—

He spun.

Everything went black, and his body drifted amid the shower of rocks.

A final, staggering impact—

Then he lay still in the darkness as pebbles, dirt, and shale thundered and clattered around him.

Alex whirled up and away from the silky blackness, then moved and coughed. His eyes flickered open, and above him, a steady patter of dirt and small pieces of shale still slid and thudded against his body.

At the top of the cliff, the silhouettes of the dogs and the men looked down to where he lay. Alex turned his head to a flurry of sound. The police vehicle charged toward him, lights on, siren kicking in.

Thank God!

The policeman had seen him fall—

Thank God!

He was coming—

To help—

The image faded.

His head fell back.

And it was black and quiet again.

Lee was the first one to leave the house. He kissed Jenny tentatively on the forehead. She smiled, knowing how uncomfortable he felt expressing affection. Just the opposite of Alex.

She watched until he was out of sight, then went in and began searching the littered rooms for the Charleston telephone book. She'd left everything scattered around the way it had been left after the robbery. This house was no longer her home, and she felt no attachment to it. It was a big hollow shell, echoing to her steps. A strange place, somebody else's house now. Until she found Alex, anyway. And then?

Jenny finally gave up looking. The creeps had even taken the damned phone book. She shook her head as tears re-formed.

"What's the difference? I'll stop somewhere when I get to Charleston. No big deal." She walked out the door and consciously left it unlocked.

"The hell with it. Let them come and take what's left, I hope they do.

"Who cares . . . now.

"They can have it all!"

Alex had the sensation of flying down a hill, skiing without skis, then whisking into an angry bank of clouds boiling and churning in space. The moisture in the thunderheads touched his face, felt cold, and electrical energy sizzled through the air all around him, leaping and crackling back and forth as a rumbling assaulted his ears. Suddenly, a strobe flashed and his body was absorbed into a lightning bolt that careened toward the ground, closer and closer—

He smashed into something hard—

Then it was silent.

His body was cold and sweating as he came awake. The light whirled and rocked to and fro, then stabilized. He concentrated on the ceiling, trying desperately to fix his eyes on something solid to keep from drifting into the maelstrom again.

Rustic wooden beams came into focus.

He closed his eyes and opened them. The beams were still there.

He reached for his forehead.

Something cold on his face.

A damp cloth?

"Dammit!" he screamed. The vibration of his voice seared his ears. He roared in frustration and anguish and slammed his fists against the pallet—

He was back in the barn!

• • •

Jenny clicked off the headlights. As she drove toward Charleston, she let her mind drift and thought about nothing. It was the only release she'd had in the last couple of days. Few cars had passed coming the other way. All of the traffic was going into Charleston. She hypnotically followed a beat-up pickup with a gun rack in the window. *If you don't like my driving, Dial 1-800 EAT SHIT,* she read on the bumper. Cute. Idiot.

Thoughts of Alex flooded her. Many nights since they'd gotten married, she'd reach out for Alex in bed and find him gone, the sheets cold where he'd been lying. Then she'd hear the soft ticking from the computer keyboard in the living room. Alex had trouble sleeping when ideas would creep up and whisper in his ear until he'd finally get up and put them on paper.

His book, which he called *Vortex,* was slowly but surely taking form. A police procedural featuring Mike Slattery, a tough-guy detective who specialized in straightening out bad attitudes and sifting the right answers out of a lot of bad choices.

"Sure could use you now, Mike," she whispered absently as tears fogged her vision again. "If only you were real." Morning mist flecked her windshield. She tapped the wiper button. They made one revolution, then came back to rest.

"So I lose a couple hours' sleep, big deal," Alex had said when she gave him a hard time about the sleep he had lost while writing. "Besides, this is good therapy. Allows me to do all the exciting things that would get me in trouble in real life."

The computer and all the floppy discs were gone. Mike Slattery was gone along with the rest of *Vortex.*

All gone.

Now in the possession of some knuckle-dragging idiot who has no idea how to even turn the equipment on, let alone run it, she thought. *Probably sell the computer and printer and all of the hundreds of hours of Alex's work*

*for fifty dollars to some other kid—to run his video
games on. Depressing. Damned depressing.*

She imagined Alex could reconstruct Mike Slattery
and his book, but only he could say for sure. She shook
her head.

Alex. Where are you? What are you doing right now?

"Try to relax." It was Manny's voice. Alex felt a hand on
his shoulder and let his head fall in that direction. From
above came the familiar sound of the birds' fluttering.

Manny's thin hairy face smiled down. His small bright
eyes showed compassion.

"Tough luck, kid. How'd they catch you?"

Alex shook his head in disbelief, almost beyond
words, and closed his eyes again when the pain intensi-
fied.

"How the hell'd I get here?" Alex finally whispered. "I
can't believe this. The cop, what happened to him? Last
thing I remember was him coming to help me."

"They brought you in early this morning. Hooked you
to the chain again. Didn't say a word. The cop went into
the house with Harley and the old lady. She returned after
you left last night. We found the key you hid, was ready
to take off when she walked in. Can you believe that
shit? We were minutes away from being out of here. We
were working so hard on getting loose, we didn't hear her
drive up in that antique."

Manny took the rag, went to the worm box, and got
some fresh cold water. He laid it on Alex's forehead
again.

"I think they're all still in the house. I been holding
cold rags on your head forever. Jesus, kid, I thought you
was gonna die sure as shit. You got an egg on your head
big as my hand."

"Thanks. Tell me again who brought me here."

"Harley and some cop."

Alex blinked open his eyelids and focused on Manny.
"What cop? What did he look like?" This was unbeliev-

able. Alex's head spun. *Must have a concussion from the fall.*

Manny described the policeman down to his paunch and Stetson hat.

Alex gasped when he finished. "You're kidding!" Alex tried to sit up, but his head whirled again, and he dropped to his elbow.

"You know him?" Manny asked.

Alex chuckled mirthlessly, and nodded. "Know him? Hell, I worked for the son of a bitch! It's the chief from Picksburg. I can't believe he's involved in this." He struggled to sit up again and failed. "Good old boy, Cody. No wonder they haven't found this barn yet. He's been in on this all along. Hell, we'll *rot* waiting for someone to come and help us."

"The local chief of police?" Incredulous, Manny leaned on his haunches, looked out the door, and whistled. "Damn! That really screws us, huh? That means we got no chance at all for the law to get us out of here."

"Sure doesn't help. My guess would be he's working alone on this. For kickbacks from the old lady, likely."

"Cops! Bastards! Wouldn't you know it!" Manny realized what he'd said, then added, "Sorry."

Alex sat up and held his forehead in his hands.

"What're we gonna do now?" Manny asked.

Alex stumbled to his feet, then wobbled to the worm box and washed his face in the ice-cold water. His body and pants still stunk from the pig droppings in spite of trying to clean himself at the cabin. He walked back and collapsed clumsily on his pallet.

"Think you should be walkin' around with that head?" Manny asked.

"Hell, this is the least of my worries." He frowned. "I was this close." Alex held up two fingers. "Thought I'd made it when I saw that damned cruiser closing in on me. Reason I got caught was because I didn't have the smarts to kill Harley when I had a chance. Had him tied, helpless, and left him in a cabin."

"Where's the girl?"

"Dead. Bastard crushed her skull like a grape."

"Dead? Holy shit! What's the old lady going to do when she finds that out?" Manny scowled and ran his fingers through his long beard.

"Don't tell her, for God's sake. She finds out, no telling who she'll kill before she calms down. Besides, she wouldn't believe us. She'll accept whatever Bigfoot tells her."

"This is bughouse. Damned if you do and damned if you don't. What the hell we going to say if she asks?"

"Nothing. Don't tell her squat. Just pretend I didn't say a word. I'll take the heat if there's any lying to be done. It's not fair to bring you in too. I shouldn't have told you in the first place."

"Balls! What happens now?"

"I don't know. I think this whole operation is going to come to a head soon. The girl told me Mae bought a house and has plans to move from here in less than a month. I can't see her taking us with her, can you?"

Manny shuddered. "Crap." He was defeated as he dropped heavily to his pallet and scowled. "Been kidding myself. Thought I could sit this thing out and someone would come along and save us." He looked at Alex. "Did I hear you say you had Harley tied up at one time?"

"Yeah. Hand and foot. In a cabin, about five miles from the road."

"And you didn't kill him?" Manny whispered. His face worked into a deeper frown.

"I know, it was stupid. If I get another chance, I won't make that mistake again."

"Fat chance. I can't believe it," Manny mumbled to himself. "You had him tied up, and you didn't kill him."

Alex shook his head and closed his eyes. His decision had seemed right at the time. It was pointless to try to justify what he'd done. In the light of morning, especially considering what had happened, it seemed stupid to him too.

Alex realized that even if he'd made the road without

someone chasing him, the odds were he'd have seen the
police vehicle.

Then he'd have run to Cody Brighton.

And he'd be right where he was right now.

No change.

No change at all.

"What's the real truth about the girl?" the chief asked
Harley. They were sitting at the table. Outside, the sky
was light, but low clouds huddled around the mountain-
tops. In the distance, thunder rolled and echoed among
the hills. Harley reached and turned off the kerosene
lamp as the chief continued. "It's time for me to get back,
and we been talkin' about everything except what we're
both thinkin' on. It's important I know where that
damned girl is. Mae believes what you said, but I been
'round the pike too many times to buy it."

"Run off, disappeared, like I said." Harley glowered as
he hunched over his coffee. "Told you that at the road,
an' told you here. Ain't changed."

"Like as not we'll find her. 'Tween you and me, I don't
give a damn whether she's alive or dead nohow, you
understand. But it'd be best you tell me the truth 'fore
Mae gets here from the henhouse with them eggs."
The chief fingered his Stetson as he talked. "Dead or
alive don't matter. But if she's dead, I need to know so's
I can pick 'er up and keep a lid on this. Damned lucky
your cousin Purdy came on you in the cabin. He knows
better'n to open his mouth, but some o' the Skaggits find
out, that'd be a different story. There'd be hell to pay."
He nodded to the door. "Ain't no need for Mae to know.
We can just let on the damned girl took off someplace,"
he finished with his voice lowered even further.

Harley sat for a long time, working on his alternatives,
then said, "At the pig farm in the valley below Cason's
Ridge. You'll find her stuffed in the outhouse behind the
cabin. The old woman in the cabin's dead. Weren't my
doing."

The chief nodded, put his hat on, and straightened it.

"Time you an' me had some plain talk about this operation and what we need to do about it, I'd say."

"That's the way I figure on it."

Mae banged in the front door. She glared, still upset about what Harley had told her earlier about Sarah up and leaving. She set the basket of eggs on the counter and busied herself with making breakfast as the men watched in silence. Her small eyes smoldered with anger.

"Why would that girl take off that way?" she mumbled. "And at the same time the cop tried to escape." She stopped in the middle of cracking eggs into the skillet and asked Harley, "Ain't no way she left with that cop, is there?"

"Mae, that didn't have nothing to do with it. She mentioned to Ellie earlier she was plannin' to light out." Harley had already told Ellie what had happened and schooled her on what to say if asked. She was sleeping now.

"Fool girl with her fool ideas. When she comes in with her tail 'twixt her legs askin' to come back I'm gonna give her a whuppin' she won't forget!" The eggs hissed as she dropped them into the hot bacon grease.

The men finished their breakfast without talking, then stood and walked out to the chief's truck. The three dogs jumped and barked until Harley shooed them away.

"She can't hear out here," the chief observed as they climbed in and slammed the doors. They were quiet for a long time, just sat and stared at the barn and picked and sucked their teeth.

The chief was the first to speak. "It's past time we shut this operation down, Harley. It was a good thing for both of us for a lot of years. You comin' and goin', not breakin' your back for some right smart money, and me pickin' up my granny fee for lookin' the other way and solvin' a minor problem here and there. But this killing's gettin' out of hand. Gonna bring some outsiders in sooner or later. More'n likely sooner. Besides, the old lady's leavin' here soon anyways, you know that, don't you?"

Harley glanced at him and smirked. "Shit, how'd you find out?"

"Ain't all that tough. I keep an eye on what's goin' on in this county. She's been dickerin' on a bit of land a ways from here for a couple months now."

"That's gonna cut into your side money a bit." Harley chuckled.

"And you're gonna be out of a job yourself, boy, but being out of a job beats the shit out of doin' time."

"Yeah, well, I got other things on the fire." Harley rolled down his window and flipped the toothpick away.

"Like livin' high on all that money she's got stashed away somewheres?" This time it was the chief who chuckled.

"What money is that?" Harley asked, trying to sound surprised. He glanced at the chief and knew he could tell it was a lie.

"Don't shit me, boy. The old lady's payin' cash for that spread over there. Costin' her something like a hundred-twenty thousand and change. She ain't cashin' in no T-bills, you know, an' she don't have accounts in no banks."

"Stupid bitch! All that money for a damned piece of dirt?"

"That's a fact."

The men stared at the barn for more long seconds, then Harley asked, "What about the cop? Why the hell did you two do something that stupid, kidnappin' those boys? Don't make no sense when everything was rollin' along with no problems."

"The young cop, Gregory, just happened to be in the way. Josh was the one we was after."

"The one 'at's dead?"

"Son of a bitch was makin' noises like he was gonna blow the whistle. Come on this setup when he picked up Jess Skaggit several months ago for rapin' that Parker girl in Picksburg. I set Josh down and tried to reason with him, then bought him off for a while with a few bucks, but the bastard started waffling on me. Talkin' about how it was wrong to be doin' what we was doin'. Didn't make no threats, but a man with a nagging conscience can cause a heap of trouble." The chief lit a cigarette, took a deep puff, and blew the smoke out his side window. "Thought at first I could set 'im up with a few planted stories about drugs, but it just got too damned complicated, too involved. Finally, seemed simpler to just get rid of him. Shit. That boy didn't leave me no choice." They sat for a long time again, then the chief added, "I want half the money she's got stashed." The words hung in the air like an ominous cloud. He turned and glared at Harley, waiting for a response.

Harley ground his teeth. This was workin' different than what he'd planned. He wanted to get this last full load of shine, get rid of the old lady, grab all the money, then burn everything to the fucking ground and disappear. Everything had seemed so simple. Now this. Only one thing to do. Can't kill him now, but—

"Don't know where it is, but you can bet I'll nose it out," Harley lied. "Why don't you meet me here tomorrow morning around ten. I'll have the last of my load of shine done, then we'll split whatever I find. After that—we close everything down."

"Mae and the kid?"

"Snap!" Harley made a twisting motion with both fists and grinned.

"The three men?"

"Same. They'll be in the ground soon's they're done with the load of shine. This truckload's worth over ten thousand dollars to me. No point in pissin' good money away."

"When this is all done, I think it'd make sense for you to disappear for a long spell."

"Why would I hang around? Ain't nothin' here what rings my bell." He smiled and rolled up the window when a few drops of rain whipped in on a gust. Distant thunder rumbled.

"Good. We understand each other. I'll be by here at ten o'clock tomorrow morning. We can split the money then." The chief started the engine, signaling he was ready to leave. "I figure the old lady's got somewheres around a couple hundred thousand, give or take. I ain't gonna quibble about pennies as long as I get me at least a hundred thousand of it. I know you wouldn't do anything stupid, like deciding to try to cut me out, now would you?" His smile was pasted on.

"Chief, ain't no way you ain't gonna get what's comin' to you." Harley dropped to the ground and grinned through the window as the chief gunned the engine.

Harley opened the gate and nodded as the truck drove off into the woods.

Yeah. Ain't no way you're not going to get what's comin' to you, you bastard, Harley thought as he walked toward the barn. He'd have to be careful. The chief trusted him the same as he trusted the chief—which was not at all. He'd have to figure on how he was gonna take him, because the chief was smart enough to realize Harley'd try to kill him to keep all the money to himself if he got the chance. Catchin' him off guard was gonna take some doing.

When the chief came with his hand out, he'd have to kill him quick, no foolin' around tryin' to be cute. Just howdy chief—bang—adios. Sweet and simple. Maybe even meet him as he's comin' up the trail. Yeah. That might work good too. Get him before he even has a chance to scratch his nose and whip out that shiny automatic of his.

Harley walked into the barn and stopped at the end of the three pallets where the men were lying. When he walked in, they stopped talking. He looked down at Alex.

"Glad to see you're okay, boy." He smiled at Alex with revived good humor now that everything was lined up right in his head again. "Here's the way it's gonna be." He turned and motioned to the vats. "We got three vats there ready to run, and three almost ready. We're gonna work straight through and finish all six by tomorrow morning early."

"Even the ones that aren't ready?" Manny asked. "Alcohol in them is pretty low right now."

"Them alkies in Atlanta'd drink snake piss if it was cheap. Run 'em."

"But we'll have to work all night," Manny complained.

"Then you'll work all night, asshole! You want to talk to the union about the conditions around here?" He guffawed, then turned to Alex again. "Y'all listen up to this. I don't know how much you told these boys, but the story about the girl is—she run away and you don't know nothin' about it. Any of you says different, I'll kill him, pure and simple. No fucking around this time. Y'all understand?" He paused a beat and walked toward the door. "You get them fires lit and get busy—now! Mae'll bring you your morning vittles. Just keep your mouths shut."

He smiled, chuckled, and was gone, not waiting for any of the men to respond. As he walked to the house, he thought about the chief saying he wanted at least a hundred thousand dollars.

Bastard! I'll give you a hundred thousand, he thought. A hundred thousand fucking worms eatin' your body!

30

Jenny pulled into the parking lot of a diner on the outskirts of Charleston. She walked to the newspaper racks and noted what she guessed were the largest papers in the area. In the telephone booth, she copied down the addresses of each, then went to her car and coordinated the information.

In the direction of the mountains, lightning crackled, and thunder grumbled a response.

Great. Rain is just what we need to make this a perfect day, she thought as she climbed into the Mustang and headed for the first newspaper. It was almost nine. She hoped they were open.

She reflected on what she had been forced to do to get the newspaper's attention, and the many movies she'd seen where the newspeople swarmed to the scene of the crime before the police. Tinseltown baloney.

At the *Post Dispatch,* a big white building with a manicured lawn, she wandered through the halls before she finally found someone who would talk to her. A secretary ushered her into a small cubicle and she sat opposite a short, round man four weeks past due for a haircut. His beard was sparse and she could see his chin behind the strands of hair. He shook her hand with such a dead-fish grip she glanced at his arm to see if he was injured. He was fine, to her surprise.

He wore a gray, air-dried suit just out of a washing

machine. It gave him a rumpled, down-at-the-heels aura she figured he hoped gave him that authentic Papa Hemingway look.

She sighed and told her story from ground zero. Crumbs from a sandwich littered his desk, probably from the prior day. He nervously bit the inside of his cheek and fingered his wire-rimmed glasses as she talked.

"You say your husband just disappeared?" he asked, repeating what she had already told him.

She nodded tiredly.

"Any evidence of foul play of any kind?"

She shook her head and twisted her hands in her lap. "Foul play? They kidnapped them with guns, for God's sake. What do you call that?"

He cleared his throat and shifted uneasily. "I meant, foul play. Like anything actually happened to them . . . other than what this woman *says* she saw. She could be mentally disturbed or something, you know?"

"The news here, seems to me, is that nobody is concerned about it, including the hick cop in Picksburg."

She watched his eyes dart up and down to the paper he was writing on. He underlined three words, then glanced up again and focused on her forehead instead of her eyes. Even though she'd been taught that it was a sign of insecurity that was supposed to elicit sympathy, people who did it really annoyed her.

The man leaned back, clicked his teeth, and bit the inside of his mouth two more times before speaking. "I mean, she says these men held a gun on them, and made them get in a truck? Geez. How do we know that happened?" The man's voice was colorless and whiny. She had him pegged as the kind of guy in a bar who uses the line "Haven't I seen you someplace before?" or "You remind me of my mother." He tapped his pencil and asked, "And what is it you'd like us to do?"

"Isn't this something that would interest your paper? Two policemen missing . . . kidnapped. It's news, isn't it? Maybe you could ask the woman or somebody else about it . . . look into it . . . talk to the chief . . . something . . . for God's sake, isn't that what newspaper people do?"

"Lady, it's only news if we know for *sure* that something has happened to these men."

"You mean, like finding their headless, naked bodies impaled on a flagpole in front of the courthouse, with all of the pertinent witnesses lined up on the lawn by height and weight . . . something like that?" She stood, too filled with energy and anger to remain seated. "And my name is Gregory. Mrs. Jenny Gregory, not 'lady.' "

"There isn't any reason to get nasty." He cleared his throat, straightened his glasses, and scanned the paper as though searching for something. It was another ploy to avoid meeting her eyes. "You said the only person who saw this alleged abduction is unavailable and you don't even have an address and telephone number for her. Now what am I supposed to do with that?"

Jenny bit off the first answer that came to mind and said, "My husband is not *allegedly* missing. He's gone, damn it. I was hoping you'd want to stand up, get in your car, and actually drive over there and ask some questions."

"We have a limited budget, you know. Do you have any proof of any of these things?" His face flushed at her barrage.

"You have the chief's testimony for starters. The woman told him what I'm telling you. You *could* call him. As far as the woman . . . these are mountain people, for God's sake. They pee in their backyard in a hole in the ground. They have no electricity and pump their own water and think Herbert Hoover is still president. We're talking bare bones here. What do you expect—for her to fax you a signed, notarized statement?"

"You can't talk to me that way. I've won awards as one of the top reporters in this—"

"If you're one of the top men, I'd sure hate to see what's below you on the food chain! This story has the potential of national exposure, can't you see that? No, you can't. You'd rather publish handouts of your Aunt Sophie's bean dip!" She glared down at him, hands spread wide on his desk.

His mouth worked as he ground his teeth and stared at the window while a spit bubble formed in the corner of his thin mouth.

"Learn to look at people when they talk to you, get a haircut, and have your suit pressed, Mr. Reporter. You look like a bum!"

Jenny left with tears in her eyes, partly from the anxiety, and partly because she was furious about being less and less able to control her emotions. After that performance, he'd die a thousand deaths before he'd print a word of this story. *Stupid!*

The second paper on Fourth Street was called *The Observer*, and her experience there was even more frustrating because she found no one at all to talk to.

Both of the full-time reporters were out on assignment, as they called it. She asked the young receptionist if she could talk to a part-timer instead. The girl blinked, cracked her gum, and told her she could call later if she wanted to, but it was obvious she hoped this strange woman would get lost so she could go back to painting her nails.

Jenny left there, went to a Denny's restaurant right next to the freeway ramp, and checked the phone book in the entrance for television and radio stations. She slammed it shut in anger and frustration, then walked in and sat at the counter and had a cup of coffee.

With her coffee half-finished, she jumped up and called her home number. *Maybe Lee has called,* she thought. It rang three times and she keyed her recall code.

The tape rewound and a voice boomed across the line: "Jenny. This is Lee. I'm in jail. A policeman collared me at the Clearys' house at seven-thirty this morning. Call an attorney to get me out. They haven't charged me with anything as yet. When I got to the house—" In the background she could hear two voices shouting at him, then he said, "Call an attorney," and the line disconnected with a bang.

"Just great!" she cried. She stood, her hand shaking, staring at the receiver in exasperation when she heard the receiver rasp again. She held it to her ear.

"Hi, cutie pie. This is your Uncle Wesley. Got my head a little straight and took to worrying about you. I don't have a phone, but you can call me on the truck radio if you want. I'll be waiting"—*scree!*

She smiled. He cared. Her line scratched again, then a metallic voice announced in a monotone, "That's the end of the messages."— *beep*.

"Thank heavens they didn't steal the answering machine. Probably didn't see it on the floor by the bed. But then, why would a burglar need an answering machine?"

She called information, and after begging the operator, had her find and read the names and telephone numbers of the two attorneys in Picksburg over the phone. She guessed they both worked out of their houses. She had an image of Festus on "Gunsmoke" when the second man answered on the third ring. Jason Billings had a resonant voice.

After ten minutes of wheedling, she talked him into going to the station and trying to help Lee. She told him she'd call as soon as she returned to Picksburg that afternoon, and hung up feeling better about her public-relations ability. She cynically told herself he'd probably accepted the job without a retainer because it was the first job he'd gotten in six months, then shook her head. Even she was getting upset with her negative disposition, but her attitude would only get worse until Alex came back.

Throwing a dollar on the counter to cover the coffee, she dashed to her car. The truck and the radio she needed to call Wesley were at home under the big tree, and he had no telephone, so there was only one thing to do.

After she started the engine, she pointed the Mustang's hood in the direction of Beckley.

12:35 p.m.

It was early afternoon in the barn, but it seemed like night as the clouds gathered over the mountains during the morning and occasionally dropped a fine mist that drifted in the door on a gust of wind. The men worked in silence with a palpable foreboding hanging in the air.

This was close to the end of the line for all of them. Alex sensed it, and he could tell by the somber demeanor of the other men that they knew it too. It was something real, as tangible as the stills they tended.

This hurry-up production of shine a day away from being ready to process was the final clue Mae and Harley were close to shutting this operation down. Had to be. Manny had told Alex yesterday they already had enough of a load for Harley, as large as he had ever taken, that there was no reason to process these remaining six vats—three not even ready to be run—

Unless . . .

"You notice? Harley didn't say nothin' about preparing any new mash in the vats like he usually does," Manny observed as he cleaned the pot for the next vat to be processed. Ti was in the storeroom getting more corn-meal for a fresh batch. They'd finished processing one vat and were now ready for the second. "We're getting low on jugs too, and he didn't say anything about that, either."

"I know," Alex answered. "It didn't escape me."

"What do you think that means, if anything?"

"Stop pretending. You know what it means as well as I do." Manny swallowed deeply and turned back to the pot he was cleaning. "If we're going to get out of here alive, we have to do something quick—tonight at the latest," Alex continued.

"You mean—"

"Yeah. It's the only choice we have left."

"Jesus!" Manny turned and walked over and sat on his

pallet, his place of refuge when he had to think. "Jesus," he echoed absently, and brushed his hair back. He sat with his shoulders hunched, like a deflated balloon, used up, tired.

Alex said, "I know we're running out of time. If one of us could get out of here, and away, there wouldn't really be any reason for them to kill the remaining men. They might take off if they felt the truth was going to come out. Why would they bother to kill them? What would it accomplish?" Alex lowered himself beside Manny. In the other room, Ti worked without noticing they had stopped.

"Sounds reasonable, but that Harley . . . that bastard. It'd be fifty-fifty he'd kill us just for fun. Only take him a few seconds if he decided to."

"Seems to me, it's better than no chance at all. If we do nothing, it looks like that's what we have. As far as jumping Harley, I expect him to be extra careful this last day and night, so ambushing him would be almost impossible. He has to know we're bright enough to suspect what's going on."

Manny's black-and-blue face twisted and Alex thought he was going to cry for a moment. Then Manny cleared his throat and asked, "Who?"

"We don't have anything to draw," Alex said. "What do you suggest?"

"Forget what we called it as kids, but we used to play a game for quarters under the West Side Highway. Played it with our hands. We could do that to decide."

"I don't know how."

Manny's eyes brightened a bit. "No problem, I can show you in a couple of minutes."

"Why not?" Alex asked. He glanced up at the knife on the beam.

Manny's gaze followed his, then he shivered.

12:45 p.m.

When Jenny climbed out of her car at the abandoned aircraft plant, the wind swirled across the concrete and blew dust in her eyes and hair. She could smell the ozone and moisture in the air. It was working up a gully-washer, as she'd heard the folks around here call it.

She was about to knock on the side door when she saw a figure out on the tarmac, leaning into the brisk morning wind, tying down the tarps that covered the helicopters. It was Wesley. He waved, jerked one last knot tight, then turned and jogged toward her. He held his collar together against the bluster. They charged into the room on a wave of leaves and whirling dust. He slammed the door and smiled.

"Don't you love it?" His eyes were bright in his bearlike face as he rubbed his hands. "Gonna have water up to our butts by morning. Maybe it'll break this goddamned heat. How about some coffee? George brews it the best, but he's down to Memphis getting some parts right now." He started making it without waiting for her response.

"Alex's dad is in jail," she said softly. "And I went to the newspapers, trying to get their help, and it . . . nothing . . . worked . . . they . . ." She bit her lip, but cried anyway.

He moved to her and held her against his chest. His coat smelled of tobacco and engine oil. Finally, he guided her to a chair and lowered her into it after brushing off a pile of papers. He combed her hair back gently with his massive hand, then went to the stove, and silently finished preparing the coffee. With it perking, he came and sat opposite her. She had dried her eyes in the meantime. She smiled and wondered how she had gotten separated from this friendly man for so many years. In spite of his profession, he had a big heart and he made her feel a lot better than anybody'd she'd met in days.

"Why'd they arrest him?" he asked. He lit a cigarette and the smoke drifted through his beard.

"I told you before about that woman who said she saw Alex. They arrested him because he went and tried to talk to her again. We didn't believe what the chief told us she said."

"You was right. It was bullshit!" he exclaimed. "What kind of man is that damned chief over there?"

"I don't know. I don't understand anything about what's going on."

She told him what had happened to date, including her abortive attempts to get the newspapers to help. He sat back, mashed out the cigarette, then got up and poured them each a cup of coffee. A frown creased his forehead.

"Just like Nam. There's always some noncom asshole fouling up the works. Damn shame you can't frag 'em here." He chugged the first cup, then stood, poured more of the strong brew, and continued talking while looking down at her. "You figure this woman and man know something, but they're keeping it from you, that it?"

She nodded.

He walked over to the window and looked out. The wind whirred past the glass and the sound of sheet metal buckling and popping came from the hangar.

"Been a long time since I've nosed into anybody's business," he mused. He sipped his coffee, reflecting. "But then, I ain't had kin to worry about 'round here, and it's been a time since I've seen anybody get jerked around as much as you and your husband." His voice drifted to silence.

The gap of time lengthened as Jenny sat and stared at the big man. Finally, beaten, she whispered: "You're . . . you're my only hope. Nobody will help me." Her voice was fading with her will to keep fighting.

He turned and stared at her for a long moment, then walked over and slammed his coffee cup into the sink and smashed it.

Jenny jerked away.

"I've had enough of this shit!" he shouted. His powerful

voice blotted out the wind. "There comes a time when you gotta stand up, bust asses, and get the job done! We'll worry about the goddamn rules later!"

He glanced back out the window, then at her, and his coarse features softened to a smile. He buttoned his jacket, and when he spoke this time, his voice was gentle and filled with affection: "Jenny, little babe. Looks like we got maybe three or four hours' flying time left at the most."

"What . . . what are you going to do?"

"*We*—girl." He held his hand out to her. "We're going to fly over and talk to that woman and man." He chuckled when she looked worried. "Trust me, girl. I got a way with people. When I get to reasoning with that man, he'll tell us what we want to know, damned sure."

"You aren't going to hurt him, are you?"

"You want Alex back?"

"Of course—"

"Then you finish that coffee and let's get out there and crank up the Huey, and you leave the persuading to me. I *guarantee* he'll tell you what you want to know. My methods bother you some, you can take a little walk in the woods while I reason with him."

31

"Quick, show me how. Let's finish this before Ti figures out what we're doing," Alex said. "The less he knows—at least until the last minute—the better."

"Okay. Here's the way you play. We count one, two, three, then we each hold a hand out. You either make a fist, two fingers, or an open palm—five fingers, that is."

Alex looked at him quizzically.

Manny continued. "See, the thing of it is, you don't know which of those three the other man is going to hold out. We decide who wins by what we each hold out. We can do it the best out of three times. The guy who loses does the wolf thing."

"How do you know who wins?"

"A fist is a rock, two fingers is called scissors, an open hand is called paper."

Alex nodded.

"Let's say I hold out a fist, for example. If you hold out two fingers, scissors, I win. Rock breaks scissors, you see. If you hold an open hand, you win. Paper covers rock."

"If I hold out two fingers—scissors?" Alex asked.

"If I hold out rock—you lose. Rock breaks scissors. I hold out paper—you win. Scissors cuts paper . . . see?"

"If I hold out paper?" Alex asked.

"If I hold out rock—you win. Paper covers rock. If I

hold out scissors, you lose. Scissors cuts paper, you see?" Manny asked.

"Seems simple. Two out of three, loser does it. Right?"

"Right."

They both moved around on their pallets and faced each other. It was a child's game, but the stakes eliminated the possibility they'd smile while they played.

"You ready?" Manny asked.

"Jesus. I can't believe we're doing this," Alex said.

"Now, we look in each other's eyes during the one, two, three . . . so's neither of us can see both hands till we both look down, okay?"

"Sure."

"Ready?"

Alex nodded again. They stared at each other for a long moment, then Manny said, "One, two . . . three!"

Both of their hands flashed out in front of them—

They glanced down.

Manny's hand was open. Paper. Alex held out a fist. Rock.

"Paper covers rock. I win." Manny said. "That's one out of three." Alex could feel his stomach turn over and tighten. He had to win both of the next two turns— Manny had to win only one. He tried to imagine himself typing with one hand, then shook his head.

"You ready?" Manny asked.

"As I'll ever be," Alex said and tried to smile, but his lips remained pressed together.

"One, two . . . THREE!" Manny shouted.

"What the hell are you guys doing?" Ti shouted from across the room. "Can I play?"

They both looked down.

Manny had a closed fist. Rock. Alex had two fingers. Scissors. Alex was confused at first, then realization dawned on him.

Manny whispered, "Rock breaks scissors. That's two out of three." He met Alex's eyes. Alex swallowed as he stared at their two hands still in position.

Manny reached out, patted Alex's shoulder, and said, "Sorry, buddy. You lose."

The helicopter ride sickened Jenny. She felt she was hurtling through a space that kept getting smaller and larger, smaller and larger. The layer of clouds above was almost within touching distance, and the green ground and trees racing below rose and fell with the undulations of the foothills. The vibration and pounding of the engine behind her added to her tension. Too frightened to breathe, she stared down with dread, consumed by the feeling that if she moved—even an inch—it would upset the delicate balance of the flying pinwheel spinning across the sky, and they'd go spiraling into the earth.

"You keep starin' at that ground, it's going to make you sick," Wesley warned as softly as he could above the throbbing engine, not wanting to scare her.

"I don't think I can move or do anything else," she said in a restricted voice.

He chuckled with good nature.

She forced her head away from the racing trees and roads below with an effort and glanced at his smiling face. Her stomach followed the motion.

"I maintain this vintage Bell Huey with great care, and I'm the best damned pilot in the whole state, okay? You've got an eleven-hundred-horsepower engine on your side back there, and we can carry three thousand pounds like nothin'. We're going to be just fine. Look straight ahead instead of down, it'll help a bit."

She did. The clouds and the ground racing toward the craft reminded her of the final scene in *2001: A Space Odyssey*—except the bright colors the astronaut saw racing toward him were now only green below, gray above—an endless green-and-gray corridor into infinity.

"Isn't it awfully dangerous? Flying in this type of weather?" she choked out, then glanced around, surprised they were still level after she'd had the effrontery to speak. A staccato of raindrops peppered the canopy, then stopped. The droplets spread from the air pressure on the plastic, and Jenny watched in fascination as they crawled up, then raced off the top of the canopy bubble in thin rivulets, clearing in seconds.

"This? This is a picnic, love," he shouted. "In Nam, we had to fly through squalls that'd take the paint off our Hueys. This is a spring day!" He laughed. "Man with a hole in his body pumpin' out his life's blood can't wait for the sun to come out." They hit a patch of turbulence. The Huey dipped slightly, then stabilized, and he laughed again like a kid on a roller coaster. She gripped her seat. If she was going to die, she'd take this damned seat into the afterlife with her.

"Comin' on Picksburg," he said. "Should be over the downtown in a half minute. Point me in the right direction when we get there." The racketing of the engine changed in pitch as he slowed perceptibly.

The white clapboard church and parking lot flashed under them. The main drag appeared with its hodge-podge of disparate retail buildings, and he banked and paralleled it. The roofs on most of the stores were covered with patched rolled roofing, making them look like temporary structures from the air.

"God, it does seem destitute. Lee was right," she exclaimed. She'd lost her rose-tinted glasses in the last couple of days and could begin to see everything as it actually was, instead of as she wanted it to be.

"Straight ahead ten miles, follow this road," she yelled. The buildings dashed under the chopper, replaced almost immediately by fast-moving trees. The ribbon of road snaked ahead and unwound faster. As they flew toward the foothills, the space they had to fly in became more and more compressed, and they moved closer and closer to the treetops.

Finally, Jenny saw the lonely tree ahead, sitting alongside the narrow road, a sentinel for the fields on either side. It was easy to spot, even from this unfamiliar angle.

"Slow down," she shouted above the sound of the engines.

Wesley did something magical at the controls, and the front end tipped up, then the whole cabin rocked. When it stopped, the tree was about forty feet below. Her nails were buried in the bottom of the seat. She glanced off to the left and could see the small cabin in the copse of trees. She pointed at the rusty-looking roof, and he nodded. He circled the house once at a distance, then found a relatively open spot in a field and did his stopping thing again in midair. He rotated the craft, then lowered it gently into the tall weeds. Out the window of the capsule, the weeds and saplings did a frenetic dance. He cut the engine and the blades still whirred above, without power now. Her ears ached in the relative silence.

"We'll walk over there—you hang back," he instructed as he unbuckled his belt. After what had happened in the past, she was willing to do it his way, gladly. They climbed out and ran across the field, out from under the still-spinning blades. In the deep weeds, she stopped for a moment, her legs weak and threatening to collapse.

"You rather wait here?" he asked.

"No. I'd worry too much just sitting here. Besides," she said, checking around her feet, "there's snakes everywhere in these fields."

"The people's names?"

"Cleary. Woman's name is Ida, I think. I forgot what the caveman's name is." He smiled, took her hand, and walked toward the trees, about thirty yards away.

"Doesn't matter, I guess," he said. "We ain't going to be exchanging a lot of amenities."

When they broke out of the trees into the clearing, Jenny noticed the limp drapes on the window jump, then swing back and forth. With the clattering of the copter overhead, sneaking up on them was out of the question.

Wesley put his hand on her shoulder and pressed down in a stay-here gesture. She bit her finger as he walked to the front door. He wore heavy boots, a camouflaged full-length outfit, and a coat that made him look even bigger than his over-six-foot height. Jenny was glad he was her friend instead of an enemy. With his beard and dark complexion, he was an ominous figure. He banged on the rickety screen door with the flat of his palm. The sound echoed in the clearing and made Jenny jump, shocked at the energy behind it.

"Go away!" came from inside the house. Cleary was home.

"I want to talk to you! Open this door!" Wesley yelled.

"I've got a gun. You get away from here!" The door opened a crack and Jenny could see Cleary's hairy face peeking out. Jenny edged back and partially hid behind a tree, watching apprehensively.

Bang!

An explosion of sound made her jump. Instead of a gunshot, she realized Wesley'd kicked the door wide with his heavy boot. He was inside the door when she looked back from flinching behind the tree.

Screaming and yelling came from inside the house—
Boom! A gunshot this time!

Jenny's heart leaped into her mouth.

He shot my uncle!

A scuffling noise came from the interior, then the sounds of something falling and crashing—

Smash!

The window exploded out and a figure came flying backwards and landed heavily on the ground in a tinkling of broken glass! Wesley looked out the empty frame to where Cleary groaned and was struggling to get up. Wesley met her eyes and smiled—

Before she could react, he was out the window and on Cleary. He moved with the grace of a man thirty years younger than he had to be. Jenny watched in wonderment as he leaned down, grabbed Cleary by his filthy shirt, and jerked him to his feet with little apparent effort.

Cleary wobbled in front of him. The discharged gun was still in the house, thank God. Cleary had a couple of minor cuts from the glass, but nothing serious that Jenny could see from where she stood. She inched closer as the men talked.

"Where's your wife?" Wesley demanded.

"Fuck you!" Cleary shouted.

Jenny saw no motion—just Cleary lifting from the ground and landing on his back with a woof of released air. She cringed at the ferocity of Wesley's attack. He smiled over at her again, then bent, and lifted the beaten man. As Wesley brushed Cleary off like an errant child, he turned to her.

"Looks like this may take a while, girl. You want to wait at the machine." She shook her head. She was torn by wanting to see this man get his, and being repulsed by the actual violence.

"Where's your wife?" Wesley insisted, this time a little louder.

"Fuck you!" Cleary said, and turned to run. Wesley caught him by his shirt, jerked him around, and hammered him onto the ground again. This time, Jenny had to glance away.

When she looked back, Cleary was standing up, being brushed off. Blood now ran freely from his nose, which she assumed was broken. His clothing was even more filthy, if possible.

"Let's try this, then," Wesley suggested. "What did your wife see happen to those two policemen down by the road?"

"Told the police! I don't have to tell you nothing!" Cleary screamed it with renewed hatred. Jenny grimaced at what she guessed was coming.

"Come with me," Wesley ordered. He imprisoned the man's arm in his meaty fist and marched him past her, Cleary stumbling to keep from being dragged. His eyes were glassy but filled with anger as he passed, trailing his cloud of disgusting body odor.

"You wait here!" Wesley demanded as he smiled at her.

"Let me come—"

"No! You stay. That's an order!" Wesley wore no smile

this time. She nodded and rubbed her hands together nervously. The men disappeared immediately through the trees in the direction of the waiting helicopter.

Jenny was frightened. Wesley would never leave without the information he came for, and she was getting nervous about what was going to happen. She wanted to know—desperately—but participating in a brutal beating or murder was something she'd never be able to live with. She struggled with whether she should dash to the helicopter and try to stop Wesley before it was too late.

What can he be doing?

In the distance, she could hear the cicadas and the chittering of restless birds. She was so used to them, they had escaped her attention when they first arrived.

A coughing sound, a bang, then the rhythmic clatter as the helicopter's engine pounded to life.

What the hell is Wesley doing? I have to stop him!

She moved as fast as she could through the trees, and as she came into the opening, the helicopter was lifting off the ground. The underbrush and grass under it danced in the prop wash as Jenny came closer, her hair flapping around her face.

Wesley was the only one in the machine! How? Where?

Then she saw it—

A rope trailed the rising machine, then the feet and body of Cleary as he hung upside down. Above the undergrowth now, she could hear him yelling, "Help, help," over the sound of the buzzing rotors.

The tone of the engine changed, and the helicopter, dangling Cleary about thirty feet below, took off toward the horizon skimming the bottom of the low clouds.

"Oh, my God," Jenny said under her breath. "Dear God, please don't let him kill him," she implored as she watched Cleary's arms flapping futilely, trying to save himself. The chopper was small on the horizon. It turned and hovered for a moment—a dot with a tiny dot hanging under it.

Jenny's body shook, sorry she'd gotten involved in

this. She felt sick inside, but was powerless to stop it now that it was set in motion.

"Alex, please give me strength," she whimpered softly. The helicopter on the horizon got larger. Buzzing louder, it raced toward her at an angle. It flashed across her field of vision at about a hundred feet, blades assaulting the air, with Cleary barely sixty or seventy feet above the ground. Jenny looked ahead of the chopper and could see it was dashing for two trees almost as high as the thundering machine. Cleary screamed constantly as he passed, his voice rising as he approached, then lowering as he zoomed away in an eerie Doppler effect.

"Pull up!" she shouted, then realized it was impossible for Wesley to hear. She screamed involuntarily as the helicopter whizzed between the tops of the two trees, and the dangling figure of Cleary brushed the middle branches, sending bough fragments and leaves to the earth in a cloud of debris.

Jenny went over and leaned on the trunk of a tree. Her legs were so weak she could hardly stand. This was turning into a nightmare. In the distance the helicopter hovered, then charged toward the other side of the same two trees.

Instead of screaming this time, Jenny held her breath as the helicopter and Cleary burst between the trees. The body of Cleary was limp as he flashed by, and his screaming had stopped. His arms flapped limply in the wind.

Jenny slid down the tree trunk to the ground, shuddered, then cried softly. Was he dead, or just unconscious? In the distance, the helicopter disappeared out of sight instead of turning and repeating the charge between the trees.

The sound of the chopper was gone for three or four minutes. She desperately searched the horizon for movement. Then, it came ripping along toward her, hugging the bottoms of the clouds. Cleary still hung under the craft. It came to the original landing site and lowered Cleary to the ground. Then Wesley deftly moved the machine a few feet to the left and clumped down and rocked heavily before settling beside the still figure.

Jenny raced toward the machine as the engine cut again. Wesley was out and on the ground hunched over Cleary when she reached him. The blades still whistled through the air, but Jenny ignored them and studied the figure on the ground.

"Is he dead?" she asked in a little-girl voice.

Cleary was soaked with water. Hair, clothing, and body dripping wet. He coughed and took in a deep rasping breath as though coming back to consciousness.

Jenny gasped herself, unaware she'd been holding her own breath. *Thank God, he's alive—*

"Took him for a dip in a lake beyond that hill," Wesley explained. "Son of a bitch smelled like he's been sleeping with goats. Wanted to neaten him up 'fore I brought him back."

"Don't . . . d-don't," Cleary coughed out.

"You ready to tell us what we want to know, or you want to go for another ride through the trees, boy?" Wesley asked.

Jenny started to say something and Wesley shushed her with a wave of his hand.

"A-Anything . . . anything . . . you want to know," Cleary forced out. Above them, the blades of the chopper came to rest and nodded up and down in a gentle breeze. The smell of hot engine oil radiated from the machine.

"Give it to us now, all of it. I don't have time to fuck with you," Wesley said. Jenny leaned forward in anticipation.

"Them two cops, stopped to talk to an old mountain woman in a car, Ida said. Had two kids with her." He coughed hard before he continued.

It was true! The chief was lying to us, she thought with a bolt of anger.

"Don't know who the people was, but she guessed they was from around here by their dress. Looked something like Skaggits from a distance, she said. Untie me, okay?"

"You just stay like you are till we know it all, then I'll decide whether you get untied. Go on!" Wesley prodded him with his foot.

He coughed again. "Young girl and a crippled little boy was with the old lady. Young girl was maybe fifteen, 'cording to Ida. Please don't take me up there, mister, I'll tell you all of it." Jenny was struck with how meek his voice was now.

"Get on with it!"

"Lady had this old car. Ida didn't know what kind, but it was real old, like the kind they used in them old movies. Long and black. Nineteen thirties kind of car. She pulled a shotgun on them two boys, made 'em get in her trunk, then drove off."

Jenny felt the muscles in her neck relax. Alex was alive. *Thank God. He is alive!* She felt warm tears of gratitude rush to her eyes.

"Anything else?" Wesley asked.

"Yeah. 'Fore she slammed the lid, she bent over and fired her shotgun into that trunk." Wesley's gaze bounced up to her, then back. Cleary smirked thinly. He'd saved that gem of information for last and had enjoyed delivering it.

"No!" Jenny shouted. "No!"

"She fired? How many times?" Wesley asked in a low voice.

"Just once. From that close, she had to kill one of them boys, no question."

"Simply drove off," Wesley said thoughtfully. Jenny's mind and heart raced. One shot. Was Alex still alive or was he the one the woman killed?

"Why'd you lie?" Wesley asked, suddenly angry.

"Didn't lie to nobody!" He held his hands out defensively. "Told the chief the truth! He threatened us to keep our mouths shut, that's all. 'Don't say nothin' to nobody,' he says. Heard later he told a different story to this lady and others, but weren't my affair." Cleary was sitting now, wiping blood from his nose on his filthy T-shirt.

"Why wouldn't you tell her the truth?" Wesley asked.

Cleary grunted and shook his head. "Chief runs everything 'round here. I'll have to live here long after them city folks is gone back to where they come from."

"Where's your wife?"

"House," Cleary said. Wesley untied his feet.

"Let's get her away from here," Jenny said. Her mind raced, thinking about Alex, but she had to take care of this poor woman first before she could let any emotion take charge of her. Cleary wobbled ahead of them to the house.

At the door, Cleary hesitated, then said, "She asked fer it. I didn't mean to hurt her."

"I'll bet. Where is she?" Jenny asked.

"Bedroom," he mumbled.

Jenny ran through the dark house into the bedroom. She searched it with her gaze, then spotted the screwdriver in the closet door. She dashed over, pulled it out, and jerked the door open.

Ida lay on the floor, her face swollen and bruised, blinking into the dim light. Wesley came in, holding Cleary by the arm. Jenny helped Ida up onto the edge of the bed.

"You want to go with us?" Jenny asked. The beaten woman looked around at Cleary, then at the floor.

"He won't hurt you. We'll protect you." It gave Jenny satisfaction to say that. The animal!

One quick glance again at Cleary, then Ida nodded yes energetically.

Wesley took Cleary into the living room and bound him tightly, so he could barely move. Cleary watched them quietly with molten hatred.

"This poor lady's going to need a head start if she's going to get away from this crazy bastard," Wesley said when she came in. Cleary lay on the floor, glaring up at them as they passed. Ida looked away, afraid to meet his eyes, but after the helicopter ride, he had obviously decided showing anger was unprofitable.

Jenny and Wesley supported Ida by each arm as they walked to the helicopter. Jenny got in first, then helped

Ida in, and shared the wide seat. Wesley climbed up. The engine coughed, and the blades spun slowly.

"I gotta get back to Beckley, girl. What do you want me to do?" Wesley asked, confused about what was going to happen with Ida.

"Can you stop in the field across from my house?"

Wesley nodded and took off straight up, slowly this time. "No problem, if you point it out."

Ida groaned and leaned into Jenny. He flew at a moderate pace as Jenny questioned Ida.

She repeated everything her husband had told them. Yes. The woman fired one shot into the trunk. Yes. The woman was definitely a mountain woman, probably a Skaggit, but she didn't know her or where she lived, but they all lived within ten miles of each other up on Cason's Ridge, didn't they? No, the old car was a mystery to her too. Black, long. Nineteen thirties vintage, she guessed.

She pointed off into the distance, showing Jenny approximately where Cason's Ridge was. Jenny followed the roads into the hills with her gaze. Where Ida pointed was miles from the main road.

Reading her thoughts, Wesley said, "I have to do a little moving this afternoon. Can't get out of it. Promised. If you can wait until tomorrow morning, we can go hunt for that car with the Huey if you want."

Jenny nodded. Any help was appreciated. His so-called moving had to do with a marijuana shipment, but she made no comment.

"I gotta finish before this narrow window of weather closes up. If it socks in any more," he explained, "might be I can't use this machine tomorrow."

"We'll have to play it by ear," Jenny said. They pounded across the sky staring at the black clouds assembling around them. Jenny was no longer sick or nervous. She had other things to think about.

Cleary's voice kept echoing through her mind:

"From that close, she had to kill one of them boys—"

"She had to kill one of them boys—"

"Had to kill one of them boys—"
"Had to kill one of them—"
"Had to kill one—"
"Kill one—"
"Kill."
"Kill."
"Kill."

32

After they touched down in the field opposite Jenny's house, Wesley lit a cigarette and waited while Jenny took Ida inside. She and Ida were about the same size. The suitcases were gone with the burglars, but all of her clothes were still there. Jenny picked out two paper grocery bags, opened them, and set them on her bed. She selected three changes of clothes for Ida from her closet along with a light jacket. Alex had bought it for her in the South Coast Plaza at the May Company. She looked at it for a long moment, absorbing its memories, then folded and stuffed it in the bag with the other clothing. Ida needed it more than Jenny needed the memories.

"I can't take this stuff, it's yorn," Ida protested.

"Yes, you will, and please don't argue," Jenny insisted gently. "It gives me pleasure to help. You don't want to take that away from me, do you?"

Ida shrugged and sat on the bed, her thin legs tight together, her face swollen black-and-blue. Wesley was waiting, or else Jenny would have tried to cover the injured places with makeup.

"You have family, or somewhere you can go?" Jenny asked.

"Just kin in Oklahoma's all." Her voice was weak. "Ain't got no way to git there, though. No car, no money. He'll kill me sure this time, if'n he ketches me."

"He isn't going to. And the money thing . . . that's

easily fixed," Jenny said as she pulled her checkbook from her nightstand drawer. It was pushed into the back and the burglars had missed it too. *At least one account I don't have to close,* she thought. She opened it and wrote a check for five hundred dollars, then ripped it up, and wrote another one for a thousand dollars. Half what they had in the bank. *The hell with it!* The more money Ida had, the better her chances were of getting away.

"I cain't pay this back nohow," Ida complained as she stared at the check dumbfounded.

"You want to pay me back, I'll tell you how." Jenny sat down next to her and put her arm around her shoulder. Ida was stiff, not used to affection. "You'll pay me in full and then some if you promise me you'll never, ever let anyone hit you, or treat you like dirt again. You're a person, a human being, entitled to be happy and live your life without pain." Ida bent and cried softly. Jenny wanted to cry too, but lifted her up instead. Wesley had to leave, and they were out of time.

At the Huey, she packed the bags behind the seat and kissed Ida on the cheek. Ida hugged her hard, urgently. From behind her, Wesley frowned questioningly.

"I'm staying here. When you get there, get her a cab for the bus station. She'll have to stop at the bank first to cash this check, but make sure she gets to the bus. She's going to Oklahoma."

"What you going to do?" Wesley asked, looking at her suspiciously. "You ain't thinkin' of going up in them hills yourself, are you? You gotta wait till I can get back."

"Of course not," Jenny assured him. She patted Ida on the cheek and smiled. "I have to clean this house, get things organized. I'll call you with the truck radio early in the morning. We can decide what to do then, okay?"

He visibly relaxed a notch and reached down to turn on the ignition. Before he hit the starter, he glanced over and said, "Stand well clear, kid. This field'll throw up a peck of dust and pebbles. I'll call the chief once the lady here's gone on the bus, an' tell 'im where to get her husband."

Shame we can't leave the bastard tied up forever, Jenny thought.

Jenny ran to the road, then looked back at the helicopter. The engine coughed blue smoke and banged. The blades spun faster and faster until the sound filled the field. Dust and sticks flew as it lifted to ten feet. Ida waved awkwardly and smiled a thin, frightened smile. A battered child on the first leg of a new, more gentle life, Jenny hoped.

The roar changed pitch. The machine tilted and dashed across the field, gaining altitude as it picked up speed, then disappeared behind a regiment of trees. Jenny stood for a long time, listening to the diminishing engine sound until it was gone. The rustling of the wind in the treetops and the incessant humming of the cicadas replaced the distant buzz of the helicopter.

Jenny suddenly felt alone, more alone than she had ever been in her life.

"Good luck, Ida," she whispered and choked back a sob. As she walked to the almost vacant house, a black depression came over her like a descending curtain. Ida was running away, away from a house and a man who had abused her in every possible way for years—her husband. And all Jenny wanted in her life right now was to see and touch and love her own husband again.

But, she had no idea where he was.

No clue at all.

Except—

Cason's Ridge, and a long, black 1930s car.

She bounded up the steps and slammed into the kitchen. She had to eat, then pack some food, shower and change, and get ready to leave.

She had to get in that damned truck—

To look for that damned car—

Up on that damned ridge.

2:25 p.m.

The day inched along second by second, minute by minute, hour by hour. Alex worked in a haze, and his mind leaped from alternative to alternative. Harley stayed in the house all morning, so deciding whether to attack him never came up.

Alex glanced down at the manacle on his left wrist. He'd made this pact with Manny, and now he had to cut off his hand and escape again. *Cut off my hand? This is insane, this can't be happening!* The whole thing seemed like a dream, something occurring to someone else, somewhere else. A movie maybe, not reality. *Things like this never happen in real life!*

If I didn't make it the first time, while I was stronger, with no loss of blood, with the advantage of a big head start—how in the hell can I hope to make it now?

It's the only chance you have! He ground his teeth as he shouted inside. *You can't sit here like a slug and die without trying!*

"You okay?" Manny asked.

Alex looked up and realized he was gritting his teeth as he poured an almost empty bucket into the still-pot instead of a full one. "Sorry." He made no excuses. Manny knew what he was thinking and remained silent. Alex walked to the vat and dipped in each of the buckets.

Mae had brought in their gruel that morning and dropped the tray on the floor with a grunt. She glared at Alex as he picked his up. He walked over and sat on his pallet. Her eyes were black and even more recessed, if that were possible. He could feel her burning stare on his back as he ate self-consciously. She suspected him of having something to do with her daughter's disappearance. It was obvious.

Hell, even if I told her what really happened and she killed Harley, I'd still be a prisoner here, no change.

Reasoning with her and trying to get her to understand

he'd meant to help Sarah, not hurt her, never entered his mind. This woman was a heartless killer who'd destroy anything or anybody who caused problems. Expecting any kind of mercy from her was a joke of the worst kind. She operated on one premise: *If it troubles you, kill it.*

As he sat under her gaze, he practiced what he'd say if she asked him about Sarah. He had to pretend he knew nothing, he had no choice.

Finally, he glanced up, and she was gone. He sighed with relief.

If I do this thing, this wolf thing, and actually escape, he thought, *that means the end of my career in law enforcement. Cops with one hand are ex-cops.*

Big deal! Who gives a damn!

His response made him stop what he was doing for a moment. He suddenly realized that being a policeman was about the last thing he wanted to be. It had been wrong from the start. Facing death constantly in the barn had made it clear how stupid it was to live his life doing what someone else wanted.

I want to be a writer, not a cop. Really never did. Dad will have to understand.

"Mike Slattery, you son of a bitch," Alex mumbled fondly. "You'd know how to get out of here. Where are you?"

"What'd you say?" Manny asked.

"Just talking to myself."

Manny nodded and Alex ambled over to the vats with his empty buckets. Alex stopped for a moment and set them down.

He walked to his pallet and sat. It was time to think about *how.* How he was going to do this *thing,* this wolf thing.

He reached over and gently explored his left wrist, feeling the tendons and bones. He pressed in his index finger at the base of his left thumb.

That's where the wrist bone stops, and the fingers start, he visualized as he rolled it between his thumb and forefinger. *That's where I'll have to cut—*

"You hurt your wrist?" Ti asked as he carried a sack by him. Ti hesitated, waiting for an answer.

"No. No, I didn't hurt it—"

Ti trudged to the vat and dropped the sacks.

"Yet," Alex finished. He turned the left wrist tentatively in his right hand, examining it again.

"Not yet."

2:34 p.m.

Gust-driven rain pattered intermittently on the windshield as Jenny drove into the foothills. The huge truck grumbled along, taking up what seemed like three-quarters of the narrow road.

It had turned into a strange sort of day. The clouds hanging low, skittering across the treetops, made it claustrophobic, almost as though her wide-open world had shrunk into a gray-green wedge. She had stopped on the edge of town and filled up at Philo's Texaco. While the pump was dinging in fifty-two dollars and some change worth of gas, she'd looked at what she could see of the hills and shivered. This was a day to read a book, or stay inside and bake some more bread, not a day to go out into a hostile area and search for a crazy woman and a gangster car.

When the pump handle popped up indicating the tank was full, she glared at the total. This monster truck had a big appetite. Good gas mileage meant nothing to the government. She instinctively bridled at that thought, something else to annoy her.

Now, driving down the gravel-covered dirt road, she had no idea what she'd do if she met a car coming the other way. She guessed she'd have to stop and hope the car could inch around her. She had packed a lunch and it sat on the seat along with her binoculars, one other item the burglars had missed under the bed.

She wore jeans, a tucked-in plaid shirt, and hiking boots. Her long black hair was tied back in a ponytail.

She'd bothered to put on lipstick because she planned to talk to people.

She felt nervous about not having a weapon, although she'd probably be more nervous if she had one. Alex's spare nine-millimeter automatic was in the hands of some mouth-breather in Beckley, probably holding up a 7-Eleven right now. Here in the woods she felt defenseless without a gun, but she had to go, and the time was too short to get another one.

To her left, what she assumed was Cason's Ridge in the distance was completely obscured in mist. She downshifted and slowed, having trouble finding the turnoff. The intersection of the narrow dirt road was unmarked. It was a thin, rutted road that led across a field, then switched back and forth and blended into the dense foliage, where it would disappear into the gray clouds somewhere in the distance. Only people who lived in those hills used it, so no markers of any kind were necessary.

She'd seen the entrance only once, when she and Carole were out sightseeing. Carole had poked her and pointed it out. She wished now she'd studied it instead of just casually glancing over. Jenny thought of California and tried to remember if she had ever been on a dirt road, or even a road with gravel. The answer was no.

It's a great place to visit, but I wouldn't want to live here flitted through her mind. Life in California had been so structured, so devoid of even the hint of problems. Here, everything was a struggle. Especially without Alex.

She yelled, "Wait—" and hit the brakes. Struggling it into reverse, she slowly backed up as she studied the woods off to the left. A small road snaked off between the trees and disappeared. She looked ahead and nothing in the road was familiar. "This has to be it," she whispered. Breathing deeply, then sighing, she pulled the gearshift into first and wrestled the large steering wheel to the left.

As Jenny drove into the dark opening between the

trees, she had the sickening feeling she was making a decision she would regret. Everything in her screamed *Go back, go back!* but she focused on the narrow rutted road.

Alex was somewhere ahead in the mist.

She knew it.

And could feel it.

33

3:15 p.m.

"Ellie, it's time you knowed what was going on, so's you don't get upset." Harley rolled over on the bed and looked at her. He rumbled up a belch from the three beers he'd just finished drinking. The bottles lined the rickety nightstand. He loved the taste of beer, but hated the trip through the woods to the creek where Mae kept them cooling. "Mae's outside somewheres, fartin' around again, so we gotta get this settled." How Ellie responded to this would decide whether he had to kill her too. If she unglued, she'd have to stay here when he left, in the barn lookin' up at dirt like the rest of them losers.

"Get what settled?" She sat up and stretched in her bra and bikini panties. He smirked. She loved to suck it up and pose, making 'em stick out as far as possible.

"You have to know when we take that money, Mae'll kick up some kinda ruckus."

"So what's she gonna do if we just take it and leave? Once we get that money, you wasn't comin' back anyways, was you?"

"You remember me tellin' you 'fore we came up here how them men in the barn was prisoners of the state we picked up from a work crew—that they was all wanted men, convicted of murder and other bad things?" She nodded and frowned. "How Mae kidnapped them off the road, from that work detail?"

318

"Yeah. 'Cept'n that cop you grabbed snoopin' around. Served him right." Snatching up a copy of *The Enquirer* from the floor, she fanned herself energetically, getting more and more disturbed. Cher's face appeared and disappeared. "Yeah, I remember all that. So what?"

"It's important you remember."

"Why you talkin' this trash?" she asked. "It ain't no nevermind to me."

"'Cause you gotta know what's gonna happen so's you don't go bullshit when it does." He sat up on the bed himself, then walked over to the window and glanced out. He scratched his naked body and ran his hand through the thick hair on his chest and stomach.

Satisfied they were alone, he returned and dropped on the edge of the bed again. The springs squeaked. *Crappy bed,* he thought. *I'll be sleepin' on goose down from now on.*

He muttered, "When we leave here, ain't nobody gonna be 'round to tell 'bout what happened."

"What do you mean?" She waved the magazine and stared at him.

"They all gotta be put down, including Mae and the kid."

"Put down?" Her eyes got larger. "What do you mean, 'put down'?"

"Dead. Snuffed. All of 'em." He studied her for a response.

Ellie got up and paced around the room, fanning herself faster. The picture of Cher came and went. "Damn it to hell! It made me sick to my stomach to have them men fight right after we got here and kill that one fella for no reason, but I don't understand *this*. Why cain't we just go to Florida or something? What's the need of any more killin'?"

"Turns out—without my knowing, of course—Mae killed several other men over the years. Wondered what happened to them. Found out she buried them in that barn." He tried to look serious, but was smiling inside. He watched her eyes carefully, judging her reaction.

He thought: The killin's got to start somewheres, and it might's well be right here and now if she don't answer right. One less worry to be done with.

"That's awful!" Her *Enquirer* flapped so fast Cher was just a blur.

He reasoned, "I know. But the worst of it is, now that she done it, we're all painted with the same brush. We take that money, she'll raise Cain sure as hell. Someone'll come snoopin' around, find out, then the law'll be lookin' for us too."

"What do you mean, us? I ain't done nothin'," she whined.

"Law don't care. They'll have us in the hoosegow whiz-bang. Then you'll have some big, fat woman-man suckin' on them pretty tits of yorn instead of me."

She shivered at that thought, then slowly fanned herself with *The Enquirer* again. Cher came back into focus.

"You gotta . . . kill 'em all? Even the men?" She froze and stared at Harley.

"'Specially the men. They seen too much."

Ellie quivered noticeably, turned, and gazed at the wall, switching the magazine now in a thoughtful manner. "And Mae?" she asked in a whisper.

He nodded, then said, "Yes," when he realized she was looking away.

"Even that piteous little boy? Not him?"

"It'd be a kindness, Lord take him." He tried to sound concerned he had to do it. No sense in takin' even a little chance was there? No tellin' how much awareness was hidden behind them dull, beady eyes.

"But when law finds 'em all dead, won't they come lookin' for us anyways?"

"Nothin' to find after I burn it all," Harley said matter-of-factly.

"Won't that draw law thick as fleas?"

"The Skaggits 'round here'll come in and pick clean what's left. Sheeit! They'll be divvyin' up this land quiet-like, quicker'n a fly leapin' on a turd."

"But they'll know who done it—ain't you scared o' that?"

"Dammit, Ellie! These Skaggits ain't been off this land nigh on two hunderd years. They'd gut-shoot me quicker'n a buck deer if'n I was dumb enough to hang around, but once we's gone, we might's well be on the moon as far as them boys is concerned. They'll sit around, get liquored up, and jaw about it for ten, fifteen years, but none of 'em'll come lookin'." He watched her carefully as he opened and closed his giant fists. *Stupid woman!*

She walked over to the window, jerked it up, bent down, and put in the piece of broomstick to hold it open, then breathed in deeply and stretched. The air outside was as close and stuffy as the air inside.

Adjusting her bra, she said, "Sure do hate this heat. Soaks right through. Hope this rain fixin' to bucket down will cool it some."

As if on cue, the sound of random heavy raindrops thumping hard on the rocky soil came through the window. The smell of the hot breeze wafting in was heavy with unspent electrical energy, and thunder grumbled in the distance, closer now.

"How do you feel about this, what I told you?" he asked. He had to have an answer to know what to do with her. He'd make the decision for her in a minute if she waffled around much longer.

She looked at the ceiling, smiled, and shifted her weight back and forth, her voice higher now. "Harley, sweetness, when we get into Miami, or wherever we're gonna go, can I have me one of them yeller outfits? You know, the kind what has them little dots on the dress, with white shoes and one of them big, white, flat hats. You know, the kind them girls wore in *Gone With the Wind*—you 'member that movie?"

She flounced around the room, her heavy breasts jiggling with the motion. "An' I want tea served out on a rollin' lawn by some Frenchy girl prancin' around tight-assed in one of them iddy-biddy white aprons and little hats. An' you an' me sittin', big as you please, in high wicker-back chairs with our pinkies stickin' out, whilst we watches boats out on the ocean, goin' away to all kinds o' exciting places, then when we finish there, we'd go on down and walk on the beach, then we'd . . ."

Ellie's voice drifted away from Harley as he relaxed back onto the bed and stared up at the ceiling. Outside, the rain changed from random drops into a constant thundering that echoed in the small room.

Women! Dammit to hell, he thought. The mind of a woman was a trip to a strange and foreign land to Harley, all filled with strange goings-on, with little side trips going nowhere. How they could put bad things aside and concentrate on crap amounting to no more'n a hill of beans was a wonderment. *Dammit to hell!* He'd let her live for now, 'cause she pleasured him some, but when they got on down the road, that'd be a different matter.

Sheeit. With that kind of money, he'd have his pick of little fillies with tight little asses, little bitches who'd whine and cry and sit up and howl when he stuck it to them. Jesus, they'd howl and beg for more. He'd do anything he wanted to them, flip 'em over and over like pink little dolls, three-hole 'em till they's loose as a goose, then shitcan 'em, or trade 'em in for a fresh one. A man with money can do anything he damned well pleases.

'Sides, Ellie here, he reasoned, *knows too much, too damned much, has too much on me.* Even more after tomorrow. *Yeah. She'll be a caution for a few days of partyin', then I'll have to turn* her *lights off too.*

Figurin' on how and when would be kind of fun in itself, with her not expecting it and all. That thought excited him so much he was getting hard. Just *wham*— out of the blue! Leave her somewhere alongside the road like a chewing-gum wrapper. The image made him smile.

Her voice filtered back. ". . . then, we have to be thinkin' on what kind of car we wanna buy. They tell me, I'm not sure, mind you, but they tell me them cars what's made in Germany is the best they is. They tell me them seats is so deep you'll sink up to your armpits, and they got. . . ."

He smiled as she droned on and on, and thought about pumping tight little asses while he snapped the cap off the last beer with his thumb.

Yeah. A man with plenty of money can do anything he damned well pleases!

4:02 p.m.

In the barn, the three men marched through their jobs in an eerie, silent cadence like sleepwalkers. Filling, emptying, filling, emptying. Bottles clinking, the still hissing and thumping. They walked back and forth endlessly without speaking.

It was darker now, and they lit two of the lanterns. The fires burning under the stills flickered and made the men's moving shadows on the far wall look otherworldly. Rain pounded the yard with a fury that accented the tension they all felt. The scent of moisture was heavy in the air along with the strong odor of burning wood, stronger than usual because the heavy rain kept it trapped in the barn.

Only about half of the birds had fluttered in out of the downpour. Alex imagined the missing ones huddled in treetops somewhere until the worst was over.

It was early evening, but it could have been late at night for all the light coming in the openings at the end of the barn roof. The dogs had retreated to cover out of sight, but they would come instantly if called.

Alex was ashamed to admit it, to even talk about it, but every time he thought about the wolf thing, his stomach grew cold and threatened to reject its contents.

Many times in his past life, in the middle of the night, he'd thought about his own mortality. He guessed that was normal, most people do at one time or another.

But the terrifying image of actually cutting off a part

of your body that was in normal condition was many times more frightening than thinking about death had ever been. Was it because *this* was real, and *that* had always been fantasy? Something in the dim future? He'd never know.

And the big question torturing him was: Could he actually do it? Actually cut his own hand off. Talking about it was one thing, but when it got down to the reality of taking that hard, unforgiving, razor-sharp hunting knife and ripping it through his live, pulsing flesh—

Then forcing—

And grinding—

And popping the bones apart!

"No!" Alex involuntarily shouted, and shivered as the vision evaporated. The other two men glanced his way, then went back to working. His face was flushed with sweat as he dipped the buckets in a vat. Manny had to know what he was thinking because it had to be what Manny was thinking about.

When the first searing pain from the amputation screamed up his arm and burned into his brain, could he actually bear it? Hold his arm still and let it happen? Even if Manny did the cutting?

God, he hoped so. Could the humiliation of finding out he was short on the courage it took be even worse than the agony and the horror of the act itself? That he seriously doubted. Nothing could possibly be worse.

If he survived this, and the odds were long against it, he knew he'd spend the rest of his life waking up in a sweat in the middle of the night.

Manny grumbled, "God, I'd sell my goddamned ass to the devil for a cigarette." The other men jumped, jerked out of their reveries.

Alex laughed in spite of himself. It was a funny, out-of-context thing to say and he would have snickered with the relief of tension if someone had simply belched.

"I didn't know you smoked," Alex said.

"I gave it up over a year ago." This time, it was Manny's turn to laugh. He bent at the still and chuckled, then roared in long, heaving convulsions that slowly turned into soft sobs. It was unsaid that they had no way to get a cigarette.

"Shit," Manny mumbled, and wiped his eyes.

"Let's take a break." Alex looked up at the frightened Ti, and added, "Relax, Ti. This won't affect your company benefits."

Ti glanced at the door apprehensively, then walked over and sat beside them.

"We're going to do the wolf tonight," Alex whispered to Ti. "You should know."

"Holy Jesus. Who? Which one?"

"Me."

"Who's gonna do the cuttin'?" Ti's eyes were big as he glanced from face to face, obviously morbidly fascinated.

"Haven't talked about it yet." Alex asked of Manny: "Can you do it for me?"

"If I have to. Probably," Manny said, then grimaced.

"Considering the pain, I don't know whether I could apply enough pressure to cut through," Alex said. His voice was a hoarse whisper now. "Once you start, though, you have to make up your mind to finish. Fast. You cut an artery and stop, I'd bleed to death. Odds are fifty-fifty I'll pass out in the process, not be able to help in spite of whether I want to or not."

"Sheesh!" Ti let out air and stared above the stills, obviously appalled at the image.

The men sat for a long time, the light from the fires flickering off their faces.

"When?" Ti asked as he turned back to Alex.

Alex shrugged. "Somewhere after midnight as near as we can estimate. I want to do it as early as possible. Give me at least an hour or so to try to recover enough before I go for the fence. We do it too late, near morning, if I'm in shock, I might not be able to recover enough to make it."

"Geez, how'd you guys decide who was gonna do it?" Ti asked Alex.

Manny screeched at him: "Shut up, we got more important things to talk about, you jerk!"

"Wha—what's wrong with you?" Ti asked. "You can't talk to me that way."

"I just did, you big tub of shit!"

"Shut up, both of you!" Alex shouted. "Knock it off." Alex leaped over and blocked Ti from moving toward Manny. "Back off, this is stupid," he demanded of Ti. "He didn't mean anything."

Ti glared across his shoulders, then lowered his bulk to his pallet.

"That's better," Alex said. "Manny, I've got an idea. In fact, it hit me before I sat down here."

"Yeah?" Manny said, still glaring at Ti and fuming with anger.

"Remember we talked about anesthetic? Using the shine? Well, listen to this. You know how when you wake up at night and your arm's asleep from lying on it for a long time. Your hand feels like someone else's hand?"

"Sure. Oh, yeah! You mean when there ain't no pain or nothin' when you touch it, that what you mean?"

"Precisely. I figure we make a tourniquet. Crank that sucker tight for about a half hour, maybe less . . . then when my arm and hand go numb, we should be able to do it with a minimum of pain. After we finish, we can let a little blood through to make sure the tissues in the arm don't die, then tighten it until it goes numb again."

"I see. Then we do the fire thing, right?" Manny said. Alex nodded.

"Fire thing?" Ti asked. "What's that?" His eyes opened wider, big and white in the firelight.

Alex explained, "We don't have anything to sew it up with. We have to try to cauterize the veins by burning them closed with coals from one of the fires. Only way to stop the blood that I know of."

All the while Alex talked, Ti's face kept getting whiter and whiter. Lightning flashed, illuminating the barn, and thunder crackled. They all jumped. The rain thundered

down harder and swept in the opening, the door creaking
and banging as it swung back and forth from the gusts.

Suddenly, Ti jumped up and ran over to the opening,
leaned far out the door, and threw up with explosive
force into the rain.

"What a wimp," Manny muttered and shook his head.
"You'd think he was actually going to have to do it
himself."

"I'm not too far away from doing the same thing,"
Alex said. "Give him some slack. I know exactly how he
feels."

"Yeah, but—"

"Drop it," Alex insisted. "You want to do something for
the cause, get one of those rags in the supply room and cut
long strips for the tourniquet. Better do enough to make at
least two of them, maybe three. We might have to cut the
first one off if it's tied too tight and we're in a hurry."

Manny stood and trudged into the dark of the supply
room. He'd been in there so many times, he knew where
the rags were by feel.

Alex looked up at the flickering fire. The thumper tubs
pounded with the unrelieved pressure and the rain
hammered on the sides of the barn. Ti still leaned out the
door into the rain and wind. Alex could sit for only a
minute longer or they'd have to clean out all the lines on
the stills.

"Jenny, I love you," he said softly. "I just hope you're
warm and safe right now. . . ."

Lightning crashed again and lit up the room. Rolling
thunder vibrated the barn as he stood to go back to work.

Idle hands, he thought. *Tomorrow, it'll be idle hand.*

He turned and glared up at that damnable knife.

It seemed alive as it taunted him.

Laughed at him—

From the beam.

*I'm up here waiting for your blood, buddy boy, and
I'm gonna get it. And I'm gonna love every minute of it—*

"Screw you," he whispered.

Firelight glinted from its hungry edge in reply.

34

Jenny lay on the seat of the truck, listening to the rain.
The rain. Where did it come from, this hard? she
wondered. It was dark now, and the roar of thudding
heavy drops on the metal roof was intimidating. In
California, months would pass before water fell from the
heavens. Then between the rare cloudbursts, she'd get a
shower of sorts, a sprinkle, a wet-your-windshield type
rain, rarely even half this hard. She rubbed her aching
right fist. It reminded her of what had happened
earlier. . . .

Through the afternoon, she had slowly crawled up into
the hills, low gear most of the way, with the branches and
leaves scraping the sides of the oversized truck, moving
ever so slowly because she never knew what was around
the next curve. A cliff? A dead end?

She had to keep reminding herself that people lived up
here, that she was going to find them eventually. Occasionally she stopped and got out to make sure she was
actually still on a road of some kind. For the first three
hours she saw only trees, and more trees. Not one person.
Not one living thing. A couple of times she heard dogs
barking in the woods, but they never came close, just
challenged her passing from the trees.

As she got farther into the hills, thirty-five miles by the
speedometer, fifteen miles at most as the crow flies—she
guessed—many of the switchbacks were so tight she had

to ease back and forth to work the truck around the corners.

When she got to the first cabins, nestled in a hollow to her left, she hesitated for a long moment. The eight or nine cabins appeared to be deserted at first. Then, here and there she saw movement, almost like shadows. Nothing definite. Just a flash of color in a window, between some trees. Why were they hiding? she wondered.

Finally, almost in answer, two old women warily creaked open a screen door and edged out on a rickety set of stairs and stood staring, frowning, wiping their hands on their aprons. Looking. Watching. But not making any other motion.

The truck, Jenny thought. *That's it. This is an army truck done in camouflage. These people have been bred to be wary of authority of any kind.*

Getting down to ask questions was risky, but that was what she'd driven this far to do.

Jenny shut off the rumbling engine. The silence was welcome. It took a few seconds before she could hear the wind and the occasional creak of thunder. She glanced out into the valley and it was a haze of gray, the trees and horizon blending with the sky, the view to the west a solid phalanx of ominous black.

If that rain comes down heavy, she thought, *I might be stuck up here for a while whether I want to stay or not.* That in itself disturbed her.

"Here goes nothing," she whispered. "I can't believe I'm doing this."

She climbed down and approached the cabins.

The swayback shacks—a better description, she decided—lined the depression on either side; some appeared to be standing only because it was too much trouble to fall.

As she looked around, the only cars she saw were rusted hulks rapidly becoming part of the landscape. Broken windows, flat tires, wheels missing. Some rusted almost through, showing no paint color at all. Three or four back in the weeds beside the cabins. And no running vehicles she could see.

As she came nearer, men and boys slunk warily out from behind the shacks, appearing like wraiths. Six, seven, eight. Barefoot. All staring at her with flat expressions as though she'd just dropped in from another planet. Two of the men carried those damnable guns of theirs. They held them by the barrel, like a walking stick.

What the hell is that? A human being or what? she could read in their eyes. *What the hell is it doing here?*

Jenny stopped in front of the porch where the two women still stood transfixed. One chewed slowly and spat something dark over the rickety railing with the assurance of long practice, never moving her eyes away from Jenny. Jenny tried not to grimace, but spitting of any kind was revolting. She hated to watch baseball on television because of it. The women's faces were leathery, arms sinewy. Their dresses hung straight down and the designs in the fabric, if any, had long since been washed out by their tubs, handmade lye soap, and washboards.

Close enough now, Jenny said weakly, "I'm looking for an old woman and a car." The women stared back as though she had said nothing.

Jenny glanced around. The men and boys had inched closer, within hearing range. Their thin faces all bore the signs of inbreeding she'd recognized on some of the other men in town. Their sunken eyes made their heads glower like skulls; their eyes were too recessed to reflect the waning light. A clan, she thought. A clan of some kind. It had a frightening sound somehow. Like *pack*—as in a vicious pack of wolves, or pride of lions.

The first spike of fear stabbed her stomach, and she had to force herself to hold her ground. Her leg muscles tightened. Running because she was scared would defeat the reason she'd come into these hills in the first place. And Alex was still out there someplace, depending on her. The moisture-spiced wind whipped her hair around her head, forcing her to hold one hand up to keep it corralled.

"I'm looking for a woman. I'm told she might be a Skaggit. Drives an old nineteen thirties kind of car. Long. Black. You know, an old one. Very old. A woman. Two youngsters. A boy and a girl. Girl's about fourteen." She self-consciously strung each word on a string like popcorn, trying to find the magic one that would get a response. She glanced around from blank expression to blank expression.

Wouldn't want to play poker with these guys, she thought, trying to lighten the weight of her growing fear.

They stared silently, as though not understanding the words. She had the sudden rush that maybe they spoke another language, then realized how foolish it was.

"Whatchoo dooin' herrre?" From the steps, the woman on the left spoke in long, uninflected syllables.

Jenny almost giggled with the relief of tension, then realized she'd better not. No telling what they'd think she meant by that. One serious misunderstanding and she'd be in deep guano.

"Friend of mine saw the old car down in town. I'm a car collector. Thought I might buy it from her and restore it. Well, actually, I don't do it. My husband does. Restore old cars, that is. I just find them for him. When I can. Then he does it. Restores them." She bit her lip because she was babbling, and knew it—always did when she was nervous.

All the way up the mountain, she'd thought about what she would say, and changed it several times, gradually softening it with each new story she made up. She went from the truth, which was a no-no, to saying she was a relative, to saying she wanted to interview the old woman for a newspaper, to the car bit. The car thing had sounded logical as hell until she said it. When spoken, it was about as credible as the dog story she'd invented for Cleary.

She sure as hell had to avoid: *My husband was kidnapped by some crazy old bitch. She might have killed him, and I've got to find her and have her thrown in the clink.*

"Sounds lak Yankee horse plop ta me." The woman's expression remained the same, as if she'd said: *"That's nice."*

One of the older boys in the back giggled.

Have to show them I'm not scared, Jenny thought.

"Why would I lie? If you don't know anything, that's fine. I'll just be on my way."

Jenny glanced back at the truck. An older boy was standing on the running board peering in the window, and that made her even more nervous.

"Din't say I din't know nothin', said it was horse plop." She grinned, apparently liking the sound of that.

"Well, will you tell me?" In spite of being scared to death, Jenny was getting annoyed. People had been leaning on her for days.

"They got old cars ever'wheres, all over God's creation. Whatchoo doin' wanderin' up hyere when it's fixin' to whomp up a storm? What's so special 'bout this'n?"

"I'll give you twenty dollars if you'll tell me where the car is," Jenny offered. She glanced behind her. The boy was gone from the truck.

The two women looked at each other, then back, as though exchanging some secret.

"How 'bout fifty dollars?" the woman asked.

"Forty."

"Done." The woman walked down to the bottom of the steps, spit again, then held out her wrinkled hand. "Money first," she insisted in the same toneless voice.

Jenny dug in her side pocket and clumsily peeled off two twenties from a small roll of bills without removing her hand from the pocket. She forced herself to smile as she held them out.

After greedily snatching the money like a monkey grabs a peanut, the woman walked to the top of the steps and turned. She carefully folded the bills and stuffed them in the side pocket of her tattered dress.

"Well? What's the woman's name?"

The woman turned to the second woman as though sharing that same secret again, then smirked wider this time.

"The woman's name," Jenny insisted.

"Puddin' tame, ast me again, I'll tell ya the same," the woman brayed, then smiled a brown, toothless smile for the first time. The men and the other children who were gathered in a tight little fist around the women burst out laughing.

"Shit!" Jenny exclaimed, and turned back to the truck accompanied by mindless cackling from behind her. Lightning flashed in the distance and a couple of heavy raindrops tapped her shoulders. She had to get the hell out of here. *Now.*

At twenty feet from the truck, two boys, about sixteen years old, stepped around from in front of the truck and blocked the driver's-side door. They leered at her.

"Let me by please, I want to leave," Jenny demanded with more conviction than she felt.

"Seed you give Miss Marsty some money. We'd like some too," the taller boy said.

Jenny measured them. Even though they were young and thin, they each outweighed her by twenty to thirty pounds.

Keep calm. Talk to them, she thought.

"Give you the same deal I did her," she said, her voice quivering slightly. "Twenty dollars for the name of the old woman who lives up here, has the old black car, and—"

"Ain't tellin' you diddly shit!" the spokesman spat. The boys moved forward and closed the gap. Jenny glanced at the truck helplessly.

Jenny stepped aside, to go around them, and the taller boy quickly moved to block her way. He was in front of her now, staring down, and his breath reeked of decaying teeth. His smirking gaze slowly lowered to her breasts.

"Shore's nice titties," Bad Breath said.

Before Jenny could react, he grabbed her left breast, and gripped it firmly, painfully.

He whooped and giggled.

Stunned, she screamed and tried to pull back, but he grabbed her right arm and held her in place with his strong hand—

Her left hand went into her pocket and grasped the small roll of bills. She jerked it out and threw it to her left, yelling: "Here—take it! A hundred fifty dollars—"

The shorter boy scrambled to the ground and began chasing the bills on his hands and knees as the wind scattered them—

Bad Breath turned to watch, yelling: "Hyeehaww! Git 'em, git 'em!" with high-pitched excitement. Looking away, he loosened his hold on her arm for a split second.

Jenny leaned forward, screamed, and smashed her knee into his groin with all her strength—

He bent, eyes wide, both hands flying down to his injury. Jenny drew back and cracked him on the bridge of his nose with her fist—he fell over the other crawling boy with a yell—

They both struggled in the red dirt as she leaped to the truck, jumped in, and banged down the lock!

Her heart trip-hammered, her breath came in gasps—

She cranked the engine, raced it once, and took off with a jerk.

The second boy crashed against the door—punching his fist on the window trying to break it.

She ducked with each impact, expecting the glass to give way.

Trees ahead—she whipped the wheel toward them—

A loud thud as she scraped against the branches—

A yell!

The boy was gone when she looked, knocked off by the tree.

Engine screaming, she barreled up the road. One boy limped along behind for a way, the other was still lying in the road. After about two miles, she slowed to a safer speed. Nothing in the rearview mirrors. Gradually, her breathing and heart rate returned to normal. Her fist ached from hitting him, but there was a quiet satisfaction in it.

He'll be waiting for me when I come back down, she thought. *I've injured a couple of them, I don't know how badly. They'll remember it forever.* That she was defending herself would make no difference to those throwbacks.

Then the rain began to really thunder down. It was black out, and the windshield wipers were falling further and further behind on their job of clearing the windshield. She had to stop.

She climbed out, getting soaked instantly, and walked off the road into the trees and found a flat spot. She climbed in the truck and carefully drove it under the trees and pulled to a stop under an umbrella-like gum tree. Even though it was protected by the branches, the rain pounded on the metal roof. She shut off the lights and the engine.

Lightning flashed. She rubbed her aching fist again and was mentally drawn back to where she now lay on the seat.

It was hours from the time she'd first parked. The trip up here had been useless so far. And it was late. She had no idea what time it was, and looking at her watch was unimportant. Nothing could happen until it got light or stopped raining.

Wesley was right. I should have waited for him in the morning, she thought. *Now I'm stuck in the woods with a couple of wild-hairs waiting for me to come down. Probably with guns this time. With no place Wesley can land to pick me up, even if he shows up.*

And I have no idea what to do.

Except to lie here and sleep.

And wait till morning.

A small red power light on the dash blinked, reminding her she had to call Wesley on the radio in the morning.

Her hand ached again, and her eyes burned.

She was wet and uncomfortable—

As she rested her eyes, hoping for sleep.

35

Everything in the barn took on a surreal quality to Alex
as the hour for the wolf thing drew nearer and nearer. He
could simply refuse to do it, but the totality of what he
thought of himself as a man and a human being was tied
up in this one act. This ultimate test.

He kept arguing with himself about *which* man had the
better chance. The one staying here, or the one who did
the wolf thing and tried to escape? Who could know?
Odds were best on both of them dying; then this decision
would be of no consequence at all. Just more pain to
endure before he died. But if he did have to die, he'd at
least have the comfort of knowing before it happened
that he had taken his best shot to try to save them all.

He stopped and stood for a long moment, staring
into the sputtering fire. Holding up his left wrist, he
studied the manacle again, trying to fathom some alternative for the thousandth time. The other men watched
him furtively as they worked. The decision of when to do
it was his. It had to be. The chain was a dark outline
against the fire. Chain. Fire. Fire. Chain.

"Welding," he mumbled. "That takes heat!"

"What?" Manny said, wanting to know what he was
thinking. He left the other still and walked over to Alex.

"You remember, I asked you about a welding torch
when I first got here?"

"Yeah?"

Alex's voice took on a tone of urgency as he continued: "Sure, we didn't find any welding tools. But how about this?" His excitement was growing, but he fought to restrain it. "When these steel links are made, they heat them and cool them fast. Once. Makes them super hard. Now, I've read somewhere that all metal becomes fatigued if it's heated and cooled repeatedly. Not once, but many times, you understand. When it expands and contracts, over and over—that destroys its normal tensile strength."

"Okay. Go on." Manny was getting infected by his enthusiasm.

"Hell, we've *got* a fire. We can heat sections of our chain, then douse them into the ice-cold water of the worm box, over and over again. Heat, cool, heat, cool. Get it? Maybe we can get the metal to fatigue and crack."

"You're shitting me. You think it would work?" Manny smiled nervously. It was way too much to hope for.

"Hell, who knows? But what do we have to lose? I have to do this wolf thing in a couple of hours from now at the latest. I'm not worried about whether we get these vats processed completely. The son of a bitch plans to kill us—he sure can't punish us any worse. Let's use those two hours and try it?"

"Howdy Doody, you just might have something there." Manny leaned down to extend a few links into the fire.

"Wait. Do it much farther away from your arm. Otherwise the links on your manacle will heat through conduction," Alex warned. He threw a couple of logs on the fire, then bent in front of the other still.

"You fucking college boys," Manny said. "Conduction! Tensile! Always usin' ten-dollar words in a dime conversation."

"You won't be such a cynic if it works." Alex turned to Ti standing by the stack of shine. "Get over here, boy. Get a few links in this fire along with us." Ti glanced around, uncomfortable with doing something that would make Harley mad.

Geez, Alex thought. *They've finally got me using the word "boy."*

Ti walked over and stood behind Alex, then pulled a length of the chain up behind him and dropped it with a clank into the fire next to Alex's without speaking. Alex smiled thinly.

"This is my last hurrah. This doesn't work right off, we'll do the wolf thing in a couple of hours," Alex whispered.

The other men were silent.

Alex glanced over. Under Manny's pallet, the pile of rolled cloth for the tourniquet waited, ripped to length, ready to use. They stood motionless, watching the fires where their chains heated, each man saying his own prayer.

Outside, the wind raised an octave, and above them, the birds rustled nervously as though absorbing the tension radiating up from the men.

Light from the lanterns reflected dully off the knife blade, still buried in the beam.

None of the men had to check if it was still there, because they could sense its presence.

The knife was like a hawk.

Feathers tickling the air currents.

Eyes focused and steady—

In its final, soundless glide.

11:15 p.m.

" 'Get what's comin' to me'!" Chief Cody Brighton selected his clothes from his closet and slammed them on his bed. "You son of a bitch! You think I'm stupid, don't you? Think I don't know you intend to leave me dead as a mackerel, like them other people. Shit, are you gonna be surprised, boy!"

He had his clothes for the morning laid out one-two-three. After he showered and ate his breakfast tomorrow, he'd pop in this spare bedroom, don these clothes, and he'd be out the door in seconds firing up his four-wheeler.

He bent and fingered the lightweight bullet-proof vest. This would be the first chance he'd had to wear it since he'd bought it at that convention up in Philadelphia two years ago. He'd never worn it before because it would be considered unmanly by the other men. But tomorrow morning, he'd be on his own. Nobody up there in the woods with him when he had to kill Harley and the rest of them people.

If he played this just right, he could end up being a legend in these parts. He'd get there about an hour early. Nine maybe. No. Make that two hours early. Take no chances. Likely Harley'd already have finished off the old lady and kid by then. That'd leave only him and that Ellie piece of trash and them men. He smiled.

It'd be simple as knockin' over them ducks at the carnival. *Pop!* Quack, quack. *Pop!* Quack, quack. That game was fun, pingin' them, then watchin' them head down the other way. If he had enough bullets he could keep 'em going all day long. Only tomorrow morning it was gonna be more than ducks.

Paper said the rain was gonna clear up first thing. With just Harley and Ellie left it'd be like that. *Ping!* Harley'd be poleaxed into the dirt instead of headin' the other way. *Bang!* And he'd put one right between Ellie's big tits. Then *bang, bang, bang,* and that'd take care of the dogs. They's so stupid, they'd run right into his sights.

So easy. Only had to be there an hour or two early while they was out in the yard still loading the truck. Easy as duck soup. *Quack, quack, you losers.* He smiled.

Then he'd get Harley's gun and *bang, bang, bang!* The men in the barn would be history. Would look like he come on the massacre and got the bad guy 'fore he got away. No need for anybody to know about the money, of course.

"Wonder how much is really there? Harley didn't

complain none when I asked for a hundred thousand dollars, which means there's a hell of a lot more than two hundred thousand there. Could be three, four hundred thousand. Jesus!

"Yes, ladies and gentlemen. We're here to honor Chief Brighton for heroism," he muttered, and chuckled. He could see himself standing on the stage, with everybody who was somebody out there in the crowd smiling on.

"Shucks, weren't nothin'," he'd say. "Anybody with brass balls the size of Utah would of done the same thing." He laughed as he laid out his tie. Man ought to wear a tie on the day he gets rich and becomes the town hero all at once. *Shit! I might even get a statue,* he thought.

He went in his bedroom, stripped to his shorts, wound his clock, and set the alarm for four A.M. just to be sure. *Want to get there in plenty of time,* he figured as he climbed under the covers.

Park the truck about a half mile away and sneak up on the barn. Take my ought-six with the telescopic sight, and a couple dozen splatter-your-guts hollow-points that'd down a bear. Gonna kick some ass.

He laughed as he switched off the light.

"Quack, quack. *Bang!* Quack, quack. *Bang!*"

12:15 a.m.

"That's fifteen times," Alex said as he held the section of chain under the cold water in the worm box. The water hissed and a cloud of steam rose as the water bubbled around it. Alex watched it with intensity, willing it to crack, bend, anything. But each time he pulled it out and banged it on the timber—before he cooled it, or after—it always looked the same.

He was sweating from sitting in front of the fire for so long. His skin glistened with hot, itchy perspiration that ran in miniature rivers down his body, and his hair was wild and matted. The other two men sat watching their sections of chain still lying in the fire. Time weighed heavily on all of them.

Alex pulled the chain out of the water and studied the section. The ten or twelve links were black and had a bluish cast from the heat.

He took the chain back to a supporting timber and slammed the links hard against it, trying to get them to crack. Nothing. Tears of frustration welled in his eyes as the inevitability of what he had to do became more and more apparent.

"If I only had some tools to work with. A vise, a hammer . . . anything," he complained. He dropped heavily to his pallet for a moment and stared at the fire, his head in his hands. "You know, every time I've seen guys working metal, it was always bright red or white-hot when they took it out of the fire. Why is it that we take these out, they're just hot, but don't change color like that?" He spoke quietly, the question meant to be rhetorical.

"Realized why after a while," Manny said without turning. Silhouetted in front of the fire, the two squatting men reminded Alex of what cavemen must have looked like—sweating before a crackling fire while a storm raged outside the cavern entrance. Their flickering shadows were huge on the far wall. A few animal paintings on the rough barn walls and the scene would be complete.

"Realized what?" Alex asked, afraid of the answer.

"Heat. Ain't hot enough," Manny answered, his voice subdued too.

"How can fire get hotter?"

"Forge," Ti interrupted. "Gotta have a forge."

"He's right, for once," Manny said, still not turning. "You have to draft the fire with oxygen to make the fire burn white-hot. Didn't think of it at first. You've seen those old movies where the blacksmith pumps a handle as he's working and the fire blows and gets white-hot?"

"Yeah? What's that?" Alex asked. The sickening feeling they were correct grew in his stomach.

"It's a bellows of some kind. Simple, really. Just blows

air into the embers and they get hotter and hotter. Kind of like air forced through a carburetor feeds the engine of a car, I guess. Fire burns oxygen. The more you can pump in, the hotter it gets. That's why turbos make a car go faster, I think. That sort of thing. Not all that complicated, I guess."

"We could make a bellows. I think I could figure it out," Ti said, his enthusiastic voice loud in the barn.

"Keep your voice down," Alex said. "We don't want Harley to hear us."

Manny stirred and scratched his head, then said, "Sure. All we need is a worktable, tools, nails or screws, something to frame it, and the material to cover the frame with—something that would contain the air. And the time to do it, of course. That's all."

"We could use cloth. It'd leak a mite, so you'd have to pump harder is all," Ti added, voice lower now but still excited.

"Forget it, Ti," Alex said, "Even if we could use cloth, we don't have any pieces big enough, and we have nothing to use to sew those rags together. Besides, the only tool we have is that damned knife up there."

Even if we had everything needed to do it, it would take days to set it up to work right. No question, Alex thought.

He glanced up.

The knife gleamed. *I'm waiting,* it seemed to say.

Alex shivered and looked back at the fire. His box was getting tiny, his back was to the wall, his choices were vanishing one by one. If he was going to come up with an answer, it had to be now.

If not, it was time for—

"The wolf thing."

12:35 a.m.

Jenny gasped as she ran through a black, deep forest. Branches whipped her arms as she passed and she was frightened, more frightened than she'd ever been in her life. She was beyond screaming and sucked in deep, wracking breaths, knowing *it* was closing in and was within striking distance now.

And she was weakening.

In back of her, branches snapped and cracked from heavy padding steps. Off to the left, a dark form loped along on four legs, effortlessly keeping pace. It was running with the ease of a wild animal, the steps sounding a casual *piddy-bump, piddy-bump*, to her desperately flailing arms and legs.

No way out, it's here, it's here!

"Jenny. Jenny." A voice reverberated her name.

How does the beast know my name?

She ran harder with her last remnants of energy. It was almost over—

Something clawed at her heel—

She threw her arms forward, was going down—

Floating, floating toward the ground.

When I hit, they'll pile on and tear me apart!

She couldn't see them, but she could feel their hot breath and knew they were waiting for her to land.

Floating, floating—

Ground closer—coming closer—

"Jenny!"

How do they know me?

She slammed hard into the ground and bounced up with a start—

"You there? Can you hear me?"

"Who? What?"

She jerked and pushed away from the damp leather seat.

It was dark and the rain still thundered on the metal roof of the truck. She was in the truck, in the forest. Still.

She ran her hand down her body. Her clothes were damp, partly from the rain, and partly from the hot sweat pouring from her skin. Disoriented, she looked around trying to locate the voice she thought she'd heard.

"Last chance, kid. You there?"

She jumped. The radio was penetrating in the silence of the cab. Wesley, it was Wesley.

Fumbling in the dark, she found the mike and pulled it to her.

She thumbed the button as he had told her, and spoke: "Hello. I'm here. Don't hang up. Can you hear me?" *Screeeech.* "Damn! Talking too loud."

Swinging her legs around, she sat up. Beyond the windows was a solid wall of black. Now that the rain was here in full force, the lightning was gone.

"What the hell you doin' in that truck this time of night?" His voice was grumpy. She smiled. He was only calling because he was worried about her. *What a sweetheart.* He had probably called her house and found she was gone.

"Don't you be grouchy with me, Papa Bear," she said with a smile. God, hearing any friendly voice sounded good. She hugged her body in the dark, then quivered. The nightmare was still with her.

"You're on that damned mountain, ain't you?"

"Stop trying to sound like a father. It doesn't become you." *Screech—*

"Damn girl. You're gonna be the death of me." The voice was gentle now. She felt as isolated as someone in a space capsule talking to a person on earth. Far away. Untouchable. Unreachable.

"Thanks." Tears filled her eyes again. They were right near the surface now, and all it took was a touch, a soft inflection of a voice, and they popped out.

"You okay?"

"Yeah, I suppose. You're right. I made it up on the mountain. Had to try to get some information on that old car she told us about. Couldn't wait. Came on a hollow. Had some trouble with some boys back there. I should be close to two miles beyond that first settlement, in some trees. Got so black with the rain, I couldn't go on. Too dangerous."

"Piss you off if I tell you how dumb that was?"

She was quiet for a long moment, then thumbed the

button again: "I love Alex. If I don't find him, I don't care what happens to me."

"Yeah. Well. I gotta meet that boy if he's important enough you'd risk your life." *Screech*— He hesitated for a moment, then went on: "I called the airport out at the junction. Have a friend works in the tower. Their Notam says it's gonna clear up 'fore light."

"Thanks for the information. That'll help."

"Wasn't meant to help you. Wanted to keep you from goin' off half-cocked." *Screech*— "Damned radio. Come light, I'll crank up the Huey. Be up there after I make one drop. Put the rest of 'em off for a couple of days. Be there around nine or a little later maybe. Want you to find an open spot on that road and park. I'll come pick you up, hear? We'll have a better chance searchin' from the air. From the ground, likely you could just drive past where the damned thing is parked."

"Nothing but trees and banks and hills up here. No place to land."

"Bull. There's always someplace to land. Keep on going up that grade. All I need is sixty to seventy feet open space. You find it and wait there, you hear?"

"Okay, I hear. I'll be waiting."

"Count on me bein' there. You wait no matter how long it takes."

"Stop naggin'. I'll do it." She smiled again.

"You got them doors locked?"

"Of course."

"Keep 'em that way. Good night." *Screech*—

"Good night. And thanks." The radio clicked in response.

She returned the mike to its holder, turned, and lay back on the seat again, cradling her head in her hands.

Exhausted, she closed her eyes. The rain was lighter on the roof now, but still hypnotic in its hollow drumming.

"Tomorrow," she whispered gently.

"Tomorrow, I'll find you, my love."

36

Alex sat sweating on the pallet as the men squatted thirty feet away watching where their chains lay in the fires. The bugs were back in full force, filling the air around the lanterns. *Looking for some shelter from the storm too, along with a little snack,* he thought.

His mind was drifting, working on a lot of disconnected thoughts. Consciously trying not to dwell on Jenny, he reflected on his childhood and on old black-and-white World War II movies that showed Japanese military men committing hari-kari. He remembered how those scenes had frightened him as a child. Walking home from the Orpheum Theater in the dark, he had been upset and replayed the ceremonies over and over in his mind. The act of killing yourself was a morbidly fascinating subject to anyone, especially the young, who have everything to live for and little concept of death.

He could understand how someone might be driven to suicide if they were terminally ill and in unbearable pain, but to kill yourself for honor? That was such a nebulous-sounding reason to a child, especially one from a different culture. Losing face. That was the hooker. The term they always used. The one abomination he'd heard the Japanese considered worse than death.

Now here he was, in a vaguely similar situation. Doing something primarily for honor. He'd given his word and now had to follow through with this agreement even though he knew it was only a last, desperate act with almost no hope for success. A desperate act by three pathetically desperate men.

A verbal contract made under duress. Was it legal? Of course not. A way out? Everything in his makeup cried out to forget it. *Don't do this stupid thing! Just tell them you've changed your mind.*

It's fine if you want to do it, guys, but I'm going to pass and take my chances. Maybe we can still pull this out some other way. God, it was so tempting.

Siren voices, cooing and whispering to him constantly in the last two hours, kept saying: *What do you care what those other men think? To hell with them! It's your hand, isn't it?*

Then a soft, reasoning voice would murmur logically in his ear: *Harley's not going to kill you in the morning. You really don't believe that, do you? You'll cut off your hand for nothing, stupid! When they come to rescue you, you'll be the only one who's maimed. And for what? Nothing, that's for what!*

Then, the hard sell that really chilled: *If I do it and don't escape . . . no way Harley's going to keep me alive. Not if I can't work until I recover. He brought me back the last time as a convenience . . . but this time? Hell, even if he doesn't kill me, Mae sure as hell will. She suspects I had something to do with her daughter disappearing anyway. If they don't shut the stills down, in a couple of days somebody else will be doing my job. Bury me tomorrow probably.*

Splooosshhhhh! The sound of the men cooling their chains in the cold water of the worm boxes jerked him back to the barn. Manny and Ti were standing now, shifting about, obviously nervous about what was coming. After they had talked about the bellows, Alex had given up on the heating and cooling idea and just sat on his pallet. Maybe if they had a week it might work, but the time was down to precious hours now.

Ti glanced back at him, then gazed self-consciously at the still. Alex knew what he was thinking. The tension was thick enough to cut. Nobody wanted to be the first to say the words that would initiate the action.

Alex rose slowly. Even though his body was soaked with sweat, his throat was dry and he had trouble swallowing.

"It's time."

"Jesus H. Christ, I sure don't want to do this," Manny mumbled as he edged over to him. He walked through the cloud of insects as though they were invisible.

"Yeah. Well, think about how *you* feel, then multiply that by ten, and you might have a vague clue how *I* feel." Alex intentionally avoided glancing at his own manacled hand.

"I hate pain," Ti said offhandedly. "Never could stand pain."

The three men looked at each other awkwardly, each not knowing what to do next. Outside, the rain had slowed to a gentle patter, and an occasional bird returned to the rafters in a wave of fluttering.

Alex told Manny: "Go over and lean out the door and check the house. See if you hear anything."

Manny moved quickly over to the door, leaned out, and listened. Shaking his head no, he walked back to them. "How do you want to do this?" he asked.

"I've been thinking that the best way would be for me to lie down. Facedown. I'll lay my wrist out. After it goes numb—I'll tell you when—you press my wrist against your pallet and cut from the outside of my wrist. Here." He pointed, making a mark with his right index finger across the outside of his left wrist.

"Mother of Jesus," Ti muttered.

"Why there first?" Manny took Alex's wrist and studied it.

"When you check your pulse, the inside of your wrist is where the big vein is. The one that you feel for. I figure that's the main vein, so we want to cut that side last. If it's going to bleed a lot, that'll delay the really bad bleeding as long as possible."

"I don't know whether I can help," Ti whined. "I'm starting to get dizzy just talking about it."

Manny shouted, "Holy shit, what a wimp—"

Alex interrupted. "Shut up, Manny! I understand how he feels. Keep it down. I don't need you two bozos at each other again. I've got enough to worry about right now. I'm having trouble keeping my own emotions under control without that." He laid his free hand on Ti's shoulder. "Look, buddy. I need you. You can help by holding my arm. Keep it from moving as much as possible. When he starts cutting, my instinct will be to try to pull away. That's where you come in."

"I'll try, but I think I'm gonna be sick," Ti muttered, then his lip quivered, and he cried softly.

Manny growled, "Try, my ass! You'll do it or I'll—"

"Give me a break, will you!" Alex yelled. Then realizing they should be more quiet, he lowered his voice. "Manny, tie the first tourniquet on my upper arm, will you? Ti, you go over and get a gallon of shine to clean the knife and my wrist, okay?" Ti walked away, head down, still snuffling. Alex had the feeling he was keeping two kindergartners apart.

"These should do it," Manny said as he picked up the first tourniquet. "I made two."

He doubled the thin strips of cloth, then wrapped them around Alex's left upper arm as Alex stared out the door. Alex concentrated: *Have to just think about other things. Think about my honeymoon, or something. Mustn't think about this—mustn't. Pretend I'm somewhere else, and this is a dream.* He remembered, as a child, when the dentist came with the needle to deaden his gum, he always cooperated by looking away, pretending he didn't see it.

Alex grimaced when Manny pinched the hairs on his muscular arm as he cinched down the cloth. It smelled of mildew from lying in the darkness for months.

"Sorry," Manny said.

"Don't worry about it. That's the least of my worries

right now." Alex tried to chuckle, but it came out a dry cough instead.

Ti set the bottle of shine down next to his pallet, kneeled, and cracked open the lid.

"Ti, you're the tallest. Walk over there and stand on tiptoe and get the knife, okay?" Ti nodded, went, and retrieved it by rocking it back and forth out of the wood. He brought it back, holding it by the tip of the handle as though it were a snake. No one questioned Alex's instructions. This was his show.

Alex felt his arm. It tingled and was getting numb from the tourniquet. He swallowed deeply. No way out now, he was committed.

"Before we get started, Manny, I think you'd better make one more tourniquet. I was thinking, we ought to have another one for just above my wrist too. To cut off any last little blood flow when we do the heat thing."

"Sure, no problem." As he went into the dark room, Ti sat beside Alex, a gleam in his eyes.

"How'd you guys decide who was going to do this? I know we didn't have any straws or anything."

Alex looked up from his tingling arm. *No harm in answering,* he thought. *Any diversion will help.*

"We played a game. I don't know what it's called. We held fingers out. A fist, two fingers, or all fingers. 'Rock, Scissors, Paper,' Manny called it. I lost."

"Oh, sure. I played that all the time as a kid. We used to play for punches on the arm mostly. Loser got punched." He laughed nervously. "Sometimes we'd play for dimes and nickels too. It was especially fun to play with the smaller kids. We'd always win their money when we taught them the game. They was too dumb to know. It was like taking candy from babies." His eyes brightened at the memory.

Manny walked into the light, holding the folded cloth. He interrupted. "Alex don't want to hear about that. Leave him alone now. He's got enough to worry about."

"I need the diversion, Manny." Alex turned to Ti. "Tell

me about the game. How did you take the money from them?"

Manny yelled. "He don't want to know that—"

"Quiet. I wouldn't have asked if I didn't want to know."

Ti's head went from Alex to Manny and back, then he smiled weakly. Behind Alex, Manny sat on his pallet heavily and started ripping the cloth.

"We allus knowed what fingers they was gonna hold out the first time after we showed them how to play," Ti continued with enthusiasm.

Rip, rip came from in back of them.

"What would they always hold out?" Alex asked.

"After you'd show them, they'd always hold out rock first, a fist, you know. We'd hold out all fingers, paper, so we'd always win that one. Strange. Always happened."

"What would they hold out second?" Alex asked. He already knew the answer.

Rip, rip, rip. Louder now.

"Every time. They'd hold out scissors the second time. It was like they was workin' up on it or something. Nothing, then two fingers, every time."

"So you'd hold out rock then."

"Sure. Always would win the first two times."

"How about after that?" Alex asked sickly.

"After that, you was on your own. Could hold out anything," Ti finished. "But we'd usually bet everything the first two times. That way we was sure to take everything from them."

"Bet everything," Alex mused. Ti smiled back. The ripping of the cloth had stopped.

Alex reached over, picked up the knife, and decisively sliced the tourniquet on his arm in two. He shook his hand to relieve the tingling, then stood and silently walked to the door and looked out into the night.

Ti glanced to him, then to Manny, and back, trying to fathom what he had said to upset him.

"What's going on?" Ti asked of Manny. "Why'd he do that?"

Manny just fingered the cloth.

"What? What's happening?" Ti asked, louder this time. Alex leaned on the doorjamb and stared into the blackness. The rain had settled into a soft humming on the dirt. In the yard where the light shone out, little rivers of water ran down the hill away from the barn. The bugs tapped on the lanterns, filling in the stillness.

Manny reached over and took a deep drink of the shine, then coughed lightly.

"You cheated him?" Ti asked in a whisper.

Manny took another drink, wiped his mouth, and slowly tore the cloth again without looking up. The silence lay like a blanket over the three men as the soft *rip, rip* filled the barn.

Alex was beaten and used up. He should be feeling some anger, but what he felt was nothing. The image of doing some noble act to help others was gone now. All that was left was the feeling of isolation, of hopelessness. They were three desperate men, all on their own. Doing what any desperate men would do. Anything to survive.

"So what?" Manny yelled, breaking the hush. "So what are you going to do? Kill me?" He stood up and waved his arms in frustration. "Shit, go ahead. I'm already dead, for Chrissakes!"

Alex turned and walked over to them. He was choked with emotion, but they had to deal with this, and the time to act was running out.

"Doesn't matter, Manny. Whether you believe it or not, I'm not mad at you. We're all doing things we wouldn't normally do." Manny fumbled with the cloth aimlessly. "We've got to get on with this if we're going to do it. You want to decide again who's going to do this?"

Manny nodded.

"You got any ideas on how we can decide this?" Alex directed the question to Ti.

Ti thought for a moment, then said, "How about, Guess Which Hand? Nobody can cheat at that."

"That okay with you, Manny?"

Manny nodded.

"Okay," Alex said as he picked up a small pebble. "Here." He handed it to Ti.

Ti was smiling now, eyes bright, anxious to be participating.

Alex continued. "We'll each pick a hand. Three times. Best two out of three wins. One who loses has to do it, okay?" Manny reluctantly stood and nodded again. He was as subdued as Alex. They were drained. "I'll go first," Alex said.

Ti put his arms behind his back and fumbled with the pebble. He held his fists out, palms down, smiling a smile only a man who was out of the game could smile.

Alex reached out and slapped his left hand.

The pebble. One.

Ti repeated the fumbling and Alex slapped the same hand nonchalantly. He had nothing to lose, having already lost the decision once before.

The pebble. Two.

Ti repeated it and held his fists out again. Manny was rocking back and forth on his heels, watching worriedly.

Alex slapped the same left fist.

Nothing. It was in the other fist. Two out of three.

"Your turn," Alex said.

The first time Manny selected the right fist, and it was blank. Zero for one.

"Damn," he said, still rocking back and forth.

The second time he selected the same fist.

The pebble. One out of two.

"One more and we're tied," Manny said absently. "Have to do it over."

The third time, Ti made a ceremony of fumbling behind his back. When he held his hands out, Manny stood for a long time as though trying to sense which hand it was in.

"That one!" He smacked Ti's same right fist again. Ti slowly turned it over.

It was empty.

Manny stared for a long moment, then ran over, leaned out the door, and threw up into the yard. After about five minutes, he came back, wiped his mouth on his shirtsleeve, and took two more deep drinks of the shine, then said, "Let's go, Howdy Doody. I wanna get the hell out of here."

It took fifteen minutes for the tourniquet to work.

"You feel that?" Alex asked as he pinched Manny's arm hard. His heart was pounding almost as hard as when he was preparing himself.

"No. Hardly anything. Just the pressure," Manny said.

"Let's give it five more minutes, just to be sure," Alex said. He sat and tied together the strips Manny had torn earlier. His hands shook from the tension. Ti had wandered off to the door again, seeming to want to distance himself from what was going to happen.

Alex went over and broke off one of the cross-tines of the mash stick and came back.

"Bite on this when we start. It should help."

Manny lay down on his stomach and flopped his limp arm out on Alex's pallet. He took the tine and held it up to his mouth.

"I'm sorry I did that to you," Manny said softly. His watery eyes reflected back the light.

"Forget it. You're a whole lot more of a man than most of the people I know." Alex patted him on the shoulder.

Alex took the rest of the shine and poured it on his arm, then carefully let it course over the gleaming knife blade.

"Get over here, Ti," Alex ordered. "It's time."

Sniffling, Ti came over and kneeled. His hands quaked as he reached down and fingered Manny's arm gently.

"Hold it firm by the manacle," Alex whispered.

Alex stared at the sharp blade, serrated at the end. It was mean-looking. He felt Manny's limp wrist, feeling for the bones in it.

"You want to change your mind?" Alex asked.

"Get on with it, dammit! Now!" Manny's body shook, and he was breathing in small gasps, his eyes clamped closed.

Alex gripped his hand.

Raised the knife—

"Dear God, help us!" Ti shouted at the ceiling. His voice was strangled with fear as he started: "The Lord is my shepherd; I shall not want—" *(Ohhhh!)* Manny bit harder—Alex held his breath and buried the blade— "He restoreth my soul; he leadeth me . . ." *(Oh! God!)* Louder now— *(Ohh! God! Ohhh!)* "Yea, though I walk through the valley" *(Shiiiit!)* "of the shadow of death" *(AAAAAWWW!)* "I will fear no evil! Oh, Mama, forgive us . . ." *(AWWaaawwww!)* "Thy rod and thy staff they comfort us . . ." *(oooohhhh . . .)* "surely, goodness and mercy shall follow" *(AAAAAAAAaaaaaaa!)* "me all the days of my life" *(Ohh—GodGodGodGod!)* "and I will dwell in the house of the Lord forever." *(oh, no! I can't, I can't . . . stand this! Jesus, hurry, hurry, hurry!)* "YES, LORD! I will dwell in the house of the Lord forever! Amen, dear God!"

Their hot breath blew like steam engines in the quiet barn. Ti continued to gaze into the ceiling as he whispered: "Are you done?"

"I think he's unconscious," Alex muttered. "Yes, I'm done." Alex reached down and slid the manacle off of Manny's bleeding stub.

Ti stood, stumbled over, leaned on the door, and looked out into the rain again, still breathing hard. Alex took the hand and wrapped it in rags, hid it in the back room, and ran back. Manny was still unconscious, not even moving.

"Let's get this searing done while he's unconscious," Alex yelled to Ti.

"I can't . . . I can't. You'll have to finish." Ti was on his knees by the door now.

"Damn," Alex said.

Have to do this fast, then release the tourniquet after I tie up the stub, he thought. *Being unconscious is a blessing.*

It took Alex ten minutes to sear the ends of Manny's wrist and bind it tightly. The stench of the burning flesh in the barn was gagging. Manny lay motionless. After

Alex was finished, and satisfied the bindings on his arm would hold, he released the tourniquet. The clublike binding showed no blood to Alex's relief.

He bent over and pressed his ear against Manny's chest. Manny's heart was fast and thready, beating way over a hundred beats a minute. Even though he was unconscious, his body had to be well aware of the damage, and was signaling its shock at the injury. Alex got some empty sugar bags, and covered Manny's body. Manny's chest was moving fast and shallow and sweat had soaked through his clothing.

"We have to keep him warm," Alex said to Ti, who finally worked up the courage to return. "I think he's in deep shock. People die of that."

"What can we do?"

"Nothing. Keep him warm. If you know any other prayers, it couldn't hurt."

The wind gusted in the door and carried the rain through, now just a light mist. Outside, two of the dogs padded by, glanced in, then continued to wherever dogs go at two in the morning.

Alex kneeled and rubbed Manny's forehead. The act gave him the settling feeling he was doing something useful.

"Damn it to hell. He was too damned frail to tolerate that. I should have been the one. I'm still strong enough," he said to Ti. He looked back at Manny. "Don't you dare die, you little creep. I was just getting to the point where I liked you," Alex whispered.

By the stills, Ti closed his eyes and moved his mouth in quiet supplication.

2:48 a.m.

"What happened?" Manny asked faintly.

Manny's eyes had just flickered open. Alex was holding Manny's head in his lap.

"You checked out for a while, buddy," Alex said.

"You finish it?"

Alex nodded.

Manny squeezed his eyes tightly, then tried to sit up and failed. He fell back, breathing hard. Tears leaked from the corners of his eyes.

"Rest for now."

"How the hell can I rest? I have to try for the fence." He tried to raise himself from the pallet.

Alex pressed him back, and said: "Don't be stupid. I doubt whether you could stand, let alone make it past those dogs, and over the fence."

"I have to try. I can't do this for nothing."

"Maybe you didn't do it for nothing."

"What are you talking about? Ohh. Jesus that hurts!"

"Be a miracle if it didn't. Look. I've been thinking while you've been snoozing. The advantage to your escaping to the men here was having Harley *think* you escaped. Whether you're actually gone or not won't make any difference to us as long as he doesn't know the difference, right?"

Manny closed his eyes and shook his head. "Keep talking. I'm listening," he said feebly.

"You're going to stay here. You wobble out in the yard, you'll be dog food in thirty seconds flat."

"Can't stay here. He'll find me."

"We'll put you up there," Alex said as he pointed to the hayloft.

"How? That's ten feet, at least. No ladder."

"You're a negative jerk, you know that." Alex smiled and laid Manny's head on the pallet and stood. "Ti. Let's move it. We've got work to do, quick!"

Ti followed him obediently into the storage room. They both grabbed 100-pound sugar sacks and carried them into the barn.

"Stack them here. We're going to need a four-foot pile fast if we're going to put him up there." Alex pointed to the hayloft.

The two men worked fast, and had their mini-mountain of sugar constructed in about a half hour. They carried Manny over and set him up on top of it. They both climbed up, then lifted Manny at arm's length to the subfloor of the hayloft. He rolled over with a groan.

"Scootch back. We can still see you."

Manny moaned as he slowly inchwormed back out of sight.

It took the two men another half hour to return the sugar bags to the storage room. They went over and sat on the pallets for a moment. The fires were dying under the kilns. They had removed the tops from the kiln pots to keep the pressure from building. The mash boiling inside was giving off a burned smell.

Alex turned to Ti. "Remember. He did the wolf thing and escaped over the fence. No matter what happens, we have to stick to that story. It's the only chance we have. Besides killing Manny if he finds him, he'll then feel free to kill us too. You have that? Our butts are on the line here too." Ti nodded. His lip quivered.

Will he have the courage to stand up to Harley's questioning? Alex wondered.

"The only chance we have for one of us to get away is for me to escape too," Alex said. "But I can't do it without you." Ti's head snapped up.

"No, not me. I can't—I can't handle any more of this. Never—never again." He waved his hands back and forth.

"I'd do it myself if I could. Someone has to do it for me. Do the actual cutting. It would only take you fifteen minutes for the whole thing."

"No. I don't care what happens. I can't—I can't. This is worse than dying. Worse than anything. I won't do it!" He stood and marched stubbornly back over to the doors again and crossed his arms. Alex shook his head. That settled that. It was impossible for him to do it himself and stay conscious.

"Relax until daylight, Ti. We're going to need whatever rest we can get. And as far as the cutting is concerned, don't feel bad about it, I understand."

Ti walked over and lay down on his pallet and rolled over. A low moan from the hayloft chilled them.

Alex sat on his pallet, looked out into the dark, and thought about that three-legged gray wolf trotting along a ridge somewhere in the night.

37

The storm was gone. It had washed the air clean, and the morning light backdropped the hills standing in stark relief. The smell of the moist red earth was heavy in the air. The forest was alive with chittering birds, and here and there dogs barked as though happy to have survived the night.

Harley rose with energy and dressed in the dark, his internal clock ticking him awake. He felt strong and his muscles quivered with tension forcing him to be up and moving. He was charged with purpose and wanted to get on with it, get the things done he'd planned for the day. The chief, Mae and the brat, then the three men, and he'd be out on the highway with the afternoon breeze blowin' through his hair. A rich man with not a care in the world shakin' off the dust of this pissant mountain. "Sheeit!" he grunted. A man with money can do anything he damned well pleases.

This morning he'd skip breakfast altogether. He'd just grab his guns and be out the door. His blood was too high to worry about heavy food. Slow him down.

"Chief, you're comin' on a wide-eyed surprise," he whispered to himself as he sat on the outhouse stool. It was black inside with the door closed. "Likely you'll be comin' early to bushwhack me, but I'll be down on the road waitin' for *you*." He chuckled. "This is the first day of the rest of your life." *Now where the hell'd I hear that?* he wondered. *For you, Chief, it's the first day and the last day all rolled into one. Damn! That's funny.*

The door to the back of the house creaked.

His mind jerked back to the present.

Someone out there—

Already finished, he buckled his belt together and froze. His skin prickled. Moving on the boards would give away where he was. *Just wait.*

The door to the outhouse creaked open. A tiny figure was in the doorway, looking in, sensing for a presence like a fawn sniffing the breeze. The luminescent moonlight highlighted his frail shoulders.

One step—

Harley gripped the boy by the throat and lifted him into the air. He made a small squealing sound, like a dying rat in a trap. The boy's thin, sinewy neck was hot and the veins pounded against his fingers. Harley hesitated for a moment. This was sweet. *One twist and he'll be a rag doll, then I'll drop him in the shithole. Right where he belongs,* he thought.

"Aaeee! Harley! Git up! Git up!"

Mae's voice—from inside the house. A loud thumping accompanied her screaming. She was beating on his bedroom door. The boy in his fist flailed silently, his struggling diminishing from lack of oxygen.

"Sheeit." He squeezed hard, felt something snap, then dropped the limp boy hard to the wood and ran into the house. Mae had a flashlight in one hand and was banging on the bedroom door with the other when he slammed into the house.

"He's 'scaped! He's 'scaped!" she screeched at Harley.

"Dammit all to hell!" Harley yelled. He opened the bedroom door and grabbed his gun, then ran to the barn. Outside the barn door, he hesitated as usual and surveyed the interior. The dogs snuffled around his feet, bounding up and down.

Two men. One gone. The little guy, Manny. He charged in the barn, sweeping the shadowed walls with his gun.

"Where is he?" Harley demanded.

Alex and Ti were sitting up now, awakened by Mae earlier. She'd been preparing to shout at them about not working when she realized Manny was missing.

"Gone," Alex said almost casually. "Over the fence in the middle of the night."

"Bullshit you say. How'd he git loose?"

Alex gazed up at the beam, and nodded.

Harley went over to the timber, studying it in the dim light, amazed that the knife was gone. He ran back and picked up Manny's empty manacle. Blood covered the outside edge and the ground. Mae stood in the background jiggling her gun restlessly, anxious to do something.

Harley raised his shotgun toward Alex, and asked, "How come them dogs din't raise no ruckus?"

"We kept them interested at the back door while he tiptoed out the front and quietly climbed the fence."

"Ain't possible, they'da heard it. 'Sides, where's his hand if'n he cut it off lak you say?"

"Back room, wrapped in some empty sugar sacks. Behind the cornmeal pile."

Harley ran in the room, rustled around in the dark, then came out. He was carrying the hand by a finger, then tossed it disdainfully in the dirt. Ti looked away with a pained expression.

"Beats all," he said slowly. "Where's the knife?" He seemed more awed than angry.

"Took it with him for protection."

Harley smiled thinly. "Thought *you* was the one so hell-fired to get out of here, cop." Another twinge of guilt hit Alex.

"We drew. He lost. Believe it or not, that's what happened." Harley glared from him to Ti, then grabbed one of the lanterns. He searched the perimeter of the barn, then the supply room.

"You didn't finish them vats," he said when he came back.

"We were busy," Alex said.

"You . . . was . . . busy," Harley muttered as he thought about what to do.

Harley thought, *Should kill 'em all now, but don't have the time. Need to git on down the mountain 'fore the chief comes by. He's my main problem right now. The only one who could screw up this whole thing.*

The two men stared back, their eyes white in the light of the lantern.

Harley smiled. *Fuck 'em! I'll kill 'em later. Take my time and enjoy it.*

"I'm usin' the truck," he announced to Mae, who lurked in the background, fingering her own gun. He walked to the door.

"Take them dogs too," she said.

"Keep 'em here," Harley said. "Like as not that biddy man'll bleed out 'fore he makes a mile. He's in piss-poor shape. Don't have a fart in a windstorm's chance o' makin' it. 'Sides, don't want any more of these heroes gittin' any ideas."

"But the dogs—"

"I said, I don't need 'em!" Harley barked.

He ran to the truck and cranked up the engine. Mae opened the gate for him, then he jostled the truck off into the shadowed forest.

"Don't matter nohow," Harley muttered to himself. "Take that pissant—even if he lives—twelve, thirteen hours to make the road. Another several hours to git some help up here 'cause the chief's gone bye-bye for good. By that time, I'll be halfway to Florida."

This is gonna be fun, he thought.

Mae had left the barn, and it was lighter out. Ti went over and shut off the hissing lanterns. He came and sat beside Alex, who was staring out into the morning.

"Why didn't he tell us to git back to work?" Ti asked.

"Wish I knew," Alex answered.

"You think he's going to let us live?"

"Probably." It was the only logical answer for Ti,

knowing how emotional he'd become. Anything else would set him off.

"'Probably'? What do you mean by that?"

"Ti, give it a rest, okay? How the hell do I know. We're just going to have to do the best we can, that's all."

"What do we do now?"

"We check on Manny."

Alex rose and walked over under the hayloft and listened for a moment for any sound or movement.

"Manny, you okay?" he asked in a low voice. "Manny?"

No answer. No movement.

God, don't let him be dead, thought Alex. Aside from his concern for Manny, he had enough guilt right now to fill a dump truck.

A cough came from above him, then a weak, dry voice: "Fuck 'em if they can't take a joke."

Alex laughed with relief.

"I need something to pee in," the voice continued.

"You in much pain?" Alex asked as he watched the door.

"That's a stupid fuckin' question," the voice grated.

He's okay, Alex thought with a grin, *back to normal.*

Alex ran over and grabbed a couple of the empty gallon jugs. He filled one with cool water from the worm box.

"Come here," Alex said to Ti after he returned to the hayloft overhang.

"Bend down. I'll jump up on your back real quick and slide these on the edge to him." Ti nodded and complied.

Alex was able to balance just long enough to slip the jugs on the edge, then he fell to the dirt. Above, a hand appeared and dragged them out of sight.

Alex walked over and opened a bottle of shine, sniffed it, and took his first real swig. He grimaced.

"Have a feeling I'm going to need this."

6:31 a.m.

The chief snapped off Hank Williams in mid-note.

"From here on, I gotta keep a sharper ear and eye," he said. He was over halfway up the mountain, about two hours ahead of the schedule Harley'd set for him. The road was getting steeper, but the Cherokee four-wheel was making good time over the wet road, slogging through the water-filled ruts with ease. Plenty early to catch them off guard. He'd be at the house at about eight-thirty while they were still loading.

"Quack, quack, *bang!* Quack, quack, *bang!*" He chuckled. The image still tickled him this morning. That big bear of a man, Harley, going back and forth in the shooting gallery, both hands out in front of him like a dog up beggin'. Now that was funny!

He reached over and patted the ought-six on the seat next to him, then touched his jingling pocket that contained the splatter-their-guts hollow-points.

"—How's 'bout cookin' somethin' up with meeee?" he sang, finishing the song. "Yeah! Always hated you, Harley, you son of a bitch! We'll be cookin' up something for you, all right. Your fucking goose! Harley, you ugly, ignorant bastard! Yeehaw!"

7:02 a.m.

Jenny awoke with a start. She jerked up in the seat and looked around, disoriented at first. Back under the huge gum tree, it was so shaded she had trouble telling whether it was still dark out or not until she glanced in her rearview mirrors and saw the light from the clearing.

"Seven-oh-two. Gotta get moving," she said as she glanced at her watch. She considered the sandwich in the sack on the seat, but her bladder was crying for relief.

She checked both mirrors again, found nothing, and climbed down to the ground. The forest floor was spongy with undigested water. It still dripped from the canopy above her, and a slight rustle of wind brought a shower tinkling down as she stepped from under the tree. She ran back into some bushes and relieved herself, then came out into the clearing. On the other side of the road was an open spot that overlooked the valley.

"Maybe I can see something from there." She went to the truck for her binoculars, then crossed the road. She walked down between several trees and came out on the other side. A rabbit scampered back into the brush and she jumped. She laughed softly.

From the promontory, it was an imposing view. The wind was still warm, but had a slight bite left by the cooling rain. High in the sky, whitecapped gray clouds raced each other across the sky. Stretched out in front of her, the green-blanketed hills rolled on and on. Not a house, not a soul anywhere. It was breathtaking. The only evidence of man was the thin ribbon of road meandering back and forth below her, revealed in just short stretches between the trees. It wouldn't have surprised her if an Indian would have stepped from behind a tree.

The wind gusted.

Then she froze—

The sound of a truck or car—

Laboring in first gear down the road above her!

She ran back to the trees and hid at a point where she had a view of the road. After ten minutes of waiting, a small, olive-green moving van lumbered by, splashing water from the ruts, and went down the hill. She sighed with relief that her own truck was hidden so well under the tree. She ran back to the edge of the cliff and watched the van wend its way down the hill below her. At the second switchback the truck came to a stop, then backed up a little and pulled back into the trees. She kneeled down in the weeds so she would be less exposed, lifted her binoculars, and watched.

Her eyes burning from watching the underbrush, she finally picked up movement. A man. He came into the clear on the road. A huge man with a beard, hunting jacket, and baseball cap, walking casually, carrying a mean-looking pump shotgun.

"Jesus. How ugly can you get! What the hell are you up to?"

The man went to the next switchback below where he'd parked the truck and stopped in the middle of the road. He studied the bushes on either side, then sighted back and forth. He finally worked his way up into the brush on the outside of the curve and leaned on a felled timber. He aimed the shotgun at the corner, about twenty feet away, then raised and lowered the gun as though lining up the sights. Satisfied, he leaned it on the log. He lit a cigarette and settled back.

"He's waiting for something," she whispered curiously. She sat on a rock and stretched her neck to look. He was out of view for the moment, but she could still see a small wisp of smoke rising from the brush behind the fallen log.

"If you're waiting, I'm waiting too, big guy," she said. Her stomach had a small hollow spot in it that told her this meant something. She'd learned to pay attention to that feeling.

Intuition or just female curiosity. Whichever. With no better ideas, she was going to wait with him for a while.

"Lester! Where the hell are you?" Mae shrieked through the small cabin. She'd searched for him everywhere, even in Harley's room. That slut was still in there, lolling around like the Queen of Sheba long after the sun was up, even while she looked in the room.

"Probably get up at noon," Mae sniffed. "Where the hell is that boy?"

She hurried out into the yard and paced the perimeter of the fence with a parade of dogs panting along behind. *Couldn't o' made it through the fence,* she thought.

When she came back around to the back, she saw the

outhouse and got a chill. It reminded her how she'd taught that boy to hold on to the edges when he did his business. *He's so skinny, he'd go through like a greased pig if'n he din't hold on tight. Worried he'd fall through someday, but never has.* Maybe this was the day. Lord, what a way to die that would be.

She opened the door. The light shone in on Lester's small body. She bent down and touched his blue face. His head was canted at an awkward angle, and his eyes were already filmed over. Dead. No question. Even before she touched him, she knew it.

Even though she'd meant to put him out of his misery herself, she was wracked with pain. Tears clouded her vision as she touched his spidery hands, cold hands, one still wedged winglike against his body.

"First my daughter, then my son. First my daughter, then my son. First my daughter, then my son, First my . . ." She rocked back and forth and repeated it slowly, hypnotically, like a mantra. The dogs lay on the ground watching, confused and whimpering.

Finally, she stood and glowered at the barn.

Decisively, she marched toward the house.

"It was that cop. He done it. It was him. Everythin' was fine 'round here till he showed up!"

She slammed into the living room and jacked two shells into the chambers of her double-barreled gun.

"First my daughter, then my son.

"Gotta get to the barn.

"Got me some killin' to do."

38

7:52 a.m.

Jenny was about to give up the wait and was nodding off when she heard it.

A vehicle, slowly working its way up the switchbacks.

The sound was what she expected. Speeding up on the straightaways, then slowing to a crawl where the road did a 180-degree turn in the other direction. She leaned forward and focused on where the big man was hiding. The smoke from the cigarette was gone.

Put it out so he wouldn't be seen, she thought.

This was no accident. The big man must be expecting this vehicle to come up the road. Then she thought of the pump shotgun he carried.

"No. That can't be possible," she whispered.

But, what else would he be hiding for? her logical mind asked.

"Naw. Don't be melodramatic."

Could be possible. Stranger things have happened.

"People don't do that!"

She concentrated the binoculars on the bushes in front of the log. Nothing. Then behind the log.

The hairy, baseball-capped head popped up, and the bill whipped in the direction of the sound, then disappeared again, like a pheasant sneaking a peek out of deep weeds, looking for danger. The vehicle was one or two switchbacks below, still hidden behind the foliage.

That hollow spot in her stomach flared out and her skin chilled.

"Maybe people do that *up here,*" she whispered.

"Yeehaw!" the chief yelled. He had gotten bored without the sound of music and had flipped it on. "Drop Kick Me, Jesus" was the funniest damned song ever was, although the little old ladies in Picksburg had complained repeatedly to the station from Charleston. "God'll git you," they loved to say. He laughed.

Another half hour of this damned mountain and he'd be where he could park the truck and work his way down through the trees to the barn.

"Shit howdy!" he yelled as the song finished.

It was gonna clear up and be a great day this afternoon and the sun'd see him a rich man in his own right. Throw in bein' a local hero to spice it up, and it'd be a day to remember.

"Yes, by God, a day to remember."

8:12 a.m.

Jenny leaned forward when the red flash of the vehicle showed between the trees. It was heading toward the switchback below the man. When the machine slowed for that final corner, the binoculars would give her an unobstructed look into the driver's window while it turned left to come back this way.

She edged forward a little, now on one knee, and concentrated the binoculars' circles of light on that sharp turn. *I'll have two to three seconds at the most,* she speculated.

The motor slowed—slower, slower.

A red Cherokee flashed into her vision—

It has lights on the top. Police lights!

The man in the window was moving his mouth—

Singing? He's singing!

"Wha—? It's the chief!" she exclaimed, then ducked down when she realized she'd said it too loud.

She raised her head cautiously and focused the binoculars on the man behind the log. His cap was gone and just his hair and eyes were above the log now, staring in the direction of the approaching car, too intense to hear anything but that machine.

The car was going fast now, approaching, then slowing again, slowing—

It reached the curve moving at a crawl.

It started its turn—

She whipped the glasses to the log.

The man leaped to his feet holding up the gun—

Bang! Bang!

Two quick explosions—

Jenny fell back on her behind from the shock—

The reports echoed and reechoed through the hills.

As she struggled to regain her footing, the air was rent with two more concussions, then came the high-pitched revving of the engine of the car—

She regained her stance and looked up just in time to see the Cherokee rolling backwards, engine racing—back, back, back—until it slammed into a tree and the engine died.

She turned her glasses back to the log—

The huge man raised up, lumbered out onto the road, and walked nonchalantly toward the now quiet car. The only sound that floated up to her was the sharp *click-click* as he inserted another shell into the chamber.

"My God, my God," she whispered. Her heart was in her throat as he leisurely approached the red car, gun trained on the windshield. He walked around to the driver's side and jerked open the door. He climbed up on the running board and struggled inside, then bent in out of sight.

Must be pushing the chief's body to the floor, she guessed. What that powerful gun had done to the chief's head from twenty feet was horrifying to imagine.

The engine started and the car slowly pulled forward. The big man drove it up to the edge of the cliff directly below her, no more than two hundred feet away, then jerked it to a stop. She scrunched as far down into the weeds as she could get and still see.

If he spots me now, I'm dead for sure.

He climbed out of the car and laid his gun on the ground. The engine was idling. He looked out over the hills and casually took out his pack of cigarettes, struck a match, cupped it in his hands, and lit a cigarette.

What a cold bastard! No more than a walk in the park for him.

After several puffs, he reached inside the window and jerked something. The Cherokee immediately started to roll toward the edge. He jumped back just as it nosed over the edge and picked up speed.

Snap! crack! bang! The popping of the saplings on the hillside came up to her in crisp reports as the bouncing car cleared a path on its downward plunge. She was fascinated and frozen in place as she watched the huge man puffing the cigarette and following the car's path.

So relaxed!

She swung the glasses back down to the car as it vaulted off a steeper slope and bounced end over end, parts flying, disassembling quickly as it disappeared into the trees below with the corpse of the chief.

She had the binoculars focused on where the car had been swallowed up—almost hypnotized—then remembering, she swung them back to the giant man—

He was looking at her!

Without thinking about it, she found herself lying in the weeds gasping for breath.

Did he see me? pounded through her brain. *I should run. I should run, but I have to know to know for sure. Don't panic, don't panic!*

She waited for long moments, then with shaking hands, she raised to take a peek. He was gone! Her heart jerked in her chest. She swept the road with her glasses and found him.

He was trudging casually up the hill finishing his
cigarette, looking down at the muddy road as he walked.
His humming drifted up to her accompanied by the
twitter of birds, both contented now that the excitement
was over.

Thank God, he didn't see me. She relaxed a little. *Have
to get back to my truck now,* she thought. *Hide under the
tree until he's gone.*

She crab-crawled back a few feet until the promontory
hid her movements, then stood and jogged as quietly
back to the truck as she could. Sound carried in these
hills, and she took care to make as little as possible. In
the truck, she gently eased the door closed until it
clicked, then slammed down the lock button on both of
them. Under the gum tree, it was quiet and shaded. She
huddled down to wait, trying to make herself as small as
possible.

*This had something to do with Alex, but what? Following
that killer on this road is impossible with the trees and the
switchbacks. Dammit! I'd have to be within feet of him to
keep him in sight.*

She thought of calling Wesley on the radio, but was
afraid to talk out loud. Even if she whispered, the sound
might carry.

Heat warmed her eyes, but she was too scared to let it
out in a real cry, a cry she needed desperately.

All she could do was listen and quiver.

Listen for the truck to go by, back up the hill, if it was
going that way.

Listen for that killer to leave.

Please God. Let him leave.

Let him leave. Please God—

Please God—

Please.

The men leaped off their pallets as Mae came storming
into the barn, gun held high. They knew instantly
something was wrong because she always came in the
door tentatively.

"You killed my boy!" she screamed at Alex.

"Your boy's dead?" he asked.

"Don' try to pretend, play innocent. Bad things been happenin' since the day I brung you here. Don't try to deny it!" The shotgun quivered in her hand and her eyes were twin black coals. Off to the side, Ti whimpered and lowered back to his pallet, trying not to be noticed.

"How could I have killed him? He hasn't been out here in a couple of days. Relax. Put that down, and let's reason this out."

"Ain't gonna relax. You're the one's gonna relax, permanent-like!" She circled slowly until she stood with her back to the storage room. "You're gonna die soon's I find out what happened to my boy and Sarah!"

Alex's peripheral vision caught movement above. His glance flitted to the dark hayloft where Manny was quietly struggling his way to his feet. Manny was gesticulating to the floor, meaning for Alex to get her below him. The edge of the overhang was about thirty feet away.

Stalling for time, Alex said, "Sarah's fine, but I don't know anything about your boy. If you'll lower that scattergun, I'll tell you where she is. She's coming back, you know."

"I knowed it! I knowed you had somethin' to do with her hightailing it! Tell me where she is, now!"

"You kill me, you'll never find out where she is." Alex had to buy time, hope she'd calm down enough to get over her killing fever.

Mae's mouth worked as she scowled at him, the shotgun still centered on his chest. Manny was standing near the edge, wobbling as he gripped a vertical support. If she turned, she'd be able to see him clearly.

If I can get her to back up, he thought. *I'll have to gamble.*

"Sarah said she loved it here, but she couldn't handle what Harley was doing to her." He took two steps closer as he talked, trying to make it appear natural. She stepped back two steps to match his, mouth ruminating.

"Stand still," she threatened.

"You see, Sarah was a very loving child. All she ever wanted to do was to live in peace here with her mom and brother." (Another step.) "We had long talks about it, about living in your new house you were buying and she wanted to make things easier for you and everything." (Another step.) "Then the other night—"

"Told you to stay still, dammit. Git on with your story and stop movin' about."

"Don't mean to upset you, Mae. Back to my story. Oh, yeah. The other night she came out here and we were talking . . . right over here, in fact—" He walked brazenly to his right to the mash box and pointed to the floor as though it had some significance.

Have to keep moving, he thought. *Keep working her back.*

"You say your boy's dead? Gee, I'm sorry about that. Where'd you find him?" As he talked, he moved a little closer. She edged back a few feet unconsciously to keep the buffer between them. Less than ten feet from the overhang now.

"Boy's bein' dead got nothin' to do with Sarah. Found him in the outhouse out back. Now git on with it."

"The outhouse. That's terrible," Alex said as he shook his head. "Must have been killed by Harley, then, right? Our chains don't reach that—"

"Shut up! He ain't got no cause. You coulda choked him and he stumbled out there! Ain't been nothin' but trouble since you got here!"

"I know that, and I'm sorry about it," Alex forced himself to say. *Keep her talking,* he thought. *Dammit!* He was too far to the side to get her back under the area of the overhang that Manny was standing on, and if he passed her to go back to where Manny was, she might look up and see him. Manny was too weak to move. "Let me show you something in here that will prove what I'm telling you," he said and walked to the right under the overhang toward the door to the supply room.

"Stop! Right where you are, dammit!" she shouted. He

avoided looking back. This was his only chance, and he had to take it.

"Look, you can shoot me in a minute, I just want to show you this note she left to prove what I say is true," he said, and continued walking. One—two—three steps. If she was going to shoot it'd be now—

"Note? What note! Girl cain't write!"

"I wrote it for her," he shouted over his back. "They're her words for you." He made the door, his body tense, waiting for the blast. *Will it be painful or will I hear it at all?* Then to his relief, he heard scurrying steps behind him. Releasing his breath, he continued on into the supply room until he was sure she was in too.

Fake it! Fake it! his mind screamed. He had to get her out under that overhang or he had just minutes at the most to live.

"Damn! I'm sorry!" he said with a snap of his fingers, as though just remembering. "I put the note under my pallet for safekeeping." He turned and smiled. Disarmingly, he hoped.

Have to lead her back under the right spot of the overhang.

"Yer jerkin' me around, you bastard," she growled. Her voice was low and malevolent now. That made him more nervous.

"I can't stop you from doing what you want to, but you should read this before you decide. That girl really thinks a lot of you." He continued to smile, but it felt pasted on—as though he were showing a chipped tooth to his dentist.

She stepped aside and silently waved the gun back toward the main room. If he was forced to look under the pallet for the nonexistent note, that would be it. No more chances.

He walked slowly back through the door. *Have to let Manny know this is our only chance—*

He continued in a loud voice: "Yeah. When I get to that pallet, and if that note isn't there, I know you'll have the right to shoot me!" He prayed Manny would hear, and would understand this was his *only* chance. "Just follow right behind me to my pallet."

He broke under the overhang where he knew Manny was and took four steps.

He stopped and turned.

Manny toppled off the edge, more fell than jumped—

Missed her, but caught her shoulder with his arm.

Alex dove to the left—

Boom! The shotgun exploded—

A hot charge flashed by his shoulder—

She squealed in pain—

Alex hit—

And bounced up with the same motion, and leaped on her.

She reached to her mouth with her fingers to whistle—

Alex smashed his fist into her face and her nose collapsed.

Her hand was at her mouth—

He drew back and pounded *(goddamn you!)* and pounded *(I'll kill you!)* and pounded *(crazy bitch!)* and pounded her face *(crazy! crazy! crazy!)* until she lay still.

Blood gushed from her nose, ears, and mouth.

Gasping for air, he kneeled over, watching her face and hands for movement as he would a poisonous snake.

"Ooohhh!" Manny groaned and rolled back and forth in pain. Alex crawled to him quickly.

"I get her?" he asked, opening his eyes.

"We got her, buddy," Alex answered. "You saved my ass. I thought I was a goner sure as hell!"

"Jim Dandy to the rescue." He smiled thinly. "She dead?" He remembered what happened with Harley.

"Still breathing. She might not make it, though," Alex said.

"What do you mean, might? Kill her, man. Drown her in a vat if you have to," Manny urged.

"Relax. She's not going anywh—"

"You made me kill that man. You made me," Ti said in a quiet voice from behind them. Alex turned. Ti had the shotgun pointed at Mae's forehead.

"Don't, Ti, don't shoot her," Alex said as reasonably as he could. "We need that gun, that shell. We can blow off a couple of our chains with it, we—" He stood slowly so as not to frighten him. Ti's eyes were glazed and he wore a frightening rictus smile.

"The Bible says, 'Thou shall not kill' . . . but you made me kill that man. God knows I didn't want to do that, and He will forgive . . . me . . . for . . . my . . . sins . . . but . . . you . . . you . . . you." Ti's voice rose as he choked each word out.

Mae's eyes blinked open, and they fluttered when she saw the barrel inches from her forehead—

She gurgled blood, trying to say something—

"Ti, don't. She'll probably die anyway. You don't need to—"

Boom! Fire erupted from the barrel—

The top of Mae's head slammed into the dirt as her body jerked into the air!

Blood sprayed them.

"Yeah!" Manny gasped. Alex lowered to his knees next to Manny, too spent to move.

"I have to go to my room now and take a nap," Ti muttered in a vacant voice. He waddled away and let the shotgun slowly slide to the ground. At his pallet, he lay down and rolled over. He settled his head on his hands and started in a high, little-boy voice: "Now I lay me down to sleep—"

The two men sat on the ground and watched him in silence for a couple of moments.

"God help him," Alex whispered. "We get out of here alive, he's gonna be makin' baskets and wallets for a long time."

"—and God, please protect and help Manny and Alex too. Amen."

"Amen. We're going to need it," Alex added.

"We're going to need it a lot."

39

Ten minutes had passed since Jenny heard the van pass
and go up the hill. She held her breath when it went by
where she was pulled back into the trees, but it kept
grinding up the grade without hesitation.

*Another ten minutes, then I'll take off, I don't know
where I'll go, but I know I have to get the hell out of here,*
she thought.

She picked up the mike, flipped on the radio, and
called: "This is Jenny. Can you hear me?" She waited,
but the radio was silent, just crackled in response.

Dumb, she thought. *Stupid!* She knew nothing about
official radio jargon. "Over and out, ten four," she
mumbled absently to herself. "Catch you on the flip-flop,
good buddy." That one she'd heard in one of those
trucker movies. But that was a CB radio. Was there any
difference? *Damn! Who knows!*

She tried twice more before she gave up. Then she
leaned back. Her breathing had slowed to normal since
the big man left. *Five more minutes, and I'm out of here,*
she guessed.

Smash! Tinkle!

Glass sprayed her from the passenger's side—

She screamed—

When she opened her eyes, the menacing barrel of a
twelve-gauge was pointed at her face. At the end of the

barrel was the giant hairy head of *the man*. He was wearing his baseball cap and a smile.

"'Morning," he called through the smashed window. "You gonna snoop some, you best not be using that spyglass. Reflects the light, girlie."

Jenny was too frightened to move, too frightened to lie, too frightened to say anything. The giant man reached in casually and flipped up the lock. He pulled the door open quickly, and moved onto the glass-strewn seat with a speed that made her cringe back. He filled the interior, his filthy cap scraping the headliner.

She found her voice. "Wha—what do you want?"

He laughed, softly at first, then louder. Finally his giant chest rocked to a stop, his eyes narrowed, and he scanned her small frame slowly, his gaze resting on her breasts, then crawling along her body. The way he did it made Jenny's legs even weaker.

"I like your truck," he said slowly, "and you."

"You want the truck?" she asked. "I'll get out—you can have it." She reached for the door handle.

"Don't."

His voice froze her. The gun was pointed at the floor, but having seen him move, she knew she would never make the ground.

When she lowered her hand from the handle, he smiled broadly.

"What you got in the back, girlie?" he asked.

"Empty."

"What you doin' up here—a soft, little ball o' city fluff like you?"

"Looking for my husband." She was out of made-up stories.

He tapped the dash with his meaty hand, surveying the size of the machine as she watched him. "Lookin' for your husband, huh?"

She nodded. "Out camping," she added. "Guess he got lost."

"You guess. Who you with?"

"There's eight of us. They're out hunting for him in

the woods. They know where I am, and will be here in a couple of minutes."

He laughed derisively. "Girlie, anybody tell you what a lousy fucking liar you are? Ain't nobody uses this kind of truck for camping. Sheeit!" His voice was harsh and it stunned her to silence.

He smirked.

His powerful arm came across, and he laid his hand on her thigh.

She screamed, "No!" and pushed it away.

The back of his hand came up and smacked hard into her nose, making her eyes water. Her head was dizzy and her heart raced. *This can't be happening!*

He moved his hand to her thigh again. She instinctively pushed it again.

The blow knocked her head back, and she felt it bounce off the back of the seat. Lights flashed in her mind, and the dash wavered, then came back into focus. The coppery taste of blood filled her mouth.

His hand was on her thigh again. She shook and started sobbing softly as he kneaded it hard—hard enough to hurt.

"Quiet! Shut up!" he shouted.

She stifled back the sobs, but her body continued to quake.

"That's better," he soothed as he rubbed her. "How you like to be fucked?" His voice was husky.

So frightened she was close to passing out, to losing complete control—she opened her mouth, but only a strangling squeak emerged. Her vocal cords were paralyzed.

"Too excited to answer, huh?" he asked in a suggestive tone. "Panties really wet 'cause you want it so bad, huh?"

In response, she choked.

"You like to be fucked with people watching?"

"N-no." Her voice finally worked.

"Great! It'll be a whole lot more fun for *me* that way," he said. He released her and leaned back as though he'd made a decision. Watching her carefully, he waited for a minute as she struggled to recover.

"Can you drive?"

She nodded, not knowing if she could, but afraid to say no. Her teeth clicked together from fear, too terrified to be embarrassed.

"Yeah. This big four-wheel'll make it down that hill just fine with a load. Was worried about the van in the mud, you know."

"Are you going to kill me?" she asked weakly.

"Shit, no, honey. Kill you? You couldn't enjoy what we're gonna do if you was dead, now could you?"

"What are you going to do to me?"

"Feel good, honey. I'm gonna make you feel *really* good. Now start this engine. I wanta get loaded! Been away too long."

9:57 a.m.

"I think the damned thing's busted," Alex said.

Manny had tried to stand, but his ankle had given way. After he'd fallen, he'd just lain on the hard-packed ground and groaned.

Ti was standing at the wall, stacking and restacking the empty glass jars to no purpose, mumbling to himself while he worked.

"I figured as much," Manny finally managed as he grimaced from the pain. "What am I gonna do?"

"Well, Harley thinks you're gone. No time to stack the bags to put you up on the hayloft again. We'll hide you in the storage room. I can make up something behind the sugar bags."

"Great. Buried in a fucking tomb. My favorite. God-damn it, that hurts!" he said as he reached futilely for his ankle with his remaining hand.

"I know. Listen, I have to get to work now before he gets back."

"How about Ti? He's not going to be able to work, you

know. That thing with Mae finished blowing out his pilot light. And what the hell you gonna do with her?" Manny motioned to Mae's body to his left.

"I'll try to bring Ti back to earth when I finish. Might have to throw a couple of bags on Mae and sink her in a vat if I don't have time to dig a shallow grave. The dirt should be pretty soft in the last one. Let me help you up. I'll take you into the storage room, out of sight. No more talking. If he comes now, we're all screwed."

Manny groaned and struggled to his feet with Alex's help. He tried to hop as Alex supported him, but ran out of gas. Alex picked him up, carried him into the room, and laid him down by the sugar bags. The bandages on Manny's left arm had bled through, but as well as Alex could tell, the bleeding was minor. Alex ran and got a jar of shine, and Manny drank some to kill the pain.

Alex made a stack of sugar bags along a blank section of the wall, about eighteen inches away. He helped Manny behind it, then stacked bags on the top, shutting him in. When he was finished, he slid two in each end, closing up the space.

"You okay?" Alex asked.

"Talk about fucking claustrophobic," Manny's muffled voice said through the cracks.

Alex ran back into the barn and looked out the door, checking for movement. Nothing. Then to the wall that contained the graves. He went to the last one and dug with his hands as fast as he could in the loose dirt. It took ten minutes to open up a space two feet deep.

He grabbed Mae's body by the hands and dragged her to the hole and dropped her in, looking away all the time. He'd seen enough gore and shit and filth to last a lifetime.

Burying her was even quicker. He stomped the sour earth down, breathed deeply, and stopped for a moment. Unaware that his heart had been racing, he was suddenly lightheaded. He realized he'd had nothing to eat today.

In the corner, a stack of jars fell and broke. Ti looked down at them, then up at Alex with a guilty look.

"Ti make boo-boo," he whined. Alex ran his fingers through his hair and tried to control his frustration.

"Listen to me, please. Do you know who I am?"

Ti shook his head and smiled. Outside the barn Alex could hear the sound of a truck approaching. A more powerful engine, not the van.

"Ti, that's probably Harley coming. Do you remember Harley?"

"Bad man," Ti said, and cringed away.

"Why don't you lay down, please? Come over here and lay down so you'll feel better, okay?" He took Ti by the arm and led him to the pallet.

"Ti lay down . . . sleep," Ti mumbled, and allowed Alex to lower him to the slats of the pallet.

"Go to sleep, Ti. You feel better in a few minutes," Alex said. Ti rolled over obediently and closed his eyes.

Alex thought, *Poor bastard. Few more days and I'll escape with you to wherever you've gone. I wonder, which one of us is better off?*

40

The barn came into view through the windshield when they broke around the last turn. Jenny was shaking, emotionally exhausted, frantically searching for a way out. This man was crazy, and after what she'd seen, there was no possibility he would let her live. Coming up the hill, she'd considered turning off a cliff a couple of times. She'd measured trying to jump clear before the truck went over, but as heavy as the doors were, and with him grabbing for her, chances of success would be zero.

"Blow the horn," he ordered as they ground to a halt in front of the twelve-foot-high gate. Jenny glared at him and hit the horn two times. The only response was more barking and bounding from the three dogs who'd arrived to greet them. "Again!" he yelled. He pounded impatiently on the dashboard with his fist. Jenny jumped. "Damn fool woman, git out here!" he bellowed through his missing window. Jenny stared at the gate, afraid to look at him.

He reached down, turned off the ignition key, and pulled it out. "You don't move," he warned. He climbed out with his shotgun, and walked to the fence. The weapon guaranteed she had no possibility of escaping. She might be able to run as fast as he could, hide in the woods maybe, but with the gun . . . no way.

He unlocked the padlock and pulled it from the big chain, then lifted the latch, and swung the door wide.

Coming back to the driver's side, he motioned for her to move over. She did. He climbed in, started the truck, and drove it through.

What a strange setup, she thought as she looked around. *A large open space with a huge barn and small adjacent cabin sitting in the middle. All surrounded by this high, locked chain-link fence. Strange—why would they enclose a barn like that, especially with not much farm country this high up?*

He drove the truck to the front door of the cabin and jerked back the emergency brake. Without speaking, he grabbed Jenny's left wrist and dragged her from the truck to the ground. He left the shotgun in the truck.

"Oww!" she complained. "You're hurting my arm." The dogs crowded around, but he kneed them back.

A barefoot woman with red hair and shorts stood at the door as he pulled Jenny into the living room.

"Where the hell you been all this time, Harley?" the woman asked. "And who the hell is she?"

"Shut up, Ellie. I got work to do and I don't wanna listen to your mouth." He threw Jenny on the filthy, blanket-covered easy chair. She sat and rubbed her injured wrist.

Ellie blurted out, "There's been a shootin' in the barn and Mae hasn't come back and I can't go out because o' them damned dogs and—"

Harley's hand flashed out and cracked Ellie across the face. She stumbled back. "Bring a rope from that kitchen," he demanded.

Ellie disappeared, and Jenny heard rustling from the kitchen. She returned, rubbing her face, and docilely handed the rope to him. Intimidated, Jenny sat and watched quietly.

"Weren't no need to hit me," Ellie whimpered. "I's just worried is all."

Harley quickly cut two sections of rope with his knife, then tied Jenny's hands and feet where she sat.

"Then worry to yourself," he grumbled as he finished. "How many shots you hear from the barn?"

"Two," Ellie said. "Wide-spaced. One, then another about two minutes later."

Harley smirked. "You stay here and keep an eye on this city woman whilst I check on things and load the truck." She nodded reluctantly, still rubbing her face.

Jenny looked up at Ellie as the giant she called Harley disappeared into the hallway. Jenny heard a loud crashing, then the splintering of boards. A few more kicking noises and more breaking of boards.

This is crazy. These people are crazy. I'm never going to get out of here, she thought.

Harley returned. He stood smiling in the doorway holding a handful of money in one hand and a heavy revolver in the other.

"Had me worried for a minute, her being gone and all. Thought for a second she might of split with the cash. Get a big bag and wrap this money and what's in the cabinet, then get our things ready to leave. I'll be back in about forty-five minutes," he said.

He spun the cylinder on the gun, then slammed out the door.

Alex was leaning against the barn door, holding the shotgun. He had one card to play, and that was it. Bluffing Harley with an empty shotgun.

The cabin door slammed. He'd been busy securing Manny's hiding place when the truck drove in the yard. Now he was ready. Exactly how this was going to play out, he had no idea. *I can probably keep him away for so long, but then what?*

Harley's steps came closer in the wet yard.

Alex stepped to the open door and leveled the shotgun at his chest. Harley kept walking, staring at him.

"Stop where you are!"

"I could play this silly-ass game with you, might even be fun, but I want to get the truck loaded," Harley said, and walked closer. Twenty feet now.

"I'll shoot," Alex warned.

"Go ahead," Harley said and kept walking. His smile got wider the closer he came.

"I'm warning you," Alex said.

Harley stopped, took the gun out of his waistband, and hefted it in his hand.

"I'm going to count to three. You throw that gun into the yard at three, or I'll have to kill you, boy," Harley said. "One, two—"

Alex threw the shotgun out into the yard, saying "Damn." *He has to know it's empty,* he thought. He felt pathetically inept.

"That's better, now back away from the door."

"How'd you know?" Alex asked as he moved back into the barn.

"I just look dumb, boy. Ellie heard two shots. Mae don't carry no more'n a double load. It's her habit. Folks don't change." He stopped at the opening and looked around. "Where'd you stuff her body?"

"What do you mean?" Alex stalled.

"Told you 'fore I was gonna kill her myself. I wanna know where she is so's I can account for her's all. Let's save time with the games, okay?"

The charade was pointless, so Alex pointed to the freshly tamped grave. Harley walked over and took a couple of steps on the newly packed earth, then smiled up at Alex.

"God, that gives me some pleasure, Mae. A-walkin' on your face under the ground." He looked serious. "Who killed her?"

"We did," Alex said. And that was the truth. She might have died from the blows he gave her. Ti had probably just hurried it along with the shotgun.

"I'm gonna back up the truck to here. You wake up your fat friend now. I want to get it loaded." Harley walked to the truck.

Alex hurried over to Ti and jostled him. "Wake up, Ti," he shouted. Ti waved at his hand in his sleep and grumbled something. "Get up, now!" If Ti refused to get up. Harley would kill him where he lay.

Finally, Ti roused and sat up, rubbing his eyes.

"Is it time to go to school?" he asked in a sleepy voice.

"Ti, stand up. We have to load the truck."

"Is breakfast ready?"

The rear of the huge truck pulled in front of the open door. The engine stopped and Alex heard steps.

"Stand up. You have to get to work or Harley'll shoot you, don't you understand?" Alex reached out and slapped him lightly in the face with his open hand. Ti looked shocked, then started crying loudly.

"What the hell's going on?" Harley asked as he approached.

"Just a disagreement," Alex said, trying to cover as long as possible.

"Stop that crying, dammit! I hate a cowardly man!"

Ti snuffled, wiped his eyes, and asked, "Can I go home now?"

Harley studied him for a moment, then looked at Alex. "He addle-brained?"

Alex shrugged. "He'll be all right. Just give him a couple of minutes."

"I don't have minutes." He turned back to Ti. "Git over there and grab hold them cases and start loading that truck!"

Ti shuffled over to the shine cases and stood wavering in front of them as though not understanding what he was supposed to do next.

"Let me help him," Alex said. "He just needs to get started." Alex picked up a case and handed it to Ti. "Take it to the truck over there, Ti," Alex said in a gentle voice, a tone he hoped Ti might respond to. Ti turned with the case and started shuffling toward the truck. Alex heaved a sigh, grabbed a case, and carried it past Ti, who was inching along, eyes glazed.

Alex lowered the tailgate, and was sliding the case in when he looked back. Ti was waddling toward his pallet with his case. Harley watched him, unbelieving. Ti set the case down gently, lay down on his pallet, and rolled over—apparently intending to go back to sleep.

"No, Ti!" Alex shouted.

Harley walked over to Ti and demanded, "Get up now, boy, and get the truck loaded!" In response, Ti settled his head in on his hands and mumbled something incoherent. His mind had apparently rejected reality completely.

"Let me try to help him!" Alex yelled. "Don't kill him!"

"Get back to work or I'll kill you both and load the truck myself!" Harley leveled the gun at Alex with a wild look. Alex backed away toward the stacks of shine.

Harley walked over to Ti and stood over him, the huge revolver pointed at Ti's head. "Last chance, boy!" A thin snore came from the pallet.

My God. He's asleep, thought Alex, then held his hand out to say stop—

The gun exploded—

Ti bounced on the pallet—

Harley whipped the barrel around to point at Alex.

"Now, can we get that fucking truck loaded?"

The shot rocked the inside of the cabin and Jenny jumped.

"What's he doing? Killing your cows?" she asked with a nervous giggle. Ellie had just walked from the bedroom, carrying two suitcases with a shopping bag under her arm.

"You wouldn't think it was so funny if you knew what he was a-doin'," Ellie said as she set her load down by the door, being extra careful with the shopping bag. She walked over and dropped to the floor in front of Jenny, then slipped her shoes on her dirty bare feet.

"Are you that man's girlfriend?"

"Harley? S'pose you'd call me that."

"Do you know he just killed a man?"

"Ain't none of my doin'." Ellie looked uncomfortable and hugged her knees.

"He killed the Picksburg chief of police in cold blood."

"Said he was gonna," Ellie said. "Ain't no way you

can stop Harley from doin' anything once he sets his cap
to it."

Jenny's mind raced. Once he was done in the barn, she
guessed that this Harley guy intended to kill *her*. He'd
have no reason to take her with them. She was confused
why he had brought her along and tied her up unless he
meant to carry out his threat to use her sexually. The
thought chilled her. That had to be what he had in
mind—keeping her prisoner for his own fun and games.

I'll die first, she thought. *He can't make me!* Even as
she thought it, she remembered his speed and strength.
Her face was still numb from where he'd hit her.

Ellie got to her feet, walked over, and leaned out the
door. The dogs barked, and Jenny could hear them
running this way. Ellie slammed the door.

"Bastards!" Ellie screamed. "Hate them damned dogs.
Cain't even stick your head out that door lest they's on
you! Cain't wait to get out of here!"

"What's he going to do with me?" Jenny asked.

Ellie shrugged as she returned and sat again.

"He's going to kill me, isn't he."

"Ain't my doin'. Harley does what he's a mind to."

"Why don't you let me go. I won't tell anyone," Jenny
said.

Ellie laughed derisively. "Firstwise, them dogs'd have
you before you made twenty feet, missy. Second, Harley'd kill me for sure if'n I did."

"You can go with me. You want to get away from here
too, don't you?"

"Why'd I want to do that?" The heavy makeup on her
forehead cracked into a frown.

"Everything I've read about psychopaths tells me that
people like him always end up killing those close to
them, don't you know that?"

"Harley? Kill me? I don't believe that." Her body
language and tortured eyes indicated she was unsure.

"Always happens. You can only keep him happy for so
long. He's probably already planning on disposing of
you, then getting another girl. Maybe killing you even

before he leaves here. Other boyfriends just drop their girlfriends, but not him. You know too much. He'll never risk you running around free. It's too easy just to kill you."

"You're lyin', tryin' to confuse me. I know what you're doin', and I ain't listenin' no more." She stood and went to the window. Her crossed arms and firm-set mouth said the subject was closed.

"Whether you want to listen or not, he'll kill you. You know it as well as I do. That's why you don't want to hear it!"

Frowning, Ellie came back and stood in front of her. Her foot was tapping and her anger was boiling over.

"How do you know so much? You don't know shit! Probably never had a real man in your life!"

"I'm married to a man, not some sadistic beast like that animal. He'll kill you sure as hell, Ellie, and you know it! That's why you're mad. Because you don't want to think about it."

"Fuck you! He will not. Harley loves me!"

"That's a laugh! A man like that never loves anyone. He doesn't have any concept of love."

"Well—we'll see who has the last laugh, honey," Ellie said with a sneer. "I hear him comin'. He's done loadin' and your skinny little ass is in deep shit!"

Ellie laughed and walked to the door.

Alex went into the storeroom and pulled a sugar bag out of the end where Manny's head was. Manny looked up and asked, "Are they gone?"

"No. Harley and his girl's still here. He killed Ti."

Manny choked and tears instantly flooded his eyes. "Son of a bitch! I was just starting to like him. He was a pain in the ass, but I was getting to like him, I really was."

"I know, so was I," Alex said. "Listen. Harley'll be back in a minute. When he leaves, he'll kill me too. Fact is, I expected him to shoot me after the truck was loaded. Anyway, I wanted to pull this bag away so you'll have a chance to try to get away after they leave. The knife's still under my pallet. Maybe you can get to the house. Who knows, he might let the dogs out of this barn area when he leaves. Maybe then you can find the keys and get that old Packard fired up. You might be the only one to get out of here alive after all."

"Don't you have any ideas? Anything you could do?"

"No. There aren't going to be any happy endings to this one. Just remember me when you're out fishing, okay? Have an extra beer for me."

"Maybe you could stab him." Manny's voice was frail and tremulous.

"He hasn't gotten within twenty feet of me, and he's always armed. Not a chance. Listen, I'd better get in there now. Can't have him find me in here. I'll stand the bag up at the end. When you hear the truck leave, you can just tip it over and crawl out."

"You've been a good friend," Manny said. "Sorry about that game thing. You forgive me?"

"Nothing to forgive. As a matter of fact, I thought it was pretty clever." Alex smiled. "I'd better go now. Remember what I said about the beer."

Manny nodded.

Alex dragged the bag over and propped it up. He angled it so that when it fell, it would fall away from the hole and make it easier for Manny to get out. Alex walked into the barn and sat on the pallet.

Should get up, do something. Get the knife. Attack him as he comes in the door. Useless, he thought.

"Now way he's going to get close enough knowing that I know he's going to kill me." Alex looked around at the wall where the long string of graves lay.

He thought, *Ten or more men including Josh. Then there was Landry. God, it seems so long ago that I came to on this pallet, reeking of carbon monoxide.*

Mae dead. Sarah dead. Landry dead, the boy dead—

He looked over where Ti lay in the same position as when Harley had shot him. He could have been sleeping except for the blood dripping to the ground.

And Ti dead—simple, harmless Ti.

And likely Manny too. In his condition, even if the dogs are gone, it's a slim chance he'll make it down the mountain even if he can get that old car started.

Alex sat up straighter.

The dogs were barking.

Harley was coming—

Alex took one last look out the hole at the top of the barn. The clouds were thinning and patches of blue were showing through. It looked like it was going to clear up.

He hoped Jenny was enjoying it, wherever she was.

"Git in there!" It was Harley's voice, but Ellie was the first one through the door. "Where is he?" Harley asked.

"Over by the other wall," she said and stepped away from the door to make room.

Harley walked in, half dragging a woman behind him—

That woman—she looks like—

Jenny?! No! Not Jenny! his mind screamed.

Alex stood up, blinked his eyes, and his jaw dropped. He was shocked and confused. Harley pushed Jenny over by the still, about thirty feet away from where Alex was standing. Harley held the heavy revolver in his left hand. Jenny was looking back at Harley in terror, unaware of the barn or who was in it.

My God. Please don't let her recognize me, he thought. *If she does, no telling what he'll do—*

"What do you think of her, cop?" Harley asked.

Jenny turned and looked at Alex, studying him closely, but there was no recognition in her eyes.

Alex suddenly realized what an apparition he must be, stripped and filthy, body raked with scratches, hair askew and matted, heavy stubble of beard.

"Alex? Alex?" Her voice was questioning and hopeful at the same time. *Damn! No way out of this now.*

"It's me. My God, Jen—what are you doing h—"

"You two know each other?" Harley demanded.

"Alex! Alex!" Jenny screamed, suddenly out of con-

trol, struggling with the powerful hand that held her.
"Alex!"

"Let her go!" Alex yelled and moved toward him.

Harley lowered the huge handgun in Alex's
direction—

Boom! It exploded.

Fire flashed from the barrel and the sound reverberated in the hollow building.

The whining bullet missed by a foot—

The concussion shook Alex.

He froze, Jenny stopped struggling.

"Don't shoot him—" Jenny cried. "Please, don't shoot
him!"

"Shut up!" Harley yelled. "How do you two know
each other?"

"She's my wife, dammit," Alex said. "Let her go—"

Jenny started crying.

"I'll be damned. Small world, ain't it? You wasn't
lying, was you, little lady?" Harley said. "You *was*
hunting for your husband."

Ellie said, "Harley, honey. We got the money and
shine. Why don't we leave now and—"

"Ellie, shut your pie hole!"

"But—"

"Quiet!"

Ellie slunk back to the still.

Harley smiled. "Well, ain't this a caution?" The
situation amused him and Alex could tell he wanted to
string it out.

"Leave her alone! She doesn't know anything—
please," Alex forced himself to say. The world *please*
stuck in his throat.

"Now, you and me'd got along a mite better if'n you'd
a used that tone 'fore now," Harley said. He turned his
head to Ellie. "Woman, go in the house and fetch that
rope we used on this woman."

Ellie started to leave, then stopped, and said, "Wait, I
cain't go out there. You know that. Them dogs—"

He raised his fingers and whistled. Loping sounds

came from outside, then all three dogs broke through the door, scanning faces, and settled on Harley. They ran to him.

"Sit!" Harley commanded. The powerful dogs whined, then obeyed, twitching their tails with barely controlled energy. "Git!" he directed to Ellie. "You only got about a couple minutes. They's mean-tempered sitting still."

Ellie trotted nervously out the door, glancing back.

"Who you got up here searchin' with you, girl?" Harley asked.

"Told you, there are eight of us!"

"Don't lie to me, girl!"

"I'm not lying. Had to have friends help. I've tried to get the chief to come up here, the newspapers, everybody—but nobody is interested, so I came with friends."

Harley laughed. "Never give up with the lies, do you? But one thing that's true, the chief sure ain't goin' to be interested."

"Let her go," Alex insisted in an even voice. Harley ignored him and looked toward the entrance.

The cabin door slammed—

The largest black dog stood and skulked toward the door—

"Satan! Come here!" The dog froze, turned, and returned to his sitting position. "Good boy."

Satan. That figures, thought Alex. *That's as close to Hitler as you can get.*

Ellie came in the door and stood transfixed, watching the dogs.

"Move to the side, girl!" Harley said. She did. "Out!" he ordered the dogs. They instantly leaped up and ran into the yard, glad to be released.

"How are you, Alex? Are you hurt?" Jenny asked. "Let me go to him, please."

"Not now," Harley said.

Not ever, thought Alex.

"Tie that boy's ankles and wrists tight as a drum," Harley said to Ellie.

"Shit, Harley. He's chained, ain't he?"

"That's a fact, but the damned thing is too long."

"Dammit, Harley. I wanna go. What we foolin' with these people for?"

"Fun, woman. I'm gonna have me some fun." He glared at her. "Do it now!"

She walked over to Alex and said, almost apologetically, "Sit down, please."

Alex glared at her, then at Harley, and said, "Go to hell!"

Harley held the gun up to Jenny's head. "Boy, you ain't got no cards left. You want her to die right now?"

"Let her go, damn you. She hasn't done anything. If there's an afterlife, I swear to God I'll find you somehow and kill you."

"I ain't scared of ghosts, I'm only scared of bullets—like you should be, boy."

Alex reluctantly dropped to his pallet and glared while Ellie tied his ankles, then his hands. She scurried back behind Harley.

"Dear God, what are you going to do to me?" Jenny asked, and started squirming in his grip again. "Dammit! Let me go!"

Harley laid the gun behind him, stood, then smacked her to the ground with a loud cracking sound. Jenny's head bounced when she hit the hard-pack. She groaned, stunned.

"You cowardly son of a bitch!" Alex screamed, and struggled with his bonds. "Leave her alone, or I'll kill you!" The rope was ripping his skin and making his hands wet with blood.

"This is gonna be fun!" Harley bellowed and laughed. In back of him, Ellie cringed behind her hands.

"Don't Harley," she squealed. "Let's go—"

"When I'm done, girl."

Harley dropped above Jenny with his knees on either side of her and patted her face. "Wake up, girl. You gotta be awake for this."

Jenny moaned, and her eyes fluttered open—

"What you gonna do, Harley? Let's get out of—"

"I ain't gonna tell you one more time, Ellie. Shut your face!"

"Don't . . . don't . . . don't . . ." Jenny said weakly, and held up her hands to defend herself.

"That's better," Harley said. He reached down and grabbed the front of her blouse and ripped it open. Jenny screamed as the buttons flew. Two more jerks and it was gone in shreds. She tried to cover herself and started kicking at him with her feet.

"Yeehaw!" he yelled, and grabbed her waist and ripped open her belt. In a smooth motion, ignoring the hands beating futilely on his chest, he pulled her jeans down. He stood and jerked them off her feet.

Jenny pulled up into a fetal position in her bra and panties, crying and begging incoherently—

Standing over her, Harley reached down and zipped down his fly and withdrew his erection—

"No! You bastard! NOOOOO!" Alex's voice was desperate as he bounced up and down on his pallet in a frenzy. "You can't! Not Jenny! No! NO! NO!"

Boom!

The explosion rocked them to silence—

Harley turned slowly, his hand still holding his erection—

Ellie stood, two hands holding the smoking gun toward the ceiling where she'd fired it. She lowered it to Harley.

"What? What you doin', girl?" Harley asked. His voice was soft now. "Put that gun down. I'll forget this, forget you done this."

Jenny still whimpered.

"No, I cain't." Ellie's lips were quivering. "I'm your girl, and you was gonna—"

"No, honey. You got it wrong. I was just tryin' to scare them is all. You know, have a little fun. You're my girl, honey. This biddy girl don't interest me none."

"Bullshit!" Ellie spat out. "What you're a-holdin' says otherwise!"

"This?" He pulled in and zipped his pants. "This don't mean nothin', you know that. Hell I can get hard lookin' at a couple dogs screw. . . ." Harley laughed nervously. "Give me the gun now, honey. We'll get in the truck and take off for Miami, just like you want. Have that tea out on the lawn and all. Right now. We'll start spendin' that—"

"Don't believe him, Ellie! He'll kill you if you give him that gun!" Alex shouted. "Don't do it! Shoot him if you want to live!"

Harley took one step toward her.

"Stop," she said, wavering.

"Shoot him, Ellie. He'll kill you if you don't," Jenny yelled. "He can't afford to let you live now, can't you—"

"Don't listen to that bullshit, baby. You know I . . . I love you," Harley said reasonably. He smiled and reached out his hand and took another step.

"He'll kill you! Shoot him!" Alex roared. "Don't believe him."

"Don't take another step, Harley," Ellie warned. He stopped with a quizzical look. "You been beatin' me and treatin' me like dirt all these months, makin' me do them awful thing in motels—an' here—"

"I thought you liked—"

"No! I hate it! I only put up with it 'cause I figured you loved me and someday things'd be different."

"They will, honey . . . why, I can—"

"No, they won't! I seed what you's really like, right here. Down in the dirt, gruntin' and ruttin' like a boar pig. That's the way you mean it to be for me from now on! Nothing's ever gonna change!" Ellie's voice was getting shriller, more out-of-control.

"You give me that gun now, woman," Harley ordered, his voice deeper. He was changing his tack. Sweet talk was failing so he was going back to what he knew. "I'll forget this if you give it to me now, but if you make me madder—"

"You'll what? Kill me? Kill me like you kill everythin' you touch! I oughta blow that off for you!" she said, looking at the lump in his crotch.

Harley took another step toward her—

She aimed the gun at his swollen pants—

"Don't move!" she screamed.

Harley took two quick steps—

Ellie shrieked—

Boom! The gun thundered—

Harley was knocked back, then dropped to his knees. Blood spurted from his crotch. He looked down questioningly and dropped both hands to try to stem the flow of blood.

"You shot me, you bitch—I'm gonna kill you for that!"

Harley struggled to his feet and lurched at her—

Boom! The gun exploded again.

The round caught him in the upper chest.

Harley stumbled back and fell like a felled oak and lay still. The two women cried in unison in the silence that followed.

"Jenny—Jenny!" Alex called. She leaped to her feet, ran over, dropped down, and put her arms around him. She kissed his face all over, then stopped.

Ellie was moaning, crying, and pointing the shaking gun at them.

Jenny screamed, "Ellie, you don't have to shoot us. That was self-defense when you shot him—any court will turn you free! Think, Ellie—"

"No! You saw it . . . he made me do it . . . I didn't want to do it . . . they'll kill me now . . . the Burris family . . . I've got to . . . I've got to." Her gaze was bounding from them to the still figure of Harley lying about thirty feet away. She was hysterical and getting worse.

"No, you're safe now. I'll help you to—"

"No! No! They'll kill me! You don't know them! They'll kill me. I've gotta take the money and run . . . run . . . run!"

Ellie turned and charged through the barn door—

Disappeared around the end of the truck.

Ellie screamed.

Padding feet—barking—

"My God," Alex yelled. "The dogs!"

Gnashing, growling, and a loud thudding against the metal side of the truck came through the door.

Continual screams now from Ellie—raising and lowering—

"Ohhh! No! Oooh! NOOOO!"

Bang! A gunshot.

A dog yelped in pain—

"She got one!" Alex said. "My God!"

Boom! Another shot—barking, screaming, and the *grr*ing and ripping sounds of dogs viciously shaking something.

"Jesus . . . owww . . . Jesus help me. . . ." Ellie's voice, faint now, fading.

Jenny huddled close to Alex, quaking uncontrollably.

Above the sounds of the snapping dogs Alex heard an approaching *thwop, thwop, thwop* sound.

"A helicopter?" he whispered. They both looked toward the door where the dogs were quieter now and the blades of the helicopter pounding the air were louder, coming nearer the barn.

"It's Wesley," Jenny said. "He made it. He'll see the truck—

"Owwww!" Jenny was rudely jerked to her feet.

Alex looked up and Harley was wavering back and forth holding Jenny's thin wrist.

Harley's pants were soaked with blood and his shirt was spotted, front and back.

"Come with me, girlie—you'll be insurance for gettin' down the mountain! Stupid bitch Ellie shoulda made sure I was dead. Faked it till she ran out that door like a chicken with its head off—"

The steady *thump, thump* of the helicopter was vibrating the timbers of the old building.

"Let her go, damn you!" Alex shouted.

"Boy, you do learn slow—" Harley winced at his pain, glared at Alex one last time, then stumbled out the door dragging Jenny with him—

41

In the yard, Jenny glanced up at the helicopter. It was about a half mile away and closing fast. It was the steel-gray color of the Huey.

"Wesley, hurry! Hurry!" she shouted even though she knew he couldn't hear.

At the truck, Ellie's unmoving body lay bleeding from the neck and arms. Jenny quivered and turned away from the gore as the two remaining dogs came to greet Harley, bored with the body. Harley took her to the passenger's side of the truck, ripped open the door, and flung her in. Jenny was amazed at his remaining strength. The shopping bag and shotgun were on the floor.

"You move from here, them dogs'll have you!" Harley said as he grabbed the shotgun, then slammed the door. "Got to put that gate up!" He went to the back of the truck.

"Jenny! Jenny! You in the truck!" came Wesley's voice from the radio. The helicopter was directly overhead now, hovering.

Jenny grabbed the mike and keyed it. "When we leave, land in the yard and get Alex out of the barn!" she yelled. "He's tied up and—"

Harley's hand came through the open window, grabbed the mike, ripped it out, and threw it hard against the barn.

"Stupid bitch!" he shouted, then limped out into the middle of the yard with the shotgun.

"Bastard! See how you like this!" he yelled. Leaning back, he fired round after round in the direction of the helicopter. The machine dipped and disappeared below the trees on the horizon.

"God, let him be all right," Jenny implored. No smoke came from the machine, it just dove out of sight. The two dogs, fresh from the kill, were in a frenzy of agitation with the new noise. They bounded around Harley. He threw the empty shotgun to the ground and picked up the revolver lying next to Ellie, then swung up into the cab.

He started the truck, raced the engine, and pulled forward, slowly picking up speed. Not bothering to stop, he accelerated through the high gate. It collapsed meekly under the wheels of the juggernaut of a truck, with barely a bump and a jostle as they rolled over it. Behind them, glass crashed to the bed of the truck. The two dogs galloped through the opening in pursuit.

"Dammit!" Harley yelled. His eyes were intent on the road as Jenny studied him. He was losing massive amounts of blood, mostly from his crotch area. The shot in his chest seemed to be a clean in-and-out wound and was bleeding, but not nearly as bad. The revolver was jammed into his belt.

I can outrun him if he didn't have that damned gun, she thought. *He has to be getting weaker and in shock. Only his bearlike disposition is keeping him conscious.* She glanced out the window at the trees flashing by and tried to gauge how much it would hurt to hit the brush in just her underwear.

"Don't try it, bitch! You'll never make it!" He glanced over through glassy eyes. Jenny could see that the light was dimmer in them.

He'll never make the bottom of the hill, she thought. *But I've still got to get away. He'll either get in a shoot-out with Wesley or will pass out and go over a cliff. Either way I'll be dead along with him.*

The huge truck skidded, wallowed in the mud, and

came near the edge of a cliff on Jenny's side. More glass crashed in the back. She squealed as the big wheels gripped and ground back into the ruts away from the yawning canyon. It was four or five hundred feet down into the mist-shrouded trees.

He laughed softly. "You don't know me, little lady. I been in tighter spots than this. I know a man who can help me, about five miles from here. Fixed up a bullet wound for me before—you'll see." He smiled, then grimaced with pain. "Woulda went back and killed that hubby of yorn if I didn't have this windmill chasin' me and blood gushin' out of my gut. Better this way. He'll shit nickels you're with me."

That means I have to bail out come hell or high water in about three miles, she thought as she studied the brush moving by the smashed open window.

No matter how this day ends, whether I live or die, when the sun sets, this animal will be dead regardless of his false confidence. He'll never kill anyone again.

That assurance, plus the fact that Alex was alive, was enough.

She calmly studied the muddy road through the spattered windshield, looking for her chance.

The longer I wait—the weaker he'll be.

"You Alex?" Wesley asked. He was carrying an M1 as he burst through the door. He swept it around the room in a professional stance.

"Nobody alive here but me and a friend in the back room. Cut me loose."

Outside the door, the Huey sat idling in the yard. The shadows of the spinning blades made the light coming in the door blink with each revolution.

Wesley pulled a knife, bent, and cut the cords at Alex's wrist, then his ankles. He glanced over at the chain. "Jesus," he exclaimed under his breath, taking in the situation.

"We have to follow the truck," Alex said.

"Of course. Put that chain on the ground."

Alex did and cringed away. Wesley pointed the M1 at it, away from them. It exploded one, two, three times. The chain jumped and the links separated.

Alex stood. He still had a three-foot section attached to the manacle.

"How about the other guy?" Wesley asked.

"I'll get him. You watch the door!" Alex dashed into the storage room and pulled the bag away from the hiding place.

Manny blinked up at the sudden light. "What the hell? You're all right? I heard shooting. What's that noise? A helicopter?"

"No time. Put your arm around my shoulder. I'll carry you."

Alex hefted him and carried him with more strength than he thought he had. Alex hesitated at the door, then realized the dogs were gone, and followed Wesley to the noisy machine. Wesley slid the large rear door open, and Alex laid Manny down gently.

"Hold this." Alex handed him a strap.

"What's going on?" Manny asked. "Are we free?"

"As a bird. Try to lay still. We'll talk more in a few minutes." He smiled, then slid the door shut.

Alex locked the door, then jumped in the copilot's seat.

Wesley pointed to the belts. Alex followed his lead and clicked them in place. Alex had never been in a chopper before. He breathed in deeply as the Huey leaped off the ground, leaving his stomach on the ground. They were silent for a couple of minutes, both knowing the danger of what was coming next.

"I'm Jenny's Uncle Wesley," the big man shouted. He smiled infectiously and held his hand out.

"Saying I'm glad to know you doesn't get it done." Alex smiled too, realizing he looked like an escapee from Devil's Island.

Wesley laughed and waved his free hand.

"Finding that truck will be duck soup," Wesley said above the thrumming engine. "Only one road. Big question is, what the hell we going to do after we catch it? Can't shoot with Jenny in there. Can't even go down and buzz him. We upset him and he goes off one of these turns, he'll take her with him."

"We just follow?"

Wesley nodded.

"For now."

Jenny concentrated on the rhythm of Harley's driving. He seemed to be getting more and more dizzy, and had trouble straightening out the wheel each time he completed one of the switchbacks. Through the open window, she could hear the *thump, thump* of the helicopter's blades approaching. She smiled. Alex was free and out of that awful barn.

"Yer friend's back," Harley said as his head wobbled to her, then back to the road. His eyes looked more out of focus. Time was on her side if he could keep the truck on the road much farther. Ahead lay a steeper hill with shorter switchbacks and more precipitous cliffs.

Soon, she thought. *Have to get out before that hill or I may not make the bottom in one piece. The helicopter is loud now. Must be right above us—*

Harley pulled the huge truck through a tight turn, then straightened it out. It was taking all of his concentration now. When he hit the ruts in the road, Jenny could hear the sloshing of liquid in the back of the truck. Whatever was back there had broken and covered the floor.

"Son of a bitch! Go away!" Harley yelled. He rolled his window down and clumsily pulled the gun out of his belt. He slowed slightly and leaned his head out the window. He stuck the gun out and fired in the air with his left hand. Jenny jumped at the cannonlike concussion of the heavy handgun.

He's in an awkward position with his head out the window, this is my chance, she realized. She glanced down at his blood-soaked pants.

Screaming, she brought both fists down on his lap as hard as she could—

Harley screeched—

His head flew forward and cracked into the edge of the window. Jenny turned her door handle—

And, in what seemed like slow motion, she leaped out into the air—

Falling, falling, falling—

Thump—ooff! She bounced in the mud on her stomach, then could feel the skin being ripped from her forearms as she tore through heavy brush—

Then tumbling down, over and over.

Arms, legs, and head whipping out of control—

A heavy, jarring collision—

Then it stopped.

Jenny's head whirled. *Have to concentrate . . . get up . . . concentrate . . . get up . . .* her mind labored. *Harley'll be coming. . . .*

Prickly bushes came into focus, and she realized she'd bounced off the road and fallen about forty feet down a steep bank into a clump of heavy brush.

She raised her head and could see the truck, slipping and sliding to a stop about one hundred feet away.

Have to move now . . . have to move now . . . have to move now! I know my body is connected if I can just make it move now. . . .

Harley slowly stumbled back up the road to where she lay, the gun dangling from his hand. *Have to move . . . have to move . . . have to move . . . Harley is coming closer, closer. . . .*

Her arm responded, then her leg, but she had to make them work together—

Have to stand and move and run . . . have to stand.

Harley was on the road above her now, looking down. He smiled and raised the gun.

Jenny closed her eyes—

Click— Click—

"Son of a bitch!" he screamed. She could see him trying to decide whether he could get down to where she lay.

Jenny opened her eyes in time to see the helicopter

coming in low, whipping the bushes and saplings into a
dance around her.

Harley threw the gun at her and it fell harmlessly in
the brush. He went wobbling back to the truck as fast as
he could and pulled himself up in the cab. He started the
engine and took off toward the next switchback.

Thank you, God, Jenny thought. *Thank you.* She
leaned her head back and watched as the helicopter
disappeared behind the ridge above her and the sound
wandered off.

"Where are you going? Follow Harley!" she shouted
to the chopper. Finding her strength, she rolled over on
her hands and knees and dragged herself slowly up the
road. Skin was torn off her legs and forearms and she had
scratches all over her stomach and body, but nothing was
broken. Wincing at the pain, she stood, testing her legs.

The helicopter thundered over her with a concussion
of sound going the other way, heading off down into the
canyon. Below she could see the truck still lazily
following the switchbacks. The sound of the engine
drifted up to her along with the buzzing of the chopper.

"Harley, you son of a bitch, we've got you now.
You're not going to get away!" she yelled, shaking her
fist. She reached up and touched her mouth. It tasted of
blood.

"Jen! Jen!" She turned. Above her, coming around the
last switchback was Alex, the length of chain dangling
from his arm as he ran. He was carrying a rifle in his left
hand. She turned and ran toward him, the vision in her
eyes immediately swimming and becoming wavy in hot
tears.

They both stopped a couple feet away from each other,
almost afraid to touch because they were both bleeding
from their arms and legs. Alex was grinning and she was
smiling and finally they were in each other's arms.

"Baby, baby, baby. I thought that crazy man was going
to kill you," he cooed in her hair.

"So did I," she said, then started sobbing softly.
Everything welled up in her—all the pain, fears, and

frustration of the last several days. She shook and moaned and sobbed with relief. He rubbed her hair with one hand and patted her back with the other. The chain jingled as he did. They rocked each other to the accompaniment of the clinking for a couple of minutes.

She leaned back and looked at him. "Love your jewelry," she said, rubbing her eyes with the back of her hand.

"Love your outfit," he said. She smiled. Having no clothes was of no importance right now. Alex held up the manacle and chain and studied it. "I'm going to save this."

"Save it?" she said. "Why?"

"Going to have it plated and mounted on a pedestal." She looked at him questioningly. "When I get to feeling overly important and all puffed up about something, this will remind me to be humble," he said.

"How'd you get out of the Huey?"

"There's a field up on the next level. Wesley let me out, and is going to follow that crazy man. We're supposed to wait for him up there."

"Harley's not going to make it, you know. He's weakening rapidly."

"Ask me if I care."

They both looked out over the valley. The truck had disappeared into the trees, but the helicopter still buzzed in the valley, moving back and forth in a constantly descending pattern. Ahead of the helicopter the ground leveled out and Jenny squinted to study the area.

"What do you see?" he asked.

"See that flat spot down there, and those cabins?"

"Yeah, why?"

"Watch it."

"Why?"

"Trust me," she said.

They stood holding each other, following the path of the helicopter as it weaved its way back and forth. Finally, the truck broke into view, climbing a small hill leading to the opening and the cabins.

"There's the truck!" Jenny shouted. Alex nodded and rubbed her back while they watched. The helicopter followed the truck's path along the road from about five hundred feet above it.

Loud cracking and explosions echoed up through the valley.

"I knew it!" Jenny squealed and jumped in the air. They watched intently as the truck veered off the road toward the valley. The cracking sounds increased.

The entire truck disappeared in a brilliant orange-and-white fireball. Two seconds later the blast wave hit them like a sonic boom.

"Wow! What was that?" Alex asked as the blazing truck slowly tumbled over the edge of the cliff. It toppled end over end down to the base of the valley, trailing fire and debris behind.

"What happened?" Alex asked again. "That shooting didn't come from the helicopter. Even if he could shoot by himself, he was too far away."

"Some friends of mine," she said smugly. "Reception committee."

"Friends? Up here?"

"Unwitting friends. I'll tell you about it later."

"That's the end of Harley, that's for sure. God, for a time there, I thought that guy was indestructible." Down below, what was left of the truck was burning furiously.

She nodded. "Let's walk up to the landing site. I don't want to miss Wesley. I have an urgent need to get off this mountain."

It took them ten minutes to walk up to the field where the helicopter was going to land. The buzzing machine approached in the distance, but they couldn't see it yet. They stood under a tree and watched the wind blow the high grass in undulating patterns, emotionally exhausted, but satisfied.

They held each other gently. It was a time for softness, for caressing after all the brutality they'd been part of.

She pushed him away and said, "My goodness, you

stink. Why do you smell so bad?" She grimaced and smiled at the same time.

"Kiss me again, I'll tell you about it later—" He smiled and rubbed her cheek gently, lovingly.

They pressed together tightly. She was warm against him, and salty tears came again and mixed with their kisses.

"I didn't think I was ever going to see you again," he said.

"I know, me too. I thought you were gone. I kept looking, trying . . . but—" Her voice cracked. She knew the tears would come and go on for days at least.

"Shhh," he said to comfort her, and kissed her soft, wet eyelids, each in turn.

"By the way, your dad's in jail in Picksburg," she whispered, smiling through her tears.

He pulled back, looked at her, and asked: "Jail—my dad? You're kidding. What's he doing here—and in jail?"

She giggled. "Technical detail. We can spring him from that tin can, easy. Kiss me again, I'll tell you about it later. . . ."

He chuckled and nuzzled her neck, languishing in the softness and the smell of her. His problems were over as long as they were together.

"I don't think I want to be a cop anymore. I want to write some books," he said as he kissed her ears and hair.

"That's great. We'll starve, you know."

"I know. Is that okay?"

"Long as we starve together. When did you decide that?"

"Kiss me again." This time their kisses were harder, more urgent.

In the field in back of them, the buzzing helicopter approached. Holding each other, they turned and watched as Wesley slowly lowered the machine to the deep grass. His smile lit the inside of the cockpit. The sun broke behind it through the few remaining clouds and reflected off the spinning rotors.

"Just realized we've got to get Manny to the hospital," Alex said.

"Wouldn't hurt us to go too, love. Who's Manny?"

"Kiss me just once more. I'll tell you all about him later, okay? Manny and I are going to do a lot of fishing together." They kissed lightly, tenderly this time.

"God," he said absently, looking around. "I hate this mountain. I can't wait to get home, clean up, have a nice meal . . . some of your bread . . . then, you know what I want to do?"

"Make passionate love to me?"

"After that."

"What?"

Wesley was smiling and waving from the open side window for them to come as the rotors idled, whistling through the air. They waved back, signaling that they'd be just a minute.

"Then, I want to get the hell out of here. I hate this mountain, I hate this town, I hate the heat and the humidity, I hate the bugs and mosquitoes, and most of all—I hate those damned cicadas buzzing in the fields. Hell, I've never even *seen* one, and I hate them. I just want to pack everything we own. Pack it all and go!"

She bent and laughed and cried and laughed some more.

"What's wrong?" He smiled, puzzled as they ambled toward the helicopter.

"We don't have to pack, my love. We don't have to pack hardly anything at all."

"What are you talking about? How the blazes are we going to leave if we don't pack?"

"Kiss me just once more when we get in that machine, my love—

"And I'll tell you about that later—

"Much later."